The Art
of
Romance

The Art of Romance

MATCHMAKERS

KAYE DACUS

OTHER BOOKS BY KAYE DACUS:

BRIDES OF BONNETERRE SERIES

Stand-In Groom
Menu for Romance
A Case of Love

THE MATCHMAKERS SERIES

Love Remains

© 2011 by Kaye Dacus

ISBN 978-1-60260-990-7

This book is a work of fiction. Names, characters, places, and incidents are either products of the author's imagination or used fictitiously. Any similarity to actual people, organizations, and/or events is purely coincidental.

Cover design: Lookout Design, Inc.

Published by Barbour Publishing, Inc., P.O. Box 719, Uhrichsville, OH 44683, www.barbourbooks.com

Our mission is to publish and distribute inspirational products offering exceptional value and biblical encouragement to the masses.

ecpa Member of the
Evangelical Christian
Publishers Association

Printed in the United States of America.

Dedication/Acknowledgment

To Julia Katherine Caylor McLellan and Edith Bradley Dacus,
my grandmothers.

Thanks to everyone who helped me with ideas for this book. For
my wonderful blog readers who helped me brainstorm story ideas:
Regina, Ruth, Sarah R., Pattie, Sylvia M., Leah, Audry, Sherrinda,
Amee, Tammy, Krista, Jennifer F., and Patricia. And Liz Johnson,
who helped name the character Emerson Bernard. Y'all rock!

Prologue

Celeste "Sassy" Evans might have had her driver's license revoked for poor eyesight, but she could clearly see something was wrong. She added artificial sweetener and creamer to her coffee and studied the faces of the two women sitting across the large table from her.

So far, only she, Trina Breitinger, and Lindy Patterson were here—because the three of them had come together.

"So they're really not getting married?" She hadn't earned the nickname Sassy in college for keeping her nose out of other people's business.

Trina's dark brows furrowed. She exchanged a glance with Lindy before answering. "Oh, they're getting married all right. Just not anytime soon."

"Apparently they think they need more time to get to know each other before they set a wedding date." Lindy dunked her tea bag in and out of her cup in a slow rhythm.

"Wait. We're talking about Zarah and Bobby here, right? The ones who were practically engaged when they were younger. Correct?" Two weeks ago at Thanksgiving dinner, Trina's granddaughter and Lindy's grandson had announced their engagement—and told the story of how they had met and dated many years before.

Sassy figured since they'd known each other for so long, the engagement would be short and the wedding soon. "What about our pact? What about our agreement that we would work to get at least

7

one of our grandchildren married so that we have a great-grandchild before. . .a certain other person in the senior adult group?"

Trina arched an eyebrow. "Lindy and I aren't the only ones with unmarried grandchildren."

"No, but at least yours are engaged. Caylor doesn't even go out on dates anymore. If it weren't for me—and Zarah and Flannery—my granddaughter would have no social life whatsoever. How am I supposed to work with that, I ask?"

Trina and Lindy were saved from answering by the arrival of the other two-fifths of the group: Helen "Perty" Bradley and Maureen O'Connor. Sassy was about to catch them up on the conversation so far then changed tacks when she caught sight of Perty's expression.

"Why the long face, Perty? I swany, between you, Trina, and Lindy, people will think we just came from a funeral."

Not even Sassy's teasing put a smile on Perty Bradley's face. "My oldest grandson has moved into our carriage house. I know, I know, that should make me happy. But from what little he's told us, there was some big scandal when the art college learned he was romantically involved with one of the deans or something. I can't get a straight answer out of him about exactly what happened. But whatever happened, he makes it sound like it's going to be nearly impossible for him to get another professorship somewhere."

The server arrived with their pitchers of pancake batter and ramekins of fruit and other toppings, the same thing they got every week when they descended upon the small, kitschy eatery in the Berry Hill neighborhood of Nashville. It had taken them awhile to settle on a regular place for their Thursday morning get-together once the coffee shop they'd been going to down in Franklin had closed. But after their first visit to the Pfunky Griddle, they'd been hooked.

"He teaches art doesn't he?" Sassy asked, lifting the jug of whole-grain batter. Perty nodded. "Caylor said something the other day about Robertson having trouble filling their adjunct positions. Get a copy of his résumé, and I'll have her pass it along to the appropriate people."

Perty smirked. "Have Caylor pass it along? All I'd have to do is pick up the phone and make one call, and he'd be hired. I was the first female president of our alma mater, if you recall."

Lindy, Trina, and Maureen exchanged looks Sassy wasn't sure she liked. More than sixty years ago, the three of them had come up with the nicknames Sassy and Perty for Celeste and Helen—nicknames that had stuck so hard even their grandchildren had picked them up and used them.

"What?" Sassy and Perty asked at the same time.

"Well, I know we're not limiting the search for partners for our grandchildren to each other's grandchildren." Maureen leaned forward to sprinkle sliced strawberries on her pancake. "But Sassy, Caylor *is* single. And Perty, your grandson—Dylan—is single. As is Dylan's younger brother. Aren't both of those boys college professors? Surely Caylor would like one of them."

Sassy shook her head. "Caylor met Paxton at the family cookout in October. Said he was a nice guy but far too young—at twenty-five, he's almost ten years younger than she."

Perty shook her head, too. "With Dylan just coming out of a relationship that cost him his job, I don't think that's a good idea."

Sassy adopted her most serious expression. "We should work on getting the already engaged couple to the altar. And Perty and I"—she looked to her best friend, who nodded in agreement—"will do what we can with our offspring. If we put our minds to it, we can accomplish anything. After all, we are the Matchmakers."

Chapter 1

"And they lived happily ever after. Period. The end." Caylor put down her favorite pen—the one with the sparkly purple ink—and twisted in her chair until her back popped in several places. She could understand her editor's wanting to get proofing on this book finished before Christmas, but to give her a due date for two weeks after Thanksgiving—which translated into the Friday before finals week—was ridiculous. She'd begged to have the deadline extended a week. Then she could have worked on the galleys while her students took their tests. But her request had been soundly, but kindly, denied.

No use fretting over something that wasn't to be. The work was done, and it would only take her another hour or so to type up a list of all the changes to e-mail back to her editor. And if she got the e-mail sent before midnight, she'd have beaten her Friday deadline by one day, technically.

But if she was going to keep working, she needed sustenance. As quietly as she could, she slipped down the stairs from her loft, skipping the third step from the bottom that squealed like a puppy with its head stuck in a fence.

She turned on the light over the sink instead of flooding the room with the original 1950s fluorescent lights. Opening the first of the three tall cabinets that served as the pantry, she pulled out the basket overflowing with packets of gourmet flavored hot chocolate. She dug through the assorted Mylar bags until she found what she wanted: sugar-free, dark-chocolate toffee. She put a mug of water in the microwave and set it for two minutes. She'd have to stop it before it beeped, lest she wake Sassy.

Next, she opened the middle cabinet. Back behind the multiple canisters of all different kinds of flour, she felt around for the Box. She and Sassy had agreed to keep it hidden behind the flour, because if Caylor didn't see it, she wouldn't want what was in it. At least not every day.

The Box wasn't there. Caylor pulled the flour bins out. Nope. No Box.

"Looking for this?"

Caylor jumped at her grandmother's soft voice, which coincided with the beeping of the microwave. Sassy held an opaque plastic storage bin, slightly larger than a shoe box, in both hands.

"I knew you had a deadline tomorrow, so when Trina, Lindy, and I stopped at Kroger on the way home from coffee this morning, I hit the Christmas candy aisle."

Caylor grinned. "Sass, I knew there was a reason I love you." Before Caylor pulled her mug out of the microwave, she grabbed the brushed stainless-steel kettle off the stove, filled it with fresh water, and put it back on over high heat. Then she fixed her own hot chocolate.

Sassy sat down at the end of the 1950s chrome and Formica table and popped the lid off the Box. Still stirring her drink, Caylor took the chair to her right and examined the booty. All kinds of miniature candy bars wrapped up in green, red, silver, and gold foil wrappers, mixed in with Hanukkah geld, a sentimental favorite Sassy got every year in honor of her Jewish grandmother. But Caylor dug through the stash, knocking at least a quarter of the candy out, until she came to what she knew her grandmother would have put on the very bottom—the chocolate-covered peanut butter Christmas trees.

"I only got a dozen of them," Sassy warned.

"For the twelve days of Christmas?" The kettle shrilled, and Caylor put the still-wrapped candy down beside her cup and got up to fix a cup of instant decaf coffee for her grandmother. "What flavor creamer?" Caylor opened the cabinet above the coffeepot only she used in the mornings.

Sassy squinted and moved her glasses around. "Belgian chocolate toffee."

Shaking her head at their similarities in taste, Caylor pulled down the canister of flavored powdered creamer and stirred two heaping spoonfuls into the double-strong instant coffee. Ever since she'd turned Sassy on to espresso-based lattes and cappuccinos, she'd insisted on having her coffee at home extra strong, extra creamy, extra sweet, and extra flavored.

Sassy took the purple mug with both hands, blew across the surface twice, and took a sip. "Ahh. . .hits the spot. I wish the restaurant would decide to serve something other than plain coffee."

"Did y'all try somewhere new today?"

Sassy gave her an incredulous look. "Do you and your friends ever try somewhere new when you get together?"

"So you went to the Pfunky Griddle."

"They have the best banana, chocolate chip, raisin, and walnut five-grain pancakes around. And with peanut butter on top, then drizzled with honey. . ." She kissed the tips of her fingers like an Italian. "Delicious."

Caylor wrinkled her nose at the combination her grandmother concocted at the make-it-yourself pancake restaurant. "Sassy, you know you aren't supposed to be overdoing it on the sugars and refined carbs."

She raised one thin eyebrow. "Look who's talking."

Caylor stopped with her teeth half sunk into the chocolate-covered peanut butter tree. She finished the bite, let the salty-sweetness saturate her mouth a moment, and swallowed. "Hey, now, I do this only on rare occasions—and I'm not the one with the blood-sugar issues."

"I know. You've been so disciplined about keeping away from it. I'm proud of you. How much weight have you lost?"

"About twenty pounds. I'm fitting back into all of my size 14s now." Though that had less to do with discipline and more to do with the fact that—between teaching, participation in the university's drama productions, and trying to get her latest book finished—the only time she wasn't running ninety-to-nothing to get her work finished was during the very few hours of sleep she got each night. Who had time to eat with a schedule like that? Of course, the healthier selections they'd started offering in the cafeteria at school helped considerably, too.

"Good for you. Now what do you want me to make for you to take to Zarah's Christmas party tomorrow night?"

"You don't have to do that. I can pick something up at the grocery store on my way."

As expected, Sassy looked thoroughly scandalized. Caylor hid her grin.

"No granddaughter of mine will go from this house taking food the likes of that." She stood and opened all three pantry doors, then moved back to lean against the table beside Caylor so she could see the contents of all three cabinets at the same time.

Caylor turned in her chair. "I told her I'd bring dessert."

"Excellent. Dessert's my middle name. Write this down."

Caylor finished off her confectionary tree and crossed the kitchen to pull the small magnetic whiteboard off the side of the fridge. She pushed the Box back and set the whiteboard on the table before resuming her seat.

Sassy mumbled to herself, pointing at things in the pantry. "Okay. Ready?"

"Ready." Caylor hovered the dry-erase pen over the clean, white surface.

"Corn syrup. Confectioners' sugar. Dark brown sugar. Oleo. Peppermint extract. Chunky peanut butter. Bittersweet and semisweet chocolate. Butterscotch. Walnuts and pecans—"

"Sassy, there will only be twelve people there. We're not feeding an army."

"Quiet. I've got friends and parties to go to also, you know. Keep writing."

Caylor chuckled and decreased the size of her handwriting to be able to fit the continual stream of ingredients onto the board. When Sassy lost her driver's license shortly after Papa passed away, Caylor had agreed to move in and become her grandmother's companion and primary source of transportation. It had been a difficult decision— Caylor so enjoyed sharing a house with her two best friends, Zarah

Mitchell and Flannery McNeill. But in the five years since then, Caylor had come to depend on Sassy as much as Sassy depended on her.

Which was why Caylor had resigned herself to the idea she would never marry—at least, not for a very long time. If she did, who would take care of Sassy?

~∞~

Dylan Bradley picked at the dried blue paint on the knuckles of his left hand. He hoped this wouldn't take long—if the canvas dried too much before he could get back to it, the painting would be ruined.

"We're happy you decided to move back to Nashville, to let us and your parents help you get back on your feet. But while you're living in the guesthouse, there are some ground rules we wanted to cover."

Rules, rules, rules. That was all anybody ever wanted to talk to him about. What good were rules when all they did was keep people from pursuing what made them happy?

Though he currently sat at his grandparents' kitchen table, the tense atmosphere created by being in the same room with a retired university president and a retired judge reminded him forcibly of the meeting he'd had just over a week ago with the president of the art college where he taught. Used to teach. It was easy enough for him to think of this as a Christmas break just like every other Christmas break—except he was here in Nashville instead of enjoying the gala art scene in Philadelphia.

Not the way he'd expected his Friday morning to go. Dylan feigned attention as his grandmother reviewed the "agreement" they expected him to sign and abide by in exchange for living rent-free in the converted carriage house behind their large Victorian home. Paying utilities. Blah, blah. Respect the historical integrity of the building. Blah, blah, blah. Find some kind of paying work. Blah, blah, blah, blah. No women spending the night.

Dylan's face burned. He'd never felt comfortable with the level to which his relationship with Rhonda had progressed—though it had been an eye-opening lesson on living outside of the rules; but he'd hoped his grandparents hadn't figured it out. In vain, obviously.

"And you are to attend church every Sunday. You can go to church with us, or you can find another church that you prefer." Perty gazed at him expectantly over the rim of her fashionable, aqua-framed reading glasses.

He should've known—his parents had freaked out two years ago when he admitted to them he no longer attended church regularly. Why wouldn't he expect the same from his grandparents? "And if I choose to go somewhere else, how will you know?"

"Dylan, dear, we're not doing this to make you feel like a child." Perty reached over and wrapped her small hand around his larger one. "We're hoping that by asking you to start attending church again, you'll regain some of the self-respect you've lost over the last couple of years."

The last couple of years? Ha. If his grandparents or parents ever learned what he'd really done to put himself through college and supplement his teaching income the first year or two, they would know he had no self-respect to rebuild.

"We would like for you, as an adult, to determine the best way to show us you're willing to abide by this agreement." Gramps should have been wearing his black judge's robe, as Dylan could not imagine his voice had sounded much different fifteen or twenty years ago when he passed sentences in civil court cases.

"We also think getting involved in church will help you meet people your age who can help you settle in to your new life here more quickly," Perty added.

And, no doubt, act as good influences on him. "Okay."

"Okay? As in okay to the entire agreement, or okay you understand this part of it?"

"Okay as in let's sign the agreement." What was the point in arguing or trying to negotiate? He didn't have a job; he didn't want to cash in his 401(k); and just paying utilities, groceries, and gas would start dwindling his savings account pretty quickly.

As instructed by Gramps, Dylan initialed and dated the bottom corner of each page of both copies of the agreement before signing and dating the last page of both beside his grandparents' signatures. Perty collated the pages and stapled each copy.

What, no notary public? No case number and surety just in case he broke the agreement?

All right. This over-the-top cynicism was starting to get to him. He put down the pen and flexed his left hand against a sensation of his skin's being too tight and not stretching correctly. He looked down. Blue. He needed to get back to his painting.

"Is that everything?" Dylan drummed his thumb against his thigh.

Gramps raised his eyebrows, but before he could speak, Perty reached over and squeezed his arm.

"I suppose," Perty said, her blue eyes twinkling, "it would be too much to ask you to cut your hair."

Dylan reached up and touched the bush of curls held back from his face with an elastic band around the crown of his head. He'd started growing it out when Rhonda mentioned how much better she thought certain male celebrities looked with long hair.

"Don't worry. We don't want to put too many unreasonable demands on you." Perty handed him his copy of the agreement. "Oh, but that reminds me, if you have your curriculum vitae ready, I can pass it along to Sassy Evans's granddaughter who teaches at James Robertson University. Caylor says they're always looking for adjuncts, especially in the art department."

Perty's suggestion surprised him. As an alumna, former professor, and the first female president of JRU, Perty could have simply made a phone call to one of her many contacts at the college and ensured Dylan the choice of any course he wished to teach.

"Maybe I should take it out myself tomorrow." Last thing he wanted was to have everyone at the college believing he'd gotten the job simply because of his grandmother's connection to the school. He was tired of taking handouts.

Perty reached around to the kitchen breakfast bar behind her and grabbed a notepad from one of the open shelves below. She scrawled something and handed the top sheet to Dylan. "This is Caylor's office number. Give her a call, and I'm sure she'd be happy to give you a tour of the campus and introduce you around."

I'm not a child, Perty. I can figure out how to get around a college campus on my own, thanks. He didn't even want to know why his grandmother had this woman's office phone number memorized. He tucked the note into his shirt pocket—where he'd probably forget about it until his next load of laundry came out with little bits of paper all over it.

He looked at them with raised brows. He shouldn't have to ask his question again. *I've eaten all my brussels sprouts. May I please be dismissed?* Actually, he liked brussels sprouts, especially the way they made them at the little German restaurant and *biergarten* near the art school. Oh how he would miss hanging out there with his graduate students after studio on Thursday and Friday evenings.

"If you don't have any questions for us"—Perty looked at Gramps then back at Dylan—"you can go do whatever it is that we took you from earlier. And you know you're welcome to join us for lunch at noon."

He graced them with a single nod of his head and left the table—only to turn back after two steps and snatch his copy of the agreement to take with him. If he was going to have to depend on his grandparents' charity for his temporary living arrangements until he could figure out where he wanted to go from here, at least he had the carriage house—set back about fifty feet from the museum-like Victorian he'd always hated visiting as a child, from being told not to touch anything. Back then, the upstairs of the carriage house had been nothing more than a big open space where he and his younger brothers could run around to their hearts' content in bad weather. Now it boasted an apartment any of those hoity-toity patrons of the art school would have been jealous of. Almost nine hundred square feet, granite and stainless kitchen, wood floors throughout, and big, airy rooms. An apartment like this in Philly would have been far out of his price range. Thus his primary reason for ignoring his conscience and moving in with Rhonda.

He entered the outbuilding through the side door. He supposed he didn't mind having his grandparents' Mercedes and Lexus as his downstairs neighbors. He crossed the garage and stepped up into the workroom—the workroom that was now his art studio.

The canvas on the easel taunted him, as if it knew what he'd just been through.

Blue. Gray. Green. No. All wrong.

He grabbed the tubes of lemon yellow and cadmium red, streaked them together on his palette, and slashed yellow-orange-red across the boring fades of blues and grays. He stepped back, dipped into the puddle of swirled brightness, and went a little Jackson Pollock on the canvas, enjoying the stark droplets of brightness against the somber background as he flicked and flung his brush to splatter and drip the paint onto the image.

Of course, the composition happening on the canvas bore absolutely no resemblance to the image he'd carried around in his head all morning. But he'd promised himself he'd never paint anything like that ever again. For now, he'd stick with the abstract, ambivalent dreck that had garnered him so much praise at the three gallery showings he'd had in Philadelphia over the past five years. *Three* gallery showings in *Philadelphia*. Friends from college had yet to land one showing anywhere.

He mashed the brush into the black paint and daubed it in lopsided polka dots across the surface, leaving plenty of texture. Rhonda had always liked the texture he created in his paintings. *Dimensionality*, she'd called it.

Child's finger painting, he'd thought it looked like. Not something he would be adding to his portfolio.

Speaking of his portfolio. . .

He grabbed the rag hanging from the top of the easel and wiped his hands while crossing to the giant-sized, economy worktable that filled the end of the room. Finished canvases of all shapes and sizes sat seven or eight deep, leaning up against the wall. He hadn't updated his portfolio since before the faculty art show back in October. He hadn't painted anything he liked since then, but he hadn't painted anything he'd liked in the last two years, so what did that matter? Rhonda said—

He supposed it didn't really matter anymore what his former department head and secret partner—she'd hated the term *girlfriend*—had said about his work. She'd been the one to make him completely change his style after hiring him as a full-time assistant professor of art.

After flipping through most of the couple of dozen canvases, he felt like throwing them all away instead of taking digital pictures of them to print and add to his portfolio.

He crouched down and pulled out one of the big cardboard boxes from under the table, the one with the address of his apartment in

18

Brooklyn written in black magic marker across the face of it. Ah, the Brooklyn years. The years when painting and drawing actually made him happy—and money. The years when art—doing, learning, and teaching it—had been about his own expression of ideas, thoughts, innovation, and creativity, not about trying to bamboozle some wealthy fat cat in Philadelphia into buying one of his paintings because it was a "conversation piece." Or to give some bored socialite high on prescription drugs the feeling that she had one-upped her rich, snotty friends by buying a one-of-a-kind, original, unique, one-and-only, exclusive, one-off work by somebody who actually looked like an artist should look: curly black hair stylishly unkempt, three days' worth of stubble, an earring, a large silver signet ring on the middle finger of his left hand, and a couple of tattoos. At least Rhonda had not put up too much of a fight over his own designs for the tattoos she insisted he get.

He pulled his watch out of his pocket. Not quite eleven o'clock in the morning. If he got cleaned up now, he could make it out to the college campus before noon. He was pretty sure this was the week before finals, so most of the professors and deans should still be on campus, even on a Friday.

And just in case his grandmother asked, he would go ahead and pop his head into the friend's granddaughter's office, just so he wouldn't have to lie about meeting her.

It wasn't as if he'd ever have to see her again.

Chapter 2

$\mathcal{D}$ylan pulled his Ford Escape into a parking space right beside another Escape. He'd wanted to get the small, hybrid SUV in white, but not a single dealer in Philly had one with the options he wanted, so he took it in blue instead. He sure did like the way it looked in white, though.

The parking tag hanging from the rearview mirror announced this SUV belonged to a member of the faculty. And the IMPROVE YOUR FUTURE—READ A BOOK TODAY bumper sticker made him suspect that faculty member was one of the English professors.

He took out his phone and used its web feature to pull up the map of the college campus again. This building should be where he would find Perty's friend's granddaughter, as long as she wasn't in class. He let himself in a side door of the stone building that looked like it had been a house, albeit a large one, in a previous life. A musty smell—one he usually associated with old people's houses—permeated the building. Not surprising, given that every window had an AC unit hanging out of it, covered with tarps to try to hold out the chilly weather.

The quiet that filled the hall pressed on Dylan's ears. The few offices on this floor were all closed up. He found the stairs. According to the school's website, Dr. Caylor Evans's office was on the second floor of Davidson Hall. He reached the top of the stairs and turned left. Yep, there it was. Room 203. But the door was closed.

She could have a student in there—or she could be in class, or even gone for the day.

He knocked.

No response.

Oh well. He could tell Perty he tried.

She had all kinds of stuff taped to her door. Quotes from Byron and Elizabeth Browning and Jane Austen and Sir Walter Scott. A final-exam schedule—and her exams were all scheduled for next week. And—

He lifted the corner of the exam schedule:

Open Auditions
Auditions for the spring production of *Much Ado about Nothing* will be held in Rutherford Auditorium January 10 & 11 from 2:30 to 6:30 p.m. Open casting call for the following roles. . .

❧

What followed was a list of the secondary characters and bit players in what was the only Shakespeare play Dylan knew well—and then only because Rhonda had loved the movie version of it so much.

He really needed to stop relating everything in his life to Rhonda. But truth be told, she'd exposed him to many things he otherwise would still be ignorant of. He wished he could get some of that innocence back. Culturally speaking, she had enriched his life.

But anyway. . .

He released the exam schedule and let it fall back over the audition announcement, then started back down the stairs. At the halfway landing, he almost ran into someone coming up.

"Sorry," they both said at the same time.

The woman he'd almost bowled over steadied herself with one hand on the railing, the other arm wrapped around a pile of books. He reached out to assist, just in case, but she regained her balance quickly. She blinked at him a couple of times.

"I know you, don't I?"

No—he was pretty sure he'd remember a gorgeous redhead who was probably the tallest woman he'd ever met—almost as tall as his own six foot three. "I don't think so."

"You look so familiar to me." She shook her head and laughed, showing slightly crooked front teeth that only made her cuter. "I'm getting to an age where I've met so many people that I'm starting to get that sensation no matter where I go—you know, the sensation that you've met the people there before?"

He couldn't really identify. And besides, she couldn't be much older than he, if at all.

"Well. . .is there someone or something I can help you find? You look a little lost."

"I. . ." He searched his pockets for the slip of paper with the name he needed. "I need to see Dr. Holtz in the art department."

"Oh, you're in the wrong building. You need to go out the front door and across the quad to Sumner Hall. That's where the art department is." The woman's blue-green eyes scrutinized him as if trying to figure out who he was and where she might know him from. "Are you a student here?"

"No. I haven't been a student for several years now."

"Oh—you're an adjunct?"

"I hope to be." He returned the note to the coin pocket of his jeans.

She shifted the pile of books into her left arm and extended her right hand. "Well, if you ever need anything, feel free to ask. I'm Dr. Caylor Evans."

Really? *She* was Caylor Evans—the woman he'd wanted to avoid? He took her outstretched hand. "Dylan Bradley."

"Brad. . ." Her eyes widened, and she held on to his hand. "You're not related to Perty—Helen—Bradley, are you?"

"She's my grandmother." He pulled away from her grasp.

"That's why you look familiar. I met your brother—oh, what was his name—the physicist?"

"Paxton?"

She snapped her fingers. "Yes Paxton. I met him at a family cookout back in October. He looks a lot like you. I hope that theoretical physics stuff is going well for him."

He liked her crooked grin, the way the right corner of her mouth came up just a little higher than the other when she smiled. "I guess it is."

He avoided getting into any kind of conversation with Pax—a

candidate for a PhD in medical physics from Vanderbilt University, though with as often as the oldest of Dylan's three younger brothers used the word *theoretically* when talking about his research, it was no surprise Caylor had misinterpreted what he did was theoretical physics.

"I couldn't understand a word of it when I met him."

She had perfectly shaped lips. He could almost feel the sweep of his pencil as he outlined them and then shaded to show their fullness.

But no. He didn't do art like that anymore.

Her smile started to falter. Probably because he hadn't said anything yet, and it was his turn. "Out the front door and across the quad to Sumner Hall?"

"What—? Oh yes. I believe Dr. Holtz's office is on the third floor." Her short hair danced in asymmetric layers and waves around her head. He would need oranges and reds and umbers and golds—

No. He did not paint people anymore. Just abstracts. That was his style. Not beautiful women he ran into, whether by design or accident.

He backed away. "Thanks."

She shifted her stack of books again. "You're welcome. It was nice to meet you."

"You, too." He went down a few steps then turned around. "Merry Christmas."

She looked down from several steps up, and the lopsided grin had returned. "Merry Christmas to you, too, Dylan."

He ran the rest of the way downstairs and hurried out the front door and down the steps from the building's porch.

There. He'd met her. She would tell her grandmother, and her grandmother would tell Perty. And everyone would be happy.

He stopped in the middle of the quad. Everyone would be happy but him. The memory of her face, her hair, her lips, the curve of her neck between her almost-square jaw and the collar of the white blouse she wore under her purple sweater—her image would haunt him. Would drive him to the brink of cracking until he gave in and drew her.

He'd met hundreds, maybe even thousands, of gorgeous women in his life. Before he met Rhonda, he'd sketched many of them. Since

Rhonda had convinced him to change his form to abstract, he'd given fleeting thoughts to drawing a beautiful specimen. But none of their images had urged him to put pencil to paper once more the way Dr. Caylor Evans's did.

No.

Trying to brush the annoyance from his mind, he started walking toward Sumner Hall again. He would not draw Caylor Evans. He would not give her one more thought. He'd done what his grandmother wanted. Now it was time to see about doing what he wanted, and that was teaching art. Dr. Evans was a passing distraction.

And as long as they never passed each other again, he might get over this urge to draw every feature he could remember—from her slightly crooked front teeth to the way her right eye squinted up just a little more than the left one when she smiled.

While JRU wasn't a huge school, it was big enough. It couldn't be too hard to avoid her. Could it?

~∞~

"Do you remember Mr. Science Guy from the family cookout back in October?" Caylor twirled a bent-open paper clip with the thumb and forefinger of her left hand.

"The tall, skinny guy with the pimply neck?" Zarah Mitchell, one of her best friends from college, asked.

"Yeah. The one who wanted to tell me all about his experiment while we were there."

"I remember him. Don't tell me he called you and asked you out."

With her cell phone tucked between ear and shoulder, Caylor used her right hand to scroll through the list of unread e-mails sitting in her Inbox to determine if any of them needed to be addressed before she left for the day. "No, he didn't call. But I met his brother Dylan a few minutes ago—his older brother, by the looks of him."

"Really?" A hint of excitement came through Zarah's voice. "How much older?"

"Probably not much. I'd say he's probably in his late twenties."

"Does he look just like the scientist?"

Caylor didn't have to search hard to recall the memory of Dylan

Bradley's looks. She hadn't been able to stop thinking about him since the run-in. "A little bit—but even cuter. Oh, and he's taller than me, too."

"That's a bonus."

Right at six feet tall—with a love of shoes with two- or three-inch heels—Caylor always noticed a man whom she had to look up to. Physically and intellectually. Today she had been wearing flats, and Dylan had been a few inches taller. His face floated before her mind's eye again. "There's something about this guy that's so familiar, and I can't put my finger on it."

"He looks like his brother?"

"Yeah. . .that's partly it. But I feel like I know him from somewhere—like we've met before." She opened an e-mail to see if it was as important as the subject made it sound, but it wasn't, so she closed it again.

"Your grandmothers are best friends. It's likely that you met him sometime when you were both younger and just don't remember it. So. . .are you going to go for it?" A teasing lilt softened Zarah's voice.

Caylor leaned back in her chair. "Go for what?"

"This guy. . .Dylan. You've been saying you might have to start taking the initiative if you're going to have any marriage prospects before you're forty. You only have five years left, dear."

The bent paper clip flew from Caylor's fingers and landed with a slight tick somewhere across the small office. "Thanks for the reminder." Actually, she had five years and six days left. "I don't think so—he's way too young for me."

"If he's in his late twenties, he can't be more than five or six years younger than you. That's nothing."

"Says the lady engaged to a man two years older. Any change on setting a wedding date?" Though haranguing her friend about her open-ended engagement took the focus off the idea of Caylor's asking a younger man out, she had to swallow back the bitterness of envy every time she talked to Zarah about the engagement or the as yet unscheduled wedding. Two years older than Zarah and a year older than their other best friend, Flannery McNeill, Caylor had always assumed she would get engaged and married first. None of them, Zarah included, had ever dreamed that Zarah would be the first engaged, first married. Of course, considering she'd met and fallen in love with the guy when she was seventeen years old, his coming back to town after so many years had given Zarah an advantage in the snag-a-man category.

She hadn't told Zarah yet, but Zarah and Bobby's experience—meeting young, falling in love, being broken up by her emotionally abusive father, resenting each other for years, and then coming back together fourteen years later—had inspired a novel idea for Caylor. And now that she had returned all of her edits on the last manuscript on her current contract, she could start working on the proposal for a new series.

"No change. We're still discussing whether I'll sell my house or he'll get rid of his condo. He likes the more urban-lifestyle feel of the apartment—reminds him of living in LA. He says my house feels too suburban for him. But I hate the idea of sharing walls—or that our floor is someone else's ceiling. It creeps me out."

Caylor picked up a pen and pulled the black vinyl-covered spiral notebook out from her messenger-style bag. She flipped open to the first blank page, about halfway through, and wrote: *Have engaged couple argue about where they're going to live? Too urban/too suburban.*

"You're writing down what I said, aren't you?"

She closed the notebook and clicked the pen closed. "Just jotting down an idea while it's fresh in my mind."

Zarah gave a long, exaggerated sigh on the other end of the phone line. "Just mention me in the acknowledgments, okay?"

"As always."

"My tour group just arrived. Everything ready for tonight?"

Oh yes, the original reason for this phone call. "Would I miss our Christmas dinner? It's been a tradition for—what?—ten, eleven years now? In fact, I need to get out of here and stop by Publix on the way home so that Sassy can—I mean, so I can finish up the desserts I'm bringing tonight."

"Oh good—you're not cooking." Zarah's voice echoed funny, and Caylor assumed she was in the stairwell headed down to the small history museum on the first floor of the Middle Tennessee Historic Preservation Commission's building.

"Ha-ha. So funny. The one time I tried to make meat loaf, and y'all will never let me live it down." She closed all of her programs and shut down the computer.

"More like a really big hockey puck. Gotta go. See you tonight around six."

"I'll be there." They said good-bye, and Caylor tossed the phone into her bag, along with everything else she might need over the weekend.

The lines at the grocery store made an ordeal out of what should have been a relatively quick stop, but she finally made it home with all of the ingredients on Sassy's list.

The sugary, cinnamony, spicy aroma of baking treats wrapped around Caylor as soon as she opened the kitchen door—though the loud music nearly forced her back out again.

Sassy danced around the kitchen singing along with Burl Ives on "A Holly Jolly Christmas." Before Caylor could get her attention, the song ended and a random 1980s hair-band rock anthem started. Caylor heaved the grocery bags onto the table, reached for the portable speakers, and turned down the volume.

"You know, I think it might have been a mistake for me to get all of Papa's vinyl transferred to digital and then give it to you on an MP3 player."

Sassy sashayed over toward her, waving a wooden spoon, and took Caylor by the hand. She led her into the middle of the room and started dancing the jitterbug. "You always say that, and then you always end up having a good time anyway."

Caylor gave in and danced with her grandmother for half a minute, then broke away. "There's cold stuff that needs to be put in the fridge."

After she put the groceries up—those that Sassy didn't need immediately—Caylor returned to her car for her school stuff, which she took upstairs to her office. While there, she changed into jeans—a pair of 16s that were on the loose side of fitting, just so she'd be as comfortable as possible tonight—and a white turtleneck with reindeer all over it. She pulled out her pine tree–green cardigan to wear over it. The weather had been mild since the cold snap just before Thanksgiving, but the forecast called for a front to come in that afternoon and make the temperature drop near freezing by nightfall.

After a cup of tomato soup and a grilled cheese sandwich, Caylor put on an apron and did what she could to help Sassy—which pretty much meant trying to stay out of her way and hand her things as she needed them.

At five thirty, Sassy put the dome over the coconut cake, and Caylor covered the pan containing the Coca-Cola cake with foil. After setting the cake carriers in the back of her small SUV—in weather definitely colder than when she'd gotten home a few hours ago—Caylor took out the large tray of cookies Sassy had covered with plastic wrap, glad she had opted for the SUV instead of the smaller car when she'd decided to get a hybrid vehicle.

She ran upstairs and got her leather jacket to put on over her sweater. Back in the kitchen, she grabbed her keys and slung her purse strap over her shoulder. "Anything else you want to send?"

"Oh—wait, the fudge!" Sassy pulled the pan of chocolaty goodness out of the fridge, cut it into one-inch squares, and arranged it on a glass plate, which she then covered loosely with plastic wrap.

Caylor's mouth watered. She loved Sassy's fudge more than anything else, and her grandmother only made it a few times during the Christmas season each year. It was so tempting to conveniently "forget" this in her car and keep it all to herself. But she didn't want to undo the good she'd done losing weight over the last few months. So she'd limit herself to one piece. Five, tops.

With the fudge safely out of reach in the back of the SUV, along with everything else, Caylor headed up to Zarah's house. In the complete darkness that was six o'clock in the evening in mid-December in Nashville, most of the houses lining Granny White Pike had their Christmas lights turned on, putting Caylor even more in the mood for the annual dinner she, Zarah, and Flannery had started when they lived together in college. They each invited three people, making an even dozen, and the three of them prepared all the food.

Flannery's car was already in the driveway when Caylor pulled up. She tapped the horn, and Zarah and Flannery came out to help carry everything in.

Just like Caylor, neither of her best friends could resist indulging in a piece of fudge as soon as Caylor uncovered it inside—and then laughed at the moaning that ensued.

Bobby, Zarah's fiancé, arrived a few minutes later—having gone home to change clothes after spending the afternoon at the house helping Zarah set up. Caylor averted her eyes when they kissed in greeting. Even though it was no more than just a peck on the lips, a surge of jealousy flared, which she couldn't control, and she didn't want them to see it.

Zarah flew around, being obsessive-compulsive over making sure everything was arranged perfectly while Caylor and Flannery chatted about whom they'd invited. With Caylor, it was the usual suspects—one of the drama professors and two of the English professors, all single, all with no family in the area.

At ten to seven, the doorbell rang. Caylor crossed to answer it, still laughing over Bobby's teasing of Zarah.

The laughter froze in her throat when she opened the door.

On the front porch, his curly dark hair mostly slicked back into a stubby ponytail, his face clean shaven, and looking handsomer than she remembered from just a few hours ago, stood Dylan Bradley.

Chapter 3

Go to a dinner party, she said. Meet some new people, she said. Start building a new life in Nashville, she said.

Had Perty known Caylor Evans would be here?

The only thing that made Dylan walk into the house was the cold air pressing behind him and the fact he was wearing no more than a leather jacket over his lightweight cashmere knit turtleneck.

"Dylan, I'm surprised to see you here." Caylor Evans extended her right hand.

He shook it, ignoring the softness of her skin. He hadn't imagined it earlier today—she was almost his height. "Dr. Evans."

"Please, it's Caylor. Come in out of the cold." Caylor ushered him into the living room, closing the door behind him.

Now that he was here, Dylan was pretty sure this was the worst idea he'd had in a long time. But he'd been back in Nashville a week and, before today, hadn't seen anybody but Perty and Gramps—and he'd been about to climb the walls being isolated from human contact like that.

He let Caylor usher him through the living room of the old, cottage-style house. While it wasn't something he could see himself living in, he liked the mix of historical and contemporary in the furnishings and décor. He internalized a sigh. He could tell already this was not going to be his scene. But it had gotten him out of the house.

"Zarah, Dylan Bradley is here." Caylor's voice still held the same note of surprise as when she'd greeted him at the door moments before.

A woman with hair as curly and bushy as his—though not nearly as dark and quite a bit longer—turned from the plate of hors d'oeuvres she'd just set down on a high side table in the dining room. She extended her hand in greeting. He started to lean forward to press his right cheek to hers—the expected greeting in the socialite circles in Philly—but when she made no reciprocal move, he released her hand and backed up slightly so he wouldn't freak her out.

"Dylan, I'm so glad you could make it tonight. When a guest canceled at the last minute, I wasn't sure what I was going to do. Fortunately, the call came in right after your grandmother had popped down to my grandmother's house while I was picking up some serving dishes and utensils." Zarah looked from Dylan to Caylor and back. "Now, I'm the kind of person who likes to be introduced around whenever I go somewhere I don't know anybody. But I know some other people actually enjoy mixing and mingling on their own, so I didn't want to presume which you would prefer."

He preferred being treated like an adult instead of led around by the hand and shown off to Rhonda's friends like a precocious child. "Thanks. I'm comfortable with just mingling." He looked down at the plate of food on the buffet table—were those sausage balls? A staple of Perty's holiday table, these were Dylan's favorite, and he hadn't eaten one in at least five years, since the last time he'd been home for Christmas his senior year of college. Oh how he had missed them. Having given in to pressure and followed the trend of becoming an organics-only almost-vegetarian upon moving to Philadelphia five years ago, his extremely high metabolism would reduce him to nothing if he didn't eat constantly. So maybe being back in Tennessee where sausage balls, cheese straws, and fried everything were staple food items wasn't a bad thing.

"Where do you want this?"

Dylan tried not to let his surprise register at the sight of the man who came into the dining room from the kitchen. Though he probably was not much, if any, taller than Dylan, the man's muscular bulk made Dylan feel scrawny in comparison. And if Dylan was ever to attempt a portrait of this guy, he was pretty sure he'd never be able to translate onto canvas the aggressiveness of the guy's square jaw.

After sliding the large tray onto the buffet where Zarah indicated, the guy turned to Dylan, hand extended. "Hey, I'm Bobby Patterson."

"Dylan Bradley." He returned the firm pressure of Bobby's handshake.

"Zarah, I think something is about to boil over or burn or something." The panicked female voice shrilled to them from the kitchen.

A look of comical surprise came over Caylor's face. "You left Flannery all alone in the kitchen? Are you nuts?"

Bobby held his hands up in front of him as if surrendering. "Mea culpa. I should have waited until Zarah got back to the kitchen before I left it." With a parting glance at Zarah that explained the large diamond on her left hand, Bobby returned to the kitchen.

"Is there anything I can do to help?" Dylan asked.

"No no. You're a guest." Zarah's gentle smile made her light-blue eyes sparkle. A little bit of silver metallic paint with one of his finest brushes might come close to replicating it. "Everyone else should be arriving shortly. Flannery can give you a tour of the house. It will get her out of the kitchen."

Moments later, he had been foisted off onto the blond woman who apparently did not want to be in the kitchen any more than the rest of them wanted her there.

"House tour. . .house tour. Well, this is the dining room. And these are the sausage balls." She picked one up, took a bite out of it, and closed her eyes in apparent bliss.

While Flannery finished enjoying the biscuity-cheesy-sausagey treat, Dylan glanced around the dining room. He had a piece a former roommate had given him in lieu of cash for rent that would go perfect with the décor and color in here.

"Are you sure you don't want one?" Flannery nodded toward the trays of hors d'oeuvres.

"I'll wait." Though he really didn't want to. He wanted to dive into their fatty, carbohydrate-laden goodness headfirst.

"Okay, well, I know they don't want me in the kitchen, so we'll go this way." She led him back into the living room—another room that would benefit from a couple of paintings he had back at the carriage house.

"Not much to see here, I guess." Flannery moved down the hall to their left, and Dylan followed. Unlike the bedroom hallway on the second floor of his grandparents' house, where the walls were covered from floor-to-ceiling with framed family photos, only two framed photo collages hung on the walls. Dylan didn't examine every picture in them, but at first glance it appeared they were all photos of Zarah, Caylor, and Flannery, not pictures of Zarah's family.

Flannery stepped through the first door on the right and flipped on the light switch. "Bathroom. Self-explanatory." She turned the light off again before he had a chance to get a good look at the room—though the candle jar on the light countertop continued its warm, gingerbread-scented glow.

She came out around him and stepped into the room across the hall. The light clicked on and revealed what had once been a small bedroom that had been converted into what looked like a professor's office, with built-in dark-wood bookcases lining the walls and even framing the windows. An antique-looking desk—the kind that looked more like a table—sat almost in the middle of the room facing the door, with a closed laptop sitting on a leather-trimmed felt desk blotter.

"This is my favorite room in the house." Flannery ran her fingertips along the spines of the books on the shelf closest to her. "You know the old joke about people looking through someone's medicine cabinet when they go to a party? Well, I look through their bookshelves. You can tell a lot about a person by the books they have."

Heat flared in Dylan's cheeks, and he turned his back on Flannery, feigning interest in the books. There were other things one could tell about people from books.

The row of mass-market-sized books on the top shelf, just above his eye level, caught his attention. The spines of several of them looked familiar. He pulled one down and flipped it so he could see the front cover—and mortification flared through his entire body. Why in the world would someone like Zarah Mitchell have books by Melanie Mason? The image of the bare-chested man being clung to by a scantily clad woman on the front cover turned his stomach. He didn't have a chance to shove the book back into its place on the upper shelf before Flannery snatched it out of his hand.

"Oh—that's not—Zarah doesn't—she met the author, so those are collectible items, not something she reads regularly." Flannery flipped the book over and looked at the back cover, then the spine, and then the front cover again. "Although I have to say, whoever this Patrick Callaghan is, he's a good artist. I wonder what other cover design work he's done." She trailed her fingertips over the embossed letters of the author's name as if reading them by Braille.

Put the book down. Please, put the book down. Don't look at the image on the cover; just put the book away.

Flannery looked up, her mouth open as if to speak. Then she frowned and looked back down at the book and her hands. "You know, if you had blond hair—and took steroids and worked out a lot—you'd look just like this guy on the cover. Well, maybe not just like him. But close." She raised up on her toes and stretched her arm all the way up to try to reshelf the book but couldn't quite reach.

Dylan took the book from her and jammed it back in the open space in the middle of all the other Melanie Mason books. Yes, he'd been correct. This was the worst idea he'd had in a very long time.

"You realize of course, that if we move into your apartment, I won't be able to host this party anymore."

Caylor grabbed the bowl of mashed potatoes and carried it into the dining room to avoid being caught in the passive-aggressive crossfire between Zarah and Bobby. Though no one had asked her opinion, after years of observing couples and coming close to marriage once herself, Caylor was pretty sure that one of the main reasons Zarah and Bobby hadn't been able to settle on a wedding date was less about getting to know each other again after fourteen years apart—the reason they had given for waiting—and more about not being able to agree on whether to live in Zarah's 1920s cottage or Bobby's new, contemporary condo.

Personally, Caylor hoped they'd keep the house.

She spent the next few minutes welcoming the rest of the guests, taking their coats in to lay across the guest bed. She stood at the end of the hallway, looking into the living room for a moment. Taller than everyone else in the room—only because Bobby wasn't in there yet—

Dylan Bradley was easy to spot. But for all he said about wanting to mix and mingle on his own, he seemed to be doing a pretty bad job of it—standing apart from the three little clusters of people in the living room.

Flannery, of course, was in her element, flitting from group to group, ensuring everyone had been introduced, and making everyone feel welcomed.

Caylor greeted her invitees—the three professors from JRU—who had been coming to this dinner every year since Zarah had bought the house, giving them room to include others in what had become a tradition for the three of them back when they roomed together in college.

Hoping Dylan did not feel as uncomfortable as he looked, Caylor motioned him over and introduced him to the other professors. "Dylan is hoping to teach art as an adjunct next semester." Caylor glanced at him for confirmation.

Dylan nodded and seemed to loosen up slightly.

"Really? Where did you go to school?" Bridget Wetzler, a drama professor, asked.

"I have my bachelor's in studio art from NYU–Steinhardt and my MFA from PAFA—Pennsylvania Academy for the Fine Arts."

"And you've taught before?" Dr. Fletcher asked. Almost seventy herself, the chair of the English department always assumed anyone under the age of forty couldn't possibly have much, if any, experience.

"I was an associate professor of art at Watts-Maxwell Institute of Fine Arts in Philadelphia for five years." His brown eyes took on a guarded look.

Sixteen different scenarios immediately ran through Caylor's head as to why talking about his previous job would bring on palpable signs of defensiveness—and it appeared to be more than just Dr. Fletcher's calling his experience into question. The firm set of his mouth was so familiar, Caylor could almost reach out and grab the memory of where she had met Dylan before.

"What kind of art do you do, Dylan?" Bridget asked.

"I've been focused on modern art—abstract painting, mostly—the last few years. But my focus in college was on portraiture." Dylan's face glowed red at this admission.

Such a strange man.

"Did I hear you say you're an artist?" Jack Colby, Flannery's boss at the publishing house, joined them.

Caylor made the introduction.

"Have you ever considered doing artwork for book covers?" Jack asked.

Though Caylor had not thought it possible, Dylan turned an even darker shade of red. "I. . .I have done some cover work before—when I was in college."

Jack reached into his shirt pocket and pulled out a business card, which he handed to Dylan. "If you're interested in discussing some freelance work, give me a call."

"While I can't offer you the promise of paying work," Bridget wedged herself in between Jack and Dylan, "if you'd like something to keep you busy, I'm sure we could use your help designing and painting the sets for the spring play."

Interest chased the residual of embarrassment from Dylan's expression. "*Much Ado about Nothing*, right?"

"Oh, so you're familiar with it?"

"My. . . I had a. . .a roommate who loved the movie and watched it all the time."

"Well, we're going Italian Renaissance with our production, so it'll be a little more elaborate than what you got used to seeing in the movie. We're kinda thinking a Tuscan villa feel for the sets."

That was news to Caylor, who'd suggested keeping the play set in the Renaissance time in which it had been written and using the Tuscan motif for the backdrops, instead of changing it to ancient Rome the way Bridget had originally wanted to do it—to reuse costumes, sets, and props from their production of *Julius Caesar* two years ago.

"I did my undergraduate art history thesis on the works of the Renaissance portraitist Titian. As part of my presentation, I did a gallery show in that style, so I should definitely be able to help." The animation in Dylan's eyes made Caylor long for a pen and paper. Her publisher and agent had been pushing her for a new series proposal. Until meeting Dylan Bradley today, ideas and inspiration had been sparse. But now, though there wasn't a full-blown character or story idea yet, the sparks were definitely kindling.

Zarah came in and greeted everyone, and then Bobby asked the blessing, praying that each person present would remember to focus on the main reason for celebrating Christmas instead of getting caught up in all the busyness and materialism of the season.

When Caylor entered the dining room, she discovered that the place cards she'd put out had been moved around. She still had Zarah's boss, Dennis Forrester, to her left. To her right now sat Jack Colby; and directly across the table from her was Dylan Bradley. Caylor looked around at all the food on the table and felt guilty. Zarah had taken the day off work to prepare dinner for twelve people, half of whom were not her friends but friends of Caylor and Flannery. In addition to the standing rib roast and baked turkey breast, Zarah had made homemade yeast rolls, sweet potato and green bean casseroles, scalloped potatoes from scratch, and a large, green salad filled with hand-cut vegetables. Sure, Caylor had brought some decadent desserts with her, but other than going to the grocery store to get some of the ingredients and then licking the spatulas and beaters as Sassy handed them to her, she hadn't done any of the hard work of preparing them. Of course, she was pretty sure that most of the appetizers had been in boxes in the freezer section at Costco a few hours ago, before Flannery picked them up on her way over here from work. But that was okay—she and Zarah encouraged Flannery to buy stuff already prepared.

Before filling her plate, Caylor visualized herself in the dark turquoise dress she wanted to wear to the faculty Christmas party. Cut to skim the figure, the dress had been a spring purchase to take with her to awards banquets at two different conferences at which her books were up for awards. She'd bought it in a size 14, telling herself she'd lose weight before the events late in the summer. The weight hadn't come off, so she'd had to resort to the black pants and sequined top she'd worn last year. But she'd pulled the dress out Wednesday night and tried it on, and it fit perfectly.

She couldn't afford to gain even two pounds in the next seven days, though, or it would be too tight. She took enough of each dish to have a taste but stuck to a larger portion of the turkey and green salad so she wouldn't feel quite so bad about eating desserts later.

Dennis Forrester held the basket of rolls for Caylor so she could take one out before passing it down the table. "I'm sure Zarah told you this, but I just want to tell you personally how much I enjoyed the production of *The Music Man* a couple of months ago. Did you ever consider taking up acting professionally?"

Pleasure heated Caylor's face. "I hadn't done any acting since my undergrad years until Dr. Wetzler"—she indicated Bridget, down the table from them—"came to Robertson to teach drama. She happened to overhear me reading James Joyce to my class in an Irish accent and then followed me all over campus for a semester, pestering me about helping out with the drama department—since I minored in it and teach so many of the classics in my classes. I finally gave in and agreed to nothing more than leading a few intensive seminars for the drama majors on Irish, Scottish, and British accents."

"After hearing you as an Irishwoman, I almost didn't believe Zarah when she told me you grew up in Nashville. She said you spent time studying over there."

Caylor nodded. "I spent a year in Oxford, working on my master's degree, and then went back for a semester at the University of Glasgow and two terms at the University of Dublin during my doctoral work."

"I would have given anything to study overseas."

Caylor wasn't sure if Dylan's comment had actually been meant for her to hear, he'd spoken with such a soft tone, almost as if to himself. Not wanting to exclude him if he had been trying to join into the conversation, Caylor turned her attention to him. "If you could take a sabbatical for a year anywhere you wanted, study anywhere you wanted, paint anywhere you wanted, where would you go?"

Dylan gave a shrug and a sardonic smile. "It sounds kind of cliché, but I'd have to pick Paris and the Sorbonne."

"I'm no artist, but I would imagine that Paris is one place where every artist should spend time, if for nothing else than the museums and galleries." Caylor mentally recorded Dylan's expressions of self-consciousness and wistful hope.

Not being able to figure out why he seemed so familiar to her irritated Caylor—she would do whatever it took to figure it out. But until then, she would find ways to keep studying him, keep observing him—as the template for the hero in her next romance novel, be it contemporary or historical. Maybe if she got to know him well enough, he might even agree to let the publishing house use his image for the front cover of the book.

Chapter 4

$\mathcal{D}$ylan checked his watch and downed the last gulp of coffee. He'd been ready to go for almost twenty minutes, but until he heard—

Under his feet, the automatic garage door opener whirred. He popped a piece of sugar-free peppermint gum in his mouth, shrugged into his sport coat, and loped down the stairs to the garage.

When he'd informed Perty yesterday he'd decided to go to church with them—this week, anyway—she'd suggested he ride with them and visit the singles class while he was at it. If he hadn't heard Zarah, Bobby, and Flannery talking about the class Friday evening, he might have balked. But at least with them there, it might not be so awkward.

Gramps nodded over the roof of his Lexus—Dylan wasn't sure if it was meant to convey a greeting or approval. Could have been both.

Whatever. If he looked up *duress* on Wikipedia, there would be a video of this situation.

"Here." Perty handed Dylan a large, gray, leather-bound Bible. "I wasn't sure if you had—if you'd unpacked yours yet or not."

Of course. Having grown up in church, he should have remembered that only heathens and backsliders went to church without a Bible big enough to choke Godzilla. He climbed into the backseat and put the book down beside him as he buckled up.

Perty surprised him by going around to Gramps's side of the car and climbing into the backseat as well.

"We're picking up Sassy Evans on the way," she explained at his questioning look.

After several long minutes of nothing but soft classical music filling the car, Perty turned to look at him. "When did Dr. Holtz think he might be able to let you know about teaching next semester?"

Dylan shrugged. "He wasn't sure. Said he needed to do some shuffling. But he probably has two classes for me."

Apparently able to see that was all she was going to get out of him, Perty turned forward again. "I hope it works out for you."

Another pause.

"Your father called this morning to let us know they're back from Chicago early and will join us for lunch after church. Pax is meeting us at the restaurant, too."

Great. Dylan *knew* he should have driven himself this morning. He'd hoped to put off the inevitable confrontation with his parents longer—a lot longer—like after he had a full-time job somewhere else and was repacking to move far, far away.

"Did Spencer come back with them?"

"No—his finals are this week, but I don't think he's planning to come home as soon as they end. He mentioned a possible ski trip to Utah with some friends in his last e-mail to me. It will be the last chance he gets to relax. I've read the final two quarters of his program are merciless in their intensity."

Dylan turned his head away from this grandmother and rolled his eyes. Paxton was getting a PhD in physics from Vanderbilt University, Spencer, an MBA from Northwestern. And the whiz kid of the family, twenty-one-year-old Tyler, had just started his PhD work in math at MIT.

One of the few things Dylan would miss about living in Philadelphia was getting together with Tyler for weekends in New Haven, Connecticut, about halfway between their homes. Tyler seemed to be the only one in the family who didn't look down on Dylan for not pursuing a "real" major in his education.

Oh, and he'd miss the cheesesteak sandwiches from Pat's King of Steaks in South Philly.

"You didn't tell us anything about Zarah Mitchell's dinner Friday night." Perty must have gotten tired of the silence again. "How was it?"

He had to give her an A+ for her effort at car banter, so how could he not reciprocate? "It was fine. I met one of the drama professors from JRU, who wants my help designing sets for their spring play. And I met an editor from Lindsley House Publishing who might want me to do some freelance design work for them."

"That would be lovely—the freelance work—if it would come through. You'll want to be sure to follow up on that this week."

Pat me on the head and give me a lollipop while you're at it, Perty. Sure, maybe he hadn't shown the highest level of maturity when he'd chosen to move in with Rhonda six months ago—knowing that having any kind of romantic relationship with her, as the chair of his department, was against institute policy, even though everyone knew about it and turned a blind eye at the time—but he was twenty-eight years old for crying out loud. Why couldn't anyone in his family treat him like an adult?

Gramps turned onto a tree-lined street and then drove about half a block and pulled into a long driveway leading to a quaint white house. A white Ford Escape hybrid sat in the carport beside a much smaller vehicle covered with a gray car cover.

Sassy Evans. Caylor Evans's grandmother.

No sooner did her name cross his mind than Caylor herself walked out onto the covered porch that connected the house to the carport.

Dylan averted his eyes, but not before the image of the statuesque redhead dressed in a vibrant purple sweater, gray skirt, and high-heeled, tall black boots was seared onto his retinas. He might have to break down and draw her just to stop having such a strong visceral reaction to her every time he saw her.

A slender, white-haired lady—who looked petite compared to Caylor's over-six-foot stature, especially with the extra height from the heels—came out behind her and locked the door.

Dylan climbed out and opened the front passenger door for her—and realized Gramps was halfway around the car to do the same thing. Gramps smiled at him and then met Sassy just under the overhang of the carport roof.

Though he tried not to, Dylan met Caylor's turquoise gaze. He inclined his head. With one arm wrapped around what looked like a notebook and a Bible—not nearly as large as the one Perty had given him—she raised her free hand and wiggled her fingers in greeting, making her keys jangle. Instead of heading toward Gramps's car, Caylor went around to her SUV and climbed in. So, she wasn't riding with them, too?

"Sassy Evans, you remember our oldest grandson, Dylan." Gramps, who'd held Sassy by the elbow the few steps from the carport to the car, handed her over to Dylan to offer her assistance getting in.

Sassy's blue eyes twinkled, and she smiled a huge, Polident-commercial-worthy smile at him. "Of course I do. It's very nice to see you again."

"Thank you, Mrs. Evans. It's nice to see you again, too." He waited until she was settled in the seat, fastening her seat belt, before closing the door and getting back into the warmth the car offered.

After Dylan fastened himself back in, Perty reached over and patted his knee. When he looked over at her, she winked at him—and in that expression, all of the memories of Perty encouraging him to draw and paint, the kits of pastels and oils she'd given him, the professors she found to teach him technique, came rushing back in. He needed to give her the benefit of the doubt. Allow for the fact that this situation was probably as awkward for them as it was for him.

Mrs. Evans turned halfway around so she could look over the seat at Perty. They started discussing their senior adult group's upcoming Christmas party.

Dylan propped his elbow on the door and watched the expensive houses along Granny White Pike roll by. He wanted to know why Caylor hadn't driven her grandmother to church this morning, but he didn't want to show undue interest in her. No, it was bad enough his own brain wouldn't leave him alone about her. He didn't need to give their grandmothers any reason to suspect he'd even noticed her turquoise eyes with the slight uptilt at the outside corners, her patrician nose, her full lips, her seductively asymmetrical smile.

Gramps pulled the luxury sedan into the small parking lot behind the contemporary, redbrick church. Dylan unfolded himself from the backseat and stretched.

"Do you want me to help you find the Sunday school room?" Perty cradled her Bible in the crook of her elbow.

Dylan ducked his head back into the car to retrieve the one she'd given him. "I think I can manage, thanks." He slid the thick Bible under his arm. "I did grow up in this church, remember?"

"I know, I just—" But whatever Perty "just" remained unsaid. "Have a good time. We'll see you afterward."

Dylan raised his hand in farewell and headed for the main entrance.

"Do you think he'll. . ."

The woman in front of Dylan sneezed, drowning out the rest of Gramps's question. According to the rest of the family, the only thing Dylan had ever done right was to get a full-time professorship at a college with a prestigious reputation—even though it was just an art school. Would there ever be a time when he didn't have to worry about what everyone else in the family was saying about him behind his back?

Trying to put that lifelong insecurity out of his mind, he walked up to the hotel-check-in-style welcome center, part of the expansion building project that had nearly split the church apart his senior year of high school—which had started him on the road to disillusionment with organized religion.

"Welcome to Acklen Avenue Fellowship," a perky, middle-aged woman greeted. "Looking for a Sunday school class?"

He couldn't remember if they'd called it by a specific name Friday night. "Yes—the class for single adults."

She picked up a thin white binder. "Hmm. . .singles? Let's see. . .Oh—here we are. How old are you?"

Yeah, he definitely didn't want to get stuck with the thirty- and fortysomething Left Behinds. "Twenty-eight."

"Okay, you're looking for the Young Professionals class. Take the stairs here up to the second floor and go to the second room on the right—number 226."

"Thanks." Well, they hadn't called it by that name, but it had to be the right one. He jogged up the stairs and found the room easily—surprised by the large size of the space. In the middle were chairs set up in rows, lecture style, and on either end of the room were six circles of eight or ten chairs.

A few people milled around a table with pump-top coffee dispensers and boxes of doughnuts. A big guy—bigger even than Bobby Patterson—moved toward him, hand outstretched.

"Hey, I'm Patrick Macdonald."

Dylan shook the meaty hand. Though Patrick wasn't but an inch or so taller, he must have weighed at least seventy-five to a hundred pounds more. "Dylan Bradley."

"Welcome, Dylan. This is my fiancée, Stacy Simms."

She was the complete opposite of Patrick—thin and short with dark hair to his bulky, tall, and blond. But she had a handshake almost as firm as his. When he returned his hand to his side, Dylan flexed it to make sure all his bones were still whole and in the right places.

Patrick ushered him over to the registration table, where Dylan filled out a visitor information slip, and then over to the food and beverage table.

"Are you new to the area, Dylan?" Patrick motioned toward the coffee and doughnuts.

Dylan raised his hand to decline. "I grew up here. In this church, actually."

Patrick eyed him. "Really? So did I, and I don't remember you. When did you graduate from high school?"

"Ten years ago."

"Ah." Patrick nodded in understanding. "You probably came up into the youth group the year I graduated. Where'd you go to school?"

"High school? Hume-Fogg."

Patrick let out a low whistle. "Ah, so you're one of those genius types. No wonder our paths never crossed."

No, his brothers were the geniuses. He was the one who'd struggled with the coursework at the academic magnet school. If it hadn't had the best art program in town, he wouldn't have worked so hard to keep his grades up and stay in.

Patrick continued without waiting for Dylan to respond. "I'm just a football mutt from Hillsboro High. So what do you do now that brought you back to Nashville?" Patrick fixed himself a cup of coffee.

Actually, the question people should be asking was what had he *done* that brought him back to Nashville. "I'm. . ." What was he, really?

Well, Dr. Holtz had all but promised him at least two courses. "I'm an art professor. I'll be teaching at James Robertson this spring."

Patrick's blond eyebrows shot up. "Robertson? I know someone who teaches there part-time. Name's Zarah Mitchell."

"I met her Friday evening at a dinner party—and her fiancé and some other friends of theirs who go here." Dylan looked around the room to see if they'd arrived yet.

"That's great—so they told you about this class?"

Dylan moved out of the way of a guy and gal—obviously a couple—trying to get to the coffee. "They mentioned something about the class's Christmas party."

An odd expression came over Patrick's face. "About. . .did they actually say it was Young Professionals?"

"Not that I remember, no."

"I see." Patrick finished off the coffee and tossed the Styrofoam cup in the small trash can under the table, then stepped out of the way of another surge of people—couples, mostly, it seemed, coming for breakfast.

Dylan moved with him, continuing to scan the crowd for anyone he'd met Friday night. There were far more paired-off couples in the room than what he expected for a singles class—and if not mistaken, he was pretty sure all of them were wearing what looked like wedding rings.

"Zarah and Bobby are in the singles class."

Frowning, Dylan turned to look at Patrick. "Right."

"This is Young Professionals—our class is for twentysomething singles and marrieds."

"It's. . .but. . .so, what's the singles class?" This was another reason he'd gotten frustrated with organized religion—all their confusing divisions and terminology.

"Singles is for folks over the age of about thirty who, well, aren't married."

So if one was unmarried and under thirty, he was considered a young professional, and if he was over thirty, he was a single? Wait—that meant Zarah and Bobby and Flannery. . .and Caylor Evans. . .might be older than he originally thought. He'd figured they were all right around his age.

46

When he'd walked out of Rhonda's apartment, her threats of revealing his most closely held secret to the school trustees echoing behind him, he'd sworn he'd never get mixed up with an older woman again.

Just one more reason for him to avoid Caylor Evans.

∽

"So do you have a boyfriend yet?"

Caylor smiled down at the little old lady—well, she was little, and she looked old, though Caylor guessed she wasn't quite as old as Sassy. "No Mrs. Morton. Not since last Sunday."

"Well, I'm praying—and I've got all the other girls in the class praying—that a nice young man will come along soon. You've got too pretty a face to stay a spinster your whole life." Mrs. Morton patted Caylor's arm and shuffled off toward the sanctuary.

Caylor continued on to the choir room, shaking her head. She loved attending the smallish church, but that was one of the drawbacks: Everyone knew about and meddled in—all in the guise of praying for each other—everyone else's business. And ever since an online article about a church where the senior adult women's praying for the single adults in their church had led to a 1,000 percent increase in marriages, or something to that effect, had gone viral among the senior women's group, and since Caylor was one of the few unmarried adults who attended regularly, they seemed to have taken her on as their special project.

No one else had arrived yet. Caylor stuck her Bible in the cubby that held her choir music and carried her ensemble notebook to the piano. Grading theses and writing finals had made it nearly impossible for her to get in the practice she'd wanted on this morning's special music.

Finding the notes on the piano whenever she wasn't confident she was hitting them correctly while practicing it a cappella, Caylor was on her second run-through of the piece before anyone else in the eight-person ensemble arrived.

Soon, the other seven women were there. Dr. Bridger, who taught German at JRU, reviewed the pronunciations with them of the opening lines of the chorale, and by the time they were all saying their vowels and consonants the same way, the organist arrived.

They moved from the choir room to the sanctuary to practice with the microphones. Caylor loved the deep, second-alto harmony of the Advent-themed song with a slight baroque lilt, especially with the organist accompanying them on the electric keyboard set to a harpsichord sound.

After the first run-through, the sound guy—one of the other few unmarried adults in the church—came forward and removed the microphone near Caylor.

Embarrassment flamed her cheeks, even though she should be accustomed by now to taking grief from Gary for the way her voice carried in the small auditorium. She usually took teasing quite well, but the idea that the senior ladies had been trying for quite some time to get him to ask her out made her uncomfortable around him— especially since she knew that the fact she towered over his less-than-average height made him uncomfortable around her.

He set the mic stand in front of the women singing first alto, so that each one had an individual microphone, which meant that, even though Caylor was alone in singing her part, she was still drowning out multiple voices on other parts. He then came over, took her by the elbows, and made her take a couple of steps to her right—away from the rest of the ensemble. The other women laughed, and Caylor joined in, even though she didn't really feel like it.

"Why don't I just go stand up in the balcony?" she asked, making an effort at keeping her tone light.

"Hey—that could work." Gary looked over his shoulder at the balcony that wrapped, U-shaped, around three sides of the sanctuary. "But it might look funny."

Again, Caylor tried laughing with everyone else as Gary went back to the soundboard at the back of the room and the music started again.

She always tried to ease off. She really did. But she couldn't help that the others in the ensemble held back and she'd been trained by her drama and singing professors in college to project her voice so well, she did it without thinking about it.

Once they'd had a few complete run-throughs and a couple of shorter sound tests, they dispersed—most to slip into their Sunday school classes for a few minutes. Caylor returned to the choir room and pulled the stack of essays out of her purse and sat down to get some grading done.

After several silent minutes, the sound of a clearing throat startled her. Her pen left a purple streak across the well-written paragraph of the comparative literature essay.

Gary stood in the doorway. "Sorry to interrupt you."

Caylor clicked her pen closed so she wouldn't mar any more of the student's paper. "It's okay. What's up?"

"I just wanted to say. . .I hope I didn't offend you out there earlier. I realized that I probably could have done that differently to keep from making it look like an insult to you." He ran his hand over his thinning dark hair.

"Probably." No sense in pretending that his teasing hadn't been a little over the top. "But it's done with now. Let's put it behind us."

"Agreed." He shoved his fists into his jeans' pockets. "Mrs. Morton asked me about you this morning."

Her cheeks started burning again. "Oh really?"

"Yeah. Asked me if I'd ever thought about asking you out." He rocked from heel to toe to heel. "Caylor, I just want you to know that I think you're a great girl—woman—but there's nothing. . . I mean, I'm not—"

"We're friends. That's not going to change." Much as she liked Gary and respected his ability to single-handedly run the church's complex audio system, she couldn't picture herself out on a date with him, much less developing romantic feelings for him. "Mrs. Morton and the senior ladies are in a phase right now."

She explained to him about the article they'd all e-mailed around to each other. "I'm their special project. I wouldn't be surprised if they show up at Robertson when school starts again in January and go from door to door meeting the faculty so they can determine who all the unmarried men there are that they can try to set me up with."

Of course, if they happened to run across someone tall with shaggy, curly dark hair, a three-day growth of stubble, and expressive brown eyes teaching an art class, Caylor might not be so resistant to their meddlesome ways.

He'd looked quite nice in the glimpse she'd gotten of him this morning in a chunky, ivory cable-knit sweater with dark-brown pants and the buttery-soft, well-worn, brown, motorcycle-style leather jacket he'd worn to the dinner party Friday night. It had taken all her resolve that night to lay that jacket across the guest bed immediately and not stand there running her hands over the supple, smooth leather.

Gary excused himself—but Caylor hardly noticed. A new image of Dylan Bradley had just popped into her mind, not in any way she'd seen him so far, but in the doublet, breeches, tall boots, cloak, and broad-brimmed, feather-adorned cavalier hat stereotypical of the Renaissance era.

She stuffed the essays back into her purse and took out the small, decorative journal she always carried and started writing. Yes. . .Dylan Bradley might just be perfect as her new muse.

Chapter 5

𝒯his church was definitely not for him. Aside from the memories that came flooding back at each familiar area of the church Dylan entered, each friend of his parents or grandparents he encountered, each reminder of why he'd grown to dislike the seemingly superficial way in which everyone here talked to each other and "worshipped," he wasn't crazy about the showy performance put on by the "worship leader" and the "praise team." He didn't know a single song that was sung. And the guest speaker, with his over-the-ear, across-the-cheek headset microphone and the three large screens behind him running a slide show of the major points of his inspirational chat—for Dylan couldn't really consider it a sermon—seemed more like a motivational speaker on an infomercial hawking his latest product. ("I wrote about this very thing in my book. . . .")

From the crossed arms and frowns on the faces of many of the older people in the congregation, Dylan inferred he wasn't the only one unimpressed by the service. With the ginormous choir loft up behind the traditional-style pulpit conspicuously empty, he had to wonder if everything about this morning was a little bit off.

He cast a quick glance down the row to his left. Bobby Patterson, Zarah Mitchell, and Flannery McNeill all appeared to be concentrating as hard as they could—almost as if willing the speaker to say something pertinent or meaningful to them. But relief showed in Bobby's profile when the man brought his talk to a close.

After the invitation and closing hymn—a brief affair, with no one going down to the front—and benediction, Dylan stood and stretched. He looked around the crowd of singles gathering around Bobby, Zarah, and Flannery. He tried to convince himself he wasn't looking for a tall redhead to join them, but he couldn't help it.

"Is Caylor meeting us for lunch?" Flannery asked Zarah as they moved past him.

His ears perked up.

"Does she ever? I think she said something about picking something up and trying to get her grading finished before we meet up for coffee this afternoon." Zarah hooked her arm through Bobby's and then smiled up at Dylan. "Are you going to join us for lunch, Dylan?"

If only he'd driven himself. "My family's expecting me."

"Have fun." Zarah's silver-flecked blue eyes twinkled at him. "Maybe next time."

"Maybe." Although he was pretty sure he wasn't going to come back to this church. But where else would he go?

He said his good-byes and excused himself, spotting Perty and Gramps not far away. If it weren't eight or nine miles, and too cold outside for his leather jacket, he'd consider walking back to Gramps and Perty's house from here. Too bad Nashville didn't have a good public transit system like Philadelphia.

Instead of heading for the back of the church and the parking lot, Gramps, Perty, and Sassy Evans headed for the front. In the wide, medieval cathedral–looking doorway, Perty turned and looked around until she saw him.

"Didn't I tell you? We're meeting them at Boscos for lunch."

Ah. That made sense—the restaurant was just a block up Twenty-First Avenue from the church.

Across the street from Acklen Avenue Fellowship stood an equally large, white-pillared church. The sign on the corner of their lot was at such an angle he couldn't read it from here, but that might be a church to check out one of these weeks.

The strong, cold wind penetrated his leather jacket and heavy wool sweater as if they were made of summer-weight cotton. Crossing the final side street, he jogged ahead to open the door of the restaurant for his grandparents and Mrs. Evans.

"Looks like Pax and your parents aren't here yet," Perty said, unwrapping her scarf from around her neck.

They waited a few minutes while the servers put two tables together for them, unbundling and discussing the cold and whether it would, indeed, snow by Christmas.

Dylan examined the flyers and announcements posted on the restaurant's community board. One in particular caught his eye:

HILLSBORO VILLAGE ART WALK
EVERY FIRST THURSDAY OF THE MONTH
5–8 P.M.

Reading the sign again, he had to smile. How many first Thursdays did they think each month had?

He'd missed it for December—it would have been last week. He'd have to look up the event online when he got home to find out what it was and, if it really was what he hoped it was, what he'd need to do to get involved next month. If he could start getting some showings and get his stuff into some of the local galleries, hopefully he could start generating some extra income selling paintings.

The hostess led them to their table. He and Gramps assisted Mrs. Evans and Perty with their chairs and coats then took the seats directly across from them, leaving the other end of the table open for Dylan's parents and brother.

Speaking of his parents. . .

Through the restaurant came a tall, distinguished man with salt-and-pepper hair—more salt now than pepper—and a woman who didn't look old enough to have four twentysomething sons, much less to have risen to the second-highest level of the state judicial system.

But there they were, his parents: Davis Bradley, the senior partner in the law firm Gramps had founded more than fifty years ago, and Grace Paxton-Bradley, the appellate court judge.

Dylan stood as they came around the table to greet him. His father shook his hand, and his mother gave him a tense hug and kissed his cheek. He held out the chair beside him for her as Dad helped her with her burgundy wool overcoat.

She reached over and rubbed Dylan's sleeve as soon as they sat down. "That sweater looks good on you."

A compliment? "Thanks, Mother."

"Are you settling in okay?" Dad asked.

Dylan nodded. "Everything's unpacked, and I've gotten some furniture." He'd either thrown out or sold all of his college-era stuff when he moved in with Rhonda, so packing, moving, and unpacking hadn't taken much effort—physically, anyway.

Mother reached into her purse and withdrew a business card, which she handed to Dylan. A business contact? Someone who might help him find a job? He looked down at it: SUITE ONE SALON.

"That's my stylist's card, but you can set up an appointment with anyone there. They do a great job." She grabbed a fistful of Dylan's hair and gave it a playful tug. "If you're going to find a job, you're going to have to look professional."

Of course. Nothing about him was ever good enough for Her Honor, not even his haircut. She'd probably flip when she found out he had tattoos on his arms that were visible when he wore short sleeves.

"It was good to see you at church this morning," Dad, across the table from Mother, said from behind the Sunday brunch menu. "I know the singles division just went through some changes, and I understand that the new Young Professionals class has been highly successful, growing each week since they started it back at the beginning of October."

"Dylan visited that class this morning." Perty turned to him with raised brows. "How did you like it?"

He shrugged. "It was fine. The guy who leads it's pretty good. But almost everyone in there is married." Or a female who seemed starved for male attention and treated the class like a last-chance saloon. He hadn't felt that uncomfortable since the meeting with the chancellor when he learned his employment was being terminated based on violation of the institute's professional conduct policies.

"It's a good place to meet quality people, Dylan." The way Mother stressed *quality*, he wondered if she had anyone particular in mind, or if it was a veiled reference to the "unquality" people he'd known and been involved with in Philadelphia. As in *art* people—like him.

No. He had to stop jumping to conclusions and getting defensive—even if just inside his own head—whenever someone said something to him.

"I'm sort of hoping for a church a little smaller." He pretended to read the menu, though he'd decided within moments of sitting down what he wanted. "Where does Pax go to church now?"

"West End United Methodist. It's close to campus and his apartment. And he likes their Young Adult program," Dad said.

Perty clucked her tongue and exchanged a glance with Mrs. Evans. "He still hasn't found himself a girlfriend, though."

"He's only twenty-six, Mama." Dad put his arm around Perty and gave her a squeeze. "Give him a chance to finish his doctorate and decide which of the jobs that he's already been offered he's going to take."

Dylan wouldn't take that as a jab at his jobless state. No. He wouldn't.

Thankfully, the waitress appeared to take their drink orders. He ordered tea, thrilled at the prospect of its already being sweetened—with real sugar—and that he didn't receive looks of confusion or ridicule for ordering *iced* tea when it was cold outside.

"You're waiting on one more?" She looked at the extra menu at the place beside Dad.

"He should be here any moment. His church lets out a few minutes later, and he has to drive over and find a place to park," Perty explained. "We'll wait to order until he gets here."

Dylan's stomach gurgled its displeasure at having to wait longer for food. He should have had some doughnuts in Sunday school to augment the four Pop Tarts he'd eaten while waiting for Gramps and Perty to be ready to leave this morning.

The subject of the guest speaker came up once the menus went down. Even though not a one of them came out and said anything overtly negative, apparently none of them had been overly impressed with him either.

"There he is."

Dylan looked up at his mom's statement. Paxton raised his hand in response to their mother's wave and wended through several tables to get to them. He came around the table and hugged Mother, then reached behind her and shook Dylan's hand.

"I heard you were back in town." Paxton sat on the other side of their mom. "Isn't it a little early for classes to be out for the semester?"

Dylan wasn't sure what was worse—assuming everyone in the family was talking about him behind his back or having to explain to them face-to-face why he was here.

"I'm sure he'll tell you all about it later." Gramps's expression and tone brooked no opposition; obviously he was as uncomfortable with the thought of Dylan explaining himself as Dylan was.

The waitress returned, and everyone ordered while Pax read the menu.

Once she left, returned to refill their drinks, and left again, Dad leaned forward and looked down the table to make sure he had everyone's attention. "Since this is as close as we're going to get to having the whole family together—and we can't wait until Christmas—Grace has an announcement she'd like to make."

Mother's brown eyes glittered with excitement. "I got a call this week from Senator Davidson. His eightieth birthday is in February, and he's decided to retire. It hasn't been officially announced yet, but there will be a special election later in the spring—and Senator Davidson has thrown his endorsement behind me. So"—she smiled a perfect photo-op smile—"I'll be running for state senate over the next several months."

Dylan leaned over and gave her a squeeze around the shoulders. "Congratulations."

Once everyone else's reactions had died down, Dad drew their attention once again. "Of course this means that the entire family is going to be under some scrutiny." He pinned Dylan with his narrowed dark eyes for a brief moment before regaining his smile. "And there will be a few events and appearances at which we'll need you boys to show up and support your mom."

Pax leaned over and kissed her cheek again. "You know I'll do whatever you need me to."

"I'll help out however I can, too," Dylan added.

Dad looked like he had a comment about that offer, but fortunately, the waitress and a helper arrived with their food.

For the next fifteen or twenty minutes, Dylan focused on his blueberry Belgian waffle and bacon while everyone else around the table talked about all the stuff Mother needed to do to get ready for the campaign.

His attention pricked up at the mention of needing design work to be done for posters, flyers, ads, yard signs, letterhead, and other products. "I could do that for you, Mother."

"Oh. . .well. . ." She rested her hand on his arm again. "Your father and I discussed it, and we think it'll be better—more ethical—to hire an outside company to do things like that so that campaign funds aren't going to family members."

"I wouldn't charge you for it."

"I know you wouldn't, dear, and that's still a problem. You see, everything needs to be clean and legal and aboveboard. No cutting corners or doing anything that might draw undue media attention." She patted his hand and returned to her egg-white omelet.

Like the mere presence of the black sheep of the family might draw undue attention? He accidentally caught Perty's eye, and she gave him a sympathetic half smile.

For the remainder of the meal, Dylan kept his thoughts and ideas to himself. Luckily, it didn't last too much longer. Mother needed to go home and work, and Pax needed to stop by his lab to check on an experiment.

Dylan withdrew his wallet to pay for his meal, but Gramps waved him off. "Sunday dinner's my treat anytime you want to come with us."

"Thanks, Gramps."

Paying with cash meant they didn't have to sit around waiting for a receipt to sign, so Dylan followed Perty's lead and pushed his chair back and stood to put his jacket on.

"Dylan, a word."

Nothing good ever followed those words from his father. Dylan sank back into the chair beside his mother, whose expression turned grim.

"We'll get the car warmed up." Gramps briefly rested his hand on

Dylan's shoulder.

"This won't take long, sir." Dad had never, in Dylan's memory, called Gramps anything other than *sir*. Not *Dad* or *Pop* or even *Father*. Always formal. Always deferential. Possibly because he'd worked under him first as an intern, then as an associate, and then as a junior partner before Gramps became a judge and Dad took over the law firm. They'd had a professional relationship longer than they'd had a true father-son relationship.

As soon as everyone else was gone, Dad moved into the chair directly across from him, where Perty had been sitting.

"I don't think we have to tell you how disappointed we are in you."

Just like Dad. Straight to the point. No sugarcoating it. "No you don't."

"We haven't told your brothers anything—only that you've moved back to Nashville. We don't want you telling anyone else what happened. If someone from the opposition's campaign gets wind of what you did, it could generate enough of a scandal to hurt your mother's campaign."

It was on the tip of Dylan's tongue to remind them that they didn't even have a clue about the work he'd done to put himself through college—but the waitress appeared to pick up the check folder and ask if they needed anything else. Dad got rid of her with a smile worthy of a politician himself and a polite, "Thank you, no."

Dylan waited until she was out of earshot, grateful her presence had kept him from revealing something his parents should never know about. "Don't worry. It's not like I'm going around telling everyone why I lost my job."

"What are you doing to find another one?" Dad leaned back in his chair as if settling in for a long conversation.

He told them about going out to campus to talk to Dr. Holtz and the potential for freelance work with Lindsley Road Publishing.

"Good. Those are respectable prospects. Grace, you want to tell him about your idea?"

Mother turned sideways in her chair to face Dylan. "The firm has a client who owns a small storefront right here in the Village. It's vacant for the moment. But we thought we could do a campaign event there." Her eyes shimmered in the way they had when she'd learned she'd been short-listed for an appellate court seat. "An art show event. We'll display your art and then have an auction, and all the proceeds will go to charity. It should generate great press."

He wanted to say no so badly his throat ached. After all these years and all the snide comments about his doodling never amounting to anything, now they wanted to use him to get what they wanted.

"Just think about it—all those wealthy campaign donors looking at your artwork, learning your name, buying your paintings." Mother reached up and brushed an errant curl back behind his ear.

And all the money going to someone other than him.

His generous side kicked in and reminded him how many people were much worse off than he. Mother was right: It was a great opportunity to get his name and work out in front of people with disposable income who loved buying art and, just like the hoity-toities in Philly, would love to know they had something by a rising new talent—as the reviewer in the Philadelphia fine arts magazine had called him.

Besides, he could get rid of all of that stuff Rhonda had encouraged him to paint and start focusing more on the kind of art he enjoyed doing. "Okay. Just let me know when, and I'll work with the building owner to get everything set up."

Mother leaned over and gave him a quick peck on the cheek. "Thank you, son. You'll actually be working with the event planner from the campaign committee. But I'm glad you're on board."

"I meant it when I said I'd help out however I can."

Across the table, his father stood and shrugged into his long, dark gray overcoat. "The event planner will be in touch with you shortly. We're thinking about February or March for the show, since the special election will most likely be in April. In the meantime, you work on getting those employment opportunities squared away. We can't have you living on your grandparents' charity for too long, can we?"

"I'm on it, Dad." Dylan helped his mother into her coat and was surprised when she turned around and hugged him.

"We may not always show it, but we're glad to see you. And especially glad you'll finally be home for Christmas this year." She gave him an extra squeeze then released him to button her coat as they walked around the table to join his father.

"We are glad to have you home, Son." Dad squeezed his shoulder. "Just remember: no more screwups."

Since his whole life seemed to be, in his father's eyes anyway, one big screwup, Dylan didn't answer beyond a tight smile and a nod.

He really should have driven himself to church this morning.

Chapter 6

∞

When the last remaining student came up to the front, put her blue book on top of the stack on the desk, and said, "Merry Christmas, Dr. Evans," Caylor looked up from the spiral-bound journal in front of her—which she strategically folded her hands atop—and returned the sentiment. In truth, the interruption had jarred her out of sixteenth-century Italy where the old-maid daughter of a wealthy aristocrat was in the process of falling in love with the handsome but poor artist hired by her father to paint her portrait so it could be used in the quest to find her a husband.

After the student left, Caylor closed the notebook with a sigh. Giovanni and Isabella would have to wait. No matter how much she loved losing herself in her fictional worlds, grading final exams must come first.

She tucked the notebook and examination booklets into her bag, pulled on her coat, and draped her baby-soft scarf—hand-knitted by one of Sassy's friends—around her neck. If possible, the temperature had dropped even more in the two hours she had been inside the classroom building. She tied the scarf into a thick knot to protect her neck from the cold, buried her hands deeply in the coat pockets, ducked her head into the icy wind, and hurried across the quad to Davidson Hall. Back in her office, she turned on the space heater under her desk before unwrapping her warm layers. She had an hour before the next exam, so she might as well get started grading.

No sooner had she settled down at her desk and opened the first exam booklet to start grading than there was a knock on her door. Dr. Wetzler stood in the doorway still in her coat, scarf, and gloves.

"What can I do for you, Bridget?" Caylor rolled the rubber grip of her pen between her forefinger and thumb.

Bridget hesitated, which was not like her at all. "I want to ask you a question, but I don't want to make things weird between us."

Caylor would have laughed if the drama professor hadn't looked so serious. "You know you can ask me anything."

Bridget cleared her throat. "Okay. . .um. . .are you going to ask Dylan Bradley to the faculty holiday party?"

Caylor pushed her bag containing her story-idea journal a little farther under her desk with her toe. "I hadn't planned to, no." Even though she'd been trying to figure out how to spend more time around him—just to observe him for the sake of her character.

"Would it bother you if I asked him?" Bridget studied the pointed toes of her black boots intently.

"Why should it bother me?"

Bridget looked up with a cautiously optimistic smile. "Because it seemed like you and he hit it off really well at the dinner the other night. I just didn't want to overstep my bounds if something was happening between the two of you."

Now Caylor did give in to the urge to laugh—though she wasn't quite sure why. "Bridget, if you want to ask Dylan Bradley to be your date to the faculty holiday party, go for it. He's too young for me; and besides, you know I don't date anymore."

Bridget held her hand out in front of her like a stop sign. "That is a conversation for a whole 'nother day. But if you're sure you don't mind, I think I will ask Mr. Bradley to come to the faculty holiday party. Not as a date, mind you—because if he's too young for you, he's definitely too young for me—but just so he can start getting to know some of the other instructors and adjuncts in case he does get a position here next semester. If you want to flirt with him while he's here, feel free—it's not like it'll be a *date* date."

"Get out of here." Caylor waved in dismissal but with a smile. Laughter trailed Bridget down the hall.

Why hadn't she thought to invite Dylan to the faculty party? She had the perfect out to keep it from sounding like she was asking him on a date—after all, their grandmothers were best friends.

After giving her last exam for the day and meetings with two of her seniors stressed out about their oral exam presentations tomorrow—on which she was certain they would do perfectly well—Caylor packed up and headed home to work on grading. Only during finals time did she envy the science and math professors who could give fill-in-the-bubble tests that could be graded by machine. Comprehensive British literature exams didn't really lend themselves to multiple-choice questions. At least the final exam for the students in her Rhetoric and Comparative Literature classes would be brief oral presentations of their theses—which she'd finished grading at two o'clock this morning.

At home, her arms full of books and folders, she struggled to open the side door into the kitchen—and was greeted with the acrid odor of something—electric?—burning.

"Sassy?" Caylor shoved the door open with her hip, hating that the door dragged on the floor, making it that much harder to open.

Her grandmother stood at the wall-mounted double ovens just inside the door, fanning smoke out of the lower oven with a dish towel.

Caylor dropped everything onto the kitchen table. "What happened?"

"Heating element shorted out. . .again." Sassy coughed into her shoulder as she continued fanning. "Fortunately, it was just preheating—I hadn't put the sponge in yet."

Caylor crossed to the fuse box behind the door. The one labeled OVENS had already been unscrewed. "I'll call Gary and see if he or one of his guys can come out tonight." She looked around at the Swiss roll pans and other ingredients Sassy had laid out on the counters, including yellow sponge-cake batter still dripping from the beaters in the old stand mixer. "Were you making Bûche de Noël?"

The holiday cake—thin yellow sponge slathered with milk chocolate buttercream, rolled, then frosted with dark chocolate buttercream and textured to resemble the Yule log for which it was named—was one of Caylor's favorite desserts of the season. Not that she'd ever met a dessert she didn't love.

"I'll call Perty, see if she has oven room for me in her kitchen."

Sassy pushed up on the oven door and let it slam closed. "Of course, she never uses that gorgeous kitchen of hers."

Relieved the house wasn't burning down around her grandmother, Caylor picked up her bag, purse, books, and folders. "You know, Sassy, the only thing that's keeping you from having a kitchen like Perty's is sheer stubbornness and the idea that you're spending your kids' inheritance. Considering you've got at least another good twenty years in you, the money you spend remodeling and modernizing this kitchen would give a better return on investment than just sitting around in a savings account."

Sassy leaned her hip against the edge of the counter near the mixer. "You only want me to remodel the kitchen so it'll be easier to sell this house when I die."

Caylor crossed the room, arms full again, and leaned down to kiss her grandmother on the cheek. "Yep, that's exactly why I want you to remodel a kitchen that now has two ovens that don't work, a five-burner stove with only three working burners, a dishwasher that leaks, and a refrigerator that's older than me. It's not because I'm concerned about your safety at all."

"You skedaddle." Sassy waved the dish towel at her. "I'll call Perty and get her to come pick me up so I can finish this over there."

"Are you sure? I can take you—"

"No, you need to work. Plus, then you can be here if you can find someone who can come out this afternoon."

"Okay. If you're sure."

At her grandmother's nod, Caylor headed upstairs to her loft, added on to the house five years ago when she'd agreed to move in to be Sassy's main means of transportation. The contractor had taken one look at the fuse box in the main house and insisted on running completely separate electrical for the office, bedroom, and bathroom that comprised Caylor's living area. The only thing the loft lacked to make it a complete apartment was a kitchen and a separate entrance— which could have been accomplished by running stairs down the back of the house from the small balcony where Caylor liked to sit and write during nice weather.

She hated it whenever Sassy talked about dying. Logically, with her grandmother having just celebrated her eighty-third birthday this year, she knew Sassy wouldn't be around another twenty years. But Caylor didn't want to think about what life would be like without her—even just a mundane thing like selling the house after she was gone. Sure, even in its original 1950s condition, the house was now worth at least a hundred times what Papa and Sassy had paid for it more than half a century ago—and it hadn't been cheap then. And Caylor had given up her freedom, living in a large house near Hillsboro Village with Flannery and Zarah five years ago, to live rent-free in Forest Hills, one of the poshest, most expensive neighborhoods in Nashville—though she did insist on paying all the utility bills.

When Caylor agreed to move in, they'd had to do a little bit of reconfiguration downstairs—they'd needed to add a staircase, after all, which had taken the main level down to two bedrooms but created a family room where one of the three original bedrooms had been, and they'd added a three-quarter bath in Sassy's room.

Caylor tossed her bag on top of the credenza at the end of her large corner desk. Her journal slid out of the top, just a little.

Oh how she'd love to spend the rest of the day in Renaissance Italy with her new characters. The image of Dylan Bradley floated before her mind's eye. As soon as the semester ended, she was going to work on figuring out where she knew him from.

❧

Sassy snapped the plastic lid onto the mixing bowl containing the double batch of cake batter for the Bûche de Noël right as a car pulled up to the house. She wiped her hands and crossed to open the door to let Perty in.

Short and plump to Sassy's tall and slim, Perty bustled from the driveway to the carport and up the steps to the porch that shared the carport's roof and connected the kitchen to the laundry-utility room.

Bundled in a silky, royal blue, quilted car coat, Perty dashed into the house. "Just heard on the radio they're thinking we might have snow by Christmas."

"They say that every year just to get children excited—and then it never happens." Sassy closed the door, shivering from the cold blast of air.

"Not never. Just rarely." Perty started recounting the handful of years in their lifetimes when there had been snow—or ice—on the ground on Christmas as she helped Sassy pack up everything she'd need for making the cakes.

The squeal of the third step from the bottom gave them a moment's notice before Caylor appeared in the kitchen.

"Hi, Dr. Bradley." Caylor winked at Perty, who never allowed anyone but Caylor to call her by her official title anymore. "I just came down to see if y'all need help carrying stuff to the car." She'd changed into jeans, a green turtleneck that emphasized her red hair, and an oversized red-and-green flannel shirt that did nothing for her perfect hourglass figure.

"Certainly. If you can get that box"—Sassy indicated the cardboard banana crate they'd picked up on one of their recent Costco trips— "out to the car, that would be wonderful."

Caylor lifted the heavy box with more ease than Sassy or Perty would have managed and took it out to Perty's car. She came back in with another blast of cold air. "I talked to Gary. He's got one of his guys working out in the area today already, so he's going to send him over as soon as he's finished with his current job."

"Who's Gary?" Perty asked.

"Our electrician." Sassy loaded the large bag of confectioners' sugar into the cloth grocery bag already holding the other ingredients for the buttercream frosting. "He goes to Caylor's church." She gave Perty an I'll-tell-you-all-about-it-in-the-car look.

After helping them finish loading everything into Perty's sleek, dark-gray Mercedes sedan, Caylor stood on the side porch and waved as Perty backed up.

"So, tell," Perty insisted as she turned the car around.

"Gary is a young man who attends Caylor's church. She's a bit frustrated that the older ladies at the church keep trying to set her up with him."

Perty headed down the long driveway. "Why won't she go out with him?"

"She says she just doesn't like him that way. I think it's less about her than it is about him—he's short, and he probably feels intimidated by her height." Sassy squinted ahead through the windshield, but even with her glasses, everything beyond about ten feet was blurred directly in front of her. Her peripheral vision, though, remained strong.

"That is problematic. I remember that even with as tall as you are, it was hard to find men as tall as you wanted."

Sassy nodded. At five foot nine, she'd always towered over the other women her age. "And when I first met Frank, I wasn't certain it would work—he was only an inch taller than me. But he told me to keep wearing my heels—that he was proud to be seen with a taller woman. He always told Caylor the same thing—to hold out for a man who would be proud to be seen with such a statuesque beauty."

"My grandsons are tall—but too young for Caylor." Perty chewed the corner of her lip.

Sassy didn't hold to such strict rules about ages in relationships as her friend, but this wasn't the time to argue. "Well, I've come up with an idea, and I'll need your help to plan it—yours and Gerald's."

"What kind of plan?" Perty turned to look at her as she waited on a traffic light to turn.

"A plan to kill two birds with one stone—introduce Caylor to some new young men and get my kitchen all fixed up at the same time."

A grin split Perty's face. "You mean, you're going to have your kitchen remodeled—but hire a contractor who's young, handsome, and single?"

"Exactly—which is why I need your help, since you and Gerald just redid your house. And if she doesn't fall for the kitchen contractor, I may have to do what you've been bugging me to do for years—have the entire house updated. There must be any number of young, handsome, unmarried contractors in this town." Sassy rubbed her hands together, already picturing the towering, muscle-bound, perfect example of manhood sweeping Caylor off her feet, like one of those medieval warrior types in the books Caylor used to write.

"If you can get that started soon, you may win the great-grandchild race before Trina and Lindy's grandkids even make it down the aisle." Perty pulled out onto Granny White Pike, headed toward her home.

"That's exactly what I was thinking. So, will you help me?"

"It would be my pleasure."

"The whole house needs to be rewired."

"Tell me something I don't know," Caylor muttered, head propped on her fist, slumped in one of the red vinyl chairs at the kitchen table.

The electrician—one she'd never met before—turned to give her a wry look over his shoulder. "We've been working over the last few years upgrading the electrical systems in most of the houses out in this area. Really helps with resale value."

"Yeah. . .not a consideration here. I just want to make sure that the wiring isn't going to short out and burn down the house one of these days—especially when my grandmother is here alone." She uncrossed her legs and recrossed them the other direction. "Can the oven be salvaged?"

He shook his blond head. Sassy would be disappointed. The guy was classically handsome as well as buff and tall—a couple of inches taller than Caylor—and she guessed he was probably close to her age. But a platinum wedding band hugged the ring finger of his left hand. He was probably married to some petite, slender thing with long hair and dark, doelike eyes. That's the kind of woman this kind of guy married in real life.

Now, if he were the hero of one of her books, she'd put him with. . .who? Average height, average build—perhaps even a little on the plump side. Maybe a contractor or. . .or an architect. Yes. An architect, and they would be at odds over a project—

"Ma'am?"

"Sorry. My mind wandered there for a moment. What did you say?" She stood and retrieved the small legal pad from beside the refrigerator to get her idea written down before she forgot it.

"What do you want me to do? The ovens aren't fixable. If I screw the fuse back in, it's likely there'll be a fire." He hooked his hand around the back of his neck and rubbed as if he had a crick.

Ooh, she needed to write that mannerism down.

"Just leave it. It's long past time that the appliances in this kitchen were replaced." She scribbled a few more notes and then flipped the notepad over so there was no danger he'd see it. She wished she could figure out a way to take a picture of him for future reference if she ever did end up using this idea.

"Okay. I'll put the panel back together and get out of your hair." He turned his attention back to the fuse box.

It was worth the risk. Caylor picked up her phone, turned the sound off, brought up the photo app, and snapped several pictures of him in the few moments it took him to finish his work and write up an invoice for her.

She wrote a check and then let him out the kitchen door. She e-mailed the images to herself so she could put them in a file on her computer with the rest of the real-world templates for characters in her story ideas.

For good measure, she printed out the three best images and opened the bottom drawer of the lateral file that extended the work surface at the right-hand end of her desk. She pulled out the TEMPLATES file.

"Hello, dear." She ran her index finger down the copy of a pencil drawing of the man who'd been the inspiration for the heroes of all of her novels to date.

She wasn't sure where the artist, Patrick Callaghan, had found the male model—whose looks he'd changed only slightly from cover to cover of her six bestselling secular romance novels, based on the hair and eye color Caylor had given him in each book. All she knew was that there was something about that man that made her want to write about falling in love—to experience vicariously through her characters something she'd never felt in real life, not even for the man she'd almost married seven years ago.

The same something now stirred up by Dylan Bradley. She stuck the images of the electrician in the folder—under her favorite Patrick Callahan drawing, which always stayed on top—

Was it her imagination, or did the model in the drawing look eerily like Dylan Bradley?

She closed the folder and returned it to the drawer. "Okay, I'm losing it. There's no way that guy is Dylan Bradley. Just wishful thinking."

Just to prove it to herself, she crossed to the bookshelves that lined the other side of the U-shaped office and pulled down a couple of her Melanie Mason books. There, on the front covers, in full-color glory, was Patrick Callaghan's artwork. And there—maybe he did resemble Dylan, slightly. But the guy on the covers was muscular, much broader through the shoulders and thighs than Dylan Bradley—who, though well built, was still rather slim.

Laughing at herself, Caylor returned to her desk and the finals she needed to grade. As if someone like Dylan Bradley would have modeled for a clench cover of a romance novel anyway. Preposterous.

Chapter 7

❧

$\mathcal{N}$ever having driven into downtown Nashville midmorning on a Tuesday before, Dylan had been uncertain what to expect. The experience once again left him wishing Nashville had a true public transit system. Traffic seemed to bombard him from every direction as soon as he got off I-40 at the Broadway exit.

It was enough to make him start praying again.

Just a couple of blocks up Broadway from the interstate was the imposing 1930s art deco building, once the main post office for Nashville, now the Frist Center for the Visual Arts, Nashville's only art museum. It had opened when he was in high school, but Dylan had been forced to wait until he was seventeen and had his driver's license before he'd been able to visit. Then every weekend when he wasn't working or studying or adding pieces to his portfolio for college entrance applications, he was at the Frist, drinking in the ever-changing art exhibits from all over the world and representing all eras and mediums.

He slung the long strap of his bag over his head so it crossed his chest, and his sketch pad and pencils rested on his right hip, ready should inspiration strike. He made it to the top of the steps leading to the main entrance before he remembered he still had his cell phone in his pocket—reminded only when it started ringing.

Diverting from entering the door, he answered it. "Hello?"

"Mr. Bradley? Please hold for Dean Holtz."

A frisson of excitement jolted through Dylan as the line went silent then clicked twice. The dean of Robertson's art department wouldn't be calling him personally if he didn't have good news.

"Dylan, Leonard Holtz here. Wanted to tell you that I do need you for the spring semester. You'll be teaching Italian Renaissance Art for the art history side and the special studies studio on portraiture for the BFA students."

Portraiture. His first art love. And the talent that had led him astray—almost as far astray as Rhonda had led him. "Thank you, Dr. Holtz."

"I understand from my secretary that you need to come in as soon as possible to fill out the paperwork and pick up the sample syllabi and curriculum requirements so you can start planning."

Dylan glanced up at the stone facade of the art museum and let out a silent sigh. "I'll be there in about twenty minutes."

"We're glad to have you on board."

Dylan echoed the dean's farewell, slipped the phone back into his pocket, and trudged down the steps and back around the side of the building to his vehicle.

His ability to draw and paint realistic—somewhat embellished—human forms had paid his way through college. And eventually had become the leverage Rhonda had needed to get him to do whatever she wanted him to do.

How was he to know that no one at Watts-Maxwell cared that he'd illustrated the covers of steamy romance novels to pay his way through school?

No, he'd taken Rhonda's word for it and allowed her to use that knowledge to coerce him into becoming her arm candy. And he'd let her because she was older, more experienced with the way the administration and school politics worked—and because she was the first person ever to show any pride in his accomplishments. Sure, after the first year or so, he'd realized it was the reflected glow of his success she wanted—*she* had discovered him; *she* had put his name on the Philadelphia art map.

At the intersection of Broadway and I-40, he considered for a moment whether surface streets or the interstate would be closer. But when he looked down Broadway to where it split at West End and saw the backed-up traffic, he made his choice. They might be farther distance-wise, but the interstates sure would be a lot faster.

Within the allotted twenty minutes, he found a parking space behind Davidson Hall, and chin tucked into the up-turned collar of his jacket—why did forty degrees in Nashville feel colder than the low teens in Philadelphia?—he started past Davidson Hall to cross the quadrangle to Sumner Hall. Halfway across, the quiet campus suddenly came alive with students pouring from the buildings, talking, laughing, calling to one another, talking on their cell phones.

Since they weren't watching where they were going, Dylan paid close attention so he wouldn't get run over or smack into anyone. He finally made it to Sumner—and to warmth. He didn't remember it getting this cold in Nashville before Christmas, but he was going to have to give up the idea that he was accustomed to a colder climate and go ahead and get out his heavy coat when he got back to the carriage house.

"Dylan?"

He looked around, unable to tell where the echoing female voice came from against the noise of the students beginning to crowd the hall on their way to and from finals.

"Dylan Bradley?" She spoke again, this time from above him. Bridget Wetzler, the drama professor, came down the last few stairs, struggling to get her scarf untangled from the stack of books and papers she carried.

"Dr. Wetzler." He took the end of the scarf from her hands, freed it from between a notebook and a textbook, and looped it loosely around her neck.

"Thanks." She settled her armload of stuff on her more-than-ample hip. "It's great that I ran into you. I was actually going to call you later on today."

She, too, had red hair—in a shoulder-length bob, and he was pretty sure that it wasn't her natural color, which, from the color of her eyebrows, he suspected was a dull, mousy brown—and she had greenish brown eyes and a white, straight smile. But nothing about her drove him mad with the desire to draw or paint her. "You were going to call me?"

"Yes. You see, the faculty holiday party is Friday evening, and I wondered if you might be interested in attending as my guest."

Dylan resisted the urge to take a step back. Not that she wasn't cute—in a plump, forty-is-the-new-thirty, cat-lady kind of way.

The drama teacher's expressive face registered she'd recognized his shock. "Now, before you get freaked out being asked out by a total stranger, I'm asking because I know you're trying to get on the faculty here, and if you do end up teaching as an adjunct in the spring, this is a great way for you to start getting to know some of the other faculty and adjuncts in a more relaxed, casual environment. You wouldn't even have to feel the need to stay with me once we're in the door. You could mingle and network as you see fit."

And he could observe Caylor Evans without her even realizing it. No. No thoughts of the English professor whose Rubenesque beauty made her the perfect muse for someone who specialized in the Italian Renaissance style of painting. "Sounds like fun."

"Great! Why don't you just meet me at my office—I'm in Davidson 215—right around seven o'clock Friday evening, and we can walk over to the dining hall together. It is kinda dressy, so you'll want to wear a suit and tie. The president always comes in a tuxedo—probably bought it for a wedding or something and figures this is the only opportunity he'll have to get any use out of it."

Dylan could relate—he could wear the two-thousand-dollar Armani suit from Boyds Rhonda had convinced him he needed. He'd bought it and paid to have it tailored (leading to his no longer being able to afford to stay in his own apartment six months ago), bought a pair of three-hundred-dollar wingtips, since none of his shoes were good enough for it, wore the ensemble out on a date with her once, and then listened in horrified disbelief when she told him a suit wasn't the right look for him.

"And the vice president?" he asked.

"She has a little black dress that would make Audrey Hepburn jealous." She looked at her watch and moved toward the doors. "I've got to run to a meeting with a student. But I'll see you Friday?"

"I'll meet you at your office at seven."

As soon as she vanished out into the wind and cold and rush of students, Dylan took the stairs up to the third floor and found the dean's suite of offices. The secretary gave him all the requisite paperwork, and he sat at the small table in the corner of her office to fill it out.

"I've got the photocopies of your transcripts that you dropped off with your curriculum vitae, but we'll need official copies as soon as you can get them sent to us."

He didn't look up from the tax form. "I've already requested them from both schools. They should be here before next semester starts."

A little while later, Dylan handed over the filled-out forms and accepted a manila folder of information about the classes he'd be teaching. Assured the secretary didn't need anything else from him, Dylan left, opening the folder to look through it as he walked down the hall. Both classes were scheduled for Mondays and Wednesdays—Italian Renaissance Art from 9:30 to 10:45 in the morning, and the portraiture studio from 12:45 to 3:30. Good. Studio needed a double period.

He read the course descriptions next. The art history class he could teach in his sleep—he'd taught it every semester for the last four years at Watts-Maxwell. The one that he hadn't taught before was portraiture, even though that had been his major field as a student.

Advanced studio work with studies from the live model.

Live model? Where was he supposed to find someone to come model for the class for three hours, two days a week? He was grateful it wasn't a class with studies from a *nude* model. He didn't consider himself a prude—and given the amount of bare flesh in Titian's work, on which he'd written his master's thesis, how could he?—but in both undergraduate and graduate school, the required drawing and painting studios that used nude models had presented some of the most uncomfortable moments of his life.

Of course, he was somewhat hypocritical with that—because drawing or painting a nude for purely artistic reasons had bothered him, but creating sensual, chest-baring, bosom-heaving images for steamy romance novels hadn't raised a single qualm for him. At least not then.

But now. . .

No one knew the pseudonym he'd painted those covers under

almost ten years ago. But those books had hit the bestseller lists. There were even a few websites dedicated to the cover art of those books, discussion forums about trying to discover the name of the male model the artist Patrick Callaghan had used for each of the six covers.

They'd be so disappointed if they learned the truth.

—◈—

"Thank you so much for your call, Dr. Holtz. And thank you for keeping this just between us." Perty turned off the cordless phone and set it on the table between the two armchairs, then picked up her knitting again, determined to get this sleeve set before lunch.

"I thought you weren't going to interfere." Gerald snapped the newspaper to straighten the pages.

"There's interfering and then there's helping out behind the scenes. I'm just helping out my grandson behind the scenes. Leonard needed additional adjuncts for the spring. I wanted to make sure he gave Dylan the consideration he deserves."

Gerald grunted. "If the boy finds out, there's no telling how he'll react."

She let the half-finished sweater fall back into her lap. "*If* he ever finds out. Hopefully if he ever does, he'll be enjoying teaching at Robertson so much that he'll be grateful instead of angry."

Her husband grunted again and flipped the page of the section.

"He's so different since he came back." Perty ran her hand along the rib-knit cuff of the extra-long sleeve. The bright blue sweater would look so good on her extra-tall oldest grandson. Perhaps even bring a smile to his face—something she hadn't seen since he'd driven in a week ago, his SUV loaded with all his worldly possessions, a world-weary forlornness in his expression that broke her heart.

"Defensive, for sure."

"Oh, if I could get my hands on that woman. . ." Perty squeezed her fists, ignoring the slight pain in her knuckles. "She had no right to do what she did to my boy."

"He's not blameless in this, remember."

"I'm not saying he's blameless. He made a stupid choice. But what did she do to him in the years before that to get him to the point where he would make a decision like that? He was raised better." For the past five years, her heart had ached just a little more each time he called to say he wasn't coming home for Christmas. "I'm not calling names or making accusations, but isolating someone from his family is something that happens in abusive relationships."

"True."

She reached for her coffee cup, discovered it was empty, and set the knitting down into the basket beside her chair. "And why else would a handsome young man like Dylan get involved with a woman in her forties unless she somehow coerced him into it?"

Gerald didn't respond. Frustrated, Perty took her coffee cup back into the kitchen to refill it. Compared to the sunroom, the kitchen was dark, the overcast sky outside not letting much light through.

Ready to settle in and enjoy her second cup—or was it her fourth? fifth?—she set the ceramic mug down on the warming plate and bent to pick up the knitting again.

Gerald looked up at her, looked down at his own empty coffee mug, and then back up at her with a comically pitiful expression.

"Oh for mercy's sake." She snatched the mug and took it in to refill it. He had, after all, made breakfast this morning and brought it to her, in her chair, on a tray.

"Thank you, my love." Gerald caught her hand and kissed the back of it when she handed the cup to him.

She settled back into the plush wing chair and propped her feet on the matching ottoman. The fragrance of coconut tickled her senses as she sipped the strong, macaroon-flavored coffee.

"Have you ever considered that Dylan fell in love with this woman?" Gerald cradled his mug between his hands, as if warming them.

"No. He didn't—he wouldn't. Not with someone almost old enough to be his mother."

"Do you remember what you always used to say about Dylan never acting his age as a boy?"

She tapped her thumbnail on the handle of the mug. "No."

"Helen. . ."

Her face ached from trying not to smile. He only used her given name whenever he was about to lose it. Which, with him, meant going totally silent for the next twelve to twenty-four hours. "Oh, all right. Dylan has always acted older than his age because he has an old soul."

"And. . . ?"

"And that it wouldn't surprise me if he ended up falling for a woman who's older than he." She set the cup back on the small electric warmer and picked up her knitting again. "But I never meant someone *that* much older. Five years, maybe ten. Not twenty. And definitely not someone who would pull him away from everything he grew up to believe in—like family and God."

"Do you know for certain that he no longer believes in God?"

"Why else would he have abandoned all his morals and moved in with that. . .woman?" Unable to focus on the intricate stitches she needed to be making, Perty rested her hands in the nest of soft cotton-rayon-blend yarn.

With a sigh, Gerald pulled his reading glasses off, folded the bows closed, and tapped one end against his chin—just as he had probably done on countless occasions when on the bench. "Do you honestly believe that the only people who make bad choices are those who aren't Christians?"

She, too, pulled off her reading glasses, letting them hang by the crystal-bejeweled chain around her neck. "Of course not. And I pray that is not the case with Dylan."

"If memory serves, he had stopped attending church regularly before he graduated from high school—back when the building program became so divisive. He has always been overly sensitive to conflict. Made me wonder then if he was choosing Sunday shifts at the restaurant just so he didn't have to witness the infighting at church."

How had she not noticed this about her favorite grandchild—the one she'd always felt took after her more than after Gerald? (Not that she meant to have favorites, of course, but these things happened.)

The security alarm beeped twice, indicating someone had opened a door and that the system was disarmed.

"Gramps? Perty?"

"In the sunroom, dear," she called.

Dylan came in, looking ruggedly windblown, his curly hair pulled back from his face with a band that hugged the crown of his head. He'd shaved for church Sunday, but not since then, apparently. Not that she minded at all. In their younger years, when on vacation, Gerald would forgo shaving, and she remembered liking that quite well.

"You left a message that you wanted to see me?" He unzipped his jacket to reveal a maroon flannel shirt over a white turtleneck. With well-worn but nice jeans, a brown belt, and brown outdoorsy lace-up boots, he could have passed for Paul Bunyan.

She pulled her feet off the ottoman and patted it, not wanting a crick in her neck from looking up at him.

He pulled off the jacket and tossed it over the footstool before sitting down.

A lump formed in Perty's throat. How many hours had he sat there, on that stool, elbows on his knees, chin on his fists, listening to her read? Yet then it had always been with a sense of excitement in his eyes, a smile never far from his lips. What did she need to do to bring that back and erase the dolefulness that hung about him like an albatross?

"I figured you'd be at the museum all day, that we wouldn't see you until later tonight."

"I got a call from Dr. Holtz at Robertson to go in and sign the paperwork to teach next semester. Renaissance art history and a portraiture studio." He ran his thumb over a worn spot in the denim near his left knee.

"That's wonderful. I know you'll love teaching there. Are they day or evening classes?"

He told her the schedule, and a bit of the melancholy left him as he talked about it, though with an economy of words. Still no smile, no sense of excitement or anticipation came to the surface by the time he finished.

"That will be a great foot in the door there if you decide you want to pursue a full-time faculty position should one come open next year." Still no flicker. Maybe he would cotton to her next idea. "I had an idea last night that I wanted to run by you. You could make a little money from it if you wanted to, but it would mostly be a free service you'd provide."

He raised his thick, dark brows—a genetic gift from her Eastern

79

European roots—which she took to mean he was amenable to listening to the idea.

"Would you be interested in teaching an art class for the senior adults at church? It can be afternoons or evenings, whatever you prefer—but daylight hours work best for most of us—and you could charge a registration fee if you really wanted to, though most people would be doing well to be able to afford basic art supplies."

His expression went through a myriad of changes—first attention, then interest, then—confusion? Confusion over what she was saying?

"Dylan?"

"Why?" He shook his head, the skin between his brows folding together in a frown.

"Why. . .what?" Now she was confused, too.

"Why do you want me to get up in front of all of your friends? As Dad pointed out Sunday, I know I'm a disappointment to everyone in the family." He shrugged as if this were an inconsequential statement.

Perty leaned forward and pressed her palms to his stubbly cheeks, forcing him to look at her. "I may be disappointed in your actions, but I am not disappointed in *you*. I love you, and I could not be prouder of your accomplishments and talents. And I want to show all of my friends just how accomplished and talented"—she pulled her hands forward until his lips began to pucker—"and handsome my grandson is. Do you think I could take Paxton to that group and have him teach them something? No one would understand a word coming out of his mouth, bless his heart. Have Spencer teach them international business structures or Tyler talk to them about math?"

His face moved under her hands, both cheeks pulling upward. Her throat constricted as Dylan slowly smiled. He captured her wrists in his hands, pulled them away from his face, and kissed her palms.

"Thank you, Perty."

"For what?"

"For proving me wrong."

Chapter 8

Caylor reached up under her glasses to rub her eyes. She would swear that she'd heard her eyes scream at the thought of putting her contact lenses in this morning. After only five hours of sleep last night, the insides of her eyelids had taken on the consistency of coarse-grit sandpaper. But with only two tests remaining to be graded, she might be able to get all of her grades recorded before the noon deadline and take a nap this afternoon.

"Knock, knock." Sassy's white hair appeared between the balusters of the railing that lined the opening for the stairs at the other end of Caylor's office. She peeked over the rim of the floor.

Caylor turned down the instrumental movie sound-track playlist running on the computer. She'd been playing it louder than usual, trying to drown out the song "Gary, Indiana" from last fall's production of *The Music Man*, which had decided to reprise, repeatedly, in her head today. "Come on up, Sassy."

Her grandmother came up the remaining few steps, a basket filled with something that smelled absolutely wonderful cradled in one arm, a coffee mug in her other hand.

"That smells like—"

Sassy pulled back the tea towel covering the contents. "Birthday cinnamon-sugar muffins!"

Caylor closed her eyes and breathed in the luscious aroma of cinnamon and nutmeg and baked goods. Wait— "Sassy, these are still

81

hot. And we don't have an oven."

"No." She set the basket down on the credenza and pulled a small paper plate out from where she'd stashed it in between the basket and the towel liner. "But we do have a toaster oven. And back before we had central air-conditioning, if I could, I'd always prefer to use the toaster oven rather than the wall ovens, to keep from heating up the whole house."

She set one of the muffins, dipped in melted butter and then in cinnamon sugar after baking, on the small plate and handed it to Caylor.

"We really shouldn't, you know."

"I only made a half dozen, since that's the size pan that fits the toaster." Sassy sat on top of the credenza next to the basket and pulled out a small plate and muffin for herself.

Caylor pulled the paper away from the bottom of one side of the fluffy muffin and bit into the top. The cinnamon sugar and butter had formed a perfect crust. Her taste buds sent up a rousing hallelujah as the spicy sweetness cascaded over her tongue.

For a few minutes, they uttered only groans of appreciation. Caylor fixed another cup of hot tea—so convenient to prepare in the mornings with the electric kettle she'd picked up in England twelve years ago—and started in on a second muffin.

"A contractor is coming in this afternoon to look at the kitchen and give us a bid on remodeling it."

Caylor inhaled when she should have swallowed, and a chunk of muffin blocked her windpipe. She coughed and sputtered, eyes watering, and reached for her tea. "I'm sorry," she rasped, "did you say you're planning on remodeling the kitchen?"

"Don't have much of a choice, do I?" Sassy brushed the excess cinnamon sugar from her fingers onto her plate and reached for another muffin. "When I was over at Perty's the other day, we looked online at what it would cost to replace the appliances, and she told me how much they'd paid to have their kitchen redone—well, an estimate, since the whole house was done at the same time—and she convinced me that it would be better just to have the whole thing gutted and replaced: floors, cabinets, appliances, countertops. I don't think I want stainless-steel appliances, though. Working in Perty's kitchen, I realized just how hard those are to keep clean. I'm thinking black. Or maybe retro red."

Caylor could only stare at her grandmother. After so many years of resisting spending any money on the house, it was strange to see the excitement gleaming from her blue eyes at the prospect of spending tens of thousands of dollars on just one room. "You realize that they're going to have to do the electrical panel as well, don't you?"

"Oh yes, I know. It'll be safer to have breakers instead of fuses. Less of a fire hazard if they rewire everything." Sassy swung her feet like a child and took a huge bite of muffin.

"Well, you know I'm all for it."

Sassy downed a gulp of coffee. "I know. And I want you to be in the meeting with the contractor so that you can have your say about what it's going to look like. You're going to have to live with it longer than I am."

Caylor grimaced and wadded the empty muffin papers before tossing them into the trash can under her desk. "Sass, don't say that."

"Why—are you planning on selling the house as soon as I die?" She grinned shamelessly and then stood and leaned over and kissed Caylor's forehead. "Happy birthday, darling granddaughter." She took the basket containing the two remaining muffins back downstairs with her.

Shaking her head, Caylor wiped up the crumbs and got back to grading. At least Sassy's revelation had knocked "Gary, Indiana" out of her—

"Oh, for Pete's sake." Caylor turned the instrumental music up again to drown out the insidious song that started echoing through her brain again.

Two and a half hours later, she dropped face-first across her bed, grading finished and reported with time to spare before the deadline.

It seemed like that was all her life was anymore—a series of deadlines. Book deadlines. Grading deadlines. Deadlines to have her syllabi written and turned in so they could be posted online for the students. Maybe Dr. Fletcher was right—maybe it was time to start putting together a proposal for a sabbatical.

She snorted and flipped over onto her back. So many English professors took a yearlong sabbatical to write *a* book. She was carrying a full teaching load, serving on several committees, assisting with the drama department's major production each semester, ministering in the music program at church, and she was writing *two* books a year and spending her summer "vacations" traveling to book signings, publishing industry trade shows, writers' conferences, and speaking events to market her books.

Of course, she wasn't writing anything that most schools would consider sabbatical-worthy. There was that research she'd been thinking about on the conventions of inspirational romance compared with general-market romances—with the gap seeming to widen yearly. When she'd first started writing, it had been okay that her books were steamy and sensual without actually getting overly graphic. In fact, she'd stopped writing them after the sixth book and the end of her contract when her publishing house kept insisting she increase the sensuality in her books—the explicitness of the scenes and how often they occurred. She'd never been completely comfortable with writing those scenes, even in very euphemistic terms, but had convinced herself it was okay because her characters were always married before they slept together. But the push toward more, more, more had pushed her right over the edge of conviction that God hadn't gifted her with the talent for storytelling to be used in such a titillating manner.

She curled up on her side and grabbed her pillow. She'd be mortified if any of the senior ladies at church discovered what she'd written before she started writing romances fit to be sold in Christian bookstores.

Her brain spun off in several directions, and she drifted to sleep.

The shrilling of her cell phone, set to a tone she could hear no matter where her phone was, ripped her out of a very pleasant dream about her Renaissance-era Italian painter who looked just like Dylan Bradley. She stumbled into the office to grab the cell phone off the desk.

"The contractor's here. Are you coming down?"

"Sassy? What—yes, I'll be down in a minute." She stepped into the bathroom, put on some foundation to cover the dark circles under her eyes, put her glasses back on, and fluffed her hair—which fell right back into lank tufts around her forehead, ears, and neck.

Whatever. It wasn't as if she had to make a great impression on this guy. Or gal, she corrected herself, remembering the story idea the electrician had given her Monday.

Deciding her JRU sweats were good enough, she headed downstairs—this time purposely hitting the third step from the bottom so it squealed. Maybe the contractor would offer to fix that for them, too.

As soon as she walked into the kitchen, she wished she could have a do-over—or that she'd skipped the third step so she could quietly escape and make another entrance after changing clothes, putting on makeup, and doing something with her hair. Standing with his back to her, measuring the existing cabinets, was someone who could easily have graced the cover of one of her books—one of her *old* books—even without knowing what his face looked like.

Dark jeans hugged him in all the right places, and the pale-blue sweater he wore rippled with every movement of his well-defined and toned muscles. And when he turned around. . .

No man was this perfect in real life. Light-brown hair, blue eyes, perfectly symmetrical features. Maybe he had crooked teeth—nope, a perfectly straight, if overly white, smile.

He held his hand out and crossed the kitchen toward her. "Riley Douglas."

"Caylor Evans." A shiver ran up her spine at the feel of his calloused hand against hers.

"I hear you're a professor out at James Robertson." A baritone voice, just as a romance novel hero should have.

"I am."

"That's fantastic." He returned to taking measurements. "Mrs. Evans tells me that you're to have the final decision on the configuration and the finishes in here."

"It'll be a collaborative effort."

"That'll be fantastic, too."

Once Mr. Fantastic's back was turned again, Sassy looked up and down Caylor with an exasperated look. Caylor gave her a look right back and dropped into one of the dinette chairs.

He finished measuring the kitchen, telling them how fantastic it was that they still had the original 1950s appliances, but what a bummer that they didn't work anymore, because retro appliances could fetch a fantastic price if they were in prime condition.

Finally, he came and sat at the table with them, hands clasped atop his clipboard. "Now, ladies, let's talk remodel. Why don't you tell me what your dream kitchen would look like, and I'll tell you if it's possible and how much it would cost."

"Caylor, why don't you start?" Sassy rested her chin in her hand and gestured with her head toward the contractor.

Caylor turned her head completely away from Riley, pursed her lips, and gave Sassy the stink eye. Sassy kicked her—gently—under the table.

Caylor turned her best I-don't-want-to-be-here smile toward Riley. "I'd just like to see new appliances. Maybe reface the cabinets, and butcher-block or granite countertops."

"Pshhh." Sassy waved her hand dismissively. "Where's the fun in that? Where's the remodeling? That's just refurbishing." She leaned forward. "I'd love to see the kitchen opened up to the dining room and family room, more of—oh, what do they call it?"

"An open concept?" Riley flashed his megawatt grin at Sassy. "That would be fantastic."

Caylor could have gagged.

"Yes. Open concept." She stood up. "If we take down this wall"— she touched the wall that separated the kitchen from the den—"and then we take down the walls between the kitchen and the dining room, and the dining room and the living room, the only thing that would keep all of the living area of the house from being completely open is the staircase, and I think that could be redone so it's a nice feature between the living room and den."

Caylor knew her mouth was hanging open, but she didn't care. Who was this woman? Tearing down walls? Making all of the common areas of the house open to each other?

Riley also stood and went around and started knocking on the walls. "We'd have to get a general contractor in here to deal with taking the walls down, but I think that's doable." He returned to the table and leaned over to scribble some notes on his clipboard. "You know, you could also enclose half of this big side porch here off the kitchen, make that your breakfast nook so you have somewhere for this table—you don't want to get rid of this, it's fantastic—and then we could build an awesome island, maybe even put your cooktop in it, with a bar for seating." He stood in the doorway between the kitchen and the den. "That would give the dining area and family room a lot more space."

"Write that down—that's a great idea. Now floors. I'm thinking bamboo throughout." Sassy made grand, sweeping gestures with her arms. "But can those be done with a darker finish?"

Caylor pulled her phone out of her pocket and texted Zarah: CALL ME ASAP.

"It can be stained as dark as you want it. But aren't there hardwoods in the other rooms?"

"There are, but they're pretty beaten up, which is why we've got the wall-to-wall carpet in the living room and den and the big area rug in the dining room. And I've seen them talk on TV about just how hard it is to match existing hardwoods. So let's just start fresh."

She turned around and seemed startled to see Caylor sitting at the table. "Caylor, dear, what do you think?"

Thank goodness, at that very moment, her cell phone rang. Caylor looked down at the screen. *Zarah Mitchell calling* scrolled across the display. "Oh, I'm sorry. I have to take this call."

She dashed from the kitchen and up the stairs, not answering until she was safely in her bedroom, where she knew Sassy couldn't hear her. "Hey, Zare."

"What's up? Your message looked urgent."

Caylor explained her need for escape. "I don't know what's gotten into her. Maybe she's been bingeing on HGTV these last few weeks while I've been at school or something."

"You said the contractor is good-looking, right?"

"That's an understatement." Caylor stepped into her closet and started looking through her wardrobe to pick out what she wanted to wear tonight.

"And he's probably around our age?"

"Yeah."

"Was he wearing a wedding ring?"

"I don't—no, I don't think so."

"Remember what Flannery said to us back at the family cookout in October?"

"Uh. . .she said a lot of things." The primary thing Caylor remembered her talking about was her dislike of Maureen O'Connor's grandson, the advertising salesman.

"She said it sounded like our grandmothers were trying to play matchmaker for us. Do you think, maybe. . . "

Caylor smacked her open palm across her forehead. "Well, duh. No wonder she looked so disgusted when I showed up down there in my sweats and no makeup."

"Hey—someone's calling on my office phone. We'll talk about this tonight with Flannery." Zarah said good-bye and hung up.

Caylor tucked the phone into the pouch pocket of her sweatshirt and got back to picking her outfit for dinner. She pulled out her favorite pair of dark jeans—a pair of talls that were actually long enough that she could wear heels with them, quite an unusual find for her—and a bright purple cashmere sweater, which she'd wear over an ivory silk camisole. She also grabbed her favorite high-heeled brown ankle boots and laid everything on her bed.

In the shower, her mind wandered—and ended up back in sixteenth-century Italy with Giovanni and Isabella.

By the time she got out, she had the perfect opening scene. Wrapped in her long, thick bathrobe, she dashed from the bathroom to the office—and came to a screeching halt.

Sassy sat in Caylor's desk chair, hands folded in her lap, legs crossed, looking for all the world like a Venus flytrap waiting for its dinner.

"Sassy?"

"So? What did you think?"

"About the kitchen remodel? I didn't realize just how ambitious your plan was until you started explaining it to what's-his-name—Mr. Fantastic."

"His name is Riley Douglas. I think he really liked you."

"Oh Sassy!" Caylor pressed both hands over her heart in a

melodramatic fashion. "My wee little heart is just all aflutter—a handsome, *fantastic* man likes little ol' me."

Sassy laughed. "Okay, so the conversation skills don't quite come up to par. But with that to look at, who cares?"

Caylor dropped the dramatics. "Wait, did you bring him here for me or for you?"

"If you don't want him. . ." Sassy winked at her. "I do need to get the kitchen remodeled—perhaps the house, depending on how much it will cost and how long it will take—and I thought it would be fun to have it done by some good-looking men. And if one of them just so happens to be single and just so happens to catch your eye, all the better."

Caylor perched on the edge of the credenza. "Look, I know you mean well, but I really don't need my grandmother acting as a matchmaker for me. I don't have time in my life right now for a man."

"You would if you met one you wanted to spend time with. Love is something you make time for." Sassy stood. "Now, I know you're supposed to be getting ready to go out with the girls, so I won't keep you any longer. But just think about what I said, and try to enter this house remodel with an open mind."

"Open about the house or about the people coming in to rip it apart and rebuild it?"

"Both." Sassy waggled her finger at Caylor, raising it above her head so it was the last thing Caylor saw as she disappeared down the stairs.

She quickly jotted down the idea for the opening scene of Giovanni and Isabella's story, then went back into the bathroom to finish getting ready to go out.

Her stomach growled, reminding her she'd slept through lunch, but since Zarah and Flannery were taking her to the Cheesecake Factory for dinner, one of her favorite restaurants, maybe skipping lunch wasn't so bad. Now she wouldn't feel quite so guilty over what she'd been planning to eat anyway.

At five thirty, she said good-bye to Sassy and left to drive up to the Mall at Green Hills. As expected, traffic on Hillsboro was horrible, and the parking lot at the mall outside the restaurant was even worse.

She parked at the very end of the overflow lot and hoofed it to the restaurant.

Flannery stood just inside the door. "I saw you out there driving around. Why didn't you just use the valet service?"

"Because I hate handing over my keys and car to a total stranger. You've seen *Ferris Bueller's Day Off*." Caylor stuck her keys into her purse.

"Oh, right, like these guys would have time to go joyriding in someone's car—and like they'd choose yours when there are people around here in luxury cars that make yours look like a Yugo in comparison." Flannery patted her front right pocket, where she must have put her valet claim ticket. "This time of year, valet is the only way to go."

"Hey, girls, sorry I'm late." Zarah breezed in, cheeks pink from the cold.

"You're not late—we're still waiting on our table." Flannery's phone started playing a pop song Caylor didn't know. Flannery lifted it out of its holster, read the screen, grimaced, then silenced the phone.

"You're not going to answer that?" Caylor exchanged a surprised look with Zarah.

"No. It's six o'clock, and I'm off work for the night—because it's my best friend's birthday." She raised the large gift bag in her left hand and waggled it in front of Caylor. "You realize, of course, now that you've turned thirty-five, you're closer to forty than you are to thirty."

Yeah, she'd realized that. But she'd also decided she wasn't going to let it bother her. She shrugged. "No biggie."

Flannery opened her mouth to say something, but the buzzer in her hand started flickering and vibrating.

"McNeill, party of three."

"That's us." Flannery followed the hostess, and Caylor and Zarah followed Flannery.

Though she usually did her best to pay no attention to it, for some reason, tonight Caylor couldn't block out the way people stared and whispered as she walked by their tables. At five foot eight and five foot nine respectively, Zarah and Flannery were by no means short. But at six feet tall—and with three-inch heels adding to that—Caylor towered over them. Fortunately, being involved in drama almost all her life had taken any shred of self-consciousness away from her.

She felt like turning around and saying, at the top of her lungs, *"Just to answer the questions I know you all have, yes, I'm very tall. No, I've never played basketball or volleyball. No, it's not a hormone abnormality or defect. Everyone in my family is tall. Deal with it and move on."* But that would mortify Zarah and give Flannery a story to tell at parties for years to come.

At their booth, Caylor slid into one side while Flannery and Zarah shared the other.

"So did you tell her before I got here?" Zarah asked.

Caylor launched into the story of Mr. Fantastic and shared with both of them the fact that Sassy confessed to the scheme afterward.

"Would you go out with him if he asked?" Flannery asked around a bite of crispy artichoke heart.

Caylor scooped up some of the lemon-garlic aioli with her piece of artichoke. "I guess so—why not? I haven't been out on a real date in years. It might be fun."

Flannery and Zarah looked at each other, then said in unison, "It would be *fantastic.*"

Chapter 9

ꗖ

Caylor set the plastic action figures of Sir Galahad and Morgana behind her desk on the shelf displaying other figures from the legend of King Arthur. Where Flannery kept coming up with these, she'd never guess. With last night's addition of these two as part of her birthday present, the collection of literary and legendary action figures was up to at least thirty.

Along with Shakespeare, Jane Austen, Charles Dickens, Oscar Wilde, and James Joyce, the collection included Henry V, Henry VIII, and Elizabeth I; King Richard the Lionheart, one standing and one on horseback; William Wallace and Robert the Bruce from the *Braveheart* movie; Sherlock Holmes; fashion dolls dressed as the Brontë sisters; and several characters from the Robin Hood legend. They were scattered throughout her office, near the books pertinent to their presence in a British literature professor's office.

She stuck two of the blank journals Flannery had also given her into the top drawer of her desk. Even though Flannery either got them as promotional marketing items from vendors or off the bargain table at bookstores, it didn't matter. She always found the most interesting and unique patterns and styles.

Caylor's gift from Zarah sat on her nightstand at home. An 1899 copy of Elizabeth Gaskell's *Cranford*. Not a first edition, but still a rare printing from one of Caylor's favorite authors. And when Caylor had protested at the extravagance of such a gift, Zarah had quieted her by telling her she'd picked it up online for next to nothing and felt bad for not spending more than she had.

The small brass clock on the desk chimed seven times. Zarah closed the office door and double-checked her appearance in the mirror on the back of it. Why, oh, why had she chosen to wear a sleeveless dress? Could her arms look any pastier and flabbier? Maybe she could just keep her coat on. But no, even though the black-and-white houndstooth trench coat was very nice, it just didn't give off the Christmas party vibe the way the slightly shimmering, dark-aqua fabric of the multitiered cocktail dress did.

Leaving her purse locked in her desk drawer, Caylor left her office, making sure the door was locked behind her. She turned toward the stairs—and her heart leaped into her throat, pounding as hard as it could.

Walking toward her, dressed in a charcoal suit that must have cost a fortune, with a purple-and-gold-patterned silk tie and a gray wool overcoat folded over his arm, was Dylan Bradley. Once again, the memory of where she knew him from was so close she could almost reach out and grab it.

"You cut your hair." Great first line.

He blushed a little and self-consciously touched the buzzed hair at the back of his head, then ran his hand up to tousle the artfully messy, longer pieces on top. "Yeah. I decided it was time."

"Oh good, Caylor. I hoped we might run into you on the way over." Bridget joined them.

Dylan turned and helped Bridget on with her coat. Caylor shrugged into hers at the same time so he didn't feel obligated to assist her as well. He put his on—and fought with the collar that caught on his suit coat's lapel and turned under.

Bridget tried to help but couldn't quite reach. Wearing low heels tonight, Caylor was still almost the same height as Dylan, so she fixed it for him. Just as Isabella would have done for Giovanni.

Her fingertips tingled as if near a live electric wire, and she snatched her hands back. Observe, but never interfere. Wasn't that the anthropologists' credo? She thought she remembered something like that from the cultural anthropology course she'd taken as an undergrad. If she were to have a creed as a writer, that would be it—at least when it came to the real world. When it came to her characters' lives, however—

"Shall we go?" Bridget started down the stairs.

Dylan motioned for Caylor to go ahead of him. "Ladies first."

"Ah, looks like I'm not the only one with this idea." Dr. Fletcher joined Dylan at the top of the stairs. "Mr. Bradley, isn't it?"

"Yes ma'am."

"Please, call me Barbara. No need to be so formal; I'm not the chair of *your* department." She graced him with a rare smile and took hold of his arm for support going down the stairs.

Caylor met Bridget at the bottom of the stairs, and they walked ahead to the doors together. "I thought you invited him so *I* could flirt with him, not Dr. Fletcher," Caylor whispered.

Bridget rolled her eyes. "He'll be lucky if he gets that arm back tonight."

Dr. Fletcher rapped the floor with her brass-tipped cane, startling both of them. Caylor was pretty sure she didn't actually need it to walk but carried it around for imperious gestures like that. "Come, girls, why are we dallying?"

Caylor held the door open for them then fell in step beside Dr. Fletcher—with Bridget walking beside Dylan. The wind had died down, but the air still froze their breath into icy fog.

"I saw on the news that it snowed in Philadelphia this week." Dr. Fletcher tapped her cane on the sidewalk as if setting a cadence. "I imagine you miss that, Dylan."

"The first snow of the season is nice. But it gets old after a few months." He seemed perfectly content escorting the older lady across campus toward the dining hall, as if this was exactly how he'd pictured the evening going.

Caylor longed for a pen and paper. Being near Dylan, observing how he treated the aristocratic Dr. Fletcher with aplomb and deference, sparked so many ideas for her story she feared they'd start leaking out her ears, and she'd lose most of them by the time she got back to her office in a couple of hours.

Inside the campus's main hub, they bypassed the large, central staircase for the elevator beyond.

Dr. Fletcher didn't let go of Dylan's arm, even in the safety of the elevator. "I hear from Leonard Holtz that you'll be joining his department as an adjunct next semester."

"Yes ma'am. I'll be teaching two classes."

"Did he tell you he has a professor going on sabbatical next year? He'll have a visiting professorship open. If you're as good as what I've heard, that position should be yours."

Caylor almost warned Dylan not to listen to any staffing predictions Dr. Fletcher made. With the exception of the positions she directly controlled, her prognostications were usually wrong. But she couldn't figure out how to tell Dylan that without insulting Dr. Fletcher.

"What have you heard about me?" Dylan's voice sounded choked— but it could have been a by-product of the noise of the opening elevator doors.

"Oh, I have my sources." She touched his arm with the head of her cane. "Nothing bad, mind you. All good. All very good."

After divesting themselves of their coats at the makeshift coat-check station outside the dining hall, they entered. The dulcet sounds of the school's madrigal choir from what sounded like this year's Christmas concert provided a soft backdrop to the sparse crowd huddled near the middle of the cavernous space.

"Will you excuse me? I see someone I need to speak to." Bridget bustled off.

"And I must go speak to the academic dean about a memo she sent out late this afternoon. Dylan, lovely to see you again. Thank you for the escort."

"My pleasure, Dr. Fletcher."

There they went, leaving Caylor standing here feeling like a sixth grader at her first school dance.

"You. . .um. . .you look really nice tonight, Caylor." Instead of the laid-back, confident man who'd escorted Dr. Fletcher over here, Dylan now seemed to have morphed into a twitchy adolescent.

Good. At least she wasn't alone in feeling uncomfortable. "Thanks. You look pretty nice yourself. Let me guess—just something you had hanging around in your closet?"

He ran his palms down the front of the jacket. "Yeah, actually. It's something I bought in Philadelphia."

She nodded. "I'll bet you had to go to a lot of gala events and show openings where you had to dress up like this." She took a glass of iced tea off the tray a server from the school's catering company brought around.

He shrugged and took a glass of tea as well. "Not really. As the artist, I wasn't expected to show up in a suit."

A flash of light took them both by surprise. Caylor blinked and then came to focus on a small, wiry guy with a huge camera anchored by a strap around his neck. "Hey, Dr. Evans. Picture for the faculty intranet newsletter. Get together and. . .and hold your glasses out like you're toasting."

"Yes, we love having *candid* pictures in the newsletter," Caylor whispered to Dylan as they stepped closer until their shoulders touched. The smooth texture of the suiting material over the warm, solid arm underneath sent goose bumps rushing all over Caylor's body.

A couple of blinding flashes later, the camera went down. "Dr. Putnam, I'd like to introduce Dylan Bradley, who's going to be joining the art department as an adjunct in the spring." She looked at Dylan. "Dr. Putnam teaches photography for both art and journalism."

The two men shook hands and exchanged pleasantries; then Dr. Putnam picked up the camera from its resting place on his chest. "Well, I'd better get back to taking photos now that more folks are arriving. I have to say, you two make a stunning couple."

❧

Atomic heat suffused Dylan's face at the photographer's statement.

Beside him, Caylor laughed. "Everyone's a matchmaker."

"What's that?" Dylan's hand shook when he raised his glass to take a sip, so he lowered it again. Too many times in his life, females had gotten the wrong idea about him and his intentions toward them simply because of an offhanded comment like Dr. Putnam's.

"Oh, I. . .It just seems like everyone in my life right now is trying to—" Caylor turned bright red. "Never mind."

He had a feeling he knew exactly what she'd been about to say.

Before his relationship with Rhonda became common knowledge, everyone in Philadelphia had tried to set him up at every available opportunity. How long would it be before people here started doing it, too?

"Caylor, I see you've met the art department's new acquisition." Dr. Holtz and his wife joined them. After extolling Dylan's qualifications to his wife, Holtz introduced them. Caylor excused herself and crossed the room to join Dr. Fletcher and the other English professor who'd come to the dinner party last week. They were quickly surrounded by several other couples. Caylor, however, could never get lost in a crowd—not standing taller than every woman and most of the men in the growing group. That, and no matter what angle Dylan viewed her from or how she positioned her body, he could clearly imagine painting her just so.

He returned his attention to Dr. Holtz's introductions of the rest of the art faculty. The other six professors seemed truly interested in everything Dylan was willing to tell them about teaching at Watts-Maxwell and the art community in Philadelphia. He had a hard time talking, though; years of Rhonda's interrupting and taking over the conversation had turned him into more of a listener than a talker at these kinds of events.

But being with other artists, other people who understood the overwhelming urge to create, the slight madness that took over at such times, made him feel happy—truly happy—for the first time since he'd returned to Nashville. No, it had been longer than that. He couldn't remember being truly happy since before Rhonda had started taking over his life—telling him what to say, what to think, what to paint; separating him from his family; making him into what she wanted him to be.

Why had it taken him so long, taken him becoming unrecognizable to himself, to realize he didn't want to be the person Rhonda wanted him to be? He just wanted to be himself. Dylan Bradley. No airs. No pretense. No pseudonyms.

He glanced back toward the center of the room—and caught Caylor looking his direction. She smiled, gave a little wave, and returned to her group's conversation.

The talk around him moved from the just-ended semester to an upcoming exhibition at the Frist of impressionist masterworks, including some big-name artists such as Monet, Manet, Degas, and Renoir. The familiar topics started relaxing him, made him start feeling like he might fit in here.

The newly shorn hairs on the back of his neck prickled with the sensation someone was watching him—an all-too-familiar tingle. He scanned the room, half expecting to see Rhonda. Instead, over near one of the food tables, his gaze caught Caylor's again. She smiled—a bit guiltily, he thought—and turned to talk to someone on her other side.

Was she checking up on him? Worried about whether he was behaving himself? Speaking only to the right people?

He mentally shook himself out of the flashback. Caylor was not Rhonda. She wasn't here to control or discipline him.

No, but she did know Perty. She could have been tasked with keeping an eye on him just to make sure he was doing okay.

"What brought you to Nashville, Dylan?" Dr. Putnam held his plate of hors d'oeuvres over his camera, which was protected from crumbs by a paper napkin draped over it.

"My family is here." When he'd practiced that answer at home, it seemed like the most logical—and least question-raising—response possible. But from the look of expectation on the photography professor's face, he realized it wasn't quite enough. "I've been away with little chance to visit with them since I graduated from high school. It was time to come home."

That seemed to be enough for Dr. Putnam, who finished off his chicken satay crostini and wiped at his goatee with another napkin. "Being near family cannot be overvalued. Good for you." He lifted the camera and snapped a photo of Dylan.

"Attention, please." At the announcement over the sound system, the crowd noise died down and everyone turned toward the stage at the other end of the dining hall.

"Oh, here we go." Dr. Putnam moved off through the crowd toward the front of the room.

Dr. Holtz took his place beside Dylan. "This is the best part of the evening."

Mrs. Holtz looked around her husband. "Do you sing, Dylan?"

"Sing?"

Dr. Holtz chuckled. "This is a liberal and fine arts school in Nashville, Tennessee. Aside from having one of the largest vocal performance and choral programs in the city—after Vanderbilt and Belmont, of course—we have a lot of talented people on this faculty."

"Happy holidays, everyone!"

Dylan joined the crowd in murmuring "Happy holidays" back to the man in the tuxedo at the microphone, the college's president, he supposed, not having seen anyone else in a tux. He glanced around, not looking for a tall redhead—and to his surprise, he didn't see the person he most definitely wasn't looking for.

"Thanks for joining us again this year for our faculty holiday celebration. I hope you all had a wonderful fall semester and are looking forward to your time off for the next few weeks. I know I am."

Mild tittering and chuckles from the crowd.

"But you didn't come here to hear me talk. So I'll turn the evening's festivities over to Dr. Edgerton in just a moment. I do want to take this opportunity to say thank you to each of you for the wonderful work you do in leading, mentoring, guiding, and teaching our students. James Robertson University wouldn't be here, wouldn't have the stellar reputation we have, without a stellar faculty. So thank you, and happy holidays!"

Applause and a few whistles emerged from the crowd that must have been over two hundred people.

A distinguished woman who looked to be in her fifties took the stage. Dressed in a red sequined dress, she commanded Dylan's attention simply by the fact he couldn't look away from the sparkly garment.

"You've been waiting and wondering for a year, while others have been plotting and planning. We had so many good submissions this year, it was hard to narrow it down to a manageable number, but somehow we did it. So let's get started. And remember, if you feel like dancing, please do so!"

The music professor introduced the musicians on the stage—a jazz quartet made up of other music department faculty, and they got things rolling with a swing version of "O Christmas Tree."

Once the music started, everyone went back to mingling and chatting. Dylan looked around again, not looking for anyone in particular. Where had she disappeared to?

He excused himself from Dr. Holtz and his wife and made his way around the outside edges of the assemblage. A few people he'd already met stopped him to introduce him to others, all of whom were quite welcoming when they learned he'd be teaching next semester. This reaction was a bit disarming to him—he couldn't remember speaking more than once or twice with any of the part-time instructors or adjuncts at Watts-Maxwell.

After several familiar holiday songs performed by vocalists and musicians from the music department, a quartet from the science department—someone told him it pretty much represented the entire full-time science faculty—got up and sang a pretty good rendition of "Silent Night," which was followed by one of the music professors who got up and sang "Eight Days of Happiness," a Hanukkah song with a Latin beat, transitioning into a more holiday-specific portion of the program.

When Dylan reached the front of the room, he looked back the way he'd come. Still no sign of the person he wasn't really looking for.

He tried to convince himself he wasn't bothered by Caylor's disappearance. He told himself that he was looking for her because he imagined Bridget Wetzler would be somewhere nearby, and since he'd come as Bridget's date, he should at least check in with her. He hoped, watching the couple of dozen couples dancing near the stage, that Bridget wouldn't expect him to ask her to dance.

Dr. Edgerton's speaking voice came as a jolt after so much uninterrupted music. "After last year's party, we had so many requests for this next group, we decided to give them the last few spots on the program. Put your hands together for the Three Redheads."

Dylan turned. There, on stage, were Caylor, Bridget, and another woman of about the same age. And though they did all have red hair, they couldn't have looked more unalike. Bridget was of average height and plump. Her dyed-red hair was pulled up into a crown of curls atop her head. The woman Dylan didn't know was even shorter than Bridget and tiny—almost frail-looking. Her red hair was long and straight and pulled around so it hung over her left shoulder in the front.

And then there was Caylor. The turquoise of her dress—almost the same color as her eyes—made her hair, in its saucy, flipped-out shortness, and her ivory skin glow with vibrancy. The dress showed off her perfect hourglass figure and long legs to perfection.

He'd already started reaching for his phone to snap a photo of her so he could reference it for the drawing of her already forming in his mind—but stopped himself. He might be tasked with teaching the students to paint portraits, but he'd stick to more mundane, less compulsion-driven subjects. After all, it had been his obsession with the artwork on the covers of the romance novels his mother kept hidden all over the house years ago that had led to his compulsion with replicating them and then to his moving on to original work in the same vein.

The keyboardist started playing something that sounded like the tinkling of a music box. Bridget sang the verses solo; then the other two came in with the harmony on the chorus, singing about "the Christmas tree angel." He'd never heard the song before but found himself swaying to the gentle swing of the rhythm. They sounded just like those sister groups from the 1940s.

Unlike during everyone else's performances, everyone paid attention when Caylor's group sang. And Dylan could see why. Though Bridget's voice alone wasn't spectacular—nowhere near as good as the music professors who'd sang—when the three of them blended together, it was dazzling. And apparently he wasn't the only one who thought so, judging by the applause and cheers they received when the song ended.

In their next song, sung by all three in perfect harmony, they extolled all of the good things about Christmas from each letter of the word—another piece he'd never heard, and another one that received the high praise of applause and cheers.

The three women shifted places—Caylor moving to the front of the stage, and the other two standing off to one side behind her. The music started, and Dylan couldn't help smiling at the Irish jig sound of the intro.

With what sounded like a perfect Irish accent and a strong alto voice he could have listened to for hours, Caylor sang "Christmas in Killarney," one of Gramps's favorite Christmas songs from Bing Crosby.

Caylor scanned the crowd as she sang, but when her eyes met Dylan's, her smile broadened and she winked at him before looking away again.

Winked at him. Though he'd jolted internally at the gesture—a good jolt—he couldn't stop the questions it raised. Why wink at him and no one else in the room? Was she flirting with him? Had she taken Dr. Putnam's comment earlier about their making a cute couple too seriously?

After she sang through the song a full time, the jazz quartet transitioned into a bridge. Caylor, Bridget, and the other woman all kicked off their shoes and began dancing an Irish jig together, laughing at their own missteps and encouraging everyone in the audience to do the same. Picking out the dance professors was pretty easy.

Worried about both his reaction to Caylor and whatever might be going through her mind about him, Dylan slipped up the side of the room and out the door. He'd send Bridget an e-mail, telling her something had come up, to try to excuse his rude behavior. Recovering his coat from the coat check, he fled the building into the cold night outside.

He'd just come out of a horrible relationship. He couldn't fall for someone else. He needed time to figure out who he was and who he wanted to become. But he liked Caylor; he couldn't deny it. Never before had the mere sight of a woman ignited the fire of inspiration in him like her presence did. And she was the kind of woman that a man would be stupid to hesitate with—because someone else would come along, see her wonderful qualities, and snatch her up.

He stopped in the middle of the quadrangle and looked up. Pinpricks of light glittered against the indigo sky. "If You're still there, God, and if I haven't burned all my bridges with You yet, You're going to have to help me out with this. Show me who I'm supposed to be and what I'm supposed to be doing. And don't let Caylor. . ."

He felt stupid saying it aloud, because he couldn't imagine that she'd want to have anything to do with him, at least not romantically, if she ever learned about his relationship with Rhonda. He wouldn't blame her one bit. But his heart still cried out, *Don't let Caylor fall in love with someone else while I'm still trying to get my head on straight.*

Chapter 10

I think it's my fault." Caylor took the lid off her cup to get to the last few drops of the peppermint-spiked hot chocolate. "He caught me staring at him a couple of times from across the room, and then when I was singing, he looked so dumbfounded, I couldn't help myself and I winked at him. Next thing I know, he's running from the room like someone pulled the fire alarm."

Flannery downed the last bit of her pumpkin pie–flavored latte. "Has Bridget heard from him?"

"She forwarded the e-mail he sent last night—said an emergency came up so he had to leave while we were singing and that's why he didn't stick around to say good-bye. She also said he called this morning to apologize." Caylor stood and tossed her cup in the trash can.

"One thing's for sure—that boy was raised right." Flannery shoved the napkins and stirrers they'd used into her cup before tossing it. "Most guys would have left it at the e-mail."

"Maybe there really was an emergency." Leave it to Zarah to give someone the benefit of the doubt. She used the water pitcher at the sugaring station to wet some napkins, then wiped off the table.

"Maybe. But after Putnam's crack about us making a nice couple, I have to wonder if that spooked Dylan." Caylor dug her Christmas shopping list out of her purse. "There are a couple of things I need to pick up here in the bookstore before we hit the other stores."

The new shopping center in Murfreesboro, with its town center style, had become one of Caylor's favorite places to shop, despite the long drive. And she was thankful Zarah and Flannery had agreed to drive down, too—especially since they couldn't come together because they all had other obligations this afternoon and wanted to have as much time for shopping as possible.

"We need to check to see if they have your books before we do anything else." Flannery headed off to the Christian fiction section.

"If they have any of my books," Caylor said to Zarah, following at a leisurely pace, "it's more likely that they'll be in the romance section, and they'll have a different name on the cover."

"Why won't they carry your new books when they'll still stock the old ones?" Zarah was always something of the odd man out when Flannery and Caylor started talking about the publishing industry, and she rarely asked questions, usually just sat and listened. So they tried not to do it too much when she was with them. But if she asked, it meant she really wanted to know and wasn't just humoring Caylor.

"Even though the six books I wrote under the pseudonym are out, because I'm writing the books for the Christian market under my own name, I'm considered a new author. I'm not cross-marketing these with the other books—in fact, the publisher and I really don't want my readers to know that the other books are out there. So it's harder for me to get picked up by the big-box stores because my sales numbers aren't high enough for them to want to take the risk of getting them in, only to have to return them when they don't sell."

"But they'd sell if they'd get them in. You're from here—well, from Nashville—and you know so many people in this area who would come in and buy your books if they carried them." Zarah's dark brows knit in consternation.

"And I'm sure those are points that the salesperson from the publishing house made. But it's a crazy business. Thank goodness for Christian bookstores and online retailers."

They caught up with Flannery, who was scanning the shelves. "D. . .D. . .D. . .E—here we go." She crouched down to read the spines of the books on the bottom shelf.

Caylor scanned the spines at the top of the next stack. "Here." She pulled the single copy of her second book off the shelf. "And this copy has been here since the last time I came down." She flipped it open to the center to reveal bookmarks for the first and third books. "I put these in here."

"If I didn't know how much publishers pay to have their authors' books faced out on the shelves, I'd tell you to put it face out." Flannery continued scanning the shelves, running her fingers along the publishing houses' logos at the bottoms, stopping whenever she came to one from Lindsley House. The Christian fiction division was Flannery's responsibility, and she took it quite seriously.

Caylor reshelved her book, tucking it between volumes from two authors she'd met at the big Christian publishing trade show this past summer. "It would look kind of silly sitting there all alone, face out."

"It would look like there had been a bunch of them and it was the only one left." Flannery crouched low again to look at the bottom shelves. She finally reached the end of the row.

"Seen enough?" Caylor stood with her elbow propped against the upper shelf of the closest bookcase. "Enough to justify writing off the mileage to drive down here, anyway?"

"Don't act like you aren't going to write it off, too." Flannery raised an eyebrow in a saucy expression.

"Can we get on with the shopping now?" Caylor asked, waving her list at Flannery.

"By all means." Flannery curtseyed—which looked quite funny in her tight jeans and tunic-length sweater.

"Girls, before we go. . .there's something I need to tell you. I've been trying to figure out how to tell you since we got here." Zarah looked so serious, so solemn.

Caylor immediately dropped her teasing demeanor. She grabbed Zarah's hand. "What is it? What's wrong?"

Flannery took Zarah's other hand in both of hers.

"Bobby and I. . ."

Oh, please, Lord, don't let them have broken up!

"We've set a wedding date. We want to get married the Saturday of Memorial Day weekend." A tremulous smile broke out on Zarah's stark-white face.

Flannery dropped Zarah's hand as if it had given her an electric shock. "Don't do that to me. I thought you were going to say y'all had broken up—or worse. I can't believe you didn't call us as soon as you decided. Or at least as soon as you walked in the door here."

Caylor pulled Zarah into a hug. She could understand a little better than Flannery where Zarah was coming from, having talked to Zarah at greater length about her relationship with Bobby since he'd returned to her life fourteen years after a bad breakup.

"I'm so happy for you." She stepped back and held Zarah's shoulders at arms' length. "Are you scared?"

"A little bit. One of Bobby's friends from work has a cousin who's a family and marriage counselor, so we're going to start going—we still have a lot of stuff to work through, both together and separately, but we know we're meant to be together. After all, if we weren't, why would God have brought us back into each other's lives the way He did?"

Flannery pushed Caylor's hands out of the way so she could hug their friend, too. "There's so much planning to do, and I want to help with everything. Oh, and I've got all those books at work about wedding planning that I helped edit. I'll grab copies of those, and we can work our way through them."

Zarah nodded. She sniffled, her eyes suspiciously wet, but her smile stretched wider than Caylor had seen it since Thanksgiving, when Zarah and Bobby had announced their engagement. Not that it had been news to Caylor and Flannery, who'd helped Bobby prepare a special evening for the proposal.

"I want you two to be my maids of honor. We're going to try to keep it somewhat small—just two attendants, a small guest list, and in the chapel, not the main sanctuary at Acklen Ave." Zarah's curly dark hair bounced on her shoulders as she looked from Caylor to Flannery and back. "You will be my maids of honor, won't you?"

"Of course we will," Caylor and Flannery answered in unison and hugged her together.

"Hey, there's a bridal store in this complex—over by the steak house, I think. Once we're finished with Caylor's Christmas shopping, we could go over there and start looking at dresses." Flannery's eyes shone with more excitement than Zarah's.

"Maybe, if we have time. But I'm not even sure about colors or how formal we're going to be yet, so it's a bit premature." Knowing Zarah, she'd want to have a complete plan in place before she set one foot in a store—and then she'd go in, order exactly what she wanted, and walk out. Ten, fifteen minutes, tops.

"Oh come on. It'll be fun just to go in and daydream."

Zarah sighed, a little overdramatically, which made them all laugh. "Fine. If there's time when we finish Christmas shopping. I have a few things I need to pick up while I'm here, too."

"And lunch. Let's not forget to leave time to eat—since it'll probably be late before any of us gets to where we're supposed to be having supper tonight." Caylor had promised herself she was going to get back on a regular eating schedule during the holidays before her crazy schedule started again in January.

After finding the few things she wanted, she'd just moved to the head of the checkout line when her phone chimed out the tone that indicated a new text message. With her arms full, she waited until she'd finished her transaction before checking it. Even if it was Sassy needing something, there wasn't much Caylor could do for her from down here.

While Zarah checked out, Caylor moved toward the door, put her bag on the floor between her feet, and pulled out her phone. She had to read the screen three times to believe what it said.

New Message from Felicity Evans.

"What is it?" Zarah asked, joining her.

"A text message from my sister." Caylor tapped the screen to open the message as Flannery finished up and rejoined them.

"Did you just say you got a text from Felicity?" Flannery asked.

"Yeah." Caylor read it—and groaned. "Y'all aren't going to believe this. FLIGHT LEAVING DENVER. IN NASHVILLE 2 P.M. MEET ME AT BAGGAGE CLAIM."

"Wait. She's coming in this afternoon? I thought you weren't expecting her until later in the week." Flannery took the phone from Caylor to read it for herself.

"That's the last I heard, though I've been e-mailing her for a week to get her to send me her itinerary." She ran her fingers through her hair, thankful that messy was the purpose of this short style. "If Mama and Daddy's flight weren't coming in so much later today, I'd tell her just to wait and I'd pick her up at the same time I pick them up."

"When do they get in?" Zarah asked.

"Six. No matter how much she frustrates me, I can't ask her to sit around waiting at the airport for four hours." Caylor took the phone back and read the message again to see if Felicity had said what airline or flight number—but no, of course not.

Flannery flipped her long blond hair over her shoulders. "Why not? She's asking you to rearrange your entire day to accommodate her. Waiting a few hours might be good for her."

"Yeah, but the security at the airport probably doesn't like people to just sit around and wait for that long." She dropped the phone back into her purse and rolled her head from side to side, trying to alleviate the sudden tightness in her neck and shoulders. "Come on. I have about an hour and a half before I have to head back to Nashville to pick her up."

⚓

Dylan sorted the canvases into four stacks—those he would use to try to get into some local galleries, perhaps the Hillsboro Village Art Walk; those he thought were high enough quality for the art auction Mother wanted to do as a campaign event; those that could possibly be recycled and painted over; and those that needed to be thrown away.

Most of the paintings going into the trash pile were those he'd painted in the past six to twelve months. His dark period, he'd call it. Crouching down beside the trash pile, he flipped through several of the pieces. Actually, he should call it his *door* period. He hadn't realized how many of his pieces involved some kind of doorway—or window or gateway.

He rocked back on his heels. Even when he hadn't been able to see it, his subconscious mind had been screaming at him that he needed to escape, needed to find a way out.

"Whatcha doing?"

Startled off balance at the sound of his brother's voice, Dylan grabbed the leg of the worktable and leveraged himself up to his feet.

Pax leaned against the doorjamb, hands in the pockets of the oversized gray fleece hoodie he wore over a blue-and-white plaid flannel shirt. It was about as rugged looking as the scientist would ever manage.

"Just doing some organizing. What brings you here?" Dylan crossed to the utility sink to wash his hands, nearly black from the years of dust on some of the boxes he'd been into this morning.

Pax lifted the shiny black laptop he'd had tucked under his arm. "Spencer, Tyler, and I had planned to talk today about Christmas gifts for Mother and Dad, Gramps and Perty, and Grandma and Grandpa Paxton. I didn't know if you had a webcam on your computer or not, so I figured it would be just as easy if I came over and we talked to them together."

In years past, Tyler had informed Dylan of the decision they'd made about their joint gifts to their parents and both sets of grandparents, and Dylan had sent however much they told him he owed to get his name on the cards.

He motioned his brother toward the stairs at the other end of the storage room that served as his art studio. "Come on up. Gramps and I just installed a new booster for the wireless a couple of days ago, so I get a strong signal and good Internet connection out here."

"Wow." Pax let out a low whistle when he reached the second-floor apartment. "You've done wonders with the place.

The one-bedroom apartment looked bigger than it probably had when Pax had lived here his first years of graduate school—mainly because Dylan didn't have the money to buy much furniture. But he'd lucked out with a few nice pieces from a thrift store in Brentwood. And he'd livened it up by hanging a few of his favorite pieces from his final showing his senior year of college—large history paintings in the style of the Renaissance masters with a bit of Romantic era color and light melded into the Venetian school tradition. In fact, one of them had been inspired by a sample cover he'd drawn for one of Melanie Mason's books, complete with the knight in shining armor and the not-so-distressed damsel fighting right along beside him.

"Where's your desk?" Pax stood in the broad, central corridor of the house, making a slow three-sixty turn.

"Uh. . .I don't have a desk. We can use the table." He pointed at the dinette set he'd picked up for twenty bucks. Gramps had helped him attach new, much sturdier legs to the table and wooden chairs. It now looked pretty good sitting in the large dormer that had once been the hayloft access of the old carriage house.

"That'll work." Pax started up the large laptop. Within moments, his video-chat program alerted him he had two calls waiting. He clicked on both of the alerts, and windows popped up containing live video feed of both Spencer and Tyler—who apparently had been talking to each other.

"Hey, Spence, Tyler." Pax adjusted the angle of the laptop screen so that the little window in the corner showed both him and Dylan. "Spence, how's Utah?"

"Cold and snowy as advertised, and almost as crowded as Chicago." The third of the Bradley brothers picked up his computer and carried it to the window. Several stories below, they could just make out the base of a ski run crawling with people. The picture bobbled, then stilled, and Spencer sat before it again. "We're leaving here Wednesday. My flight gets in around three in the afternoon. Can one of you pick me up?"

"We'll come get you. I got the itinerary you e-mailed, and I have it in my calendar. Don't forget, we have to go out to Mother and Dad's for the family photo shoot. The campaign publicist should have e-mailed each of you the information." When had Pax become the authoritative, responsible one? Growing up, he'd never been one to think beyond his next science experiment. "Tyler—I saw Boston's getting hit with a big winter storm this weekend. You all bundled up and keeping your toes and nose warm?"

Their youngest brother rolled his eyes. Warmth trickled down into Dylan's stomach. Oh how he'd missed seeing Tyler grow up. Why had he let himself be pulled away from them? He and his brothers had all gotten along pretty well as kids. The idea he might have lost that sliced into his gut like a broadsword.

"I'm keeping warm." Tyler contorted himself to lift one foot to show them his thick woolen sock—the toe of which flopped around with extra room, as a little kid's would. "They should have the snow cleared out before I head to the airport Monday. Dylan, are you picking me up?"

111

Surprised at the request, Dylan glanced at Pax, who shrugged. Dylan turned back to the computer screen. "Yeah, li'l brother, I can come get you. Just send me your flight info." His cell phone buzzed almost immediately with a new text message.

"Now that we've got that all squared away. . ." Pax reached out and made a millimeter adjustment to the angle of the screen. "Guys, Dylan thinks that we're supposed to be talking about the gifts for Mother and Dad and the grands."

"You didn't tell him?" Tyler's voice cracked. His face reddened, and he took off his wire-rim glasses and cleaned them on the tail of his long-sleeved Boston Harbor tourist T-shirt.

"Tell me what?" Dylan studied Pax's profile, then the averted gazes of Spencer and Tyler, whose glasses seemed to be terminally dirty. "What's going on?"

Pax cleared his throat. "We, uh, wanted to talk to you before everyone got here and things got crazy with the holidays and Mother's campaign stuff."

Tyler slid his glasses back on. "Dylan, we're worried about you. I probably know more than Pax and Spencer, only because we've spent time together over the last few years. But dude, we all grew up in the same house. We know you—or at least we used to; and even though we don't know all the specifics, we know something's wrong."

"We know Mother and Dad never made life easy on you." Spencer leaned closer to his computer, making his nose look strangely enlarged. "We heard all the 'debates' "—he enclosed the word with finger quotes—"about your desire to major in art and that they wouldn't support you financially if you chose to go that route."

Dylan twisted the carved silver ring around his left thumb, every nerve in his body firing mixed signals of anxiety and relief.

Pax turned to look at him. "We're your brothers. We love you and respect you. And we'd like to help you. If you'll let us in, tell us what happened, so we can help you come up with a solution. And no, we won't tell Mother and Dad or anyone else. It's just us—the Bradley brothers."

Dylan's throat squeezed nearly shut with the desire to unburden himself and the fear of their reaction to the truth. He looked each of his brothers in the eyes then took a deep breath. "It started. . .in New York. I had that good scholarship but no money to live on. So I started looking for freelance work, thinking I could make money and expand my portfolio. I got requests for samples at a couple of places; then, through someone at school, I got hooked up with an agent. She took a look at all of my work, even my sketchbooks."

Mortification boiled up his neck and across his face. "Y'all don't know this, but one of the reasons Mother and Dad didn't want me pursuing art is because of some of the drawings in those sketchbooks. Mother liked to read steamy romance novels. When I was about twelve or thirteen, I found some of them hidden around the house. I became obsessed with the artwork on the front. That was before they started using photos, like so many of them do now."

Tyler's mouth hung open. "You were drawing. . .*porn?*"

"No Tyler, that's not what he's saying." Spencer's face went blank after his immediate defense of his big brother. "That's not what you were saying, was it, D?"

Pax got up and went into the kitchen.

"No, that's not what I'm saying. One of the things that drew me to them is that they had some similarity to the artwork from the Renaissance era—the castles and landscapes, the realistic renderings of the people, the characters."

Pax returned and handed Dylan a glass of water. "Guys, I think the problem was less about the fact Dylan had done drawings like that and more because Mother was horrified that Dylan had discovered her dirty little secret—that she liked reading raunchy romance novels and that she was afraid somehow, from his imitating the covers in his artwork, the whole world would find out."

Dylan stared, open-mouthed, at his brother.

"We shared a room, bro. And I spent a lot of time sitting in the hallway outside our room. Those doors weren't all that thick." Bright red patches illuminated his cheeks. "And what you and Mother never knew, and I'll deny it with my last breath, is that while you just liked the covers, I liked reading them myself."

Spencer and Tyler guffawed—but Dylan gave Pax a sympathetic squeeze on the shoulder. His admission would draw all kinds of harassment from their two younger brothers for years to come.

To take the heat off Pax, Dylan continued his story. "The agent who picked me up in college got me a chance to pitch cover ideas to one of the big romance novel publishers in New York. When I saw how much they would pay, I knew I had to do whatever it took to get that job. I have a pretty good imagination, but like most portrait artists, it's better to have a real world image to create from. I couldn't afford to pay any models, but one of my roommates had a girlfriend who shared our post office box. But she only came by once a week to get her mail. So her clothing catalogs would sit around on the coffee table all week. That gave me the perfect—free—resource for female images. For the men—"

Dylan grabbed the glass of water and took a big swig. Other than Rhonda, he'd never shared this with anyone. "For the men, I used. . .I used myself as the model."

Chapter 11

∞

$\mathcal{S}$urprisingly, the peanut gallery remained silent after Dylan's revelations, but looks of shock and—was that respect?—came from all three. "I disguised myself—more heavily muscled, different hair color or eye color—but it's me on the front of six romance novels that hit the bestseller list. I used a pseudonym, so except for the agent and whoever paid the bills at the publisher, no one knows I did them."

"But that's not what made you pull away from the family, is it?" Pax asked.

Dylan sighed. In for a penny, in for a pound. "No. The last cover I did was after I got the assistant professor position at Watts-Maxwell. My thesis adviser in graduate school thought it was funny that I'd been doing romance novel covers in the style of the Venetian master artist I'd been studying. So I didn't think anything of renting studio space at Watts to work on it. The chair of my department saw me working on it one night and warned me never to tell anyone else there about it because I could be in danger of losing my job—said they wouldn't want any of their professors to be involved in anything like that."

Here came the hard part. "Dr. Kramer, the department chair, decided that the work I'd done—the work I'd been encouraged to do as a student—was hindering my growth as an artist. She had me take several of her modern and postmodern classes—yes, even though I was already a professor—and insisted I work only in that style, closely supervised by her. She took me to all of the gala events in the Philadelphia art community—and even to New York a few times for gallery and exhibit openings."

His hands shook, remembering not the fun he'd had in the beginning, experiencing things someone of that age rarely got to experience, but how things ended. "She convinced me I didn't know as much about art as I thought, and she took a systematic approach to reteaching me everything—about art and about myself."

How—why had he fallen for her? He could see it so clearly now: she'd fed him a meal of lies, and he'd licked the plate clean.

"When did it turn into a relationship?" Tyler asked.

"Wait—what?" Spencer's heavy brows met over his nose. "You had a relationship with the chair of your department? Don't most schools have rules about instructors or professors and department chairs and deans? In businesses, it falls under the nepotism rules."

"It does in academia, too," Pax said.

"She had me so convinced that she knew best, that anything she did was okay, I didn't worry about it. She told me that I needed to stay in Philadelphia during all my school breaks—made sure I had showings scheduled or that there were events for us to attend during the summers or over the holidays—so that I wouldn't be able to come home." He rubbed the inside of his right elbow, where he'd gotten his first tattoo. "She played on my desire to have someone, anyone in a position of authority over me, approve of what I was doing, and she used it to her advantage."

Just saying the words aloud flooded him with new understanding of her and of himself. "She had me living a lifestyle that was far beyond my financial means—and after a couple of years of that, I was on the verge of losing everything. Until she suggested I move in with her."

"Were you in love with her?" Tyler pushed his glasses up the bridge of his nose and leaned forward.

"I don't know. I thought so. But at the same time, my conscience kept bothering me, telling me it was wrong, that I shouldn't be sleeping with a woman I wasn't married to." A grim chuckle bubbled in his chest. No matter how many times he'd heard at church that God wanted him to save himself sexually for marriage, whenever he'd had misgivings about living with Rhonda, the remonstrances always came in Perty's voice.

"When I told her at Thanksgiving that I wanted to come home for Christmas, that it had been five years since I'd had Christmas with my family, she told me that she was my family and she was the only one who mattered. It was like something snapped inside of me. The next day, I called a buddy—the guy I'd bought my truck from, as a matter of fact—and asked him if I could crash at his place. I told Rhonda I was moving out. And then she snapped. Started screaming at me, crying, telling me how ungrateful I was, how she'd made me, how I would be nothing if it weren't for her. Then she went to the human resources department and told them that we'd been having a relationship. She's the chair of a department. I was an assistant professor without tenure. So. . .here I am. Jobless. Homeless. And feeling pretty stupid."

He downed the rest of his water. Speaking that much for the first time in a month strained his vocal cords. Admitting to his weakness, his stupidity, and his sordid choices left him completely drained.

"Well, you're not homeless, because Gramps and Perty will let you live there however long you want to—you've always been Perty's favorite." Spencer softened his accusation with a grin.

"And Perty said something at lunch last Sunday about the possibility of you picking up a couple of classes at Robertson in the spring, so it doesn't sound like you're completely jobless," Pax said.

"As to stupidity. . ." Tyler started, then grinned, still looking like the eleven-year-old he'd been when Dylan left for college. If anyone in the family had the right to call Dylan stupid, it was the certified genius. "You know what they say about those of us in the higher IQ brackets—to pack in all that extra intelligence, God had to leave something out. He had to make the *common sense* choice."

And to prove the point about his limited common sense, Dylan had actually considered *not* telling his brothers anything.

"There's one more thing we want to talk to you about." From the grim set of Pax's mouth, Dylan steeled himself for something even more unpleasant than what he'd just been through. "Even though we weren't sure what had happened while you were away, we were pretty sure it was bad—just from what Tyler shared with us about how you'd changed whenever y'all got together. I have a really good friend from church who'll be doing his practicum this spring for his master's in marriage and family therapy over at Trevecca. He has to carry a client load of something like eight people that he's counseling over the semester. It's a win-win situation—he rounds out the number of clients he needs; you get free therapy." Pax ended with a nervous laugh.

The canvases with images of doors, windows, and gateways scrolled through Dylan's mind—along with the few things he remembered from the art therapy course he'd taken as an undergrad. It couldn't hurt—and it would probably help. "That sounds like a good idea."

As one, his three brothers let out relieved breaths.

"Now, I thought we were supposed to be talking about gifts for Mother and Dad and the grands." The gamut of emotions he'd just run left him as limp as the filaments of a squirrel-hair paintbrush.

Pax clapped him on the shoulder. "We got their gifts when Spencer and Tyler were here at Thanksgiving. Don't worry. I brought the cards with me for you to sign, and I'll tell you how much you owe."

Spencer looked away from his computer and spoke to someone off camera. "Hey, guys, if we're done, I've got some serious snowboarding to get to."

"And I've got plans to go into the city this afternoon with some of the guys." Tyler started typing something on his computer.

"See you two next week." Pax pulled the laptop closer to him.

Dylan raised his hand in farewell before his brothers each severed the connection. Pax shut down and closed the laptop.

"I heard that Mrs. Evans is over here using Perty's kitchen." Pax brushed his unruly curls back from his eyes. "Let's go see if there's anything we can sample."

"Okay." Dylan grabbed his leather jacket off the arm of the oversized easy chair that demarcated the beginning of the living room area of the apartment. "And hey, Pax?"

His brother stopped at the head of the stairs. "Yeah?"

"Thanks. I know this"—Dylan jerked his head toward the table—"couldn't have been easy on you, especially."

"You're my big brother. What else could I do?" Pax shrugged then tromped down the stairs.

Dylan looked up at the ceiling, but his heart looked even higher.

After so many years of systematically cutting himself off from his family, his brothers had been willing to stage an intervention to drag him, kicking and screaming if necessary, back into the fold. Maybe it was time for him to see if God was willing to do the same thing.

∞

Caylor sang along with a 1950s stage performance sound track from *Oklahoma!*, the musical she'd been begging Bridget to choose as their fall musical next school year. Of course, Bridget had seen through her request—Caylor wanted to play the role of Aunt Eller so she could be on stage instead of behind the scenes. In high school and college performances, she'd played Ado Annie.

And just like the girl who couldn't say no when a man started talking "purty" to her, that was how Caylor had ended up with her first—and last—broken heart. No, she much preferred the role of Aunt Eller, the stalwart spinster aunt of the musical's female lead. She'd save the starry-eyed dreams of falling in love for the heroines of her romance novels.

In the middle of belting out "I Cain't Say No," and ignoring the looks she was sure she was getting from the other people waiting impatiently in the crowded cell phone lot at the Nashville International Airport, Caylor's phone chimed with a new text message.

Finally.

PLN LANDED. GTNG OFF NOW. BGG CLAIM #8.

Caylor pulled up the airport's website on her phone and located the map for the baggage claim area of the terminal. Carousel number eight should put Felicity coming out at one of the first two doors from the direction Caylor would approach the building.

TEXT ME WHEN YOU GET TO BAGGAGE CLAIM AND CAROUSEL STARTS RUNNING. She punched SEND on the message but wasn't certain Felicity would—

The phone chirped.

K

Well, maybe Felicity would remember to follow through. Caylor started the SUV and turned the music back on, though at a reduced volume. Several cars pulled out of the lot. Caylor waited. Two more songs. Three.

HERE. CARSEL MOVING.

Caylor pulled out of the waiting lot and into the traffic, trying to navigate the many forking lanes of the airport's access road. With as many times a year as Caylor picked up and dropped off her parents or flew in and out herself, she knew which lanes went where, so she could concentrate on not getting into a wreck instead of having to read the signs.

Oh, lucky day. Someone pulled away from the curb just between the two doors closest to carousel eight as Caylor drove up. She whipped into the spot, put the Escape in PARK, got out, and went around the back to open the tailgate of the small SUV.

Just in time, too. The airport's glass doors slid open, and a young woman with long, stringy red hair exited, dragging a huge duffel bag and suitcase behind her. Caylor didn't even want to know how much the enormous, and probably overweight, bags had cost her to check.

She waved. Felicity acknowledged her by raising her chin and moving in her direction. Not wanting to leave her still-running vehicle unattended, Caylor waited for her sister at the curb but took the rolling suitcase from her as soon as she got there.

"Mercy—how much stuff did you think you were going to need for a couple of weeks at home?" She was pretty sure she felt something in her back pull when she hefted the suitcase up into the SUV.

"And hello to you, too." Same Felicity, always grumpy after traveling.

"I'm sorry." Caylor helped her sister get the duffel in then turned and drew her into a hug. "Hello, Felicity. Welcome home."

"Sage."

Caylor stepped back, and reached for the tailgate to close it. "What's that?"

"I'm going by Sage now."

"O–oh." This was all Mama and Daddy's fault. Hadn't they realized when they named their younger daughter Felicity Sage that it would have an effect on her? "Let's go, then, Sage."

Caylor had to remind *Sage* to put her seat belt on before she would pull out into the flow of traffic, which she managed to do right before the traffic cop with the mean face reached them.

"How come you decided to fly in a few days early?" Caylor again kept her attention on the other cars—and decided to take the back exit out onto Donelson Pike to get to the interstate instead of going all the way around to I-40 on the airport access road.

"I knew Mama and Daddy were coming in today, and I thought it would make a nice surprise if I was already here when they got here. It means I'll get to spend as much time with them this year as you do."

Was that a hint of jealousy, of sibling rivalry, Caylor detected? Well, she wasn't the one who'd dropped out of college in the middle of her sophomore year, after losing all her scholarships the year before from poor grades, and decided to bounce from job to job, from place to place, landing who knew where.

"So, Portland, Oregon, huh?" That was the last city Felic—Sage had listed as her current city on Facebook.

"Yeah. But I liked Eugene and Salem a lot better. Portland was too big, too expensive."

Judging by the grungy look of her clothing, she seemed to have assimilated into the West Coast, crunchy granola crowd. "What were you doing in Portland?"

"I worked as a receptionist at a salon for a while." She twisted one dingy strand of hair around a finger. "They fired me because I wouldn't give in to their establishmentarian ideals of personal appearance."

Yep. Just as Caylor suspected. Not that her sister had ever really cared much for what other people thought of her appearance or behavior. And if Caylor could hold her breath for the almost thirty-minute drive to Forest Hills, she could survive her sister's slept-on-a-floor-in-a-gym-for-a-week odor. She felt sorry for the people who'd had to be mushed up against her for hours on the flights from Portland to Denver and Denver to Nashville.

"Sassy is over at Mrs. Bradley's house, baking this afternoon. I thought we could go straight there so you can see her." Caylor took the exit from I-40 to get onto the I-440 parkway.

"Actually, can we stop at the house first? I'd really like to take a shower. It's been a few days since I've been able to get one, and I know I smell pretty ripe." After the bravado she'd shown at the airport, Sage seemed to shrink into herself—and the shapeless oatmeal-colored sweater.

"What's going on, sis?"

Sage shrugged, her eyes pointed out the side window. "It's a long story, and I don't want to have to tell it several times. Let's just wait until after Mama and Daddy get here."

Stopping at home first, they unloaded Sage's luggage, which they dragged into the den, where she'd be sleeping on the sofa, and while Sage went into the bathroom off the guest bedroom downstairs, Caylor carried all of her shopping bags upstairs to the loft.

Assuming all of Sage's clothes were in pretty near the same condition as the ones she'd been wearing—if not worse—Caylor pulled out a sweater and T-shirt that had shrunk up in the wash and were way too tight for her now and a pair of warm socks, then went down to Sassy's room and pulled out a pair of jeans Sassy rarely wore because they were too long for her. With Sage being between their heights, at just over five foot ten, but with a slenderer build than Caylor's, hopefully the clothes would fit.

Laying the clothes out on the end of the bed in the guest bedroom where her sister would be sure to see them, she then went back upstairs to send a quick e-mail to Zarah and Flannery to let them know "Sage" had arrived safely.

She archived a few e-mails from students complaining about their final grades—she'd deal with those later.

The third step squealed.

"Hey, Caylor?"

She shut down the computer and headed for the stairs. Sage stood on the betraying third step. "That sweater looks good on you, if a bit too big. Sorry about that. Do the jeans fit? They're Sassy's."

"Yeah, thanks."

"Sorry I couldn't supply you with underwear."

Sage stepped down into the den but turned and held up something wadded in plastic in her hand. "I was able to take a few dollars and get a pack of new underwear at a discount store before I left. That's one thing I definitely refuse to live without—clean undies."

Even with her hair still wrapped in a towel, Sage looked 100 percent better.

"I've got some body sprays up in my bathroom if you want to borrow one." Caylor listed the scents she could remember off the top of her head. Students and faculty and staff loved to give either bath product gift baskets or candles for gifts, so she had a stockpile of both.

"Ooh, jasmine pear sounds great."

Caylor went back upstairs to dig through all of the travel-size bottles until she found that particular scent. She had three, so she took two of them down to Sage. "Here. I've got several. You can have these."

Tears sprang to Sage's hazel eyes. "Thanks."

Since her sister had already indicated she didn't want to discuss her problems right now, Caylor gave her a quick hug then pretended nothing out of the ordinary had happened. "Ready to go?"

Sage pulled her damp hair back into a ponytail holder, leaving the length of it tucked under in a loose approximation of a bun at her nape. Having washed away the smudged eye makeup that had made her look like she hadn't slept in weeks, she looked so much younger than her thirty-one years. "Yep. Let's go."

Back in the car—this time Caylor didn't have to remind her to buckle up—Sage kicked off her black mules and pulled her heels up onto the edge of the seat and wrapped her arms around her knees. "How come Sassy is cooking over at Mrs. Bradley's house?"

Caylor told her about the second oven giving up the ghost—and about Sassy's elaborate plans for remodeling the house, including the arrival of Mr. Fantastic. By the time she pulled up the long driveway to the Bradleys' grand Victorian home, Sage was actually laughing.

Caylor parked the car, but before turning it off, she reached over and clasped her sister's hand. "You know I love you, right?"

Sage squeezed her hand back. "I know. I love you, too."

"And you can tell me anything."

"I know."

"Just wanted to make sure we're on the same page." She gave Sage's hand a quick double squeeze then reached for the keys and killed the engine. "Come on. I'm sure Sassy has some bowls or spatulas for us to lick."

She led Sage up the steps of the side porch, and the door opened before Caylor could knock.

The young, long-necked scientist from the family cookout back in October stood in the doorway, smiling. "Caylor, right?"

"Yes—you're Paxton?"

"Pax, yeah."

She shook his hand and walked past him into the warm, heavenly smelling kitchen. "This is my sister, Sage Evans."

Pax didn't say anything for a moment, his gaze fixed on Sage's clean, angelic face. He seemed to recover himself as soon as her foot hit the threshold. "Hi, it's nice to meet you, Sage."

"Felicity? Is that you?" Sassy dropped her wooden spoon into the bowl of batter she was mixing and rushed across the kitchen to hug her younger granddaughter. "Why didn't you tell me you were coming in early?"

"I wanted it to be a surprise." Sage looked like she might burst into tears when Sassy pulled her into a rib-crushing hug. Caylor moved around until she could catch Sage's eye and tried to send waves of calmness to her sister. Apparently it worked, because Sage relaxed, blinked a few times, and regained her smile.

"Felicity is going by her middle name now, Sassy. I like it. I think Sage suits her, don't you?" Caylor moved closer to her sister and grandmother.

"Yes. In fact, I'm the one who suggested that to your mother." Sassy patted Sage's cheek. "Now, Sage, I don't know if you've ever met Perty's oldest grandson. This is Dylan Bradley."

Caylor whirled around. Behind her, sliding off one of the breakfast-bar stools, Dylan stood and moved toward them.

She seriously wished she could take a page out of his book and flee the room.

Chapter 12

Caylor did a good job of hiding her initial shock at seeing Dylan. He went around the end of the bar to shake hands with Sage Evans. She had the same red hair as Caylor—though hers was long and pulled back instead of framing her face like a spunky elf.

The buzzing oven timer was the only thing that could pull Mrs. Evans away from fawning over her younger granddaughter.

"Sit, stay awhile." Perty waved them toward the four stools at the breakfast bar. Dylan returned to the one on the far side. Caylor, who wouldn't make eye contact with him, took the one on the opposite end. Paxton helped Sage get situated in the one next to Caylor before he sat down.

Dylan wasn't sure what to say to Caylor—if he got the chance today. She seemed embarrassed to see him. Embarrassed that she'd taken what Dr. Putnam said the wrong way? Or embarrassed over the scene Dylan had caused by misinterpreting what could have been simple friendly gestures from her?

Perty handed them each a mug of cider from the slow cooker on the counter. Mrs. Evans slid the batch of cookies from the baking sheet onto a cooling rack, plated four of them, and brought them over to the bar.

She held the plate in front of Caylor first. "Toffee chip. Your favorite."

Caylor picked up the hot cookie and slid it onto a napkin then set

125

it down to cool for a few minutes.

"How were your flights?" Mrs. Evans asked Sage, returning to stirring the mincemeat pie filling she'd been working on when they arrived.

"Fine. Long. I had to be at the airport a little after four this morning—that's what, six o'clock this time zone?—so it's been a long day for me already." She punctuated the statement with a yawn.

"Where do you live?" Pax seemed oblivious to the fact there was a tempting cookie and a cup of hot cider in front of him.

"I came in from Portland, Oregon." Sage took a bite of the hot cookie. "You really should try these—they're Sassy's signature cookie."

"What—oh." Pax picked his up, took a bite, and then puckered his lips and started blowing to keep the hot bite from burning his tongue, bringing him momentarily out of his Sage-induced euphoria.

Choking back a laugh, Caylor accidentally caught Dylan's eye. He smiled back, despite the heat rising up his neck into his cheeks, then looked away again.

Sage and Pax started talking about Christmas movies, and Perty and Mrs. Evans joined in. Sassy brought up Bing Crosby's *White Christmas*. She turned her beaming smile onto Caylor—who was shaking her head—and Sage.

"Oh girls, you must do it."

"Sassy—no, they don't want to hear that." Caylor crossed her arms and set her jaw in a stubborn expression.

Perty seemed to catch on to what Mrs. Evans wanted them to do. "Oh yes girls. It's been so long since I've seen you do it. Please?"

Sage groaned. But she slid off her stool. "I think I remember all the words and movements."

Caylor lodged one more protest but moved into the open area between the bar and the breakfast nook. "It won't be the same without the big feathered fans."

Dylan turned to watch them. Feathered fans? What were they talking about?

She hummed the introduction, and then she and Sage started singing a song called "Sisters." Wait. Dylan had heard this song before. But he remembered that two guys had done it. Of course Bing Crosby and. . .some other guy in *White Christmas*. Perty used to make them watch it every year. Apparently Caylor and Sage's grandparents had not only made them watch it, but get up and sing and dance with it, too.

Dylan had only been to a few shows on Broadway in the years he'd lived in New York and Philadelphia, but he was pretty sure he hadn't seen anyone on stage there who was a better performer than Caylor Evans.

Oops, she caught him staring at her again. This time, though, she didn't wink, and she almost hid her smile until she had her back turned to him.

Caylor and Sage got their signals crossed at the end and had to grab hold of each other—laughing hysterically—to keep from falling over. Dylan joined in the laughter and applause. He needed to apologize to Caylor for last night, for giving her any reason to feel uncomfortable.

Pax jumped up as if his seat were spring-loaded and assisted Sage with her bar stool again. Dylan sipped his cider to hide his amusement. None of the four of them had ever been very adept with women. But in the last few years, Spencer seemed to have come into Dad's suavity, and his popularity with women simply from his inheriting all the good looks couldn't be denied.

Then Sage did it. She asked *the question*.

"So, Pax, what do you do?"

"I'm a doctoral candidate in medical physics at Vanderbilt." And away he went, explaining exactly what medical physics was and how important it was to the advancement of medical science and health care.

Caylor moved into the kitchen and had a hushed conversation with Sassy about sleeping arrangements at their house. On the pretext of getting something cold to drink, Dylan went to the fridge, getting away from Pax's theory of physics monologue.

"So I can either take y'all home and then go pick them up; or I can get them, take them to the house, drop them off, and then come pick you up." Caylor leaned against the edge of the counter over the dishwasher.

Mrs. Evans looked at the oven timer then around at everything laid out on the large prep island. "But this won't be finished before you need to leave to get them."

Dylan stepped forward. "I can take your sister and grandmother home, if that helps." Would she understand his implied apology in the offer?

"Are you sure?"

"Yeah, it's not a problem. And I have enough room for all of the food, too." He looked around at the bakery's worth of pies, cakes, and cookies on plates, platters, and pedestals around the kitchen.

"That would be wonderful and save me a little time. Speaking of. . ." Caylor looked at the silver bracelet watch on her left wrist. "I should probably get going in a few minutes. I got a text alert a little over an hour ago that their flight from Washington DC left on time, and that's only a two-hour flight."

"So your parents live in DC?" Dylan bent over and leaned his elbows on the cool marble of the island.

"No. Geneva, Switzerland. My mother's a doctor working on cancer research with the World Health Organization. Daddy's a software designer for international banks and businesses."

Wow. And he thought Mother and Dad had given him and his brothers a lot to live up to.

"You know, this kitchen is getting awfully crowded. Dylan, why don't you take them over and give them a tour of the carriage house. Maybe show them some of your artwork." Perty put her arm around his waist and gave him a squeeze as she slipped past him to get to the fridge.

Knowing the sketches he'd been working on early this morning—when he'd woken before dawn and hadn't had the willpower not to draw—were well hidden, how could he not agree? "Sure, come on over. I just got some of my favorite pieces up on the wall day before yesterday."

"Okay." Caylor followed him out of the kitchen. He had to physically touch Pax on the shoulder to get his attention and tell him what they were doing. He assumed Sage would be grateful for the interruption, but as they shrugged into jackets to make the trek across the side yard to the outbuilding, Sage kept peppering Pax with questions about his research.

Caylor shrugged and shook her head as if to say, *There's no accounting for tastes.*

Dylan held the door until Pax took over to hold it for Sage, then fell into step beside Caylor. "I'm sorry I had to leave early last night. Something. . .came up."

"Bridget told me. I hope everything's okay now." She buttoned her purple wool peacoat against the cold wind. The color, like the dark aqua she'd worn last night, nearly drove him to the brink of seizures with the need to try to capture her red hair, ivory skin, and turquoise eyes. Sage's eyes were a much plainer hazel—and set slightly too close together.

"Everything seems to be fine now." At least, he hoped it was. He was comfortable around Caylor. He didn't want to do anything to jeopardize that until he got himself straightened out and figured out if they were supposed to be friends or if there was a possibility at a chance of more than that. That she was older than him—how much he wasn't quite sure—did give him pause. But he liked her. And that crossed all age boundaries.

He sped his last few steps to open the door into the workroom beside the garage portion of the building.

She stepped up into the room. "What a great work space. Complete with laundry for if you get paint all over your clothes?"

That crooked smile of hers would be his undoing. He'd almost captured it in his sketchbook this morning but now noticed that she pulled the left side of her bottom lip down just a little bit less than he'd drawn it.

"Gramps and Perty had those installed when Pax lived here a few years ago. I think Perty was tired of doing his laundry for him." He gave his brother's shoulder a playful fist bump.

"Perty offered to do it for me. I was the one who pointed out there are hookups in here. Next thing I knew, they had someone out here installing a washer and dryer." Pax wandered over to the stacks of canvases Dylan had been sorting when he arrived earlier. He crouched down and seemed to study all of them, then looked up at Dylan. "I don't get it."

"Don't get what?"

Pax indicated the paintings with a wave of his hand. "This. When you can do what you do, why do this kind of. . .stuff?"

"Because it was what I'd been told was the kind of art I should be doing. But I'm going back to the other style."

Caylor and Sage moved over beside Pax. Sage knelt down and started flipping through the images of doors, windows, and gateways. "I love these," she breathed. "These really speak to me."

Maybe he should suggest she go into counseling with Pax's friend, too. "If you see anything in there you want, take it. I was planning to throw those away."

Sage looked over her shoulder at him. "Really? But these are brilliant. I can feel the raw emotion in them."

She sounded sort of like those half-off-their-rocker art critics who saw deep meaning in everything, even when it was something Dylan had slapped together with no more thought than if he'd dipped a dog's tail in a can of paint and then held a sausage treat in front of him.

But as the paintings Sage held in her hands had come out of one of the darkest times of his life, maybe there was something in them that spoke to something dark inside of her. If it helped her, he'd be more than happy for her to take them. "Sure. Take that whole stack if you want them."

"Don't tempt me." She flipped through them and pulled out a painting of a blue door in a black wall. Rhonda had loved the texture and juxtaposition of the bright blue against the black. "I like this one best. Are you sure you don't mind me taking it?"

"Have it." The fewer things he had around to remind him of Rhonda, the better.

"Why don't you show them what you can really do?" Pax went back toward the door and started up the stairs.

He motioned Caylor and Sage to follow. He almost asked Caylor what she thought of the stuff down here, but he was pretty sure if she'd liked it, she would have said something by now.

Pax stood in the wide area at the top of the stairs under the three enormous history paintings. "This is the kind of stuff Dylan does best."

"Oh wow—it looks so real. Almost like a photograph." Sage moved closer.

Dylan stood to the side where he could see Caylor's face. Her eyes moved over the paintings, and she stood transfixed, the way he'd probably looked the time he'd seen his first Titian painting on display at the Metropolitan Museum of Art in New York.

A warm glow settled in his chest.

Then, all color drained from her face. She frowned and moved closer, leaning her head back to study the center piece. She swallowed a couple of times, blinked, and took a jagged breath. When she looked at him, she forced a smile. "These are amazing, Dylan." She looked at her watch. "I hate to run, but I don't want to be late to pick up my parents."

With that, she turned and practically ran down the stairs.

What had he done now?

Caylor's heart didn't return to a normal rhythm until she pulled off I-40 at the airport. It had to be a coincidence. Had to be.

Her phone rang. She jabbed the button on the steering wheel to answer it. "Hello?"

"Hey, sweetie, it's Mama." Her mother's voice filled the car. "We're picking up our luggage right now."

"I'm just getting off the interstate, so you shouldn't have to wait long. What carousel are you at?" She merged, with extreme caution, back onto the airport access road and got into the lane for passenger pickup.

"Nine. We're coming out the door at the close end of the building."

Caylor pulled over into the right lane as she approached the building. She slowed down before she got there, waiting to see if someone might pull out, but no one did, so she pulled up into one of the temporary, for-loading-only, spaces across the driving lanes from the sidewalk.

"I see you. We'll be right there." Mama hung up.

Caylor jumped out and popped the tailgate. Hadn't she just been here doing this? Why had she insisted on taking Sage over to see Sassy? She could have waited until later.

Mama, her bobbed red hair getting lighter each time Caylor saw her, and Daddy, his short curly hair long since turned silver from the medium brown she remembered from her childhood, came jogging across the driving lanes as soon as the traffic cop stopped the two lanes of cars for them. They each pulled one large suitcase behind them.

Mama released hers as soon as she drew up to the car, and she pulled Caylor into a hug. Daddy put his arms around both of them and squeezed them tightly before disengaging to put the suitcases in the Escape.

Stepping back, Mama adjusted the collar of Caylor's coat. "That color is so good on you." Searching Caylor's face, she frowned. "Is everything okay?"

Caylor shook off the bothersome suspicions and thoughts. "Yes. Everything is wonderful now that y'all are here." She glanced over her shoulder. The traffic cop tapped his wristwatch. "We'd better go before they arrest us for impeding the flow of traffic or something."

Daddy climbed into the front seat, Mama in the back, and Caylor once again took the Donelson exit out of the back of the airport. Her parents kept the conversation going with tales of the people they'd seen in the Geneva airport and on the nine-and-a-half-hour flight from Geneva to Washington's Dulles Airport. Of course, getting through customs with a suitcase full of Christmas gifts always generated stories, and Caylor had almost forgotten what she'd seen in Dylan's apartment by the time she pulled up under the carport at home.

Sassy and Sage greeted them at the door, and Caylor stood back, enjoying Mama and Daddy's surprise at Sage's appearance several days earlier than expected.

After the joyous reunion, Mama and Daddy took their baggage off to the guest bedroom on the far end of the house. Sage went out to the laundry room to put her first load of clothes in the dryer and start a second load, and Caylor went upstairs to change into something a little nicer to wear out to dinner.

As soon as she hit the landing at the top of the stairs, though, she didn't go straight through across to her bedroom. She turned right into the office. From the top shelf of the inside-most bookcase along the wall behind her desk, she pulled out six books. She went through the first three quickly; then, at the fourth one, her knees gave out, and she sank into her office chair.

She opened the cabinet below the bookshelves and pulled out a banker's box. Opening it, she reached for the large folder standing upright along the side of the box and pulled it out onto her desk.

Taking a deep breath, she opened the folder and looked at the glossy copy of Patrick Callaghan's artwork for the cover of her fourth Melanie Mason book. She closed her eyes, pressed the heels of her hands to her temples, and then looked at it again.

It wasn't the twelfth-century armor worn by the hero, holding tightly to his side the heroine, in an elaborate bliaut with flowing sleeves and elaborate gold embroidery that drew her eye. It was the large brown dog standing his ground beside them as they faced the oncoming column of knights in the far distant landscape that grabbed her by the throat.

The exact same dog had been beside the hero in later-period armor in the middle painting hanging on Dylan's wall.

She turned to the credenza and pulled out the folder labeled TEMPLATES. Shuffling through all of the pages of printed images of men who inspired her to think about romantic heroes, she pulled out every drawing or painting of the model who graced the cover of each of the six Melanie Mason books.

Laying them out side by side with the books, she could no longer deny her suspicion.

Sliding down in her chair until her head rested against the midheight back, she stared up at the eggshell ceiling. "You know, God, I knew You had a sick sense of humor. I knew I was making trouble by allowing myself to obsess over that cover model. But *this*? Seriously? How am I going to be able to look him in the eye ever again? What exactly is it You're trying to tell me here?"

God apparently didn't feel like chatting, because He didn't split the ceiling and come down to have a heart-to-heart with her.

Dylan Bradley was Patrick Callaghan. But not only that, Dylan Bradley was the cover model who had inspired every hero in the novels she'd written in the past eight years, including four of the Mason books—the cover model she'd fallen in love with a little more with each book she'd written.

Chapter 13

❦

"Thanks for the loan, D."

Dylan glanced in the rearview mirror in time to see Spencer pull off the *Utah!* sweatshirt he'd worn on the plane. Mother would've had a cow if her favorite child hadn't shown up in the mandated uniform today. "No problem."

"So we're really going to be in her campaign ads?" Spencer pulled the button-down shirt off the hanger and thrust his arms into the sleeves.

"And on her website and in her print ads. That's why she wanted all of us in white shirts, nice jeans, and casual brown shoes or boots." Tyler kicked the back of Dylan's seat with one of his brown lace-up boots. Poor kid, having to squeeze in behind the driver's seat. But no way would all of them have fit in Pax's two-door Mini Cooper.

"And shorn and shaved." Pax ran his hand over his newly trimmed hair, making Dylan glad he'd decided on his own to get his cut before the Robertson holiday party last week.

Oh man, he'd meant *not* to think about anything having to do with JRU or any of their faculty. He'd made it almost a solid four hours without being plagued by questions about Caylor's reaction to seeing his paintings Saturday.

He'd studied the painting that had caused her reaction. Sure, the style was similar to the covers he used to do, but why would that have bothered Caylor? No way she knew about those. Perty had shown him the books Caylor wrote. No one who wrote squeaky-clean stuff for the Christian market ever could have read books like Melanie Mason's.

Though. . .her friend Zarah did have copies of them on her bookshelf. Maybe she'd seen them there? But she'd have to have a photographic memory—and be able to extrapolate quite a bit stylistically—to figure out he was the same artist.

"So where are we going to eat after the photo shoot?" Spencer finished buttoning his shirt.

"No can do, brother. We have to stay and have dinner with Mother and Dad—photos of *family time*." Pax angled in the front seat so he could see all three of them. "We've got to do indoor and outdoor, video and still, and somehow make like it's not the beginning of winter, since most of these ads will run in the spring. Mother suggested we'd probably be there till late."

Tyler and Spencer groaned. Dylan changed lanes to take the I-40 West split at the end of the I-440 Parkway. "How do you know all this?"

Pax shrugged. "I asked. That's the foundation of the scientific method. If you don't ask the questions, you'll never learn the answers."

This would be the first time Dylan would sit down to dinner with his entire immediate family since the last time he came home for Christmas, his senior year of college. The year after that, Mother and Dad had torn down the home he'd grown up in and built a new house.

He wasn't certain what to expect, except what he'd seen in the few photos his brothers had sent him over the years. The sun started angling toward the western horizon as Dylan navigated the old, winding roads through Belle Meade. Amazing how, after all these years, everything seemed the same—yet different. The small ranch houses and bungalows and cottages that had been the mainstay of this area when he was growing up had, by and large, been razed to make way for starter mansions and mini-estates. But the roads, and the trees lining them, all felt familiar.

His heart hammered when he signaled his turn onto their street. Here the houses were far apart, each one on at least two acres. He slowed then turned into the fifth driveway, which wound a few hundred feet through crepe myrtle trees—now bare—before straightening to reveal the house.

The place where Dylan had grown up—but not. Farther back on the property from where the original low, sprawling ranch had been now stood a tall, imposing cream-colored French chateau, complete with multiple gables, arched windows with decorative masonry details, and iron-fenced Juliet balconies on the two square turrets on either side of a small courtyard to the right of the massive main entrance.

He started to park in the wide, paved area at the base of the steps up to the path leading to the columned front porch.

"Don't park here," Pax said. "Pull around to the side of the house."

Sure enough, a secondary cobblestone driveway led straight to—no *through*—the house. He drove through the archway that connected the main part of the house to what turned out to be one of two double garages with a large parking area between them.

He parked and pulled the key out of the ignition. He'd always thought Gramps and Perty's house grandiose. But their historical Victorian, no matter how nicely remodeled inside, seemed understated and humble compared to this.

"You coming?" Tyler opened his door.

Dylan slid out and pocketed his keys. "Yeah, just taking it all in."

"Massive, huh?"

Dylan turned, taking in the stucco walls surrounding the basketball court–sized parking area on three sides. Though they had plenty of windows, keeping it from looking quite so much like a fortress, other than the closed garage doors to his left and right, he didn't see a single entrance into the house.

"Come on." Tyler pulled his sleeve, and they followed Spencer and Pax back toward the portico he'd driven through. A glass-paned door opened into a kitchen—a kitchen smaller than Perty's, though fancier, with moldings and finials decorating the light cabinetry and small central island. The six-burner industrial range appeared to be in unused, straight-from-the-showroom condition. And the soapstone tiles of the backsplash looked hand hewn.

"It's about time." Mother stood from the table in the tiled, window-surrounded eating area just beyond the kitchen's stubby breakfast bar. "We only have about an hour to do the outdoor shoots." She immediately flung open a french door to a covered patio that connected the house to a swimming pool.

A swimming pool? His parents hated swimming, had refused to let them take swimming lessons or compete on swim team in school because they didn't want to have to sit in the natatorium near all that chlorinated water.

Pax turned and looked over his shoulder at Dylan. "I know, right?"

Beyond the house—which extended in almost a V-shape well beyond the pool on both sides—in the enormous yard where Dylan and his brothers had built forts, played hide-and-seek, chased each other, and climbed the old silver maple and hickory trees, at least a dozen people scurried around setting up cameras and lights. In addition to the equipment, a bunch of potted flowering plants and shrubs behind a blanket spread over the dead grass created a vignette in one area near the still cameras.

"Stop!" A middle-aged woman with a clipboard came running toward them just as Dylan was about to step from the paved pool deck onto the grass. "Jackets off and all of you come over here"— she pointed at the side yard just beyond the rear garage—"and group around Grace."

Mother, dressed in her jeans—which probably cost more than the amount of Dylan's final paycheck—and white shirt led the way and then positioned all of the rest of them around her. Dylan, of course, was farthest away, with Tyler and Spencer between him and her.

The video crew came over.

"Walk toward the camera," Clipboard Lady shouted, "but don't look at the camera. Talk and laugh, but be natural, all attention on Grace."

Dylan couldn't help but smile, remembering Caylor's murmured aside to him when Dr. Putnam took the "candid" picture of them last week. She should have been here; she'd be able to demonstrate how to put on a good show without giving one thought to being self-conscious.

"Stop, stop, stop! You there, on the end—left side—my left side."

Naturally, he'd be the one to be singled out. "Sorry?"

"Get a little closer and act like you're actually part of the family. The smiling was perfect—spot on—but just act like you like your brothers."

Once again, off in his own little world, which, if they were going for a genuine family dynamic, having him isolated off to the side would have been just about right.

But whose fault was that?

On a whim, he moved behind Tyler and Spencer and draped his arms around their shoulders.

"End guy, that's perfect. Now walk toward the camera. Mom is saying something so funny, you love her so much. Grace and Davis, hold hands."

After a few attempts, Clipboard Lady declared they'd gotten the footage they needed and told them to go over to the blanket by the bushes. She positioned Mother in the center front with Dad behind her. Spencer, the best-looking of the four of them, got prime positioning at Mother's right hand. They had to put Tyler to her left— he was too small to hold his own on the outside or in the back. First, they had Pax and Dylan kneel behind everyone, but after a few shots, Clipboard Lady didn't like it, so she had them move to the sides and sit beside their brothers, leaning toward Mother.

This setup must have worked, because the only instructions Clipboard Lady gave after that were minor tweaks: chin up, head angled, don't make a fist, look at Grace.

"Now, since these are running in the spring, boys, I want you to roll up your sleeves."

Dylan stopped his roll midforearm. Apparently that wasn't to Clipboard Lady's liking, because she came over, set her clipboard down, and rolled and pushed his right sleeve up over his elbow—and promptly gasped.

"What is it?" Mother's head whirled around.

Clipboard Lady jerked Dylan's arm forward. "I didn't mind the jewelry, but this—it just won't do."

Just below the bend of Dylan's elbow, stark against his indoor-kinda-guy pale skin, was the tattoo of his own somewhat simplified rendering of Titian's "Allegory of Prudence" with three faces—one facing left, one forward, one right—depicting the three ages of man. Below it in a calligraphic script was the motto Titian had included over the heads in his painting.

"A tattoo?" Fury blotched Mother's face. "A tattoo? I should have known."

"Should have known what?" Spencer came up on his knees, unbuttoned his shirt, pulled it off his left shoulder, and pushed up the sleeve of his undershirt to reveal a tattoo of an intricately designed Celtic cross on his muscular upper arm. "That getting ink is something everyone does now?"

Mother looked like she was about to cry.

Clipboard Lady released Dylan's wrist and stepped back off the blanket. "Boys, sleeves rolled up, but no tattoos showing. Grace Paxton-Bradley, future state senator, has good, clean-cut sons."

Tyler rolled his eyes at Dylan and patted his right upper arm. Tyler, of all people? Dylan, who hadn't thought he'd be able to force it, smiled freely for the remainder of the outdoor portion of the photo shoot.

On the way back into the house for the family dinner scene, Tyler asked to see Dylan's tattoo. He angled Dylan's arm so it caught the waning beams of the sunset.

"*Ex praeterito praesens prudenter agit ne futura action—deturpet.*" He read the words below the image. "Latin for: 'From the past, the present acts prudently, to not blacken future actions.'"

"Ironic that I'd have that permanently engraved on my body, huh?" Dylan rolled down his sleeve, lest he raise Mother's ire again. "You'll have to show me yours while you're here."

"It's a proud declaration of my nerdhood. You know those tribal or barbed-wire armbands that people get around their upper arm? Well, mine looks like that, but it's actually Schrödinger's equation for a single particle with potential energy." He held the door open for Dylan. "Everyone in my study group freshman year chose a different piece of the equation to get as an armband."

"And the tattoo artist was able to do it for you?"

Tyler grinned his goofy grin and pushed his glasses up. "It's a tattoo place just off the MIT campus. You should *see* some of the photos of their work that they have hanging on their walls."

Dinner was even more uncomfortable than the outdoor session. The publicist—Clipboard Lady—had them change into the colored polo shirts they'd been instructed to bring (Mother had Spencer trade shirts with Pax, since the short-sleeved blue polo didn't quite cover the bottom of Spencer's tattoo), and once again, they were instructed to talk and laugh and pretend like they were having a good time.

Dylan was about good-timed out. And as to dinner—by the time they were actually allowed to put a bite in their mouths for the video shoot, it was so cold as to be inedible. After that came working and laughing and talking in the kitchen while Mother washed the dishes.

All four of them watched this very closely, since it was something they'd never seen her do before.

"I think that's a wrap on the boys." The publicist consulted her clipboard. "Yes, thanks Grace's sons. That's all we need from you."

"Hallelujah," Pax murmured. "I'm starving."

Dylan nodded. His stomach had been rumbling—loudly—for the past hour. They grabbed their white shirts and jackets and fled before anyone could decide they were still needed for something more.

"Where are we going to eat?" Tyler asked as soon as the kitchen door closed behind them.

Dylan checked the time on his cell phone. "It's after seven thirty. What's close?"

"And fast," Tyler added. "I don't know if I can wait on a sit-down place. But I don't want fast food either."

Pax responded after they all climbed in and Dylan got the engine—and the heater—started. "What about Whitt's Barbecue? We can pick it up and take it back to Gramps and Perty's and watch movies or something."

"That's perfect. I haven't had Whitt's in ages." Spencer blocked Dylan's view of the parking courtyard through the rearview mirror as he struggled back into his sweatshirt.

"I think they close at eight, so we'll need to hurry. It's just out on Highway 70S—so take a left at the end of Harding Place, and it'll be almost immediately on the right." Pax zipped up his jacket before putting on his seat belt.

Dylan navigated back out to the road carefully. Even with the low fixtures lighting the edges of the driveways, the dark was almost absolute under the low, tight overhang of trees.

As the last customers of the night, they got their order from the drive-thru barbecue place quickly. Pax made Dylan wait until he'd checked to make sure they'd gotten everything, and Dylan had to knock on the pickup window to get the tub of spicy sauce. Getting home without that would have been a travesty.

"Drive fast, bro." Spencer leaned forward and drew in a deep breath through his nose. "I don't think I can stand smelling that but not eating it for too long."

Less than fifteen minutes later, he pulled up beside the side porch that led into Perty's kitchen.

The food came out of the white paper bags as soon as they got to the table. Pax retrieved paper plates from one of the overhead cabinets near the stove and four glasses from another. Dylan took the glasses and filled them with ice from the fancy, stainless-steel refrigerator.

With no need for talking, they began the process of building their sandwiches. Dylan soaked the tops of the three hamburger buns with the hot, vinegar-based sauce and the bottoms with the mild. Then he piled on the pulled pork, followed by coleslaw and more hot sauce. He set the tops of the buns on the sandwiches and squished them down with the palm of his hand.

Pouring himself a glass of Whitt's iced tea—so sweet, some said, it could be used for pancake syrup—he sat down, tucked a napkin into the collar of his blue polo shirt, and shoved as much of his first sandwich into his mouth as he could.

"I thought y'all were having dinner at your parents' house."

They all looked up at Perty, cheeks bulging. Dylan cleared his bite first. "We didn't get much to eat."

Spencer gulped down his bite, stood, and hugged their grandmother. "Hey, Perty. Sorry I didn't come in and say hi when we got here."

She kissed his cheek then pushed him back toward his chair. "I raised two boys of my own. I know you forget everything when you're hungry." She picked up a piece of meat that had fallen onto Spencer's plate and ate it. "And you know even I can never pass up Whitt's."

"Want a sandwich?" Tyler reached for the bag of buns, which still

141

had four left after they'd all fixed three sandwiches to start with.

"No, Gramps and I ate at church a little while ago." She went around the table and gave the rest of them a kiss on the cheek as well. "What do you boys have planned for the rest of the night?"

"We thought we might watch movies."

"Feel free to use the game room up on your floor. Even if it weren't two floors above our bedroom, we made sure to have everything soundproofed when we remodeled the house." She went into the kitchen, filled a large ceramic mug with water, and stuck it in the microwave.

Dylan finished his first sandwich and started on the second.

Gramps came in. Spencer choked down the huge bite he'd just taken and stood to greet their grandfather.

With their nightly mugs of hot tea, Gramps and Perty said good night and left them to their own devices.

After his third sandwich, Dylan leaned back and finished off his glass of tea. Tyler, now starting his fourth, pushed the bag containing the three remaining buns toward him.

"I think I'll save my extra sandwich for breakfast in the morning." He threw the several wadded napkins he'd used onto his plate.

"Sounds like a plan." Spencer laced his fingers over his abdomen. "So. . .movies? Oh—how about *A Christmas Story*? I haven't watched that one yet this year." He looked at Dylan and cuffed him on the shoulder. "Watching that together every year just hasn't been the same without you."

Dylan returned his brother's gesture. "Hey, thanks for getting my back with Mother earlier."

"No problem."

"Tyler's got one, too." Dylan turned to look directly across the table. "So, Pax, that just leaves you. Anything you want to tell us?"

"I thought about getting one once, but then my old car broke down and I had to buy a new one, so the money I would have spent on it went to the down payment." He put the lids back onto the tubs of sauce.

"What would you have gotten?"

"Actually, it would have been a lot like Tyler's—he's the one who got me started thinking about it. It would have been Newton's Third

Law in Latin designed into an armband: *Actioni contrariam semper et æqualem esse reactionem.* For every action—"

"There is an equal and opposite reaction," Dylan, Tyler, and Spencer finished the physics principle along with him.

Following his brothers up to the third floor where three guest bedrooms surrounded a bonus room housing several cushy chairs and sofas and a big-screen TV, Dylan thought about that Newtonian principle—and the Latin permanently etched in his own skin.

Every action created a consequence. But the wise man learned from the past and acted prudently in the present so he wouldn't ruin his future.

And it seemed as if Someone had gone to great lengths to make sure Dylan had a chance to do just that.

Over the next few days, as Dylan spent time getting to know his brothers again—mostly over cutthroat video game competitions—the idea of actions creating consequences, of learning from the past to keep from blackening his future, made him run through every major decision, every choice, every turn he'd ever made. As he reviewed each one, he made a mental list of the consequences—and the lessons he should learn from them.

On Christmas Day, watching his parents sit back like beneficent royalty as their sons opened gifts of expensive wallets, sweaters, and ties, along with gift cards to a major electronics store, Dylan resigned himself to his position as the black sheep of the family.

When Mother determined it was time for the boys to exchange their gifts to each other, Dylan exchanged glances with his brothers. They all ended up looking at Spencer—who was, after all, Mother's favorite.

"We decided this year that we're all going to treat each other to dinner at the Stock-Yard Steakhouse instead of buying physical gifts. We don't get to spend a lot of time together, and we all rarely get to eat out at a fancy restaurant like that." Spencer's no-nonsense tone invited no questions.

She rolled her eyes but did not argue.

Spencer took that as the sign to pull out their joint gifts for their parents. If Mother didn't like the designer purse, she was a

143

better actress than Dylan had ever imagined. And Dad got pretty excited over the digital golf scorekeeper, personalized golf balls, and monogrammed medallions that would attach to the end of his golf clubs so everyone would know whose they were. At least that's what Spencer had told them when he ordered them.

The rest of the day, spent at Gramps and Perty's house, was much merrier, especially with the addition of their father's older, bachelor brother, Donald, who raised pashmina and cashmere goats on a farm near Bell Buckle, Tennessee. Like Dylan, Donny didn't meet with the approval of Davis and Grace Paxton-Bradley, but he'd always been a favorite at family gatherings for the boys.

Though their parents flew up to Cleveland for the obligatory four-day visit to Mother's parents the day after Christmas, Dylan and his brothers chose to save money and drive. And eighteen hours in the car with his brothers more than made up for the time they had to spend with Grandma and Grandpa Paxton and the rest of the Paxton family—who made Mother look humble and self-effacing in comparison. Every time he started to get upset over the way his grandparents, aunts and uncles, and cousins ignored or patronized him, Dylan rubbed his hand over the inside of his elbow.

From the past, the present acts prudently, to not blacken future actions.

Until now, he'd always avoided making New Year's resolutions, but as he and his brothers drove back to Nashville the day before New Year's Eve, he vowed to himself that this next year would be the one in which he learned from the mistakes of the past so he could start building a better future.

Chapter 14

❧

"So, here's where I'm not sure the story is actually working for me anymore."

Sassy paused and looked up from the box of kitchen items she was packing. "What do you mean? It sounds like a wonderful story."

Caylor shrugged and reached for the stack of glass serving platters on a top shelf. "Well, after I got into it, I started realizing that Giovanni—the artist—may not be who I thought he was in the beginning."

"Who's he turning out to be?" Susan asked her daughter, stepping off the stepstool with an armful of plastic food-storage containers.

Sassy hoped she knew who the artist was—at least in real life, anyway—but she said nothing.

"I don't know. I feel like there's an identity, a part of himself, he's keeping hidden. A secret past—something he's done, something he's created or painted in the past—that would totally change the way Isabella sees him if she ever found out. So he has to keep her from finding out. But somehow, she realizes what's going on, realizes that whatever this thing is that he did in his past could put any hope of finding happiness together at risk—because if she reveals to him she knows his secret, she'll be revealing a secret of her own. . . ." Caylor's voice drifted off, and her eyes took on that spaced-out look she got whenever one of her story ideas took over.

"But that sounds like just what you need to happen in a perfect romance. Lots of conflict. Leave us worried about if they'll ever be able to work things out so that they can live happily ever after." Sassy finished taping the box then wrote BAKING PANS AND CASSEROLES on the top and side with a black marker.

"What's that?" Caylor turned around, and her eyes slowly refocused. "Oh, right. But I'm just not sure that Isabella will be able to understand or overcome whatever it is that Giovanni did in his past—nor he hers."

Sassy handed Caylor the tape gun then patted her cheek. "You'll figure out a way to give them a happy ending. You always do."

But the worried expression didn't leave her face. Sassy knew better than to push Caylor when she was in the development stage of a story idea—or when she was in the final throes of writing it later on down the line. Caylor simply needed time to think through and work out the details. A few days from now, Sassy was certain, Caylor would be euphoric over having figured out how to get her characters together at the end of the book.

Sage bounced into the room, long red hair swinging from a high ponytail. "What are y'all still doing in here packing? I thought you said we were supposed to be leaving for the Bradleys' open house at two."

Sassy looked for the clock—which was no longer hanging on the wall but packed in a box. "What time is it?"

"It's twenty of." Sage, famous for always being the last one ready to go anywhere, planted her fists on her hips. "And here I thought you'd be waiting for me to be ready to go."

"I think, actually, you slipped out to change clothes to get out of helping to pack up the kitchen." Caylor smirked at her younger sister.

"Yeah, well, that, too."

Sassy stretched her aching back. "Don't worry. There will be plenty left to do when we get home."

Sage followed Caylor upstairs when she left to change clothes for the Bradleys' New Year's Day open house. Sage had been doing that quite a bit—going up to Caylor's loft—and Sassy was glad to see her granddaughters getting along and spending time together after several years of virtual estrangement.

The only thing that would have made Christmas perfect would have been if Sassy's younger child, Samantha, and her husband and children had been able to come. But they could not leave Peter's elderly, infirm parents, with whom they lived.

That reminded her, she needed to get on the computer tonight, confirm her reservation, and check in for her flight to Maine tomorrow. She used a scrap piece of packing paper and the black marker to write herself a note, which she carried into her bedroom with her so she wouldn't forget. She pulled out a favorite pink sweater set and gray slacks and changed into them. Perty wouldn't mind if Sassy showed up in blue jeans, like most others did, but Sassy wouldn't disrespect her best friend in that way.

She dressed and went into her bathroom to put on some lipstick and fluff her hair.

"Sassy, can I talk to you for a minute?" Sage hovered in the doorway to Sassy's room.

Sassy stepped out of the bathroom and motioned Sage to enter the bedroom and have a seat in the desk chair. Sassy sat on the cedar chest so she could put her stockings and shoes on.

"Has Caylor told you?" Sage twisted a strand of her long, straight red hair around her finger.

"If you've shared anything with your sister, she hasn't broken your confidence." Sassy pulled the thin trouser socks up to her knees then slipped on the black loafers.

"I didn't tell her she couldn't." Sage sighed. "I need to stay here for a while, Sassy."

She crossed her legs and clasped her hands around her knee. "All right."

"I mean for *a while*. I can't go back to Oregon. I. . .well, I lost everything. My car was repossessed, and I was evicted from my apartment. All I have with me is what I was able to get out of the apartment before they threw everything out on the street and the scavengers took it all."

Sassy didn't want to know what kind of neighborhood her offspring had been living in that all of her furniture and belongings would disappear like that. "You've told Caylor this already?"

"Yes ma'am. She said it was okay with her if I stayed here indefinitely, but that I needed to clear it with you."

Indefinitely. The way Sage treated everything in her life. "There will be stipulations if you stay."

"Stipulations?" Sage caught her bottom lip between her teeth. "Like rules?"

"Like rules. First and foremost is that if you're going to stay here, you'll get a job. Full-time or part-time—in this economy, I'm not picky. Then, once you have a job, you'll help pay utilities, as much as you can afford each month. Your sister pays them all now, so it's only fair you chip in toward the extra cost having another person in the house will generate."

Sage's chin trembled as if she were about to burst into tears. "Okay."

"You will commit to me that once you find a job, you'll stay in it for at least six months."

"I've never"—Sage cleared her throat—"I've never held a job that long, but okay. I can commit to that."

"And finally, I want you to go back to college and start working toward your degree. I'd like you taking at least one class every semester. Talk to Caylor, talk to some of her friends at Robertson about the different majors there." An idea struck, remembering the way Sage had flirted with a certain young man the day she arrived in Nashville. "Talk to Paxton Bradley about programs at Vanderbilt, too. Until you can afford to pay for it yourself, whether through saving money now while you're living here or by student loans, grants, or scholarships, I will pay for you to take one class each semester at Robertson or however many classes that same amount of money would cover at one of the state universities or community colleges."

The hazel eyes that had been dull and listless for the past two weeks finally sparked to life. "Really? Sassy that would be—I promise you, I won't disappoint you."

"I know." At least she hoped so. Sassy stood and went to her dresser where she pulled a key ring out of the top drawer. She kissed the silver locket that dangled from it—the locket holding pictures of herself and Frank from their wedding—and handed it to Sage. "You're going to need to get around, so you can use the Falcon."

Sage's eyes widened as she accepted the keys. "I'll take such good care of it, Sassy."

"Please do. That was the first car your grandfather and I ever bought brand new, back in 1963. Right up until the end, one of his favorite things to do was to put the top down and drive around out in the country on a Sunday afternoon, even after we had newer, more comfortable cars." A lump grew in Sassy's throat. The day when Frank had been too weak, too tired to take her for their Sunday afternoon drive had been when she'd known he wouldn't be with her much longer. Caylor had come over and taken them for their drive, Frank sitting in the backseat with Sassy, holding her hand, reminiscing over times long past.

Though Sassy hadn't found out until later from Caylor, that was the night Frank had asked Caylor to move in and take care of her after he was gone. He'd slipped away in his sleep three days later. She didn't know how she would have survived that first year if it hadn't been for Caylor. Now she was afraid her granddaughter had given up on ever having a life of her own.

Not if she had anything to say about it!

"You girls ready?" Dean stuck his head in the room.

"We're ready." Sassy put her arm around Sage's waist and walked with her out to the driveway.

Sassy let her son assist her up into the front seat of the giant SUV he'd rented for the month he and Susan would be in the States. Sage slid into the center of the middle seat, flanked by her mother and sister.

The weather had turned warmer since Christmas, but Sassy still appreciated the heated seat, which Dean turned on for her. She pulled down the sun visor, ostensibly to check her lipstick in the mirror, but she looked at her two granddaughters' reflections.

Unless she was completely mistaken, she and Perty might just be about to one-up Lindy and Trina by each having *two* of their grandchildren fall in love and get married.

∞

Perty tried to focus herself on the guests who were arriving, not the ones who hadn't shown up yet. It wasn't like Sassy to be late. In fact, Perty had hoped her best friend would show up early so she could share her excitement.

The Breitingers arrived—Trina glowing like a lighthouse, telling anyone who might care that her granddaughter would be getting married Memorial Day weekend. Though when Trina and Lindy had taken them aside at the Christmas Eve service last week and announced this news, a flash of jealousy had hit before Perty could stop it, with what she knew now, she was able to smile and feel genuinely happy for her friends.

Lindy and Greely Patterson came in next, Lindy joining Trina in spreading their joy, Greeley joining the rest of the men in the second-floor family room to watch football.

Well, almost all the men. Perty wandered into the formal sitting room to the right of the entry hall. Dylan sat in front of the bay window, his easel in front of him, sketching whoever would sit for him. Perty had started him doing this when he was only twelve or thirteen years old—after she'd noticed him sitting in a quiet corner sketching their guests surreptitiously. For several years, it had been one of the highlights of the Bradleys' open house—that the guests got a souvenir to take home. She was so pleased Dylan had suggested reviving the practice. Especially since it had allowed her to see—

The front door opened again, and the Evanses came in. Gerald appeared to greet them, and Perty tried to tell Sassy with just her eyes that she had something important to tell her. But first she wanted to witness. . .

Dylan finished his current sketch and handed it to the pastor's wife. He stood to greet the Evanses—and Perty caught her bottom lip between her teeth. The stiff greeting between Dylan and Caylor seemed only to prove Perty's speculation correct.

Grace came over to glad-hand everyone, though she'd promised she wouldn't be campaigning today, and Perty slipped her arm through Sassy's and led her down the hall, through the kitchen, and to the mudroom, where they could have some privacy.

"What is it?" Sassy pushed up the sleeves of her pink cardigan.

Perty reached into her pocket and pulled out a folded piece of white paper. "I found this on the floor in the garage workroom that Dylan's using for a studio."

Sassy unfolded the page. Perty moved so she, too, could see the delicate pencil drawing of Caylor's face in profile. Sassy's blue eyes danced when she looked up from the sketch. "I knew it!"

"Knew what?"

Sassy shared the idea of the new novel Caylor was working on. "Don't you see—the hero, the artist, it's Dylan. Caylor is falling in love with him; that's why she's writing a romance novel about an artist."

"And he's drawing pictures of her." Perty caught the tip of her tongue between her teeth. "You know what this means, don't you?"

"That they're attracted to each other. They are both creative types after all, and so they may not even see what their subconscious minds are telling them." Sassy looked at the drawing one more time then refolded it and handed it back to Perty. "Of course, if your Dylan is anything like my Caylor, they may never do anything about it."

"Then it's up to us to make sure they do."

"How?"

"Well. . ." Perty thought for a moment. "Oh—Dylan has agreed to teach an art class at church for the senior group on Tuesday afternoons starting in a couple of weeks. Make sure that Caylor doesn't just drop you off—make sure she stays. And, well, I'm sure more opportunities like that, for us to get our families together, will arise over the next few months."

"And then there's Sage and Pax to think about, as well."

"Sage and Pax?" With as much as Perty loved Sassy and her family, she wasn't certain she liked the idea of Pax—or any of her grandsons—falling for Sassy's flighty, irresponsible granddaughter. He'd probably end up with his heart broken when Sage lost interest and moved on, as she always did.

"Yes. Didn't you see them flirting that afternoon when I was over here baking? Instant chemistry." Sassy seemed quite pleased with herself.

"Won't she be heading back to Oregon soon?"

"No—she's staying here for the foreseeable future. She's going to get a job and go back to school."

Well, if Sage was actually growing up, maturing, maybe it wouldn't be such a bad match. "Pax will receive his doctorate in May, so there's no hurry on that front. Let Sage get settled in before we start doing any matchmaking there. For now, let's concentrate on Dylan and Caylor." She held out the pinky finger of her right hand.

Sassy grinned and hooked her pinky finger around Perty's. "Caylor and Dylan. I'm thinking a Christmas wedding."

"That sounds like a great New Year's resolution to me." And then maybe a year from today they'd be speculating on how soon they could expect their first great-grandchild.

Chapter 15

❧

"Sage, can I see you upstairs for a minute?" Caylor paused on the bottom step leading up to her loft. Though she had expected the Bradleys' New Year's Day open house to be uncomfortable—being the first time she would see Dylan since recognizing the dog in the painting—it had been worse than she possibly could have imagined.

Blissfully unaware that she had created any problems, Sage followed her up the stairs. Caylor waited until Sage gained the landing at the top before turning to confront her.

"How could you do that to Pax Bradley?" Even though she knew it was the melodramatic thing to do, Caylor planted her fists on her hips.

Sage's mouth dropped open, and confusion flooded her eyes. "What are you talking about? I didn't do anything to Pax—I hardly even talked to him."

"That's exactly what I'm talking about. You spent hours two weeks ago flirting with Pax, giving him reason to believe that you like him—and then today, you hardly give him the time of day because his better-looking younger brother happens to be there."

The confusion left Sage's expression, replaced by dreamy remembrance. "Spencer is good-looking, isn't he?"

Caylor wanted to scream. How could Sage do this again? Was she truly so self-absorbed that she couldn't see how damaging her narcissistic flirting could be?

"It's not like I'm ever going to see Spencer again. He's going back

153

to Chicago this week. Anyway, I don't see how it's your business who I flirt with." She picked at her fingernails as if to indicate she was totally over this conversation. "Sounds to me like you're still mad because you think it's my fault Bryan broke up with you." Sage dropped her hands to her sides. "It was ten years ago, Caylor. Get over it." With those hurtful parting words, Sage flounced down the stairs.

Caylor sank into her desk chair, stunned. How could Sage not realize it had been her fault? Bryan *told* Sage he broke up with Caylor for her. And had Sage apologized or even tried to make things right? Had she tried explaining to Bryan that she was a compulsive flirt and didn't feel anything for him? No, of course not. In the middle of the night, she had thrown all of her stuff into her car and taken off without even leaving a note for Mama and Daddy. Leaving behind Caylor, as always, to clean up her mess.

She once again sent up a quick prayer of gratitude to God for putting Zarah and Flannery in her life. In fact. . .

Twenty minutes later, Caylor sent the e-mail in which she vented all of her frustrations about her sister to her two best friends. She changed back into her old jeans and ratty T-shirt and went back downstairs to burn off the rest of her frustration by helping Sassy and Mama finish packing up the kitchen.

Next morning, Caylor got up early to have breakfast with Sassy and Mama and Daddy. Sage, who was sleeping in the den, made a disgruntled appearance when their hushed conversation woke her up. Sassy toasted some waffles for her, which she was still eating when Caylor left to drive Sassy to the airport and Mama and Daddy left to drive to Atlanta, where Mama would be speaking at a conference later in the week. From the airport, Caylor drove straight to campus.

Silence rang through the corridors of Davidson Hall—just what Caylor wanted. She pulled her laptop out of her bag and set it up on her desk then started writing.

When she finally came up for air, it was fully dark outside—though a check of the clock showed her it was only 4:45 p.m. But she had gotten the first two chapters of Giovanni and Isabella's story written. Now all she had to do was write one more chapter and get the synopsis finished—figure out what the artist's secret was and how they would overcome it—then come up with some general ideas for at least two more similar books, and she'd send the proposal off to her agent.

At home Sage sprawled sleeping on the sofa with the TV blaring. She woke up as soon as Caylor turned it off.

"Hey, I was watching that." Sage rubbed her eyes.

Caylor set the remote down on the end table. "Really? Tell me what was on."

"Um. . .*House Hunters*?"

"Nice try, but you weren't even on the right channel for that." Caylor dropped into the plush leather recliner. "The moving truck will be here between eight and nine tomorrow morning. And the crew is supposed to be here around nine to start getting all the furniture moved out so they can start tearing down walls and whatever. We need to move the microwave and toaster oven out into the laundry room so we at least have those while the kitchen is torn up and unusable."

"What about the refrigerator?"

"We need to empty it tomorrow morning, and they'll move it out into the laundry room for us." Of course, once they started building the new breakfast room in front of the laundry room, it wouldn't matter if the fridge, toaster oven, and microwave were out there. They might not be able to access it anyway. "Once the cafeteria opens up next week, I'll get you a meal card and you can come up to school to eat, since we won't be able to eat here."

"So am I going to have to be here all day every day when the contractors are working?" Sage asked.

"No, they have a key to let themselves in and out. So except for tomorrow when everything is getting moved out, it would probably be better if you weren't here, because they're going to be tearing up the entire living portion of the house." The idea of people being in the house with no one here to watch over them bugged Caylor. But Riley Douglas had assured her when he came out last week to get the extra key that all of his subcontractors were bonded and had never posed a problem.

"What am I supposed to do?"

"The public library has computers where you can use the Internet for free. You could start looking for a job." Caylor had fully concurred with Sassy's list of stipulations that Sage had to abide by when living with them.

Sage rolled her eyes, but she didn't argue.

On Tuesday morning Caylor had to go in and physically shake Sage awake to get her up to help clean everything out of the refrigerator so Riley's guys could move it out into the laundry room. Sage took one step out of her room dressed in sweats with her long hair pulled back in a ponytail and no makeup, caught sight of the kitchen contractor, and went right back into her room and slammed the door. Fifteen minutes later, she came back out dressed in jeans and a bright green sweater with a little bit of makeup on—quite different from the person who claimed she did not care what other people thought of her appearance. She turned on all the charm for the contractor—who thought it was *fantastic* that she had been living on the West Coast for the last few years but had decided to come home to help take care of her aging grandmother.

Caylor jammed a bag of frozen green peas down into the cooler. More like Sage came home for Sassy to take care of her.

She stood and pushed the lid of the cooler hard to shut it. Unfortunately, it didn't make much noise. "Riley, the fridge and freezer are empty, so it's ready to go out to the laundry room."

"Fantastic. I'll get the guys on that right now." He turned back to Sage and extended his right hand. "It was fantastic to meet you, Sadie."

Caylor's suppressed laughed came out as a snort, which she tried to hide with a cough. From the indignant look on her sister's face, she knew she'd failed.

By ten o'clock, when Caylor left to go out to campus to work in peace and quiet, the general contractor and his crew had arrived and were already tearing the drywall off the walls to examine the underlying structure and wiring.

It was after six when she got home, and upon seeing the light on in the laundry room, she stepped in to turn it off before entering the house. Instead, she found Sage standing in front of the dryer on top of which was the toaster oven.

Sage turned and looked over her shoulder. "Hey, sis. I made supper. Honey-cheese toast." She picked up the plastic honey bear and drizzled what looked like half the bottle over the two pieces of toast with American cheese melted on top. "And I made dessert, or salad, or whatever you want to call it." She pointed to the two small paper bowls sitting on top of the washing machine. Each held half of a canned pear, the hole in the center filled with a glop of mayonnaise and topped with grated cheddar cheese.

Caylor laughed. "A true gourmand."

"Don't knock it." Sage licked a drip of honey off the heel of her hand. "This was the meal I always made whenever I got homesick. And honey-cheese toast, ramen noodles, and dollar frozen pizzas are how I survived sometimes when money was really tight. Oh, and big five-pound bags of white potatoes." She handed Caylor one of the plates of honey-cheese toast, and Caylor picked up one of the small bowls.

They crossed the porch to the kitchen door, and when Caylor stepped into the house, she nearly choked. The walls were gone—replaced by framed, temporary walls until they installed the new support beams.

Caylor led the way upstairs, where they sat at the kitchen table—now shoved up against the stair banister and wall in her office, leaving two sides open for them to sit at to eat.

"That contractor—Riley—he didn't stick around for very long after you left this morning." Sage cut her two pieces of honey-cheese toast into small squares before beginning to eat.

"No, he won't be here all the time—he has other jobs he has to oversee as well, so he'll be in and out throughout the whole project." Caylor closed her eyes and took a moment to enjoy the rough texture of the toast juxtaposed to the creamy cheese and viscous honey, the contrast of the salty and the sweet on her tongue. It had been too long since she'd indulged in this childhood favorite—one of the dinners Mama would make at least a couple of times a week when her work in the oncology department at Vanderbilt-Ingram Cancer Center left her too exhausted, mentally or physically, to cook. As soon as Caylor was old enough to understand this, she'd asked Sassy to teach her how to cook so she could help out.

"He asked about you." Sage took a loud gulp from her cup of milk.

"Who?" Caylor dragged her mind back from the past.

"Riley Douglas. Asked if you have a boyfriend." She swirled a bite around in the puddle of honey that had formed in the center of her plate.

"Oh?" Caylor tried to get excited, to feel some sort of thrill at the idea of a romance-cover-worthy guy acting interested in her. "What did you tell him?"

"That I didn't think so. I offered to give him your phone number, but he said he already had it. Did he call you?"

"Just about the fact the house needs two I beams instead of one." Hmm. If he'd been interested enough to ask Sage about her but hadn't said anything personal to Caylor on the phone, was he genuinely interested, or had he used it as a tactic to throw Sage off her incessant flirting? Caylor finished off her honey-cheese toast and started on her pear. Another childhood favorite too long neglected.

Sage muttered something under her breath.

"What's that?"

"Nothing." With a slurp, Sage finished off the last bite of pear. "So are you going to be leaving me alone here all day every day?"

"I have to work, Sage—get my syllabi written, get lessons planned, homework and reading assignments written up. I can't do that here with the construction noise." Or Sage's constant complaining about how she was bored, as she'd been doing the last two weeks—and that had been with Sassy, Mama, and Daddy here.

"Can I come up to school with you, then?"

Caylor turned to toss the paper plate and bowl into the kitchen trash can, which she'd also brought up here for the duration. She stood and pushed her chair in. "No, I don't think that would be a very good idea. I really need uninterrupted quiet in which to work." And to get that proposal finished. "As I said, go to the library—the closest one's in Green Hills, not far from campus—and use their computers to start looking for a job."

Sage propped her cheek on her fist and leaned over the table, her expression petulant. "Sassy told me that you could probably get me a job at Robertson."

Caylor knew Sassy well enough to know she absolutely had *not* said that to Sage but probably suggested she ask Caylor if there were any job openings at Robertson for which she was qualified. Which would be—what? "Log on to the school's website when you go to the library. There's a link at the bottom of the page for job openings."

Before Sage could work herself up into a full pout, Caylor's phone rang. Flannery. Thank goodness. "I've got to take this call, Sage." She motioned with her head toward the stairs.

Leaving her plate, bowl, and cup on the table, Sage stomped down the stairs.

"Hey, Flan." Below her bedroom, the door to the guest room slammed.

"How'd it go with the contractors this morning?"

Caylor gave Flannery a blow-by-blow account of her day. She picked up Sage's trash—taking the cup into the bathroom to dump the remaining milk down the sink—then went into her bedroom and sank into the embrace of her overstuffed chair-and-a-half. She actually started feeling relaxed by the time she got to Sage's little tantrum.

"I wish we had some openings here she was somewhat qualified for. But they're talking about not refilling the two customer service positions that came open at the end of the year." Flannery sighed. "For someone with her limited qualifications, she's going to have a tough time finding anything."

"Sassy's going to pay for her to go back to college—one class per semester at Robertson or however many hours that would cover at another school—but told her she has to get at least a part-time job for as long as she lives here."

"How long do you think that'll be?"

Caylor yawned, curled up, and snuggled farther down into the chair, resting her head on the high, plush arm. "I have no idea. But she'll stay however long Sassy lets her or until she decides to run away again."

"This could be the time that God works on her to change her, to help her grow up."

Caylor rolled her eyes heavenward. "Yeah, He's been beating me over the head with that thought. It's just hard to imagine even He could get through to her."

"Speaking as a younger child with two older siblings whose lives are hard to live up to—give her a chance. For me?"

Caylor hated it when Flannery pulled out the baby-of-the-family card. Especially when she did it in that high-pitched, innocent voice. "Oh, all right. I'll give her a chance."

❦

Dylan stopped in the aisle and turned to take in the panorama of the auditorium. He vaguely remembered coming to see plays and musicals here back before Perty retired. But with the exception of the rows and rows of ornate wooden pews, the venue bore little resemblance to the churchlike setting he'd come to. Though not nearly as state-of-the-art as a professional performing arts center, Rutherford Auditorium did the small, liberal-arts college proud.

He pulled his sketchbook out of his bag and tucked a pencil behind his ear, ready to get started helping the students work on designing backdrops.

"Dylan, so glad you could make it out today." Bridget came down to the edge of the stage. "Come on up, and I'll give you the grand tour."

He skirted the orchestra pit and mounted the stairs on the side of the broad stage. Bridget held out her hands and turned in a slow circle. "What do you think? Everything's state of the art—or as state of the art as we could get in an old building like this."

"It's great."

She motioned him to follow her to the back of the stage area. "We are a full-fly theater"—she looked down from the area that opened up what seemed hundreds of feet above them and must have seen his confusion—"that means that we can raise the backdrops up fully so that they can't be seen from anywhere in the auditorium. We also use scenery wagons, lifts, and stagehands to move smaller pieces in and out."

He followed her backstage, through the bowels of the theater, and finally out into a long corridor. She entered the third door on the left. He stepped into a large workshop where at least a dozen people were working.

"As you can see, we've been working on our set pieces and backdrops for a while. We do four major productions each year, along with the interdepartment Christmas show and a revue at the end of the spring semester, so that all of the undergraduate and MFA students can get the experience they need. You'll be working mainly with the MFA students—and the graduate student who's the scenic designer for this production—on the flying backdrops."

Looking around at the smaller set pieces that were in various phases of completion, images started forming in Dylan's head—images inspired by the masterworks of the Venetian period and his own work inspired by those artists.

"I can see from the look in your eyes that you're already coming up with ideas." Bridget grinned at him. "Come on back and meet the team."

Within half an hour, Dylan realized he would most definitely be in the learner role, not the instructor role, in this project. First, there was the vastness of the scale—what Dylan could imagine on a smaller scale wouldn't necessarily translate to what people sitting at the back of the balcony would be able to see.

"Let's go out front," Malique, the scenic designer, said, grabbing his sketchpad. "I find I can sometimes visualize these things better looking at it from the audience's perspective—and sometimes hearing the actors reading the lines helps, too, even if it is the same passages over and over and over again in auditions."

The two graduate students serving as Malique's assistants came with them. He took Dylan down a series of hallways and into the auditorium through one of the main entrances instead of back through the labyrinth behind the stage.

Before they could enter, though, a student rushed in from outside. "I'm so sorry I'm late. My relief didn't show up on time for her shift, so I was late leaving the restaurant."

Malique stopped to give the student directions on her project. Dylan stepped into the auditorium—but turned when someone tugged on his sleeve.

He turned. "Sage? Hey. What are you doing here?"

She smiled and lowered her chin in a flirtatious gesture. "Just came up to see my sister. What are you doing here?"

Dylan stiffened. He'd seen her in action with both Pax and Spencer. He wasn't about to let her do the same to him. "I'm going to try to help with the scenery design."

"Sage—what are you doing here?"

Dylan relaxed a bit at the sound of Caylor's voice. He tried to step back, but Sage kept hold of his sleeve.

"I tried to come up for lunch, but they told me I couldn't get anything to eat." Sage's lips puckered into a pout.

Zarah looked at her watch. "It's almost two thirty. They stop serving lunch at two o'clock. What time did you get there?"

"Just now. So, since they're closed, I came to find you to get some money so I can go get lunch." Sage's pout turned to girlish innocence when she looked at Dylan again. Like Caylor, she was only a few inches shorter than he, which made the little-girl act even more bizarre and uncomfortable. "Our house is being remodeled, so we have no kitchen."

Caylor looked like she was about ready to give physical egress to the frustration building behind her turquoise eyes. "No, but there is a toaster oven and a microwave and plenty of stuff in the fridge and freezer that can you can eat."

Sage heaved a dramatic sigh. "Do you know how bad all that processed, chemical-laden food is for you? And it's full of sodium and fat." She looked her sister up and down with a smirk.

Dylan prayed the floor would come alive and eat him. He wouldn't have blamed Caylor if she'd slapped her sister. If one of his brothers had insulted him like that in front of someone—But his brothers would never do that.

Caylor, amazingly, kept her cool. She gave her sister a benign shrug. "If you don't have money to go buy your own food or go out to eat, I guess you'll either have to risk the stuff that's already there, or you'll just have to go hungry."

"But I've been looking for jobs all morning, Caylor. I can't find anything I'm qualified for."

Bridget called Caylor's name from the front of the auditorium.

"I've got to go. Sage, just go home, get something to eat there, and remember tomorrow to get here before two o'clock so you can get lunch on the lunch card I gave you."

With an apologetic glance at Dylan, Caylor escaped to the front of the auditorium.

Sage adopted her flirty expression again. "You don't happen to know of any positions open here at the school you could recommend me for, do you?"

"I'm not. . . I'm new here, and I'll only be teaching part-time. What are your qualifications?"

She shrugged. "I have about a year of college. I did some clerical work and some modeling."

Modeling? Dylan still hadn't figured out how he'd find a live model for his portraiture studio. "I may actually have a job to offer you. It would only be six hours a week at minimum wage—well, only three hours for the first two weeks—but it would be better than nothing."

Something akin to real interest flickered in Sage's hazel eyes. "Really? What is it?"

He explained the need for a live model to sit for his class. "So really, there are no qualifications necessary except just sitting there. But it would only be for eight weeks, starting day after tomorrow."

"Dylan, that would be wonderful—it will get Caylor off my back and give me time to figure out what I'm going to do for a real job." She threw her arms around him and kissed his cheek then skipped toward the door.

Malique and his assistants had to step out of the way as she twirled on her way through the double doors. All three of them turned to watch her walk away.

Dylan turned the opposite direction—and caught Caylor looking away from him, the corners of her mouth and eyes tight.

Great. The job might get Caylor off Sage's back, but the weight of Caylor's ire fell heavily on Dylan.

Chapter 16

After a morning filled with advising late-registering students and an English department lunch meeting that lasted all afternoon, Caylor entered the construction zone at home, wanting nothing more than to go up to her loft and curl up in her chair for an hour and veg out. She still had a lot of work to do on finalizing her first few lectures for the composition class dumped in her lap today because the adjunct who'd taught the freshman course the last ten years suddenly moved out of state, but that could wait until after she'd let her brain rest for an hour.

The crew seemed to have made good progress with the breakfast room addition. The new little room that connected the kitchen to the laundry room looked finished outside, with white siding and trim to match the rest of the house. Inside, a couple of guys troweled mud over the seams of the drywall they'd installed. It would be so nice to be able to go to and from the laundry room and stay nice and warm—or cool during the summer—instead of having to exit the house to get there.

Sassy, who had returned from Maine that morning, stood with the site foreman in the kitchen, which was stripped down to the shells of the cabinets with all of the appliances now gone.

"Oh good, Caylor." Sassy motioned her over. "Jerry was telling me that they plan to install the island and refinish the cabinets tomorrow. Then on Thursday, they're going to start on the floors, so that's the night we won't be able to stay at home."

"Okay. I'll call Zarah and let her know. You and Sage are still staying with the Bradleys?" Caylor shifted the load of books and paperwork from one arm to the other.

"Yes. I talked to Perty this afternoon. She'd love for you to come stay also. They've got six extra bedrooms, you know."

"I know. But Zarah and Flannery and I have talked about ordering in Chinese food and working on wedding stuff whatever night I get kicked out of the house. It may be the only chance we have before spring break." Caylor covered a yawn with the back of her hand. "I'm going to go upstairs and get some work done." After resting for a while.

"You can't—I have a new class starting at church at five thirty. Sage is out with some high school friends, so I'll need you to take me."

Though working in the comfort of her big chair upstairs would be preferable, she'd save time by staying at the church and working there instead of driving up to the church twice. "Okay. Let me change clothes, and I'll be ready to go."

Upstairs, Caylor set her books and laptop case on the desk and resisted the urge to drop into the desk chair and groan out her frustration.

Instead, she stepped into the walk-in closet and changed from her trousers, jacket, and blouse into jeans and a comfy, slightly oversized turtleneck sweater—which, naturally, snagged on her watch, creating a pull across the front.

She yanked the sweater off and tossed it in the to-be-mended pile, grabbed a long-sleeved brown T-shirt off a shelf, and topped that with an old, oatmeal-colored, duster-style bulky cardigan—the sweater she usually wore around the house during the winter when she knew she wouldn't be seeing anyone but Sassy.

She needed chocolate. She needed the Box. But where. . . ? Caylor closed her eyes and tried to remember where they'd put the bin filled with candy.

Grabbing her laptop bag and digging the composition textbook and grammar handbook out of the pile on her desk, she went back downstairs, through the now empty kitchen and breakfast room, and into the laundry room.

There, in the cabinet in the corner beyond the utility sink—almost out of reach due to the position of the washer—was the Box. She'd been careful to ration the twelve chocolate-covered peanut butter Christmas trees, and tonight was the night for the last one. She set the box atop the washer and popped the lid off.

It seemed emptier than last time she'd been into it. She shifted it from side to side to move the mostly red- and green- and gold-wrapped candy around, but she didn't see the last Christmas tree.

Her frustration increased. Someone—and she had a pretty good idea who—had been in the Box and had taken her last Christmas tree. She picked out five miniature peanut butter cups, snapped the lid on, and stuck the container back in the cabinet.

Sassy came out of the kitchen door carrying a plastic bin filled with what looked like school supplies. Caylor dropped the candy into the outside pocket of her bag and joined Sassy at the new door to the porch.

"What's in there?" Caylor went out first and held the door open for Sassy.

"Supplies for class."

Caylor used her remote to unlock the SUV then returned to the kitchen to turn off the lights—a couple of naked bulbs hanging from the wiring pulled down after the old fixtures were removed.

Sassy chattered about her flight back from Maine and how she'd been excited to come home and see how much work had been accomplished on the remodel. Caylor listened with half an ear as her mind whirled with everything she needed to get done tonight to be prepared to face a classroom full of freshmen at eight o'clock tomorrow morning in a class most of them didn't want to take.

Several cars already sat in the parking lot behind Acklen Avenue Fellowship. Caylor looked up at the three-story redbrick exterior with a sigh. She'd visited this church off and on over the years, but even with Flannery and Zarah urging her to come with them all those years they'd lived together, she'd never felt called to leave the church she grew up in. Sure, it was small, but she couldn't imagine being just another face in the crowd of the thousand people who squeezed into Acklen Ave.'s three different worship services. She much preferred knowing—and being known by—almost everyone at her church of fewer than two hundred.

She followed Sassy across the courtyard to the back door, carefully watching her grandmother cross the slick, wet concrete. But she needn't have worried. Sassy, her supply box wrapped securely in her arms, marched right to the door and managed to get it open before Caylor could get it for her.

Sassy went directly to one of the large rooms behind the sanctuary—larger, in fact, than any of the classrooms at Robertson except for the theater-style lecture halls.

Caylor stopped just inside the door and stared. Before she'd made the decision to come and work here, she should have asked Sassy what kind of class this was. At the front of the room stood two rows of low wooden easels, each with a canvas on it. Three plastic banquet tables covered with newspaper divided the easels into groups of four. And padded metal folding chairs sat poised at each easel, ready for a student.

Sassy went to an easel in the front row, across one of the tables from where Perty was setting out tubes of paint and paintbrushes. Sassy started doing the same.

Caylor dropped her computer bag onto one of the chairs in the rows that faced the lectern to her right on this end of the large room.

Then she saw him. Dressed in a dark T-shirt and jeans, Dylan Bradley stood at the heavy-duty easel in front of all the others, arranging his own supplies on a newspaper-covered side table. He looked up, and their eyes met.

Her scalp tingled, and the sensation worked its way all the way down to her hot-pink toenails. In the past twenty-four hours, the spectacle of Sage throwing her arms around Dylan's neck and kissing him on the cheek had replayed in Caylor's head every time she'd allowed herself to think about it—like during the four-hour-long lunch meeting this afternoon.

And every time it played back, she couldn't help noticing that he'd stiffened and looked extremely uncomfortable when it happened. She couldn't blame him for Sage's actions.

Dylan left his easel and, after greeting Sassy, moved toward Caylor.

She wanted to run, wanted to get away from him, from the guilt and embarrassment of having pictured him—well, his likeness anyway—years ago when she was writing books she never should have written. Yet like a June bug to a porch light, she couldn't resist the draw she felt toward him.

"I didn't know you were coming." He extended his hand.

Though she knew it was a *really* bad idea, she placed her hand in his. Long, soft, strong fingers wrapped around her hand, and her breath caught in her chest. "I just brought Sassy up since Sage wasn't available to drive her."

Dylan released his grip, and their hands slid across each other's in a slow, agonizing separation.

What was wrong with her?

She really needed to write all this down.

"How were auditions this afternoon?" Dylan tucked his hands into his jeans' pockets and rocked from heel to toe on his bare feet.

Bare feet? It was forty degrees outside.

He wiggled his toes. "Yeah. . .for some reason, I feel more creative without shoes on."

"I was in a meeting that lasted all afternoon and didn't make it to the audition session." Caylor blushed, embarrassed he'd caught her looking at his feet.

What a great character quirk for Giovanni. How did the Renaissance-era Venetians feel about bare feet? She needed to write that question down and see if she could find any research resources on that.

Dylan excused himself when two other ladies walked into the room. Caylor sat and pulled out her laptop, then turned her chair at an angle, giving herself a better view of the other end of the room.

At 5:35, those two ladies were the only other students besides Sassy and Mrs. Bradley who'd come. Sassy turned and caught her eye and motioned Caylor forward.

Caylor shook her head.

Sassy put on her mean face.

Caylor sighed, closed the computer, and wove through the rows of chairs to sit at the easel to Sassy's right.

~∽~

The disappointment Dylan had been trying to hide eased when Caylor came forward and took a position at one of the student easels Perty had found in a storage closet in the children's wing of the church.

Caylor took the handful of brushes and a palette her grandmother handed to her. She laid them out on the table to her right.

As soon as she looked up, Dylan bent to adjust the blue-and-white-striped vase holding a nosegay of daisies that sat on a small table between him and his students. He'd been uncertain about trying to teach a beginning painting class to people who'd never picked up a paintbrush before—all his experience with "beginners" was with students who'd had to show a certain level of existing proficiency to be able to get into art school. But now, with Caylor looking on in expectation, a sense of determination overwhelmed him—to make this the most engaging and fun class he could to make sure she'd come back.

He started talking about drawing and painting and the different types of supplies and materials they could use—though Perty had purchased a classroom-size kit of scholastic-grade acrylics for everyone to work with—and about his own background with painting. He showed two small canvases he'd done for his MFA gallery show, handpicked by Perty, but told the ladies looking up at him that they shouldn't expect to have similar results.

"Acrylics dry quickly and don't rehydrate once they are dry, so let's go ahead and learn how to do a background wash. Pick a color you want for the background of your still life. . . ." He walked them through the steps of thinning the paint and using one of the large brushes to cover their small, square canvases with the color—showing them how they could add depth by gradating the darkness of the color.

Most of the ladies chose muted shades for the background—white with touches of brown or yellow mixed in for ivories and creams—but when Caylor got up and went to Perty's table to pick a color, she squeezed a glop of Brilliant Orange and a little bit of Chrome Yellow onto her palette.

Once they'd all covered the square canvases with the background wash—Caylor's looking like the surface of the sun in its brightness compared to that of the others—he talked a little bit about light and shadow, perspective, and shapes and then let them ask questions.

"Where can we see the rest of your paintings?" One of the ladies—Edith, he was pretty sure—asked.

"I don't have any exhibited anywhere yet, but I'll be having a show soon—a show and charity auction. I'm certain my grandmother will fill you in on the details as soon as they're finalized." He smiled at his grandmother.

"Why do you paint barefoot?"

When he turned to look at her, Caylor grinned shamelessly at him.

Heat chased goose bumps up his spine. "Probably because when I started painting as a kid, I had to do it outside, and I liked the feel of the grass under my feet. Plus, if the paint drips, it keeps me from ruining my shoes."

He reached over and touched Perty's canvas. Dry. "Now that your backgrounds are dry, you can sketch the vase and flowers onto your canvas in pencil and then start painting it."

He returned to his easel and started on his sketch. Out of the corner of his left eye, he watched Caylor as she sat for a while and contemplated her canvas, a distant look in her eyes.

A slow smile spread across her face. She jumped from her seat and rushed to the back of the room where she pulled a notepad out of her computer case and started scribbling. She filled one page of the legal pad and turned to the next—and the more she wrote, the broader her smile grew.

"She does that when she gets a story idea," Mrs. Evans said in a low tone.

Dylan snapped his attention back to the ladies in front of him. "What? Oh yes. I can get that way too when an idea for a piece strikes." He finished the rough outline of his vase and started on the flowers.

Satisfaction gleaming from her eyes, Caylor returned to her easel a few minutes later.

"Good story idea?" Sassy leaned over and whispered.

"I just figured out the main conflict for the hero and how to resolve the story." Caylor sighed. "Of course, I won't have time to work on it until this weekend, but I should be able to get the synopsis finished and then get the proposal off to my agent."

"Good for you." Sassy returned to her painting.

Caylor sat and stared at her canvas. And the longer she sat there, the more disconcerted she appeared.

Dylan left his easel and went down to sit across the table from her. "What's wrong?"

Caylor twisted her mouth to the side. "I'm no artist. When I doodle, I draw lines and boxes. There's no way I'm going to be able to draw—much less paint—anything that bears any resemblance to that flower arrangement."

"Art doesn't always have to be about making an exact replica of something. Art is about translating what something makes you feel on the inside. When you look at that vase, at those flowers, how do they make you feel?" He looked at her canvas. "Why did you choose such a bright color for your background?"

She shrugged. "I liked the way Brilliant Orange and Chrome Yellow looked in the tubes. They're happy colors."

"So do something with your painting that makes you happy. How can you take the vase and flowers in front of you and make something happy on your canvas?" He should probably be giving credit to his counselor here. He'd only had one session with him so far, and Dylan's biggest breakthrough had come when he'd admitted the art he'd been doing the last four years hadn't made him happy. "So what if it doesn't come out perfect? If it makes you happy, that's what matters."

"What makes me happy, huh?" She looked at him, turned bright red, and looked back at the flowers. "Okay. I'll come up with something."

Back at his own easel, Dylan painted the blue-and-white vase and mixed flowers with mechanical ease. In his mind, however, he composed a portrait of Caylor Evans—and no matter how authentic to the Renaissance era he tried to make the gown he pictured her in, he could not, for the life of him, picture her with long hair.

A few minutes later, Caylor started drawing on the canvas, her hand movements showing that her image was loose and free-flowing.

She got up and went to the table between their grandmothers and picked up several tubes of the brightest-colored paint, which she took back to her table.

He wished he had the freedom she did to drop this project and give in to the creative impulse pushing at the back of his mind. He wanted—no *needed*—to draw her, to paint her, to explore the minute details of her face, of her anatomy.

Now he was the one turning bright red, he was certain. He'd tried not to be prudish when it had come to the figure drawing studios in undergrad and graduate school in which they'd had to do studies from live, nude models. As he'd learned as a child, God had designed the human form, and it wasn't until sin entered the world that there was any shame attached to it. He understood the need for artists to have a good knowledge and understanding of human anatomy. Arms and legs could bend only certain ways, and needed to be in a certain proportion to the rest of the body. Learning those lessons had greatly helped him when creating the covers for the Melanie Mason novels, since he hadn't had live models to draw from—well, except his own reflection in the mirror, and even then, he'd changed his own proportions and features slightly.

He had to stop thinking about Caylor, and the only way he could do it would be to go ahead and paint her portrait. Once he did that, he could stop thinking about her constantly. Stop dreaming about her. Stop wondering if she might ever be able to fall for someone who'd made the mistakes he'd made. Stop praying that God would give him a future he knew he didn't deserve.

Chapter 17

∞

Caylor hit the button on the wireless mouse and looked up at the screen behind her. "Your first assignment—for next Wednesday, since we don't have classes Monday in observance of Martin Luther King Jr. Day—is to read chapter 1 in your theory of criticism book and 'A Good Man Is Hard to Find' by Flannery O'Connor, which you can find in the class folder on the school intranet. The password to access the folder is on your syllabus."

"Dr. Evans, do we have to turn in a Monday Paper next week?"

Caylor surveyed the class of eighteen senior-level English majors. When would they learn how to read? "No. As it shows on the daily assignment breakdown, the first Monday Paper is due on the first Monday we actually have class, which is week after next." And to stave off the next inevitable question, even though she'd been over it already, she added, "It should be a minimum of 250 and no more than 500 words of a personal reaction to one of the literary reading assignments from the week before. If there aren't any other questions. . ."

The students shook their heads.

"I'll see you next Wednesday, then. My office hours are on the front of the syllabus, and I do expect to see every one of you there before February 28 so we can discuss ideas for your thesis project. There's a sign-up sheet on the bulletin board next to my door. So if you want to make sure you can put it off until the very last minute, you'd better go sign up today to get one of those last spots." She had to raise her voice to be heard above the students' scramble to get out of the classroom. Since she was letting them go about fifteen minutes early, they probably hoped they'd beat all the other students to the cafeteria for lunch.

She detached the projector cord from her laptop, unplugged it, and stuck it back in her bag, along with the few extra copies of the syllabus, her record book, and the textbook.

The bottleneck at the door worsened momentarily, until someone pushed his way through the exiting students into the room.

No, not someone. Dylan.

"Dr. Evans, I need your help." Panic edged his voice.

"What's wrong?" She swung the strap of her bag up onto her shoulder.

"Sage canceled. I need someone to sit for my class." Even though his voice betrayed his frantic worry, only a small V between his brows and tightness around his mouth betrayed any distress.

Caylor's own anxiety rose at the mention of her sister's name. "Sage canceled. . .what?"

Dylan took a deep breath. "When I saw your sister at the auditions Monday, I asked her to be the model for my portraiture studio until spring break. She agreed and came by yesterday to fill out the employment paperwork. I got a text from her twenty minutes ago that said something came up and she couldn't make it today." He turned and paced the length of the room, running his fingers through his hair.

He returned to the front of the room and dropped his arms to his side. "If I don't have a model for the class to work with today, I won't be able to analyze the students' skill levels to determine what I need to work on with them."

She knew better than to trust Sage would change. She should have warned Dylan—if she'd known he was thinking of offering her a job. "I'm finished with classes for the day. What time does your studio start, and how long will you need me there?"

The crease between his eyebrows eased as they rose in surprise. "Oh—I didn't mean for you. . . I only hoped you could recommend someone."

"She's my sister, and I've been used to cleaning up her messes my whole life. Why stop now?" She led the way out of the classroom. "What are the times?"

Dylan looked at his watch. "Studio starts at twelve forty-five, but I'll spend a few minutes going over the syllabus and course expectations. So if you could be there around one o'clock, that would be perfect. It's 408 Sumner Hall. The class goes until three thirty."

Caylor took hold of his arm to look at his watch. Not quite twelve fifteen yet. "That gives me plenty of time to go back to my office and put a note on my door that I won't be there for office hours this afternoon."

"I can't tell you how much I appreciate this." Dylan's brown eyes locked with hers, and for a moment, the entire world went silent.

Was he leaning toward her, or was she leaning toward him?

"Dr. Evans, I have a question about the thesis project." A very unobservant student walked into the room, bringing Caylor back to reality.

"Mr. Bradley, I'll see you in a little while." Caylor breathed in slowly, trying to ease her pounding heart.

"Thank you, Dr. Evans." Dylan looked more shaken now than he had when he'd first entered the classroom.

Caylor made the student walk back to her office with her as they discussed the thesis paper all of the Lit Crit students would have to write and present by the end of the semester. Thank goodness it was a project she assigned every year in this course, because her mind wasn't on literary criticism, resources, citations, or MLA style.

The student parted company with her as soon as she reached the front steps to Davidson Hall. Caylor charged up the stairs and into her office, forcing herself to be pleasant to the two students from the early morning composition class who stood outside her door waiting.

Both students had the same question—about testing out of freshman comp—and she gave them the photocopied directions to the testing center, which got rid of them posthaste. She quickly wrote a note canceling today's office hours and hung it on her door so it covered her schedule.

Shutting herself into the office, she picked up her cell phone and hit the speed dial for Sage.

Her sister picked up on the second ring. "Hey, Caylor. What's up?"

The cheerful chirp in Sage's voice only added fuel to the flames of Caylor's annoyance. "What's up? Do you realize what you've done? How much Dylan Bradley was depending on you? You always do this—you commit to something, make people believe they can rely on you, and then leave them in the lurch when you flake out on them."

"I feel totally bad about having to cancel on him today—but it's the first day of class. He couldn't have needed me for much anyway. I promised him that I'd be there starting next week, rain or shine."

"Sage—"

"I *had* to, Caylor. One of the girls from high school I went out with last night works in the registrar's office at the community college. She said if I could get over there today with all of my transcripts, I could probably get registered. I did some figuring last night. I can go to school full-time there for about a thousand dollars less than what it would cost Sassy to pay for one class at Robertson. I started at seven this morning, calling the high school and MTSU to let them know I'd be coming in to get official copies of my transcripts. But it took a lot longer than I expected. I'm almost out at the community college, and I know this will take a couple of hours."

Caylor rubbed her forehead against the oncoming headache. "So you've decided to go to school full-time?"

"Yes. I'm going to go for my associate's degree in office management. It's not as glamorous as being an English professor, sure, but it'll mean I'll be qualified for all those jobs I couldn't apply for before." Road noise filled the empty space when Sage paused. "Cay, I really need your support on this."

Flannery's admonition to give Sage a chance rang through Caylor's mind. "I think it's wonderful that you've decided to go back to school. And I'll help you in whatever way I can."

"Great—because if I can get in, I'll be taking Composition and Business English this semester, which means lots of papers to write, and I'll need someone to look over them for me before I turn them in."

Caylor had to laugh. "We'll see."

"Beg Dylan's forgiveness for me, and tell him I will definitely be there next Wednesday and every day after that. Gotta go. I just pulled into the parking lot. Bye."

Caylor dropped her head down onto the desk. Give her one more chance, everyone always said. But how many chances could a person burn through until there wasn't one more?

***

"So when we come back from spring break, you should have decided on the live model or form you want to use for your final project of the semester and bring in plenty of photos so we can decide how best to proceed." Dylan looked up from the printed syllabus page in front of him—just in time to see Caylor slip into the back of the classroom.

His chest tightened. He still couldn't believe how close he'd come to giving into his whim and kissing her earlier. His counselor would definitely be hearing about that.

Caylor took a seat in the back while he answered questions from the eight students, all in their last semester for their bachelor of fine arts, their final project in here one of the several they'd be creating in their different studio courses for the art show in April. Only too keenly aware of how one piece could ruin a collection—as had happened to one of his undergrad roommates, who'd tried to phone in his sculpture piece and hadn't graduated with the rest of them—Dylan determined to help each student as much as he could to work to the best of his or her ability to paint portraits that would earn high-pass marks.

And that started today. "If there are no other questions, get your sketch pads and pencils ready."

Over the scraping of stools against the old, scarred, paint-splattered wood floors, Dylan motioned Caylor to the front of the soaring studio space. Students secured their sketch pads on the large metal easels—though the three guys in the room had trouble doing this and watching Caylor walk past at the same time.

"Thanks so much for coming." He indicated the stool on the dais.

Caylor had removed the dark purple blazer she'd been wearing earlier and looked unbelievably sensuous in a tailored white button-down shirt and gray tweed trousers that looked like they'd come straight off a 1940s Katharine Hepburn, with the high waist and wide legs. "I talked to Sage. She asked me to beg your forgiveness and assure you she'll be here every day from now on. I'll explain later why she couldn't make it today."

Dylan's hand shook as he reached out to straighten her collar. He really would prefer Caylor sit here in his classroom six hours a week for the next two months, but he couldn't ask that of her. "Tell her she owes you one."

"Oh, don't worry. She'll find that out." Caylor perched on the stool. "Where do you want me?"

"You're going to want to sit—you'll be here for more than two hours." It felt strange looking down at her—he was so accustomed to looking her almost directly in the eye, something he'd come to appreciate. He took her hands in his, ignoring the tingle at the back of his neck. She'd crossed her legs, so he arranged her hands on her knee, left over right. "Relax your shoulders and hold your head at a comfortable angle. Don't smile. Relax your face, but don't let it go slack."

A smile forced its way through his concentrated effort to remain neutral with her. "Think happy thoughts. Like the ones from last night that led you to paint fluorescent daisies with smiley faces in the middle."

Caylor grinned that lopsided grin that twisted his insides, but then flexed her jaw, opening and closing her mouth to erase the amusement. "Do I have to hold completely still?"

"As still as you can manage. We'll take a break every so often so you can get up and stretch." He stepped over to adjust the lights to flatter Caylor's bone structure—not hard to do—and eliminate unnecessary shadows. "Ready?"

"Ready." She smiled, pressed her lips together, smiled again, then wiped her expression clear, though her eyes continued to dance with amusement.

He turned to the class, his back fully to her before he let his own smile show again. "Since our regular model couldn't be here today, we have a substitute—Dr. Evans from the English department was kind enough to volunteer to sit for us. Remember, today we're concentrating on studies. By the end of the period, I want from each of you at least five studies—one must be the face, one must be the eyes, and one must be the hands. The other two are up to you. Concentrate on underlying structure, but don't neglect shading and toning. If you can't do it in pencil, it'll be that much harder to do in oils."

Dylan set up shop at one of the long, high worktables just behind the students where he could see all eight easels—and Caylor. He opened his sketchbook to the middle and turned through the few pages he'd filled the last few days. All images of Caylor—though they'd been done from memory, not from life.

Looking up, he caught Caylor's gaze. A slight lift of her left eyebrow was the only change in her expression. There, that intensity— that was what he hadn't been able to capture before. He immediately put graphite to paper and began his own study of her eyes—which started to turn into a full sketch of her face.

But he couldn't just concentrate on his own drawing. Much as he hated to walk away from it—just when he thought he might finally capture the exact shape of her mouth—he got up and went from student to student, watching technique, praising what was well done, making suggestions on what needed improvement.

With a quick break every thirty minutes for Caylor to move and stretch, and between his own drawing and working with each of the students, the time went by far too fast.

At three twenty, Dylan went around to each student and checked the five studies, pleased with the skill level of each of them—especially considering they were undergraduates rather than the grad students he'd worked with at Watts-Maxwell. He dismissed them and went back to the worktable to clean up his own supplies.

"I notice you kept your shoes on today." After touching several colorful spots on the table to make sure they were dry, Caylor leaned her elbows on it across from him.

"Well, I do try to keep some manner of professionalism in an academic setting." He tucked his pencils back into their box and slid it into an outside pocket of his bag.

"I want to see it."

His heart thudded against his ribs. "See what?"

She reached over and rested her hand on the cover of his sketchbook. "I know you were drawing me, too. I didn't get to see any of the students' work, so I want to see yours."

Swallowing hard, he picked up the book and angled it so she couldn't see anything else as he flipped open to the appropriate page. He turned it around, set it down on the table, and slid it toward her, catching his bottom lip between his teeth.

Caylor studied the drawing for quite some time—long enough for him to hear her stomach rumble several times. When she looked up, extra moisture pooled along her lower lash line. She blinked several times to clear it. "It's beautiful, Dylan. You've truly been blessed with a gift from God."

If she truly believed that, why did she look so confused, so conflicted, when she said it? "Thank you." He retrieved the book before she decided to flip through the rest of it. "I don't suppose you had time to eat lunch before you came?"

Caylor straightened and went to the back of the room to put her blazer and coat back on. "Nope. I'll probably just pick something up on my way home."

Don't let her walk away. "Would you be interested in going over to Green Hills and grabbing a sandwich at Provence with me? I've got to go to an art store over there for some supplies this afternoon."

"I love Provence. I can't stay long, but that sounds great." Caylor looped a fluffy pink scarf around her neck. "I've got to go back to my office and get everything I need to take home tonight. Why don't I meet you at the restaurant?"

Dylan nodded—maybe a little too enthusiastically, so he stopped. "I'll see you there, then."

Other than getting him to admit—out loud—that the kind of art he'd been painting to please Rhonda the last four years had been making him miserable, the other piece of advice his counselor had given Dylan in their first meeting was to start communicating better. To stop assigning motives and start asking people what they really meant and thought and felt.

He needed to know what had spooked Caylor about his painting back before Christmas. Especially after her reaction to his drawing of her this afternoon.

The parking garage at the town-center-style shopping area had quite a few empty spaces. Dylan thought about leaving his jacket behind but changed his mind after noticing the wind that whipped up the main driveway into the structure. Caylor pulled in and parked across from him. She'd added fuzzy gloves to complete her look—pink scarf, purple peacoat, pink gloves, gray trousers, black boots. She could have stepped out of a catalog.

"You know, I figured you'd be used to this kind of weather—and worse—but you look just as miserable as I feel in this cold." Caylor dropped her keys into her coat pocket and rubbed the fuzzy gloves together, shivering.

He motioned her toward the side exit closest to the café. "I never did get used to the cold up there. And I'm seriously considering pulling my parka out if it gets as cold as they're predicting for this weekend."

"I spent two winters overseas when I was in school—one in England and one in Ireland. I'll take a Tennessee winter over those any day."

As they stood in line and then waited for their food, they chatted about growing up in Nashville—Caylor had attended Harpeth Hall, so she shared several anecdotes about attending an all-girls private school.

Not ready to launch into a serious topic when they sat down and started eating, Dylan cast around for something to keep the conversation light. "So what TV shows do you watch?"

"Pretty much only stuff that's available to watch season by season online or on DVD." Caylor pulled a corner off her grilled cheese panini and dipped it into her tomato-basil soup. "I don't really have a lot of time to watch anything during the school year—between school, participating in the drama department's productions, and writing—so when I'm traveling in the summer, it's nice to be able to chill in the hotel in the evenings and catch up with shows a couple of episodes at a time on my laptop."

Ah, another topic. "How long have you been writing?"

The mischievous sparkle he'd seen in her eyes when she'd been painting her fluorescent flowers last night returned. "How long have you been drawing and painting?"

"Touché." Oh how he loved it when she grinned like that.

"I finished my first novel when I was eighteen. It garnered me a drawer full of rejections, but also a lot of feedback and suggestions on how to improve. So I joined a couple of writing groups, studied the industry, and kept at it." She finished off her tomato-basil soup.

"How long did it take you to get published?" He left the crust from his ham and cheese sandwich on the plate and started on the potato salad. The need to ask her about the painting kept getting drowned out by the joy of sitting and carrying on a civil conversation with a woman about something other than what he should or shouldn't be doing.

"A few years." She laid the last corner of her sandwich down on the plate and pushed it back. "What's the equivalent in the art world to getting published?"

"Probably getting into certain galleries or museums for showings." He explained a little about the competition between artists to gain recognition through shows and reviews. "Mostly, a lot of it comes down to connections—it's who you know and who they know."

"It's a little like that in publishing, but I can only imagine how much worse the subjectivity is in your field." Caylor looked at her watch. "Oh, I didn't realize how late it's getting. I've got to run—I have a meeting at church at five thirty."

Dylan grabbed her plate and bowl and stacked it with his to carry to the busing station. She was in the process of buttoning her coat when he returned to the table.

"Thanks again for filling in for your sister today." He shoved his arms into his jacket, annoyed with himself for not following through on his counselor's advice.

"Not a problem. I'm always happy to help out another instructor."

He opened the door for her, and she waited on the other side to walk back to the garage with him.

"Do you have any pets, Dylan?"

Her question came out of the blue, making him wonder where she was going with it. "No. My mother is allergic, so we never had pets. I had a roommate in New York who had a dog, though."

"What kind?" Caylor pulled her keys out of her pocket and pointed the remote at her SUV.

"An Irish wolfhound. Let me tell you, not an easy dog to deal with in a small Brooklyn flat." He leaned against the front fender of his truck, losing himself momentarily in admiration of the statuesque beauty before him.

Caylor nodded, lips pressed together, all her former humor gone. "Oh. Well. . .I guess I'll be seeing you around." She opened the door and climbed into her vehicle.

"See you." Confused, Dylan didn't move until Caylor's brake lights disappeared around the corner. How had such a pleasant afternoon ended on such a sour note? What was it he kept doing wrong to make Caylor react so strangely?

Maybe by the next time he saw her, he'd have worked up the courage to ask.

Chapter 18

$\mathcal{C}$aylor let out a low moan and rubbed her eyes. Though her earliest class today hadn't started until ten thirty, she'd still been on campus by seven—between wanting to avoid the worst of morning rush hour, be out of the house by the time the construction crew arrived, and get to campus in time to grab breakfast before most of the students descended on the cafeteria.

She hadn't taught four classes in a semester since being promoted to associate professor, gaining tenure, and taking on responsibilities advising and mentoring grad students. And with one of her courses being freshman composition filled to maximum with thirty students, she had the sinking feeling that this semester was going to be a lot harder than she'd initially expected. Of course, she had a couple of graduate students who weren't yet ready for full teaching assistantships who would be helping out considerably with the comp class—doing some teaching and helping to grade the eight essay assignments throughout the semester—but then, that also meant she had her graduate students to work with and oversee.

Leaning against the edge of the counter in Zarah's guest bathroom, Caylor wiped her makeup off with a disposable wipe—from the pack she'd had in her travel kit for last summer's frenetic travels. As much as she loved Zarah and Flannery, she really wished she were at home tonight, in the quiet of her own loft, in the comfort of her big chair, in the space where she could deal with the chaos whirling through her head.

Freshman Comp. Graduate Rhetoric. Brit Lit. Literary Criticism. Essay, thesis, and dissertation topics. Student meetings. Committee meetings. Meetings about meetings.

Sassy and the house remodel.

Accents, pronunciations, and connotation of Shakespeare's words in *Much Ado about Nothing*.

Sage.

Choir practice. Choir council. Meetings to choose Easter music. Ensemble practice.

Edits, revisions, cover art suggestions, marketing, fan mail, monthly newsletters, and blogging.

Dylan.

Ah, yes. Before she'd met him, all of these other issues—with the exception of Sage—had been manageable. Nonchaotic. Normal.

But then along came this tall, handsome artist with his messy hair, bad-boy accessories (which she suspected included at least one tattoo), facial scruff, and penetrating eyes—who might be the man in the drawings she'd thought about, dreamed about, and fantasized about for years—and her well-balanced life spun out of control.

She tossed the wipe into the small trash can, grabbed her glasses, and turned the light off before she could look at herself in the mirror again. Thinking about him—especially the amount of time she'd allowed herself to do it—created the problem. Therefore, all she had to do was make herself stop thinking about him.

"You look like you're much more relaxed and comfortable now." Zarah straightened from looking at something in the oven.

Having exchanged her slightly too-small navy pencil skirt, tights, tall brown boots, suede blazer, and blue shell for her oldest, most comfortable pair of jeans, thick socks and cushiony leather mules, and a french terry tunic, she definitely felt more comfortable now. Relaxed—well, she'd work on it. "What can I help with?"

"There's a bag of dinner rolls in the freezer—you could get six of those out and put them on a pan." Zarah glanced at the clock on the back of the range. "Flannery should be here in about ten minutes, and those take about fifteen with the oven on 350."

Happy to feel useful, Caylor found the bag of roll dough—

185

homemade by Zarah's grandmother, she was pretty sure—broke the rolls apart, and set them on the cookie sheet Zarah handed her. Though she'd worked up a pretty good craving through the day for the Chinese food they'd talked about ordering in tonight, arriving to the pungent aroma of Zarah's Italian casserole baking in the oven had immediately put thoughts of General Tso and his sweet and spicy chicken right out of her head.

"How did your first week of classes go?" Caylor opened the oven, closing her eyes against the initial blast of hot—though delicious-smelling—air. She slid the pan in and closed it.

"I haven't started yet—the Middle Tennessee History class at Robertson was canceled because of low registration numbers. Now I don't have to worry about missing church on Wednesday nights all semester, and the regular Tennessee History class at the community college meets on Tuesdays, so our first class is next week." Zarah handed Caylor a large serving bowl, then went to the fridge and started passing her fixings for a green salad.

"Sage went out there yesterday to register. She's decided to go to school full time and get her associate's degree in office management." Caylor opened the bag of romaine hearts, rinsed them, and started pulling off leaves and tearing them into the bowl.

"Really? That's all she wants to do?" At eighteen years old, when Zarah arrived in Nashville to attend Vanderbilt and Caylor met her for the first time, Zarah had a singular goal in view: getting her PhD in history and working in that field in some capacity. Her undergraduate internship had led her to the Middle Tennessee Historic Preservation Commission, which had detoured her slightly—to a PhD in historic preservation from Robertson—finishing her bachelor's, master's, and doctorate degrees in a total of six years.

"I know. . . . It bugs me that she seems to have no ambition for her life. And believe me, if some guy comes along who makes enough money to support her and asks her to marry him, she'd do it in a heartbeat and forget this whole school idea. She just wants to be taken care of." Caylor ripped the lettuce leaves apart with more force than the poor vegetable deserved.

"Hmm. . .could that be because her big sister always took care of her growing up?" Zarah brought red and yellow bell peppers over and set them on the cutting board beside Caylor. "You have to admit, you have a tendency to do that."

"Just like you have a tendency to work yourself to death at a party instead of having a good time?" Having lived together for seven years, they knew each other's strengths and weaknesses too well.

"Yeah, something like that."

They both turned when the front door opened and closed.

"I'm here—the party can start now." Flannery breezed into the kitchen, a large bakery box in her arms.

Caylor tossed the sliced cucumber into the bowl and clapped her hands. "Yay—you remembered!"

"Of course I remembered. Any excuse to go to Gigi's." Flannery slid the box onto the small kitchen table.

Zarah looked from one to the other. "Gigi's. . .the cupcake place over on Broadway?"

Flannery flipped the box lid open. "The very one. Caylor and I figured we'd be planning your bridal shower, so we decided there was no time like the present to taste-test cupcakes to decide which ones we want to serve at it."

Caylor reached toward one of the high, fluffy clouds of buttercream frosting with tiny pearl sprinkles on top, but Flannery flipped the lid closed. "After dinner."

"Spoil sport." Caylor went back to chopping the rest of the vegetables.

"Excuse me." Zarah fled the room

Caylor dropped the knife and followed her, Flannery right on her heels.

Zarah stood beside the sofa end table, dabbing her eyes with a tissue.

"What's wrong?" Caylor laid her hand on Zarah's shoulder—her trembling shoulder.

Zarah's face contorted. She rolled her eyes and wiped away more escaping tears. "I hate this. Every time someone does something for me related to the wedding, I burst into tears. You should have seen me Sunday evening at Pops and Kiki's house. Kiki took me into her bedroom and opened the cedar chest at the end of her bed and pulled out the box that had all of her wedding stuff in it—including her veil, which she gave me."

"And her wedding dress? I've always admired it in the picture over the fireplace." Caylor handed her another tissue.

"She donated it to the Historic Textiles department at JRU twenty years ago because the fabric was starting to degrade." Zarah blew her nose and took a few deep breaths.

"I can ask Dr. Cloud if you can borrow it back."

"No. I had another meltdown earlier this week when Beth—Bobby's mother—called and told me she wants to take all three of us to Manhattan to shop for dresses for the wedding." She managed to smile through the waterworks that continued flooding her eyes. "Bobby's an only child, so the Pattersons have offered to pay for everything since they always wanted a daughter."

"Why do you think you're freaking out every time someone brings up the wedding?" Flannery looped her arm through Zarah's and led her back to the kitchen, where she pulled a hand towel out of a drawer, wetted it at the sink, and handed it to Zarah.

Zarah pressed the damp cloth to her forehead and then to her cheeks. "It's not at the mention of the wedding—it's whenever someone offers to do something for us. . .well, for me, particularly. I guess I just don't feel like I deserve it."

Caylor and Flannery both started to protest, but Zarah stopped them with a raised hand. "I know, I know. I need to take joy in letting others serve me, just as I take joy in serving others. In addition to going through a few months of premarital counseling with Bobby, I've started seeing my therapist again. I asked Pops to walk me down the aisle. And I haven't decided if I'm going to invite the general and my stepmother to the wedding."

The timer beeped, and Zarah put down the towel and crossed to the range, where she put on an oven mitt and pulled the dish of pasta casserole out.

Caylor's mouth watered and her stomach growled at the sight and aroma of the bubbling tomatoey-cheesy concoction.

"Even if I invite them and they say they'll come, they probably will forget to show up again." Zarah set the glass pan down on a cork trivet and leaned back down for the bread.

Having just said good-bye to her own parents on Monday as they headed back to Geneva, Caylor's heart broke for her friend, whose emotionally abusive father had done all he could to break Zarah's spirit as a child—and as an adult, with his latest offense toward her just a few months ago. Thank goodness Bobby had been there to help Zarah hold it together. As always, God's timing in bringing the one-time sweethearts back together after fourteen years had been perfect.

Flannery grabbed plates and flatware to set the dining room table, and Caylor and Zarah followed with the food. Flannery started the blessing before Caylor was fully in her seat, and it was over almost as quickly as she started.

"Someone's hungry." Zarah handed the first plate of casserole—made from several different types of pastas she'd cooked the night before, layered with spaghetti sauce, pepperoni, and lots and lots of mozzarella cheese—to Flannery.

Caylor cut open one of the hot rolls and slathered butter on the soft insides. "Is it safe to talk about the wedding now?"

"Just don't offer to do anything for her." Flannery put a little bit of salad onto her plate and drowned it in ranch dressing.

"Yeah, it's safe. I'll try to keep from getting all weepy at the table." Zarah took a large serving of salad and handed the bowl to Caylor. "Beth and Tank—"

Caylor almost choked on her bread. "Tank?"

Zarah's expression went soft. "Oh, sorry. Andrew—Bobby's dad. He played pro football for a few years after college, and that was his nickname."

"Fitting that Bobby's football nickname was Diesel, then." Flannery pursed her lips to the side, eyes dancing.

"Really?" Caylor filled the empty three-quarters of her plate with greenery, then dressed it with Zarah's homemade dressing—olive oil, pomegranate-infused red wine vinegar, and herbs and spices. "Apple doesn't fall far, huh? Okay, so anyway, sorry I interrupted, Zare."

"It's okay. I keep forgetting that even though you and Flannery have known each other most of your lives, you didn't go to school or church together." Zarah looked from one to the other. "I can't believe I'm about to ask this, after knowing you as long as I have. How did you know each other growing up if you didn't go to school or church together?"

"Our moms were friends from when they were med students together at Vandy." Caylor took a bite of salad and let the slightly sweet and very tart flavor of the vinegar permeate her mouth. "They loved being able to share the expense of a babysitter, so we were pretty much constantly together the first five years of our lives."

"It was one of those situations where we were destined to either hate each other or love each other when we grew up." Flannery smiled at Caylor. "God knew what He was doing when He threw our moms together." She turned and looked at Zarah. "Because without the two of us, where would you be?"

"I don't even want to think about it. Because I can't imagine any-one else as my maids of honor. Which reminds me. . .Bobby's parents have convinced us to increase the size of the wedding. That means"— she sighed heavily—"I also have to increase the number of attendants. Because, as Beth pointed out, having only two people standing up there with me, and Bobby's two—Patrick and Chase, a guy he works with— was fine for the chapel but would look pretty scrawny in Acklen's main sanctuary."

"So who else are you going to ask?" While Caylor knew Zarah had other friends, there wasn't anyone she ever talked about as being close enough to want in her wedding. After all of the emotional turmoil Zarah had been through in her life, Caylor couldn't blame her for not making friends easily.

"I was thinking maybe Stacy—Patrick's fiancée. And Debbie from work. Bobby's thinking about asking the two other agents on his team." She pushed her pasta around on the plate. "It's pretty sad that we're each having trouble coming up with four people to ask to be in our wedding."

Caylor suddenly had a full mental image of Dylan and his three brothers, all dressed in tuxedoes, standing at the front of the much smaller sanctuary at her church. Wow, they all looked good in tuxes.

Wait—no. She couldn't allow herself to think about him like

that. She had enough guilt from just having used that drawing of him. . .*maybe* him. . .for inspiration when writing novels that, while not explicit, were titillating. She'd fantasized enough about the man in those samples and covers back then. She didn't need to compound her embarrassment every time she saw him now by continuing to have inappropriately romantic thoughts about him.

As Zarah talked about the tentative plans and ideas for the wedding, the phrase, "Beth suggested" or "Beth said" seemed to be repeated quite often.

"Aren't you letting your future mother-in-law make an awful lot of decisions about this wedding that aren't necessarily what you want?" Caylor wiped up the last of the tomato sauce from her plate with the heel of her roll.

"I am compromising on some things, but Bobby's not letting his mom dictate anything. He knows me well enough to know that I'll do anything to make Beth happy. He's looking out for me. Don't worry."

After a quick cleanup, they moved into the living room with the box of cupcakes.

"I got three each of four different flavors." Flannery lifted the lid and referred to a small piece of notepaper. "The two white ones with pearl sprinkles are different—the one with the fluted frosting is Champagne, the one with the frosting that looks like ice cream from Dairy Queen is Wedding Cake. The one with toasted coconut on it is Italian Cream Wedding Cake. And the White Midnight Magic has the dark chocolate cake, cream cheese frosting, and chocolate chips. And that's the one I'm trying first."

Caylor took one of the Italian Cream cupcakes onto her dessert plate and settled back into the corner of the sofa, curling her feet up onto the cushion beside her.

After a couple of bites of the decadent dessert, Caylor set it aside and rested her head on the arm of the sofa. She wished she'd had the drawing of the cover model with her after sitting for Dylan's class yesterday. She could have whipped it out and held it beside the pencil drawing he'd done of her to see if they shared as many similarities as she imagined they did.

And then there was the dog. She'd written in *Lady Knight* that the heroine had a large hound—with no specific breed given—but she'd pictured it as a wolfhound and had mentioned that in the cover information she'd sent to her editor to be passed along to Patrick Callaghan. Just to be certain she had her dogs right, she'd gotten online as soon as she got home last night and searched for images of Irish wolfhounds. Though she'd had little doubt before, the photos that came up proved that the dog on the cover of the book was the same as the dog in the painting at Dylan's apartment, which was the kind of dog his roommate owned.

"For late May, I was thinking either a pink or a green—though we'll have to be careful with the shade of pink, to make sure it looks good on both of you." Zarah flipped through the pages in the thick, three-ring binder on the coffee table in front of her, the box of cupcakes having been closed and moved to the floor. "And we're talking an evening wedding, now. So super formal, which means floor-length dresses for you."

Caylor sat up when Zarah looked over at her with concern in her gaze. She moved closer and leaned forward, bracing her elbows on her knees, to look at the pictures of dresses Zarah had found online and printed for reference.

"You're just trouble all the way around, Caylor. Red hair. Six feet tall." Flannery pulled the notebook closer and studied the photos of the bridesmaid dresses.

Of course, it could be pure coincidence that Dylan had painted a wolfhound in his piece at home that looked just like the dog on the cover. After all, both he and Patrick Callaghan painted in an almost photorealistic style. Online, one Irish wolfhound had looked just like the next, so maybe the same was true in paintings, too.

Based on seeing him in that close-fitting, black T-shirt Tuesday night at the seniors' painting class, Dylan was nowhere near as broad through the shoulders or as muscular as the guy on the covers of her Mason novels—though he could hold his own when it came to broad shoulders and strong arms, from what she'd observed. And she *had* observed.

"Caylor?"

"Uh-huh." But what if Dylan *was* Patrick Callaghan? Her editor told her that Patrick Callaghan said he read every word in Melanie Mason's manuscripts, which was what inspired his cover art for them. What would Dylan think if he found out Caylor was the one who'd written them? No nice guy like Dylan would be interested in someone who'd spent five or six years letting her imagination go to places she would never dream of letting herself go in reality—not until she was married, anyway. Which meant she definitely shouldn't have been thinking about it, much less writing about it for public consumption.

"Caylor."

She jumped at the sound of the notebook slamming closed. "What?"

"We've been trying to get your attention for five minutes now. What is going on with you?" Zarah pushed back the notebook and put the cupcake box back on the table, and she and Flannery each helped themselves to another.

Caylor started to explain but then realized she needed visual aids. She stood, stepped over Zarah's feet, and went down the hall to the office. When she returned, she set each of the six Melanie Mason books down on the table.

"Don't tell me you're thinking about going back to writing this kind of novel." Flannery, who'd been a great help in getting Caylor connected with editors and agents in the Christian publishing industry, looked offended.

"No. It's not that. I'm perfectly happy writing sweet and inspirational romances." She picked up *Lady Knight* and handed it to Flannery. "Look really close at the guy on the front cover."

She got her phone out of her pocket and pulled up the picture of Dylan she'd secretly snapped during one of the breaks they'd taken in his class yesterday. "Tell me that the guy on these covers doesn't look like Dylan Bradley."

"You mean your cover model you've been in love with for the last ten years?" Flannery smirked, but she obliged and picked up each of the books in turn and held it up to the phone she and Zarah now held between them.

"Eight years. But yes, that guy."

"I told him when he was here for the Christmas dinner that he looked like this guy." Flannery exchanged the books and phone for the tall cloud of white frosting atop her cupcake.

Caylor's stomach dropped to her knees. "You did *what*? When were you talking to him about these books? You didn't tell him I wrote them, did you?"

"He pulled one off the shelf in the office. We were talking about book cover design, and he said he had some experience. I looked at the book—um. . .I think it was *Knight Fall*—and remarked on the resemblance between him and the cover model. Except the cover model is bulkier and the nose is different." Flannery wiped the frosting from her lips with a napkin. "Wait, you don't think that Dylan Bradley was the model for these, do you?"

Caylor rubbed her forehead then removed her glasses and rubbed her eyes. "Not only do I think he's the model, but I'm pretty sure he's the artist. Which means he's read all of these books. Which means that if he ever learns I wrote them, he'll probably figure out that I was picturing the cover model—him—when I was writing them, especially the scenes that get pretty steamy, because I tend to have the heroine noticing little details of his appearance—details I got from the sketches and sample covers Patrick Callaghan did."

She curled up in the corner of the sofa again and flung her forearm across her forehead. "Y'all. . .I feel horrible about it. When I wrote those books, those scenes especially, I could so clearly picture that guy in my head."

"You never went over the edge with what you wrote though." Zarah stacked the books in two piles of three, perfectly square and aligned.

"Not with what I wrote, no. But I shouldn't have been writing stuff like that or allowing myself to imagine it, especially once I became fixated on him. On Dylan."

"So what if it is him? I think it's highly unlikely." Flannery licked the last bit of frosting off the white cupcake. "But if it is, you two have something in common."

Caylor sat up a little straighter and dropped her arm to her lap. "Oh yeah, what's that?"

"You wrote steamy novels. . . . He not only drew the clench covers for steamy novels; he put himself *on* the covers of steamy novels. I know you regret having written the books—even though, in the grand scheme of where the general-market romance novel has gone in the past ten years, yours are positively tame—and so maybe he regrets having created the covers. These books came out between five and eight years ago. If Dylan is as young as I think he is, he was probably in college when he started doing these, assuming they are indeed his."

Caylor slapped her hands over her ears. "La-la-la-la-la. I can't hear that. I can't think like that. I can't think that I might have been fantasizing about someone that much younger than me."

"He's got to be in his late twenties—he said he was a full-time professor for more than four years—so he can't be that much younger than you. Maybe seven or eight years."

"That's quite a bit."

"He'd have been twenty or twenty-one when the first book came out. That's not too young." Flannery set the half-eaten cake back onto the plate and on the table. "I think there's another component to this you aren't admitting, even to yourself."

Caylor reached over and swiped a glob of frosting from her mostly uneaten cupcake and stuck her finger in her mouth, enjoying the richness of the cream cheese frosting. "What's that?"

"I think you like Dylan Bradley. I think you're falling for him, and you're coming up with excuses why you shouldn't—like he's too young, or you're too embarrassed over the whole book thing. You've managed to scuttle every chance you've had at a relationship in the past five years, since you moved in with your grandmother. I'm not going to let you do it again."

Caylor stared at the woman she'd known since before she could remember. She liked Dylan? Oh no. She *liked* Dylan. No. That was wrong. She couldn't like Dylan. "He's too young. Besides, he just came out of a bad relationship. The last thing he needs to be thinking about is getting involved with someone else."

Zarah reached over and laid her hand lightly on Caylor's knee. "What were you thinking about when we were looking at the wedding book?"

Caylor pressed her lips closed. No way was she admitting to it.

Flannery released a dramatic sigh. "Look, the only way you're

195

ever going to find out the truth is if you tell him the truth. Tell him you wrote those books. Tell him you think he looks like the guy on the cover. Ask him if it's him—ask him if he painted them. Otherwise, you're just going to keep torturing yourself, and us, about this until you've run him off. And Caylor, sweetie, I don't think I need to remind you that you're now officially closer to forty than you are to thirty. So, tick-tock, honey."

Except for maybe Sassy, there wasn't another person in the world who would get away with saying something like that to Caylor. "But I like him, even if he is quite a bit younger than me. I'm starting to get comfortable with him. I like spending time with him. What if telling him the truth ruins everything? What if he's so embarrassed or offended that he no longer wants to have anything to do with me?"

Zarah gave her knee a slight squeeze. "You'll never know until you ask. And if you can't tell him the truth about yourself—the whole truth—there's not really a lot of hope for much of a future between you anyway."

Confront Dylan about the covers—tell him she was Melanie Mason?

She'd never been good at direct confrontations, not when she was coming from a position of weakness or vulnerability. Usually she chose to approach it in writing.

That's what she could do. She'd send him an e-mail. Then she wouldn't have to see his face turn from delight to dismay to disgust when she told him everything.

Chapter 19

❧

*A*fter an impromptu lesson on Renaissance-era art and architecture that drew the attention and participation of everyone in the workshop in Rutherford Hall, Dylan picked up a brush and started painting—at the direction of the graduate student whose master's degree depended on the outcome of all of the set and scenery pieces for this production.

At first, when he'd learned that JRU scheduled all their classes Monday through Thursday, Dylan wasn't certain he'd like it—after all, teaching a fifty-minute class three times a week required quite different preparation than teaching an hour-and-twenty-minute class twice a week. But after three weeks, he'd decided he liked the four-day class schedule. It allowed all of the meetings that typically happened either at the crack of dawn or late in the evening to happen at a more reasonable hour on Friday, and it gave art students an extra full day to work on projects uninterrupted by classes.

"Hey, Dylan. I didn't realize you were coming in today." Bridget Wetzler skirted around a large set piece to get to where he knelt over the top part of the canvas, working on the sky of the outdoor backdrop.

"I saw a couple of your students at the art majors meeting this morning—I guess some of the set design majors are also considered art majors—and they asked if I'd come talk about translating the style of the era to what they're doing. I figured as long as I'm here, I'd lend a hand where needed." He stippled a bit more blue in the quadrant he'd been working on then rocked back on his heels and pushed up to his feet.

"It's all looking pretty good for only being three weeks out." The drama professor made a slow turn, looking around the busy workshop. She stopped when she faced Dylan again. "You don't sew, too, do you? The soft props and costumes group needs a lot of help on this production."

"No. . .you're talking to the person who'll wear his shirt unbuttoned rather than pick up a needle and thread to sew on a missing button." He pointed to the gap in the buttons on the flannel shirt he wore over his black T-shirt.

"Well, I had to ask, right?" She tucked a strand of fire-engine red hair behind her ear and started strolling between the long rows of workbenches looking at props and set pieces. "I couldn't get to you before you disappeared, but I saw you at my church last Sunday. I didn't know you were going there."

Following her, Dylan almost shuddered at the memory of the enormous church. "Two Rivers? It was the first time I'd been there."

"What did you think?" She looked over her shoulder at him.

He clasped his hands behind his back and took a moment to compose his thoughts.

Bridget laughed. "Yeah, it's not for everyone. We do have a great singles group."

After his experience with the age-divided singles at Acklen Ave., he again had to suppress a shudder. "I think I need something smaller."

"You should try Providence Chapel." Bridget stopped to answer a student's question before continuing on down the row.

"Where's Providence Chapel?"

"It's that old stone-looking building just north of campus—the one with the trees lining the driveway."

"That's a church?" He'd seen it every day he'd been to campus, driving past it coming and going. He imagined painting it in the spring when all the trees around it were in bloom.

"Yep. Several of the faculty attend there. It's small, only a couple hundred people. But if the big churches aren't doing it for you, that might be an option. I've heard they have a fantastic music program."

He liked music. Actually, he'd always enjoyed music more than talking at church. There was something about those old hymns sung to the accompaniment of an organ, and maybe a piano, that made him feel like God was near, like God would actually listen to someone like him.

Bridget's cell phone rang. "Oh, this is a call I've been waiting for from another program that has costumes we might be able to use. It was good to see you, Dylan."

He checked his watch. Oops, he'd better get out of here. After answering a few more questions about a building in the background on one of the pieces, Dylan left the workshop.

Just north of campus, he pulled into the driveway of Providence Chapel—how had he never noticed the low, stone sign at the road?—and stopped just in front where he could read the notice board beside the front door. Sunday school at 9:15, service at 10:30. Good. That meant he would get out in time to still be able to meet Perty and Gramps and Pax—and Mother and Dad—for lunch afterward.

Even though Perty and Gramps never asked, Dylan always made a point of telling them all about the church he'd visited each week. He'd resented the implication—his perception of the implication—when they'd first gone over the rental agreement and told him he would have to attend church every week. Now, however, six weeks later, he not only appreciated the nudge, but a desire grew in him to find a church where he fit in, where he could once again start learning how to make pursuing God a regular part of his life.

He'd tried out the big churches since he'd been in town: Acklen Ave., Belmont, West End United Methodist, Christ Church Cathedral, First Baptist, and Two Rivers. But aside from his feeling like part of a cattle herd in a stockyard, he thought they'd all been either too casual and contemporary or too formal and traditional. He needed something in between, and he needed a place where he didn't just meld into the background.

After snapping a couple of pictures of the building with his phone, he headed toward Trevecca. The modern-Gothic style of the church would look great in the background of the new historic piece he'd started.

He was able to find a parking space pretty close to the building when he arrived at the smaller university and took the stairs two at a time to get up to the second-floor therapy department. Someone came out of the room where he and Ken usually met, gave Dylan a tight smile, and hurried away down the hall.

The door opened again, and Ken stepped out into the hall. "Go on in and have a seat. I'm going to grab a bottle of water. Want one?"

"No, I'm good, thanks." Dylan pulled the strap of his messenger-style bag over his head and set it down beside the low-backed armchair he always sat in.

Ken was back within seconds. "Thanks for waiting. My last session was being recorded for review by my faculty mentor, and we had technical issues with the video camera, so that's why we ran a few minutes over." He took a swig of water, screwed the lid on, and set the bottle on the floor beside the chair.

"No problem." Dylan wiped his hands down his thighs. No matter that he'd done this before; it still wracked his nerves—and his sessions weren't even being recorded.

Ken pulled a folder out of the expanding file beside him on the floor, set the folder on his lap, then picked up his legal pad from the low table between them. "Ready to get started?"

Dylan nodded. "Sure."

Ken opened the folder and looked at a page fastened to the left side of the folder with a two-prong metal fastener. "Last time we discussed your grandparents. We talked about how you tend to react defensively to things they say to you. Did you do your assignment?"

"Write down all the times I automatically assumed that what they were saying to me was negative or belittling?" Dylan nodded. "I did. After a few days, I was able to recognize it and stop it before it could start. I realized I'd already begun to stop myself from doing that—but only after the full-blown reaction. Now it's getting easier to stop it before I roll over into the defensive reaction."

Ken made notes on his legal pad. "That's great progress. Keep writing those things down—and if your initial reactions start to change, write that down, too. Now, you were also supposed to make a list of things you wanted to tell them about what happened to you and what you did while you lived in Philadelphia. Did you do that this week?"

Dylan slouched a little lower in the chair. He'd had dinner with

Gramps and Perty three times since the last session, but each time he thought about bringing up the topic of his relationship with Rhonda, how it had gone from mentor to physical—had it ever been romantic?—he clammed up and the opportunity bypassed him.

"I made the list, but I haven't talked to them about that yet." He reached down and pulled a small brown journal out of his bag. He flipped it open to the first blank page and started writing.

Tell Gramps and Perty about Rhonda.

"You hold your grandparents in very high regard. Out of anyone in your life, it's the idea of disappointing them that drives most of your actions now. Do you think it would help if you talked to one of your brothers about your relationship with the older woman before you talk to your grandparents?"

He shook his head. "My brothers. . .before Christmas they confronted me and got me to tell them about what happened that led to me moving home. After all, they're the ones who helped me see I needed therapy."

"You told them the facts of what happened, but have you actually talked *about* it? Have you shared with them your thoughts, your emotions—both from when you were going through it and now that you're a few months removed from it and have the benefit of hindsight?"

Talk to his brothers about his emotions? He was an artist, not a girl. "No, I haven't told them anything like that."

"You don't need to do it all at once, but you need to find someone with whom you can be open and honest about everything—past, present, and future."

An image of Caylor danced before his mind's eye, her eyes slightly squinted, head cocked a little to the right as they talked over sandwiches the last time he'd seen her. Well, he had caught a couple of glimpses at her running in and out of rehearsals for *Much Ado*, but she'd appeared far too busy and harried to stop and talk, even just to say hi.

"Do you have someone in mind?"

"My brother who lives in town." Because if he couldn't talk to Pax, how was he ever going to be able to talk to Caylor. . .or Gramps and Perty?

Ken made some notes on his legal pad. "Do you think before our next session you can set up a meeting with your brother—coffee or a meal—at which you can begin sharing with him? You don't have to tell him everything all at once; start small then build on that. Once again, make a list before you talk to him. Will you make that commitment?"

"Yeah. . .yes, I can do that." Dylan wrote it down so he wouldn't forget. *Coffee or dinner with Pax to talk about emotions.* Wouldn't Pax just love that?

"How did your job interview at JRU go last week?" Ken smiled at him, as if giving him a reward for being a good boy by agreeing to rip his insides out and show them to his younger brother.

"I feel like all of the elements of it went well. The panel seemed to like my teaching presentation, and they didn't ask me anything I couldn't easily answer. I'm supposed to be hearing something soon." After only three weeks of teaching part-time at Robertson, Dylan thought the invitation to interview for a full-time assistant professorship seemed like the hand of God coming down from the sky and telling him he was right where he was supposed to be.

Ken made more notes. "Now. . .let's talk about your parents."

Dylan fell face-first onto the secondhand sofa in his living room as soon as he walked in the door. The sessions with Ken left him as wrung out as if he'd run the New York City Marathon—without the benefit of warming up first.

A state of hazy relaxation settled over him—but vanished when his phone started ringing. His bag was too far away to reach, so he had to push himself up off the couch to reach it before the call rolled to voice mail.

"Pax?"

"Hey, D. I know it's short notice, but some of the guys at church decided to go out tonight. Want to go with us?"

"Go out to do what?"

"I'm not sure. But we're definitely going to Manny's House of Pizza downtown for supper first. From there. . .who knows? We find we have more fun most of the time if we just wing it instead of planning it all out ahead of time."

While he preferred having a plan, what else was there to do tonight if he didn't go? Sit in front of the TV and flip through the channels and complain that there was never anything worth watching on a Friday night? "Sure. What time?"

"Six. Dress comfortably. We could be doing anything—walking around downtown to listen to music or going bowling or going to a movie."

"I'll meet you there, then."

Comfortable for Dylan included paint-splattered jeans and T-shirt and no shoes. Instead, he dressed warmly, wearing the soft blue sweater Perty had given him for Christmas, along with nice jeans and his brown, rugged-looking boots he would never consider wearing anywhere the leather might get damaged—they'd cost way too much for that.

The group consisted of six guys other than Dylan and Pax. They were all younger than him, but Dylan did have a good time. He hadn't been bowling in at least five years, and though rusty at first, it came back to him pretty quickly—and Pax and his friends were stiff competition, pushing him to concentrate on his form so that his scores improved each round.

Walking out to their cars after saying good-bye to everyone else, Dylan seized the opportunity. "Hey, Pax, want to come over for a little while? We haven't really had the chance to sit and talk—just the two of us—since I got back."

Pax shrugged his thin shoulders. "Sure. You got any junk food at your place?"

"Only if condiments count—I haven't been to the grocery store this week. Funds are starting to run a little low." Yet one more reason why he hoped—and maybe prayed, just a little—that Robertson offered him the full-time position.

"Why don't I stop at the grocery store on the way? I'd suggest we go over to my place, but my three housemates invited a bunch of guys over for a video game tournament. Plus, I need somewhere to store my stash of junk food. It gets eaten both at home and at the lab no matter where I try to hide it."

Dylan opened the front door of his SUV and hooked his arm over the top of it. "Gets eaten. . .by you?"

Pax grinned. "Guilty. Besides, if it's stored at your place, I'll have more reason to come over and hang out with my big bro. You go on over and make sure it's presentable, and I'll be there in a little bit with grub."

"See you in a little bit, then." Dylan headed back to Gramps and Perty's place. He stuck his head in the living room at the main house to say good night and let them know Pax was coming over. He also told them about Bridget's recommendation he visit Providence Chapel Sunday. Though an odd look flashed in Perty's eyes at the mention of it, both she and Gramps claimed not to know much about the church.

Suspicious, but not assertive enough to push the matter—he knew *assertive* was the correct term, because that's what Ken had told him was part of his problem, he wasn't *assertive enough* in his communication— Dylan said his good nights and walked back to the carriage house.

In the downstairs workroom, he flipped the light on so Pax wouldn't hurt himself going up the steep stairs. The large canvas on his easel caught his eye. He crossed to it and turned on the floor lamp beside it. The scene he'd started sketching on the white background went from tentative pencil lines to a full-color image in his mind. Of course, the image in his mind included a figure of a man looking upon the woman, the central focus of the painting, with admiration and longing—the way he imagined he looked when he watched Caylor when certain no one else was observing him.

But as Ken had warned—and as his own mind tried to tell him—it was too soon to be thinking about another romantic relationship. He needed time to work through everything that had happened in the last few years, to figure out who he really was instead of who Rhonda had made him. He needed to stand on his own again. He needed—

"Hey, are we hanging or are you painting tonight?" Pax's voice startled Dylan out of his thoughts.

"We're hanging." He snapped off the lamp and followed his brother up the stairs.

One step at a time. Ken's constant refrain echoed with the rhythm of Dylan's feet on the stairs. Step one was talking to Pax about what happened with Rhonda. He wasn't quite sure exactly how many steps he'd need to take between tonight and when he might be ready to express his feelings to Caylor. But he had a feeling it was a pretty high number—one he wasn't certain he'd ever attain. He only hoped she'd still be around—and available—by then.

Chapter 20

◈

$\mathcal{O}$f course, one of the problems with having the art show and auction in Hillsboro Village would be parking. Dylan circled the block of buildings again, hoping someone would have pulled out by the time he got back around to the small lots between the buildings and the alley that ran parallel to Twenty-First Avenue.

With all of the cars displaying flags and banners for Vanderbilt and the University of South Carolina, he realized he should have checked Vandy's basketball schedule before agreeing to the first weekend in February to meet with Mother, her publicist, and the event planner at the location chosen for the showing. If he'd known about the game, he'd have suggested a weeknight or even later in the day.

Oh, finally, a parking space. He whipped into the narrow slot as soon as the other car cleared it, lest someone else beat him to it. He had to squeeze out the door, because the cars on either side were on or over the line, but at least he'd found a spot.

He popped the tailgate and pulled out his portfolio. Supposedly, this Emerson guy, the event planner, had some background in art, so Mother had wanted him to go through the pieces before the final decision was made on what would be shown.

After almost entering a coffee shop's kitchen, Dylan managed to find the correct rear entrance for the vacant building owned by one of the Bradley law firm's clients.

"Hello?" He entered what looked like it had originally been a combination storage area and break room.

Clipboard Lady—Mother's publicist—flung open the door. "Finally. We don't have all day, you know."

Dylan didn't even bother forcing a smile. There was just no pleasing some people. She turned on her heel and marched back into the front room of the building.

The space looked like it had been a clothing store in its previous life—with some of the racks and hardware for displaying clothing still hanging on the walls. A glass display case ran down the center of the wooden floor. Dylan set the portfolio down on it.

"We can put the bar here, on the cashier's desk"—Mother's voice echoed through the empty space—"and set up the auctioneer's stand here."

"I thought we were doing a silent auction," another female voice responded.

He turned and found himself looking upon an ethereal beauty— small, blond, pale—in an expensive-looking business suit with shoes that could have doubled as weapons, between the thick soles in the front and the death-defyingly high, thin heels.

Panic prickled his skin.

"Oh good, Dylan, you're here." Mother came over and made him lean down so she could press her cheek against his and make a kissing sound. "You brought your pictures with you?"

He motioned toward the portfolio with his head.

"Good. The art appraiser should be here momentarily."

The young blond woman stepped forward, hand extended. "I'm Emerson Bernard, the event planner. You can call me Ems."

Dylan wiped his palm down the leg of his jeans before shaking hands with her. *This* was Emerson? The *guy* he was supposed to be working with to set up this show? He wracked his brain, trying to remember if his mother had ever mentioned that Emerson was a woman.

Emerson zipped open the large leather binder and started flipping through the color printouts of his pieces. She dug a pad of sticky notes out of a briefcase on the display cabinet and started marking pages. After she went through the inventory, she flipped back to one of the images she'd marked, leaving the portfolio open there. "These are fantastic. We'll have a nice big check to donate to charity."

Dylan caught the left corner of his mouth between his teeth.

The banging of the front door as it closed behind someone saved him from having to respond to the siren.

"Ah good. Ricardo's here." Mother gave the tall, balding man an air kiss and ushered him over to Dylan's portfolio.

Like the good boy he'd been trained to be—by Rhonda—Dylan stepped aside and allowed his mother, the publicist, and Emerson to discuss his art with the appraiser as if he weren't in the room.

Instead, he pulled the strap of his messenger bag over his head, set it on what had once been the cashier's station, and pulled out his tape measure and pad of graph paper to start measuring the space.

"Here, let me help you with that."

Dylan nearly jumped out of his skin when Emerson's soft fingertips brushed his hand. She took the end of the tape and walked down to the other end of the wall with it, heels making a strangely hollow tapping sound on the floor that echoed over the hushed voices of Mother and her publicist and appraiser, still huddled over the portfolio.

Shaking himself, he pressed the metal casing against the wall and wrote down the measurement—22' 8'—at the top of the page. Without a word from him, Emerson moved to the next wall and the next, enabling him to get an accurate measure of the space in half the amount of time it would have taken him on his own.

But then she sidled up beside him when he set the graph pad down on the cashier stand to draw a rough sketch of the space.

"You seem to be an old pro at doing this." She leaned back against the high counter, crossing her arms and looking over her shoulder at his handiwork.

"I—I've done it a few times." His voice came out hoarse, wobbly. He cleared his throat.

"We have access to several portable panels so that we can display more artwork in the middle of the room. The owner is going to get the display case out of here on Wednesday, so we'll have full use of the space—unless you have some three-dimensional artwork you'd like displayed under glass."

He shook his head. She smelled like flowers—with a splash of musk. Not overpowering, nor unpleasant, but noticeable. Caylor, on the other hand, sometimes smelled like apples, sometimes like coconut, and on the night of Robertson's faculty party, she'd smelled like warm, spicy gingerbread. He much preferred fruity and spicy aromas to an imitation of flowers.

"I understand you just moved back here from Philadelphia." Emerson turned and leaned the side of her arm against the counter, facing him. "Are you enjoying being home?"

He kept sketching. "Yes."

"And you're teaching at James Robertson?"

"Yes." He turned the pad and drew in the long, uninterrupted wall, counting the number of squares on the grid to make sure he drew it the correct length.

"What kinds of things do you like to do in your spare time—other than art, obviously?"

From the corner of his eye, he could see Emerson's perfect, overly white smile. "I like watching hockey and basketball."

"What about baseball? My dad has season tickets to Vanderbilt's games. If you'd like to go sometime, I can try to finagle them from him." She tucked her thick, wavy hair behind her ear with her fine-boned fingers.

"Not really a big baseball fan. Do you know the size of the panels you have access to?"

Emerson let out a tiny sigh. "They're three feet wide, six feet tall. Fabric covered."

Dylan turned and let his eyes rove over the open room, imagining how best to feed traffic through. He sketched in the freestanding panels—just two, one on each wall, offset from each other near the front of the room so that it wouldn't be too crowded back here near the bar and auctioneer's stand—then took the graph pad over to the art appraiser.

Over the next couple of hours, the appraiser, Mother, Emerson, and the publicist dickered back and forth about which pieces to display, how to frame them, and where they should be hung. Dylan gave little input—this was their baby; he was merely the vendor.

"What do you think, Dylan?"

At Emerson's question, Dylan had to force himself out of the landscape of the new project and back into reality. "I'm sorry?"

"What do you think about grouping the paintings this way? You're the artist; you should have the final approval on how the pieces are displayed." Emerson raised pale brows and waited for him to answer.

"Um. . ." Perspiration tickled his upper lip. After years of Rhonda's talking over him or completely ignoring his ideas, he'd stopped developing opinions on how to do anything other than the grunt work of setting up his own exhibitions. She'd always determined which pieces to display and where to hang them.

"This is our highest-ticket painting." Mother flipped the portfolio open to one of Dylan's least-favorite pieces. "It should be hung prominently in the front so people see it when they come in."

"No." Dylan's heart leaped into his throat as if he'd just slipped off the edge of a cliff. He took a shaky breath and tried to keep his body—and voice—from trembling over this monumental step forward in his emotional healing. "The most desirable pieces should be placed in the back—that way people have to walk past, and look at, everything else on their way back to it. Feature it on the cover or just inside the front of the auction catalog. That's what will drive interest."

His mother pressed her hands to his cheeks, and he stiffened. "That's my brilliant boy." She ended the contact—he wondered if it felt as strange to her as it did to him—and turned to the event planner. "Ems, make sure to tell the graphic designer that."

"Yes ma'am." Emerson wrote the note with a stylus on her pad-style computer. "Dylan, I'll need you to e-mail high-quality digital photos of each piece, along with all of the specifications—such as size, media, title—to the graphic designer"—she handed him a business card—"so she can get the catalog completed by the end of the week. I don't think I need to point out what a quick turnaround we're on here."

He tucked the card into his shirt pocket. Emerson double-checked the list of paintings to be displayed and the estimated sales price with the appraiser, then handed the several sheets of legal pad paper to Dylan. He stuck it in the front of the portfolio and zipped it closed.

Before he could leave, though, the publicist, who'd stepped into the back room to take a phone call, returned. "Great news. Mr. and Mrs. Adams have five extra tickets to the hockey game Tuesday night and would like to offer them to your family, Grace."

"That's lovely. So that would be me, Davis, Pax, Dylan, and. . ." Mother put her arm around Emerson's tiny waist. "Ems, would you like to go to the hockey game with us? You've done so much, and I'd love you to come and meet the rest of the family."

Emerson beamed a high-wattage smile. "I'd love to, Mrs. Bradley."

A moment of excitement over the prospect of attending a live hockey game crashed down when Dylan processed the information that the game was on Tuesday night. "You'll need to find another guest, Mother. I have a standing commitment on Tuesday evenings."

All pretense and true traces of pleasure vanished from his mother's face. "What could you possibly have to do that's more important than face time with one of my most important financial supporters?"

Dylan took his mother by the elbow. "Excuse us for a moment, please."

He escorted her to the storage room in the back, feeling her grow stiffer and angrier by the second. "Mother, I'm teaching a class on Tuesday nights."

She yanked her elbow out of his grasp. "You told me your adjunct classes are on Mondays and Wednesdays during the daytime."

The frown on his mother's face transported him back to being seven years old again, standing in front of her, waiting to receive his punishment for the mural he'd drawn on the basement wall. In permanent ink. "The ones I'm teaching at the school are. But I'm also teaching a painting class at Acklen Avenue for the senior adult group."

"Cancel it." Mother headed toward the door, as if all were settled.

Dylan's breath caught in his throat. No wonder he'd allowed Rhonda to walk all over him the last few years. His mother had trained him for it quite well. He tried to catch a deep breath in the thinning air. "No."

She stopped with her hand on the doorknob. "What did you say?"

"No. I won't cancel the class. I've made a commitment, and I intend to follow through on it." No matter how much he'd really rather go to the hockey game.

Mother stalked back over to him. "You *will* cancel, and you *will* attend the game."

Assertive. Be assertive. "Mother, it's a hockey game. And while I understand that you don't think my commitment to teaching Perty and her friends how to paint is important, it is—because it's important to them, and it's important to me. I'm an artist. I'm a teacher. And I know you've never been happy with those choices. But this is who I am. I know I'm not the son you've always wished I would be, but I'm the son God gave you; and I hope you can find it in your heart some day to accept me and love me the way I am. Because I love you."

He squeezed her shoulders; then, taking a tiny bit of pleasure in her stunned silence, he left her in the storage room and returned to the front to retrieve his portfolio.

Rather than risk another run-in with Mother, he exited the front of the store and walked around the block to his car. But it wasn't until he got home, pulling the small SUV up under the old hickory tree beside the carriage house, that he allowed himself to process what had just happened.

He'd confronted his mother. He'd resisted her commands the way he'd imagined doing with Rhonda so many times. He'd been assertive, and he'd finally shared his heart with his mother, finally stood up for himself and the life he'd chosen—the life God had called him to.

Inside the workroom, he set the portfolio down on the table at the end and then went and stood in front of his easel, letting his gaze—and his imagination—roam over the pencil lines, letting the image take shape in his head.

Several minutes later, he picked up the pencil and started sketching—no hesitation, no doubt. The image of the man looking upon the central figure of the woman, who just happened to look like Caylor Evans, needed to be there.

Because if he wanted Mother to take him seriously as an artist and accept him for who he was, he needed to be true to his calling and be the artist God was calling him to be. Not one who worried about what others might think, but one who stayed true to the vision God gave him.

Even if that meant revealing his secret past by putting his own face on canvas again.

Chapter 21

∞

$\mathcal{C}$aylor's heart sped as the choir's call to worship came to a rousing end. Though she'd sung special music dozens, if not hundreds, of times over her lifetime in this church, the nervous flutterings in the pit of her stomach never failed to start just before she rose to sing.

During the pastor's welcoming remarks to members and guests, Caylor slipped out of the back row of the choir loft, exited, and entered the sanctuary through a side door near the stage. She bowed with everyone else for the prayer—though the first line of the song ran through her head over and over—stepped up onto the platform, placed the sheet with the words of the song on the podium, stepped to the side of it, and nodded to the pianist.

And then she looked up.

Dylan Bradley stood just inside the back doors on the left side of the sanctuary, glancing around as if to find a place to sit.

An immense buzzing filled her ears, and all coherent thought fled her mind. She could do no more than stare as he made his way around to the far side and quickly seated himself at the end of a pew—a spot that usually stayed empty due to its partially blocked view of the front of the church. But she could still see him clearly past the pillar that stood between them.

A loud chord on the piano caught her attention. Certain her face glowed incandescent with embarrassment, Caylor looked down at the piece of paper on the podium, finding there words that seemed at

213

once familiar and strange.

The pianist seamlessly repeated the introduction, and Caylor pulled herself together and opened her mouth to start singing. After the first verse, the meaning of the words pulled her back into a spirit of worship, and she almost forgot the tall, handsome man sitting toward the back of the room.

To a murmur of soft amens from the congregation, Caylor forced herself to walk—not run—down the steps to the door. Once in the hallway, she leaned against the wall, hand pressed to her chest over her pounding heart.

She hadn't seen Dylan in weeks—at least not at less than a distance across campus. But avoiding him had backfired; she'd thought about him more, letting him derail her thoughts frequently since they'd last spoken. And trying to channel those thoughts into writing Isabella and Giovanni's story only made matters worse. Every time she wrote a scene, she could clearly picture Dylan as Giovanni—just as clearly as she had pictured him as the hero of every previous book she'd written.

Hoping her longer-than-usual absence wouldn't be noted, she sneaked back into her place in the choir loft during the offertory hymn.

When the choir stood to sing the anthem just before the sermon, Caylor resisted the urge to look past the choir director's right shoulder toward the back of the sanctuary. She wouldn't have to adjust her gaze much—wouldn't even have to change the angle of her head. But she put all of her discipline into practice and kept her focus on the waving hands of the director, even though he was two beats behind the organ and piano.

The pastor's sermon on Jesus' parable of the hidden treasure and the pearl of great price, one of Caylor's favorite passages from scripture, managed to occupy and challenge her mind—most of it—for the remainder of the worship time.

Church ended. Caylor escaped to the safety of the choir room.

But why? Why didn't she want to see him?

Um, it could have something to do with the fact she'd been having romantic—clean, wholesome, but romantic nonetheless—fantasies about him. And the fear that he might be able to see it in her eyes if they came within a few feet of each other. And the fear that she might actually follow through on Zarah and Flannery's advice and ask him about the book covers.

"Caylor, dear." Mrs. Morton's sing-song voice cut through the low chatter of the other choir members hanging their robes and retrieving personal items and making lunch plans.

She summoned up a smile, preparing for the inevitable conversation— the same conversation they had every week. "Good morning, Mrs. . . ."

No. This couldn't be happening.

Beside the elderly woman stood Dylan, looking as uncomfortable as Caylor suddenly felt.

"I wanted to introduce you to this nice young man who's visiting with us this morning." Mrs. Morton propelled Dylan forward with her famous iron grip. Caylor's arm twinged in sympathy.

"Actually, Mrs. Morton, Dylan and I already know each other." But just to get her to release Dylan's arm, Caylor extended her right hand. She forced herself to drag her gaze to his. "It's good to see you."

The silver rings he wore on his thumb and middle finger created a hard contrast to the soft strength of his hand. "It's good to see you, too."

She wouldn't have been surprised to see blue bolts of electricity arcing between their hands as they pulled away from each other. "What brings you to Providence Chapel?"

"Dr. Wetzler suggested it when I mentioned to her I hadn't found any of the larger churches in town to be a good fit for me." Dylan moved his arms behind his back and rocked from heel to toe.

"Well, Providence Chapel is a wonderful place to worship. We have many activities for young people, a wonderful music program, and the pastor has a good wind in the pulpit." Mrs. Morton's husband had owned a car dealership for more than fifty years, and many people credited her sales skills with its early and continued success. "I'm certain Caylor would be more than happy to give you a tour of the building and tell you all about it."

Caylor almost asked her if she'd been talking to Sassy but settled for acknowledging her knowing wink with a benign smile.

"I've got to be off, but you two stay and talk awhile." The doyenne of the senior adult group bustled off—no doubt to tell the others she'd just accomplished matchmaking success.

"I would be pleased to show you around the church," Caylor swung her purse strap up on her shoulder, "but I've got to run myself. If I'm late to Sassy's birthday lunch, she'll never let me forget it."

"Lunch at Giovanni's, right?"

Just hearing the restaurant name in Dylan's mellow, rich voice was enough to send Caylor into a swoon. But she held herself together. "Right, up on Twentieth Avenue, between Grand and Division."

"I'm heading that direction myself." He rocked back and forth again. "Um. . .since we'd both have to drive right back past the church, and I know parking in that area of midtown is scarce, why don't you just ride with me?"

She would ride with him anywhere. . . . No, wait, that was a reaction one of the silly heroines of one of her silly romance novels would have. He wasn't Giovanni Vendelino, and she wasn't Isabella Foscari. No matter how much she wanted them to be.

But the expression of innocent supplication on his handsome face proved to be her undoing. "That sounds like a good idea. Let me drop the rest of my stuff in my car so I don't have to tote it around with me."

He walked with her to the exit—drawing speculative looks from the few people still lingering in the foyer behind the sanctuary. Great. She'd be trying to stamp out rumors for weeks—months—to come.

Just before they got to the door, she indulged herself—she drew in a deep breath through her nose, tingling all over at the light, spicy scent of Dylan's cologne. She wouldn't mind smelling that every day. All day.

Stop. She had to stop doing this to herself.

"I'm parked over there." Dylan pointed to the back corner of the lot.

"I'm right here under the tree." She motioned toward the white SUV parked in the farthest aisle but only a few spaces back.

"I'll swing around and pick you up." He grinned at her and then took off across the lot in a long, loping stride.

Once again, Caylor reveled in allowing herself to appreciate his lean form, his broad shoulders—but not as broad as on the covers of the Mason books. A cold shiver shook her out of her unproductive admiration, and she hurried over to put her music and Bible on the passenger seat of her Escape.

Man, she'd missed talking to him and spending time with him. She paused, hand resting atop the supple leather cover of her Bible.

Could it be that she was truly falling for Dylan, the man, and not just for his handsome face?

No, that couldn't happen. She'd committed herself to living with and taking care of Sassy. A relationship—especially the kind of lifelong relationship she was starting to allow herself to imagine with Dylan Bradley—was out of the question.

∞

Cherry pie.

Dylan couldn't get the smell out of his nose or the smile off his face. Unless his senses deceived him, Caylor smelled like cherry pie today. Yes, he definitely preferred the down-to-earth, homey fragrances Caylor wore to the fancy stuff Emerson Bernard favored.

He pulled into the spot next to her SUV, but before he could get out and open the door for her, she climbed in.

"Thanks for offering to drive. I hate trying to find parking in midtown." She fastened her seat belt.

Dylan took in another slow, appreciative breath. "No problem. Parking here will never be as bad as in Philly." He backed out and headed north toward central Nashville.

"I figured Philadelphia was one of those cities where people didn't even bother with cars, since there's good public transportation." Caylor crossed her long legs, her knee almost touching the dashboard, though he knew the seat was as far back as it would go, due to Pax riding around with him occasionally.

"A lot of people depend solely on the transit system, but I guess I'm too much of a small-town boy—the thought of giving up the independence of my own vehicle almost made me sick."

Her elbow, resting lightly on the padded top of the center console, was mere inches from his. He only had to shift, just a little, and they'd be touching.

"I thought it would drive me crazy to be dependent on public transportation—buses, undergrounds, taxis—when I was in the UK

217

and Ireland, but it was amazing how fast I got used to it. I actually miss it sometimes, not having the maintenance headaches or stopping for gas in the middle of a thunderstorm or driving in rush-hour traffic. Though having to ride a bus with a bunch of drunken soccer fans through Dublin after a semifinal game for the World Cup—I was wishing for a car that night."

Dylan chuckled and pulled to a stop at a red light. "You were probably safer on the bus than you would have been driving with all of the other drunk fans out on the road." He glanced at her. "So, are you a soccer fan?"

"I tried to become one when I lived there, but it didn't take. I was a big baseball fan when I was at Vanderbilt. . . ." Her face reddened, and she turned to look out her window. After a brief moment, she turned back to look at him. "But I don't really enjoy it much anymore."

He could easily guess she'd been a baseball fan because she'd been dating a baseball player. But exes were apparently still off the table for casual conversation. Good.

"Since I started teaching at Robertson, though, I've become a big basketball fan. Our team always does well in our little conference, and because I've always had a few of the players in one class or another, it makes it more fun. I just don't get to go as often as I'd like—especially when we're ramping up for a drama production I'm involved in."

"I wondered why I hadn't seen you at any of the games. You're right. They're very good players." There was so much other than sports he wanted to talk to her about. He wanted to fast-track everything—get through all of his therapy stuff, get to a place where he felt comfortable talking to everyone about everything—and move on with making Caylor fall as much in love with him as he was falling in love with her.

"The final set pieces look fantastic. I know the kids are grateful for your guidance and help."

"I'm looking forward to seeing the production. It's hard to believe something of this scale can be pulled together in just six weeks." The residential area began to transition to a more commercial district as Granny White Pike turned into Twelfth Avenue South. The area had changed so much over the last few years. In addition to all of the new casual restaurants, coffee shops, and stores, it was geographically central to almost everything in Nashville. And only about five or ten minutes from Robertson—at least the part where Zarah Mitchell lived.

"Don't let the production date fool you—Bridget and her students started working on this production last semester. The drama department is always working on at least three productions at once—the one that's about to be on stage and the next two coming down the pipeline. The main roles were cast and began table-reads when they were still in rehearsals for the holiday variety show last fall. They split it up between the different professors as to who's in charge of which production. Bridget usually does the spring musical. But since one of the other professors chose *The Music Man* for his production last fall, she had to go with Shakespeare."

"Sounds like a lot of work." Dylan designated more of his attention to navigating through the numbered and occasionally one-way streets as Caylor talked more about the drama department's process.

He found an on-street parking space less than a block from the restaurant. This time he hopped out of the car and got around to the passenger door just as she turned to get out.

At first, she looked surprised, but then she smiled. "Thanks."

"Of course." He resisted the urge to put his arm around her and settle his hand possessively on the small of her back as they crossed the street.

"I heard a full-time position came open in your department," Caylor said, transitioning the conversation. "Are you going to apply?"

"I've already interviewed for it." He took the five steps at the entrance in two bounds and opened the door for her.

"I hope you get it. You'll be such an asset to the school."

So this was what it was like to have a woman see value in him—and not because it would be of any benefit or advantage to herself.

The hostess led them back to where a large table was already mostly filled with their families and a few other older couples—friends of Perty and Sassy Evans's. He didn't even care that Mother and Dad were here.

Pax stood and greeted Caylor with a handshake. Caylor's sister, Sage, sat next to his brother, but neither seemed pleased by the arrangement. Dylan, though, was more than pleased to see that there were only two chairs left, and they were side by side across from their siblings.

Caylor set her purse on the chair beside one of the older men and went to where her grandmother sat in the middle of the table. "Happy birthday, Sassy. Sorry I had to leave the house so early this morning that I didn't get to say it to you then."

Mrs. Evans kissed Caylor's cheeks. "I knew I'd get to see you eventually, so I wasn't too fussed about it."

Dylan waved from his position by their chairs. "Happy birthday, Mrs. Evans."

"Thank you for coming, Dylan—and you have my permission to call me Sassy." She grinned at him—and it was almost an exact replica of Caylor's endearingly crooked smile.

Caylor returned to her seat—which Dylan held for her and waited until she was situated before sitting down himself and opening his menu.

He almost choked at the prices, knowing Gramps intended to pick up the bill for everyone.

"Good night—I'd forgotten how expensive this place is," Caylor whispered. "That ravioli better be filled with diamonds and pearls for that price."

Dylan stifled his laugh behind his menu and leaned a little closer. "And the pizza covered in rubies and opals?"

Caylor's arm pressed against his. "Something like that. Oh. . ." The last syllable came out in an awed tone. "I just saw what I want. I totally shouldn't eat it, but when am I ever going to see that again? Coffee-flavored french toast made with brioche and topped with blueberries and dark chocolate shavings."

Dylan's mouth started watering, and he set his menu down. "Sign me up for that."

Across the table from them, Pax and Sage looked desperate for someone, anyone to come to their rescue and engage them in conversation. Dylan didn't feel like obliging. He had Caylor's attention, and he was going to keep it as long as he could without being rude—to anyone but Pax or Sage.

"Did I tell you I talked to Jack Colby this week about creating some sample cover artwork for Lindsley House?" Oops. . .maybe bringing up his cover design work wasn't the most intelligent thing to do.

Caylor straightened, her expression hardening a bit. "No. That's exciting. What kinds of books does he want you working on?"

"Some nonfiction right now—so some general landscape and iconographic work for books that don't lend themselves to photographs. Your. . .your books all use photos, don't they?" He'd only seen one of her books—on the table beside Perty's chair in the sunroom—and though well designed, to him it had been apparent the publisher had used stock photography.

"Yes, my inspirational romances use photographs."

The way she said it made him wonder why she'd emphasized the fact she wrote inspirational romances. Was she embarrassed—used to people assuming that because she wrote romances they were the steamy kind?

Like the kind his face and artwork appeared on.

"Is that the kind of cover work you did before? Nonfiction? Landscapes and graphics?" Caylor unfolded her napkin and draped it across her lap.

"Um. . .no. I've done some fiction covers as well. But it seems most publishers have gone to photographs for all fiction. It's hard to get freelance gigs as a painter these days."

As if in answer to the prayer for intervention crying from his heart, the waitress arrived to begin taking orders. Dylan was able to calm his mind, center himself, and really think about the current topic of conversation.

He should tell her.

At lunch? In front of family—and nonfamily?

It guaranteed she wouldn't have an explosive reaction—Caylor was a consummate actress, or so he'd heard; she'd know how to cover her shock and outrage over learning something so horrible about him.

But if he told her, others would find out.

He looked down the table at his parents at the other end. No more screwups. Nothing that might cause a scandal for his mother's campaign.

Caylor could be trusted to keep the secret. He needed her to know. Because if he couldn't tell her about the covers, how was he ever going to tell her about Rhonda?

Not here. Not where others might overhear them.

He engaged Sage in conversation about her classes at the community college, and Caylor gave Pax the only encouragement he needed by asking what he was up to these days.

Though it had been presented beautifully and he ate everything on the plate, by the time lunch was over, Dylan couldn't remember what it tasted like. But Caylor raved about it, so it must have been good.

Sage offered to take Caylor back to get her car in the little red convertible that had belonged to their grandparents.

Before she could answer, Caylor was interrupted by one of the older ladies, Lindy Patterson, who kissed her on the cheek and whispered something in her ear. Their grandmothers' friend walked away, and Dylan caught Caylor's elbow.

"Before you go—I. . .I need to talk to you about something." His heart played leapfrog with his stomach when Caylor turned to look at him, curiosity in her turquoise eyes.

"All right." She told her sister to wait for her then followed him down the sidewalk away from the valet stand so they could have some privacy.

Turning to face her, he instantly regretted this decision.

After a few moments, she broke the uncomfortable silence. "So what is it you wanted to talk about?"

"I wanted to tell you something about me. Something that may change the way you feel. . .the way you think about me." He kept his eyes down, watching the toe of his shoe as he traced a crack in the sidewalk.

"I doubt that."

Oh, she wouldn't even hear the half of it today, and he had a feeling once he was done she wasn't going to want to have anything to do with him.

Assertive and straightforward. That was all he had to do. Be assertive and straightforward.

"I started freelancing book covers when I was in college to make extra money. I did a few small projects, and then I was given a chance to do some artwork on spec for a new, up-and-coming novelist. I submitted my pieces and waited. A few weeks later, I learned that not only had my work been chosen, but the author and her editor requested that I do the art for all of her books."

He wiped his hands down his chinos. "Because I was a broke college student, I couldn't afford to pay models for the covers I'd been contracted to create. So I used catalog models for the girls. . .and myself for the guys. You see—I'd been hired to paint the covers of romance novels. Not the kind you write. The other kind. So my image is on the cover of half a dozen novels I'd be embarrassed for my grandmother to read."

The sound of his parents' car driving past filled the gap between them.

Caylor paused for a moment. "Your grandmother has read them."

He looked up so fast his neck cricked. "What are you talking about? My grandmother would never read those kinds of books."

She couldn't turn any redder if she'd tried, and something—fear? embarrassment?—filled her eyes. "I know your grandmother has read them. I gave them to her."

Even though the books were sensual without falling off the edge into dirty, he still couldn't imagine Perty reading anything like them. "Why would you do that?"

"Because I wrote them. Dylan. . .I'm Melanie Mason."

"Right." But how would she know the name unless. . . "You're serious?"

He took a step back. Not Caylor—sweet, innocent, *Christian* Caylor. Someone like her shouldn't even know about books like that— or be thinking about the things in those books.

"I am serious. I wrote six general-market romance novels under the penname Melanie Mason. I handpicked the artist Patrick Callaghan for the cover work. And. . ." Caylor's voice choked, and she worked at clearing her throat, her eyes downcast. "And I picked the artist Patrick Callaghan because. . .because the male model he used was good-looking and he. . .inspired me to keep writing more books."

Dylan wasn't sure if he should take the compliment or if he should press his hands over his ears.

"Caylor—come on!" Sage called from across the street.

Caylor backed away from him. "I probably shouldn't have told you that. I. . .um. . ." She pressed her lips together. "We'll talk later?"

"Yeah. Later." Dylan raised his hand in a weak wave as she jogged across the street, her high-heeled shoes making a strange clattering sound against the pavement. She climbed into the backseat of the classic, two-door convertible and shoved on a pair of large sunglasses.

Though he could no longer see her eyes, her face left him in no doubt over her displeasure with discovering his alter ego. If she couldn't handle the revelation of his pseudonym, how could he ever tell her about Rhonda?

He trudged toward his car, got in, and stuck the key in the ignition. But he didn't start it, wanting to give the Evanses a good head start on him.

Caylor had written titillating romance novels. And he'd enjoyed reading them. Maybe he was once again assigning meaning that wasn't there by believing her negative reaction was to learning he was Patrick Callaghan. Maybe she was embarrassed about having written the books.

The corners of his mouth started to pull up, almost against his will. She'd found the somewhat disguised likenesses of him *inspiring*. Could that mean. . . ?

He started the engine and headed toward Gramps and Perty's.

No matter what either of them had done in the past, in the present, he and Caylor were attracted to each other. And if he was going to win the heart of a romance novelist, he had some research to do—and he knew just where to start.

Chapter 22

Sassy hurried around the end of the aisle to catch up with Perty. She didn't really need to go through all of the organic spices again just to see if anything new had come in since last week.

"Did you enjoy your birthday luncheon yesterday?" Perty raised her reading glasses to peer through them at the label on a canister of oatmeal.

"It was the best one ever." Sassy's heart warmed with the memory of seeing Caylor and Dylan walk in together, sit together, and then stand on the sidewalk talking for several minutes before going home.

"Did Caylor tell you what they talked about afterward?" Perty dropped the glasses, letting them hang from their jeweled chain. "Dylan was in a strange mood yesterday afternoon—asked me if he could borrow all of Caylor's books."

"No—Caylor kept to herself on the ride home. To tell the truth, she seemed a bit upset—but I figured that was because she's leaving to go out of town this week and maybe she'd had to turn down an invitation from him or something." Sassy hoped they'd been discussing a date or get-together, since many young folks today apparently didn't "date" anymore, but just "hung out" until they decided to get married.

"I'm worried about Dylan." Perty slid her glasses back on and compared two boxes of cereal bars side by side.

Sassy threw a couple of boxes of frosted cherry and chocolate toaster pastries in her basket. Sage seemed happy to eat them any time of day—but thankfully she liked the store brand just fine. "What has you concerned?"

"Well. . ." Perty placed one of the boxes back on the shelf and put the other in her cart before moving on down the aisle to the cold cereals. "He's been in therapy for almost two months now, and I can see that he's making great strides in dealing with some. . .issues and problems in his life. But it's also meant that he's been opening up to us more about the relationship he had that ended and led to his moving home."

Perty left her basket and came around Sassy's to stand close to her, lowering her voice. "I love Caylor. You know I'd like nothing more than to see a marriage connection between our families. But I don't know if Dylan is emotionally ready, if he's taken adequate time to heal from this broken relationship. I'm afraid he's—oh, what do they call it—bouncing?"

"On the rebound?" Sassy tapped her fingernails against the handle of the cart. How could Perty even begin to compare Dylan's relationship with Caylor to the one he'd had before he moved back home?

"Yes—that's it. I'm concerned that if he jumps immediately into another relationship that he's never going to truly grow and develop into the man he's supposed to be." Perty rested her hand on Sassy's arm. "This isn't coming out the way I want it to. I think Dylan and Caylor would be great—perfect—together. I just think they need to take it much slower—wait until Dylan has had time to adjust to his new life, has had time to explore his renewed relationship with God. Because"—and Perty's smile beamed—"he has made an almost miraculous turnaround when it comes to his attitude toward church and toward God."

"That's good to hear." Sassy wasn't sure how to respond. She could understand that, only a few months out of a bad relationship, Dylan might still have some issues to work through, but Caylor could help him do that.

They finished their shopping and hurried to get Sassy home and her groceries unloaded from Perty's car before the threatening rain started. Sure enough, the first few drops splattered on Perty's windshield as she backed out of the driveway.

Sassy stood for a brief moment in the new breakfast room and breathed in the new-room smell, then returned to the kitchen to put the food away.

A little before four o'clock, Sage hurried into the kitchen, hair, coat, and jeans pretty well drenched.

"Forgot to take your umbrella again today?" Sassy wedged a package of spinach into the packed freezer.

"At least I remembered to put the top up on the car. But I left the umbrella in the backseat. Got soaked coming back across campus." She grabbed the dish towel from the refrigerator handle and squeezed it around her sodden ponytail.

"It only takes getting wet a couple of times to remember to pay attention."

"I know, I know." Sage opened the box of chocolate toaster pastries and took out a package. "Caylor asked me to tell you she's going to be later that usual getting home tonight. She had some meeting rescheduled to this afternoon from Friday."

"I figured she'd be putting in some extra hours this week before she goes out of town."

Sage heaved a deep sigh then chomped into the pastry, sprinkling crumbs all over the floor Sassy had just mopped that morning. "Manhattan in the springtime. I wish I could go on this wedding dress shopping excursion with them."

Sassy turned to put cans in the pantry so she didn't have to see more crumbs soil her brand-new bamboo floor. "It's not really even springtime here. . . . It's definitely not springtime up there."

"That's right." Sage's disappointed tone was followed by the sound of a zipper. "I'm going to throw my coat in the dryer." The door banged closed behind her.

Sassy sighed. She loved her younger granddaughter. Truly she did. But she wasn't certain she always *liked* her. She couldn't pinpoint it to anything specific—other than Sage's seeming inability to commit to anything or plan anything in her life—but she and Sage just didn't click the way she and Caylor did.

Yet if her plan for Caylor was going to work, Sassy would need to start getting along with Sage better—much better.

Sage came back and perched on one of the tall chairs at the bar on the far side of the new kitchen island. Sassy looked around at the bags of groceries still on the countertops.

"I think I'll call some of the girls and see if they want to study tonight." Sage started on her second pastry then glanced up and caught Sassy looking at her. "What?"

Sassy shook her head in defeat and moved on to the next bag. "Nothing. I think it's wonderful that you've made friends in your classes."

"I know. I can't believe how much I'm actually enjoying going to school," Sage said around a mouthful of chocolate.

Squeezing her eyes shut against the sight of half-chewed food, Sassy pulled the bag containing salad vegetables off the island and put it on the counter beside the fridge. She hadn't been certain she would like having the freezer on the bottom, but she loved the double doors of the fridge section on top. She could fit all of her serving and party trays in with no problem. Not that she'd need them again until Easter, when she had all the girls' families over for dinner after church. Perty had tried usurping Sassy's Easter dinner last year when the remodel of their house was finished, but then Gerald had come down with the flu and they'd all ended up back at Sassy's house. She couldn't wait for Trina, Lindy, and Maureen to see the new open layout of the house.

She did find herself wishing it had taken longer than a month, though, as the whole point of the remodel was to throw Caylor and Riley Douglas together as often as possible.

"What's wrong, Sassy?"

"Wrong?" She turned, the pack of mushrooms still in her hand.

"You sighed."

"Oh. . .I didn't realize. Do you think you'll eat supper here before you go or after you come home?" She set the mushrooms on the counter, thinking about making a stir-fry for supper.

"I'll probably pick something up while I'm out." Sage brushed the remaining crumbs of her toaster pastries onto the floor and slid down from the chair. "I'm going to go get out of these wet clothes and take a shower, and then I'll probably be off."

As soon as Sassy heard the water start running, she pulled the small, lightweight duster-vacuum out of the laundry room and got rid of all traces of crumbs from the floor—not that she could actually see the chocolate against the darkly stained wood. But she couldn't live with the knowledge the crumbs lay on her floor.

Shortly after Sage left to meet her friends to study—or go out to eat or drink coffee or whatever it was they were really doing—Caylor got home. She immediately set her coat and bags down at the foot of the stairs and came back to the kitchen sink to wash her hands.

"What can I help with?" She hung the dish towel she used back on the hook under the upper cabinet beside the sink. The one Sage had used still sat in a wad on the island.

Yes, Sassy thought, she and Caylor got along much better. Maybe it would simply be a matter of reminding Sage to help out around the house. "Slice the peppers and mushrooms, if you don't mind."

"I'd love to." Caylor pulled out a cutting board and a favorite prep knife and set to work. Though not a fantastic cook herself, she was fabulous at cutting everything quickly and into precise, uniform pieces.

She finished, and Sassy shooed her off upstairs to change into something more comfortable.

"Thanks, Sassy. Unless you'll need me again in the next thirty or forty-five minutes, I have some e-mails I really need to get written and sent." Caylor frowned at the towel on the island and then picked it up, sighing when she felt how wet it was.

"I think I have everything under control here. I just put the rice on, so that'll give you the forty-five minutes you need." Sassy looked at the clock. That would put them eating around six thirty—a little later than she usually liked to have supper ready, but anything to accommodate Caylor.

"Thanks, Sassy." Caylor carried Sage's wet dish towel out to the laundry room then gathered all her stuff and headed upstairs.

Sassy stopped chopping the onion and closed her eyes. "Father, Caylor deserves more than this. She deserves to fall madly, passionately in love and experience having someone love her the way Frank loved me for so many years. Teach me to appreciate Sage and the unique and lovely things about her that I have yet to understand or experience.

229

Because when You answer my prayer for Caylor, I know I'll be stuck with—I'll be depending on—Sage." She clucked her tongue at herself. "Show me how to help both of my granddaughters find the blessings You have in store for them."

"Who are you talking to? And why are you crying?"

Sassy jumped at the sound of Caylor's voice. Maybe having the squeak in the third step fixed hadn't been such a great idea. "Just chopping onions and having a little chat with God." She went back to the task at hand, hoping Caylor hadn't heard anything specific she'd been praying about.

"I figured it would be just as easy to bring my laptop down here to work and keep you company at the same time. Looks like the right decision if you're starting to use onions and prayer as covers for crying while talking to yourself." Caylor winked at her, settled in to one of the bar chairs, and flipped open her shiny purple laptop.

Sassy reminded herself not to hum and disturb Caylor, who was now wearing her glasses—meaning she was tired and had most likely stayed up too late last night, writing.

The next half hour was filled with the intermittent tapping of Caylor's fingers on the keyboard as she worked. When she finally arched her back and stretched her long arms over her head, Sassy took that to mean she'd come to a stopping point. "Is that writing stuff or school stuff?"

"School stuff. Dr. Fletcher reassigned two more graduate students to me today. Apparently they weren't quite ready to be teaching on their own, after all. But she did take the freshman comp class from me and give it to one of her other teaching assistants, so at least that's off my plate." Caylor rubbed the bridge of her nose under the nose pads of the rimless glasses.

"It's unusual to make those kinds of changes midsemester, isn't it?" Sassy dropped the cubed-up chicken into the hot iron skillet on the stove.

"A bit. It means these two are at least one semester further behind on their PhDs now—and that I've got to set meetings with them to discuss their dissertations and figure out where they are and how much they still need to do. But both are in my Literary Criticism class, so that makes it a little easier to connect with them." Caylor went back to typing.

The small pieces of chicken had browned quickly, so Sassy tossed the onions into the pan with them. She hoped it wouldn't take too much longer to get the hang of this professional-grade gas stove—the cast-iron pans got hot so much faster on it, which was changing the cooking time of a lot of her dishes.

Caylor's cell phone rang—the general ring, not one of the assigned tones for her friends. She made a frustrated sound in the back of her throat before answering. Must be someone from school or something.

"Hello? . . . No, it's fine. I was just finishing up something for work."

For *work*, not for *school*? No, maybe not someone from the university.

"This weekend? I can't—I'm going to be out of town."

Someone asking Caylor if she was available this weekend? Perhaps Dylan Bradley? With her back turned to Caylor, Sassy didn't bother trying to hide her smile.

"Next Tuesday night—a week from tomorrow? Sure. I think I could do that."

Sassy wanted to grab the phone and remind Dylan he was teaching the painting class at Acklen Ave. But maybe he wanted to do something with her afterward.

"Six. Okay, I can meet you—" Caylor paused, obviously interrupted by the person who was not Dylan Bradley. "Why don't you pick me up on campus, then? That'll be closer to downtown."

Excited—but consternated—Sassy composed herself before turning around to face Caylor as she made her farewell and hung up.

"That was Riley Douglas." She set the phone down beside the computer. "He wants to take me to hear one of his favorite bands that's playing at the Wildhorse next Tuesday."

"And that's why he asked you about this weekend?" Disappointment oozed in, squelching Sassy's earlier excitement.

"He originally wanted to take me to a hockey game."

"Oh—that's too bad. I know you've enjoyed that the few times you've been."

"I'm still learning the sport, but going to the games is a lot of fun.

So that's kind of disappointing." She narrowed her eyes and scrutinized Sassy. "What?"

"What what?" Sassy tried to feign the excitement from earlier.

"I can tell from your expression that you don't like the fact I've just made a date with Mr. Fantastic. Why?" Caylor leaned back and crossed her arms.

"No—I'm happy."

"You're a bad actress. And a bad liar. Why aren't you happy that I finally have a date?"

Sassy turned around, scraped the chicken and onions off the bottom of the pan where they'd stuck, and then turned back to face her granddaughter. "Okay—fine. I'm not thrilled that you have a date with Riley."

Shock filled Caylor's face, and she made sounds like she was choking. "You did all this"—she stretched out her arms as if to encompass the entirety of the kitchen, family room, living room, and dining room—"to throw Riley into my path, hoping that he'd ask me out. Now he has, and you aren't happy about it. And I want to know why."

How honest could she be with her granddaughter? Sassy scraped the very brown chicken and onions from the bottom of the skillet again and tapped the metal spatula against the side of the skillet. The clang sounded like the bell between rounds at a boxing match. Oh. . .how Frank had loved watching his boxing.

And Riley Douglas was no Frank. Because of that, Sassy needed to be honest with Caylor. "I'm very happy you've agreed to go out on a date. But I just wish it was with someone else."

Caylor pressed her fingertips to her temples. "After all that"—she heaved a long, dramatic sigh—"who do you wish I was going out with?"

"I. . .I don't want to tell you."

"*Excuse* me?" Caylor looked like she wanted to bang her head against the granite countertop. "You're disappointed that I accepted a date with Riley—with whom you purposely threw me together, at quite a financial cost, I might add—but now you don't want to tell me whom you *do* want me to go out with?"

Caylor was right—taking down all the walls and installing hard floors throughout the living areas made everything so much louder in here. "You'll just get madder at me if I do tell you."

"Sassy!" Caylor's voice hadn't gone that high-pitched since she was a teenager. "If you don't tell me, I'm not taking you anywhere for. . .a month! A month—do you hear? You'll have to rely on Sage to get you where you want to go."

"I'm already going to have to rely on her while you're in New York this weekend."

"Yeah, well, see how you like it and then get back to me." The corners of Caylor's mouth twitched, but she kept her expression serious otherwise. She closed her computer, stood, and tucked her phone in the back pocket of her jeans.

Oh how Sassy loved this child—loved that even in a heated discussion like this, Caylor still found the humor in the situation. "Okay, fine. I'll tell you."

Caylor tucked the laptop in the crook of her arm and planted the other fist on her hip. "Do tell."

"I wish you were going out with Dylan Bradley." Sassy watched Caylor's expression carefully.

A bit of color drained from Caylor's face, and her lips flattened out.

"What—don't you like Dylan? I thought on Sunday. . ." Defeat weighed Sassy's shoulders down.

"There are. . .obstacles between us. Obstacles I don't know if we can surmount." Caylor sank back onto the bar chair. "Sassy—he's the artist who did the covers of my Melanie Mason books."

Sassy pulled the skillet off the burner—the onions and chicken well past done. "He's the—he's the face?"

Caylor nodded. "He's been my muse for years, and I didn't even know it. And he wigged out a little when I told him so on Sunday after he revealed his pseudonym to me. I don't think he wants anything to do with someone who could write books like that."

"But you don't. . .not anymore. And he's no angel himself." Sassy pressed her lips together, angry with herself for almost revealing too much.

Caylor's eyes snapped up in surprise. "What do you mean?"

"Nothing. I shouldn't have said anything. He needs to tell you about his past, not me. But suffice it to say that if he's going to condemn you for writing steamy romance novels years ago, he's not the man I thought he was." Sassy pulled the pan of overcooked rice off the stove. "See what you've made me do? There's no way we can eat this now. You go put some shoes on while I dispose of this mess. We're going out for dinner."

Though she looked like she wanted to try to weasel the information about Dylan out of her, Caylor turned and went back upstairs.

Sassy looked up at the newly smooth ceiling. "Okay, Lord. Now I have a starting point. Thanks."

Chapter 23

Dylan stood in the wide aisle between the front and back sections of the main floor of Rutherford auditorium and studied the set pieces and backdrop on the stage.

"Good job, Malique." Dylan extended his hand to the graduate student.

The scenic designer—born in the Caribbean and raised by adoptive parents in Minnesota—grinned and pumped Dylan's hand up and down. "Thanks. Your input was so valuable, Mr. Bradley."

Dylan still couldn't get over how formal everything at Robertson was. But it had given him more of a sense of authority over the students—many of whom were within a few years of his age—that he hadn't always felt at Watts-Maxwell where, because of his familiarity and camaraderie with the students, even the faculty hadn't afforded him the respect due a professor.

Malique jogged up to the stage to make a few changes to locations of smaller props, and Dylan turned to leave. Even though he didn't teach on Thursdays, he'd started coming up to campus almost every day of the week—at first to help with painting the backdrops and set pieces, but then simply because he realized how much he missed being on a university campus. Maybe he should take Tyler's suggestion and start working on a PhD if he didn't have a full-time job offer soon.

His phone beeped—a timer reminding him of a meeting with one of the students from his portraiture studio. He jogged over to Sumner

Hall and up to the third-floor studio. Instead of having a portfolio, the student had brought his small netbook on which he showed Dylan every piece of art he'd created, and Dylan helped him choose the pieces for his collection for the seniors' art show, which opened in April.

Oh yeah—the graphic designer should be sending him the catalog to proof today. He pulled out his phone and put a note-to-self memo in his calendar to follow up with an e-mail if nothing came by the end of the day.

With the student's fears over his showpieces alleviated, he tucked the minicomputer into his bag and hurried off to meet up with a study group. Dylan sat a few minutes longer, checking e-mail on his phone just to see if the catalog for Mother's auction had arrived—it hadn't. Still laughing over a series of crazy photos Spencer had forwarded to his brothers, Dylan tucked his phone in his pocket and decided to head home. If he had an office here where he could keep his painting supplies, he could use one of the individual studio rooms to work on his new piece.

"Mr. Bradley?" Dr. Holtz's secretary rushed down the hall after him.

He turned at the top of the stairs. "Hi, Joyce."

"I'm so glad I caught you—I had just picked up the phone to call you when I saw you go past the door. Dr. Holtz would like a word, if you have a minute." The fortysomething woman led him back to her office and motioned him to sit in the guest chair beside the hall door while she stuck her head into the dean's office.

"Come on in, Dylan," Dr. Holtz called.

Joyce gave Dylan a furtive glance as he stood aside for her to exit the inner office. Uh-oh. That didn't look good. And she'd asked him if he had a *minute*. That was about how long it took to tell someone he wasn't being offered a job he wanted.

"Close the door behind you, will you?" Dr. Holtz closed a manila folder and set it down on top of a stack.

Yep. That looked like a pile of rejections. Dylan turned his back on the dean to close the door—and compose himself so he wouldn't betray his disappointment when Dr. Holtz broke the bad news to him. He wanted to stay here, to make Nashville his home again. . .to see if he had any kind of chance at building a relationship with a certain statuesque redhead. But he needed a full-time job, and since none of the other colleges and universities in the area had any openings for full-time art faculty, it meant looking elsewhere and moving away again.

With what he hoped was a neutral expression, he sank into the chair across the desk from the art department dean. Why hadn't he worn something other than paint-stained jeans and a long-sleeved, black T-shirt with a hockey team logo on it to the drama workshop today?

Dr. Holtz pulled another file out of his desk and opened it—with it angled so that Dylan couldn't see anything in it. Of course, he didn't need to see the piece of paper on top to know it was the thanks-but-no-thanks letter. Though Dylan hadn't used Rhonda as a professional reference, every ounce of his being told him Rhonda carried enough influence with everyone else in the department that they'd all given him sketchy, if not outright bad, letters of recommendation.

"I'm glad you were here so that I could tell you in person. After reviewing all of the applicants' qualifications, interviews, and teaching sessions, the committee has decided to offer you the position of assistant professor of art to begin in the fall semester."

Maybe if he found a job in southern Kentucky or northern Alabama it wouldn't be—"Excuse me, sir?" Dylan noticed Dr. Holtz had extended his right hand over his desk. "You're offering me the job?"

Dr. Holtz laughed. "Yes. You're just the kind of young, energetic professor we're looking for. Don't tell me you've decided you don't want it."

"No! No sir. I definitely want it." He thrust his arm out and pumped the dean's hand a little more vigorously than necessary.

After setting up a time to come back and find out everything the job offer entailed, Dylan fairly skipped out of the dean's office. Joyce congratulated him and told him she'd have a packet of paperwork for him to fill out when he came back to meet with Dr. Holtz.

Outside, the chill air held a faint hint of spring—or was that his imagination? He shrugged into his jacket and pulled out his phone. He had to tell someone—and walking across the quad gave him time to make one quick phone call.

But Pax's voice mail picked up. He left a message for his brother to call when time allowed. Dylan tucked the phone back in his pocket just as he reached the top of the stairs in Davidson Hall. He turned left—and Caylor's office door stood shut.

A yellow piece of paper hung at eye level—well, the average person's eye level, but Dylan's chin level—over several other things on the door. He bent his head to read it more easily:

DR. EVANS'S CLASSES AND OFFICE HOURS ON THURSDAY AND FRIDAY THIS WEEK HAVE BEEN CANCELED. IF YOU CANNOT WAIT UNTIL MONDAY, PLEASE SEE DR. FLETCHER IN DAVIDSON 212.

How could she not be here when he wanted—needed—to see her?

He hoped she wasn't sick. But no, wait. She'd said something to Pax at Sassy's birthday lunch Sunday about going to New York to help her friend Zarah shop for a wedding dress. Was that this weekend?

Feeling somewhat deflated, he exited the back of the office building and headed to his car.

He'd be teaching at Robertson full-time starting in August. After believing for months he'd never be able to secure another professorship anywhere, he'd been offered a job at the place he'd come to love in such a short time.

Take that, Rhonda.

All her predictions that he'd never work in academia again came rushing back in—idle threats. He'd believed her delusions of grandeur, her self-aggrandizing claims that she held vast sway over the deans of university art departments all over the country.

And he was the one in therapy.

Oh, he needed to remember to write down his reactions, his emotions in his feelings journal so he could tell Ken all about it in their session tomorrow.

He pulled up his SUV under the hickory tree, but instead of going into the carriage house, he went straight to Gramps and Perty's kitchen door and entered without knocking. They'd apparently just sat down to lunch at the small table in the alcove, as they had big bowls of soup and sandwiches only partially eaten in front of them.

"You look like the cow that jumped over the moon." Perty stood. "Can I make you a sandwich and bowl of soup?"

"No, I'll grab something at my place." He might still have a pack of ramen noodles over there. "There's something I need to tell you."

He waited until Perty regained her seat before taking the same chair he'd sat in two months ago when they'd reviewed the living arrangement agreement with him.

Had it really been two months already? Well, in some ways, it seemed even longer than that—because he felt as if he'd known Caylor for years.

"I can tell it's something good by the way your eyes are gleaming. What's going on, Dylan?" Perty tore a corner off her sandwich and dipped it in her soup before eating it.

"I just came from Dr. Holtz's office. Starting in August, I'll be teaching full-time at James Robertson University." He chewed the corner of his bottom lip and looked from Perty to Gramps.

Perty beamed—though didn't look as excited as she probably should have.

Gramps, always hard to read, smiled and nodded his head. "Well done."

"Well, it shouldn't have been a surprise. You were the top candidate—" Perty clamped her lips together.

Caylor's absence had begun the leak in the balloon of his excitement; Perty's statement popped it altogether. "Perty—did you. . . ? You didn't interfere, did you?" He closed his eyes and covered them with both hands. "Please tell me you didn't intervene on my behalf as the former president of the university and encourage Dr. Holtz to hire me."

He couldn't go through this again. He couldn't allow someone else—a female authority figure in his life—to arrange things, make things happen for him without allowing him the chance to succeed or fail on his own. If that's what had happened, he'd call Dr. Holtz immediately and turn down the offer.

"Helen?" An edge of surprise laced Gramps's voice.

Dylan dropped his hands, shocked at his grandfather's betrayal of his true feelings.

"Of course I didn't." Perty pressed her open palms on the place mat under her soup bowl.

"Then how did you know Dylan was the top candidate? You talked to someone, didn't you?" Now the judge facade had come back, masking Gramps's emotions again.

"I didn't do anything to influence the decision. I had lunch with the school president and a few key alumni from my time to discuss an endowment. Leonard Holtz happened to be at the same restaurant. I simply asked him how the search was going." Perty's cheeks turned almost magenta. "I admit, I was planning to put in a good word for you, Dylan. Not because I don't feel like you have the qualifications to get the job on your own, but because I wanted to. . .well, to support my grandson. But Leonard offered the information that you were their top candidate by far and he was fairly certain the entire committee felt that way."

"And then what did you say?" Beads of perspiration tickled the back of his neck. He hated that he got all sweaty when he was nervous. "What did you tell him about me?"

Perty reached across the table and patted his clenched hands. "I promise you, I didn't say anything else. I wished him all the best with the search and returned to my group. Dylan, *you* got the job for yourself. You can be assured that you were hired based on your own merits."

Shaking, but feeling better—and not like he wanted to call Dr. Holtz and turn down the job anymore—Dylan excused himself and returned to the carriage house. He needed to paint to clear his head.

Using his wireless headset when Pax called him back, Dylan managed to finish most of the background details of the large painting while telling his brother everything—even his accusing Perty of arranging it for him.

"Have you told Mother and Dad yet?" Pax asked.

Dylan put a finishing touch on the medieval Italian castle in the background. "No. I thought I'd save that for lunch on Sunday."

"Better make sure Perty and Gramps know not to say anything."

He swirled his brush in the small jar of turpentine and then cleaned it thoroughly. His earpiece beeped, and he wiped his hands and pulled the phone out of his back pocket. "I have another call coming in. I'll see you tomorrow night."

As soon as Pax was gone, Dylan answered the incoming call.

"Dylan? This is Ems Bernard. I'm the event planner for your mother's campaign. We met last weekend."

Right. As if he could forget someone like Emerson Bernard. "Yes, I remember. Is everything okay? I haven't seen the auction catalog to proof yet. I sent the designer an e-mail earlier."

"Oh, that's not why I'm calling—but I did talk to her earlier, and she said it'll be later this evening before she can get that over to you. Sorry about the short turnaround on that."

He put his brushes on a rack to dry then washed his hands in the utility sink. "That's okay. I have time to give it the immediate attention it needs."

"Why I am calling is because my brother-in-law got two tickets from work to the hockey game Saturday night. But he forgot that it's their anniversary, so needless to say, he can't use the tickets. He gave them to me, and I remember how disappointed you were that you couldn't go to the game on Tuesday. I thought I'd see if you'd like to go with me. They're fifth row up from the rink."

Tuesday night, as he'd walked around correcting the five elderly ladies' brush techniques, he'd been able to clearly visualize himself at the game. Except he hadn't been in the luxury suite with Mother and Dad and the publicist and Emerson. He'd been in a seat near the ice, and a tall redhead had been at his side.

Well, one out of two would have to do. It had been far too long since he'd been to a hockey game—as that was yet another of the things Rhonda had tried to change about him. "I'd enjoy that. Is there a good place where I can meet you at the arena?"

"Oh—I hadn't thought about that. Um. . .why don't we meet at the base of the sign out in front of the arena? The pillar closest to the building. The game starts at seven—but the doors open at five thirty, according to the tickets. Want to meet around six fifteen? We can grab hot dogs or something at the concession stand for supper. I have to admit I have a secret addiction to concession stand food at sporting events." Emerson's laugh tinkled through the phone, a high-pitched sound that, while not loud, did grate a bit on Dylan's nerves. Though after everything else he'd been through today, that could be more a reflection on the state of his nerves and have nothing to do with Emerson.

"Okay. I'll meet you under the sign at six fifteen on Saturday."

"See you then." She said good-bye and got off the phone quickly, which he appreciated.

Cleaning up his paints and supplies, Dylan paused a moment to review the work he'd accomplished. There, in the center of the four-by three-foot canvas was the pencil sketch of Caylor. And beside and below her, an artist at a rustic easel, ready to paint the beautiful woman—a Renaissance artist with the profile of twenty-first-century Dylan Bradley.

He could never let anyone see this painting. Except maybe Caylor. But then only once he knew for certain she felt the same for him as he felt for her.

⚬⚬

Caylor gladly closed her notebook and stuffed it in her bag as the black car rolled to a stop before the Plaza Hotel. She reached for the door handle, but someone opened it before she could. She stepped out and thanked the uniformed doorman, then turned to take her suitcase from the driver.

He looked at her as if snakes had sprouted from her scalp. The uniformed man—maybe a bellhop and not a doorman?—took the suitcase and, almost bowing and scraping, ushered her into the hotel lobby.

She tried not to gawk at the opulence surrounding her. Once she'd learned Zarah's mother-in-law-to-be had booked them into the landmark hotel, Caylor had looked up images online, trying to prepare herself. But nothing could have prepared her for the real marble, chandeliers, and gilded, ornate ceiling. And this was just the lobby.

The hotel clerk handed Caylor a note to read while she got checked in. She instantly recognized Zarah's handwriting:

Beth, Kiki, Lindy, and I are having lunch "uptown" with some of Beth's friends. She said we shouldn't expect to be back before

*suppertime. There is a car on call to take you anywhere you want to
go. Beth suggested shopping. I thought the New York Public Library
would be of more interest to you (though I think we may go there
when we're sightseeing on Saturday). We have dinner reservations
at seven and will meet you in the lobby near the concierge desk.*

Z

P.S. Remind me again why I agreed to this?

Caylor smiled and tucked the note into her blazer pocket. Zarah
and her grandmother, along with Bobby's mother and grandmother,
had flown in last night. She was already overwhelmed, and they hadn't
even gotten to the bridal salon yet. Sage had watched a program on
cable that showed women going into the store at which Beth had
made the appointment to buy the wedding dress. Caylor had stopped
and watched a few minutes of the show with her last weekend. She
had a feeling that tomorrow was going to be a very emotionally trying
day for Zarah, whose only reason for agreeing to this trip was to please
Beth Patterson.

"This way, please, ma'am." The bellhop led her toward the elevators.
As unobtrusively as she could, Caylor pulled money out for a tip, which
she gave to the man as soon as he set her suitcase on the luggage rack
in the closet.

At first she thought his affronted expression was because she
hadn't tipped him enough. "Do you not want assistance in unpacking,
ma'am?"

"What—no, thank you very much. I believe I can handle it." Um,
no, she didn't want a stranger—man or woman—going through her
personal items.

"Very good, ma'am. The butler service is available anytime you
need anything."

Butler service? At a hotel? Good grief, she was really out of her
element now. "Thank you."

He finally left, and Caylor dropped into the armchair at the
end of the luxurious, king-size bed. A glance at the clock informed
her she had more than six hours to kill before meeting everyone else
for dinner. Flannery would be tied up all day, too—she'd flown up

243

earlier this week to meet with authors and agents and vendors in the area, and today was her day to wrap everything up.

The New York Public Library was a place that any English professor worth her salt should visit. But if they were all going together on Saturday, why go by herself today?

She stood and crossed to the window—out of which she had a view of a very busy street lined with piles of dirty snow, tons of buildings, and a gray sky above it all. She wished her room overlooked Central Park—but couldn't imagine how expensive that view was.

The Metropolitan Museum of Art wasn't too far away—at least not from what she'd seen on the map online. Dylan had mentioned a few times how much he enjoyed visiting the art museum when he lived here, even though it had taken him almost an hour to get to it from his apartment in Brooklyn.

She leaned her head against the cool glass. What would it have been like to have her first experience visiting New York with someone who'd lived here—someone who'd experienced the city as a college student, as someone who couldn't afford the Plaza and a car on call and designer wedding dresses at a boutique so famous it had its own TV show? What a different experience seeing New York through Dylan's eyes would have been. She had a feeling she probably would have enjoyed it more.

Once she figured out she'd have to pay for Internet service, she pulled her phone out and used her rarely accessed web connection to look up information about the art museum.

If she couldn't see New York with Dylan, she'd at least make sure she saw a part of the city he loved. It might be one of the last threads of contact she had with him, given his reaction to her revelation on Sunday.

The same black luxury car picked her up outside the hotel and drove her straight to the Eighty-Second Street entrance of the art museum. She arranged with the driver to be picked up at five o'clock and then entered the enormous museum.

Once she paid her admission fee and entered the great hall, the magnificence of the place made her consider running all the way back to the hills of Tennessee from whence she came—the same feeling that had struck her the first time she'd toured Buckingham Palace in London. Drawing a deep breath, she looked down at the map they'd given her and saw European Paintings marked in several wings of the gallery on the second floor.

She needed to see Titian's paintings, but she didn't know how to go about finding them. Or if the museum actually had any.

Entering the European gallery, Caylor started out going from painting to painting, more interested in reading the placards beside each framed masterpiece than in the paintings themselves.

"Are you looking for something in particular?"

She turned at the masculine voice. A young man—who looked every inch the artist, from his long hair to his full beard to the paint stains on his hands—stood a few steps from her.

"Do you work here?" She turned her back on the painting by someone named El Greco.

"No, but I'm here often enough they should hire me. I'm pretty familiar with what they have here." He hooked his thumbs in the frayed pockets of his jeans.

"Okay—I'm looking for paintings by the Italian painter Titian."

His grayish eyes lit up. "I know exactly where those are. Follow me." He led her to a room with red walls. "These are the Italian masters. And there is *Venus and the Lute Player*."

Caylor glanced at the painting he indicated—and nearly choked. "Did. . .did Titian paint a lot of nudes?"

"Yes—as did most of the Italian masters of the Renaissance—though he created plenty of history paintings, some religious scenes, and portraits in which everyone is clothed. Why the interest in Titian?" The guy moved around until he stood almost between Caylor and the painting.

"I know. . .someone, an art professor at the university where I teach, who studied Titian in school. He's talked quite a bit about how Titian is one of his greatest influences, so I thought while I was in New York I'd take the time to see Titian's work for myself." She averted her eyes from the painting. "Now I'm not quite so sure I wanted to know that much about Dylan."

"Dylan. . .not Dylan Bradley?" He looked around sheepishly at the way his raised voice echoed in the almost empty chamber.

"Yes. How do you know him?"

He scrubbed his fingers in his beard. "We shared a flat when we were undergrads at Steinhardt. I'm Wyatt Oakes."

Out of however many million people lived in New York, she had to run into someone connected to the man who currently served as the biggest complication in her life. "Caylor Evans. You don't happen to own an Irish wolfhound, do you?"

Wyatt threw back his head and laughed. "He told you about the dog?"

"I've seen it in his paintings." She rubbed her forehead.

"Of all days for me to visit the museum to get inspiration. When did you last see Dylan?" He led her to the bench in the middle of the room.

"I just saw him Sunday."

"Really? Wow—that woman must really have eased up on his restrictions. For a while there, she was keeping him on a very short leash. Last time I tried calling him—about four or five months ago— she answered his phone and told me to stop calling him, that he needed to concentrate on his art." Wyatt dropped onto the bench beside her. "So if you teach with Dylan, I guess you know Rhonda, too."

If Caylor hadn't been sitting, she might have fallen down. All the strength left her body. "N–no. I've never met Rhonda. Dylan is teaching at James Robertson University in Nashville now. That's where I know him from." There and from the mental image she'd built of him from his self-portraits and the person he'd presented himself to be over the past couple of months.

"Oh. Dylan's back in Nashville? Well, he must have finally seen the light and broken up with that b—that woman. Since he'd just moved in with her last time I talked to him, I assumed this was going to be a long-term thing. Of course, I did warn him about getting involved with someone he worked with that closely." Wyatt's pocket buzzed. He pulled out a cell phone. "Oops, that's my alarm to remind me I've got to run. It was nice to meet you, Caylor Evans."

"You, too." But that was a lie. She managed to hold her smile until Wyatt disappeared into the next gallery. Then she doubled over, arms wrapped around her stomach.

Dylan had been living with a woman—apparently one he'd worked with at the art school in Philadelphia—as recently as four or five months ago. A woman who, it seemed, did a fair job of controlling everything he did.

And he was upset at the fact Caylor had written six steamy romance novels more than five years ago?

Sassy was right. He wasn't the man she thought he was.

Chapter 24

❧

$\mathcal{A}$ sharp pain in Caylor's shoulder made her blink—and realize the limo had stopped in front of the bridal boutique. She'd have a bruise in the shape of Flannery's fist on her arm tomorrow.

The frigid mid-February air bit her nose and cheeks, and she hurried into the store, not caring how far behind her any of the others were—and not wanting Flannery to question her again about why she couldn't focus today. The excuse that she just hadn't slept well would only work for so long.

She waited inside the lobby area in the enormous store until the others joined her. Beth Patterson marched past her to the front counter. "We have an eleven o'clock appointment with Jessica. Bride's name is Zarah Mitchell."

"Please have a seat right over there, and your sales consultant will be right with you."

The area looked like a hotel lobby with clusters of sofas and chairs, though here, each grouping was gathered in a semicircle around a dais—no doubt where the bride showed off her dress. And even though it was a Friday, every section seemed to be full of customers.

A young woman dressed all in black came over and welcomed them to the store. "I'm Jessica. Who's my bride?"

They all looked at Zarah, who stood. "Zarah Mitchell."

"Congratulations." The sales consultant smiled a too-perfect smile and looked around at the other five women. "And who did you bring with you today?"

Zarah turned and motioned to each in turn. "My fiancé's mother, Beth Patterson; his grandmother, Lindy Patterson; my grandmother, Trina Breitinger; and my best friends and maids of honor, Flannery McNeill and Caylor Evans."

"So nice to meet all of you." Jessica turned to Zarah again. "When's your wedding?"

"Memorial Day weekend. So we're on kind of a tight turnaround."

"But the fees to have the order and alterations expedited are not a problem," Beth stated, standing up beside Zarah.

Jessica's brows raised slightly. "Okay. So tell me, Zarah, how do you picture yourself on your wedding day?"

At the other end of the semicircle, Caylor could almost feel the heat radiating from Zarah's face, she turned so red.

"Um. . .well, I had been picturing a small wedding, but things have changed and we're having a big church wedding now. So I'm not sure." Zarah turned to look at her future mother-in-law.

"She needs something elegant but that makes a statement."

Jessica nodded then looked at Flannery and Caylor. "Best friends, what do you see her in?"

"Nothing strapless." Caylor looked at Flannery, who nodded. "Nothing low cut. Something almost old-fashioned or Victorian. Zarah doesn't like anything flashy. But not pouffy or frilly either. No princess ball gowns."

"Lace," Flannery added. "And exquisite detailing, because she is a very detail-oriented person."

From the expression on Zarah's face, she was about to lose it again. But Beth put her arm around Zarah's waist and gave her a little squeeze, which seemed to help.

Jessica turned to the grandmothers then, and they reiterated much of what Beth, Caylor, and Flannery had said.

"And what's our budget?" Jessica looked at Zarah—who looked at Beth.

"There is no budget," Beth answered. "And Zarah is not to be told how much the gowns cost when you put them on her. I'm paying for everything, so she doesn't need to know how much it costs."

The consultant's eyes gleamed. Caylor was a little surprised she didn't rub her hands together at the thought of getting Zarah into one of their most expensive gowns and the commission that would bring.

"All right, then. Zarah, you're with me. Ladies, as soon as I get her into a dress, we'll be back to show it to you." Jessica looked down at the clipboard in her hand. "Oh, I see we're booked for a double appointment time. Excellent. Just that many more options we can explore." She ushered Zarah off.

Caylor looked around the store at the several other groups of women either waiting for their bride to come back in a gown or critiquing the girl standing in front of them in a wedding dress. If Caylor believed in romance anymore, she might find this a fascinating place and be curious as to how each of these women met and fell in love with their fiancés.

But after yesterday. . .

She slumped a little in the baroque reproduction armchair. Shortly after Wyatt disappeared, Caylor had left the art museum and walked back to the hotel where she'd gotten on the computer and agreed to the exorbitant daily Internet access fee so she could do some research. She'd found only one Rhonda listed at the art institute in Philadelphia— Dr. Rhonda Kramer, chair of the painting department. The woman's picture had been flattering but couldn't hide the fact that she must be at least ten years older than Caylor. Why would Dylan have been romantically involved not only with the chair of his department, but with someone that much older than him?

"He's no angel himself." Sassy's voice rang through her memory.

Wyatt said Dylan had moved in with Rhonda. Rhonda had answered Dylan's phone—Caylor assumed his cell phone. All signs pointed to the answer that Dylan and Rhonda had not been platonic roommates just trying to save money.

Movement caught her eye, and Caylor dragged her brain back to the present. Zarah walked toward them in an empire-waist gown with gold and dusty rose embroidery covering the bust and cap sleeves, and a sheer tulle over the silk skirt on the bottom. With her hair clipped up in the back and a few curls falling down in front of her ears, she looked like a character from a Jane Austen novel.

"Ladies, what do you think?"

On the few minutes of the television program about this shop that Caylor had seen, she had been dismayed at the way the bride's large entourage had disparaged not only the gown, but also the way the bride looked in it. Zarah couldn't survive anything like that. Not that any of them would do it.

"It is a lovely gown." Zarah's grandmother, Kiki, scooted to the edge of the sofa seat. "But I don't know that it's quite the right style for Zarah. She looks like she's dressed for a Jane Austen masquerade ball, not a wedding."

"What do you think, Zarah?" Flannery asked.

"Kiki's right. It's a beautiful dress, and I like the way it looks on me—except that it shows my upper arms too much—but it isn't quite what I was picturing." Zarah tried to shield her quite nice upper arms with her hands.

Jessica nodded. "All right, let's get you in another dress."

Two hours later, they seemed to be no closer to finding something that suited both Zarah's sensibilities and Beth's vision of something grand that would make a statement in the enormous auditorium at Acklen Avenue. Flannery had gotten a call from work and was pacing the lobby area while she talked on the phone.

After half an hour with no reappearance from Zarah—Caylor imagined she was discarding multiple dresses without even bothering to come up and show them—Beth stood, a determined expression on her face.

"Caylor, come with me." She headed toward one of the gated-off display rooms beyond the showroom.

Startled, Caylor rose and followed Bobby's mother.

Beth started going through the dresses hanging on the rack. "We're going to find a dress for Zarah, even if I have to look through every one of the thousands of gowns they have here. You know Zarah's tastes. Find something that looks like her but has a sense of presence about it."

They looked through a few of the galleries—one of the clerks tagging along behind them and taking the few dresses Beth pulled as possibilities.

As soon as she entered the third gallery, Caylor stopped and stared at the dress on the mannequin in the center of the room. The ivory gown had an empire waist—though one in which the champagne-colored satin ribbon sash angled down from a small rhinestone accent in the center. The gown had a V-neck with a lace insert serving as a modesty panel, and—unlike most of the strapless gowns they'd put on Zarah with a lace or satin shrug, promising they could alter it to add sleeves—this dress had cap sleeves, which Zarah had said she could deal with. The skirt was A-line, though nowhere near as full as most of the supposed A-lines they'd been putting her in, with the beautiful floral lace continuing all the way down to the floor.

Caylor held her breath as she rounded the dress and, for the moment, forgot all about Dylan and this woman named Rhonda. "Beth, I think I've found it."

Beth entered the room. "It's pretty, but. . ." Then she walked around behind it. She grabbed Caylor's wrist, bouncing on her toes like a teenager. "I think you're right."

She asked the clerk to take the dress off the mannequin and take it to the dressing room. She then hooked her arm through Caylor's and led her back toward the showroom. "Thank you for helping me. I probably would have walked right past that gown."

"My pleasure."

"When are you going to be doing this kind of shopping for yourself?"

"Me? I'll probably never marry." Especially now. "I live with my grandmother and take care of her—she can't drive anymore, so someone has to be there."

Always before when she'd thought about living with Sassy and the sacrifice she'd willingly made five years ago, along with the decision to forgo serious relationships to avoid complications, she'd been content with it. But today the future felt bleak and empty.

Flannery still hadn't returned when Caylor slouched back into the chair. Which was probably a good thing—it gave Caylor time to compose herself and cajole herself into a better mood so that Zarah and Flannery wouldn't pester her about what was wrong. She should work this out on her own. No need to drag them into a mess of her own making.

Lord, I'm confused. At first I thought You wanted me to stay single and take care of Sassy. Then I thought You might be telling me You wanted me to fall in love with Dylan. Now it's looking like that's not going to happen, yet I can't imagine spending the next fifteen or so years—or the rest of my life—alone. A little help here would be appreciated.

Flannery made it back to her seat just as Zarah came around the corner. "Ooh, that's pretty."

"Just wait," Caylor whispered.

The style of the dress was perfect for Zarah's size 14 figure, even if the sample gown was a little small for her, just as Caylor had envisioned. But when she stepped up on the dais, turning her back to them—Kiki, Lindy, and Flannery all gasped. Beth reached for the box of tissues on the end table beside her chair and dabbed her eyes.

If the front of the dress was all about Zarah and her sensibilities, the back of the dress—four tiers of bustle leading to an almost cathedral length, detachable train—was all about Beth and her desire for something grand.

Along with the four women seated beside her and the bride standing in front of them, Caylor couldn't hold back her tears. Or her guilt over the fact that the tears were more for herself than from the pleasure of seeing Zarah's joy at having found the perfect wedding dress.

⚶

A day spent at the Frist Center followed by a hockey game. Could there be a more perfect Saturday?

Yes, as a matter of fact. Caylor's presence could definitely have improved it.

Dylan leaned against the pillar holding up the electronic sign announcing upcoming events at the downtown arena. The temptation to call Caylor and tell her about the job offer and ask her out to coffee sometime when they would have time to sit and talk—truly talk—made his fingers twitch. But after talking to Ken yesterday about his immediate desire to tell Caylor about the job—even before his grandparents or parents—he decided to take the therapist's advice and try to distance himself from the infatuation he felt for Caylor (even though he tried to explain to Ken that *infatuation* couldn't even begin to describe how he felt for Caylor) and give himself time to adjust to being newly single and explore his rekindling relationship with God before diving headfirst into another romantic entanglement.

But he still wished Caylor were here.

He straightened at the sight of a beautiful blond coming toward him. Nervousness twisted his stomach—why did beautiful women do this to him? Well, all beautiful women but one. Admiration and longing were the only visceral reactions he had whenever he saw Caylor.

"Hey, Dylan!" Emerson jogged the last few yards toward him. He closed his eyes against the sight of the ugly sheepskin-lined tan boots she'd tucked her too-tight jeans into. When he opened them again, he focused on her angelic face. Yes, he could probably use her as a model for an angel if he ever took a piece that direction.

"Hi, Emerson."

"Ems, remember?" She grinned, and he had to wonder if she'd had her teeth capped, because no one had teeth that perfectly straight and symmetrical naturally.

Was it the right or left side on which Caylor had a tooth with a tiny chip out of one corner?

He followed Ems into the arena. She seemed to know her way around, so this must be something she did regularly.

Did Caylor like hockey?

Okay, he seriously needed to get Caylor Evans off his mind. But at least he wasn't comparing everyone he came in contact with to Rhonda anymore.

Chattering at him the whole time, Ems led him to the concession stand nearest the section their seats were in. She ordered two of everything—hot dogs, french fries, and bottled water. Dylan pulled out his wallet to pay, but Ems waved him off. "My treat."

"Really, you should let me, since you got the tickets."

"But I didn't have to pay for them." She handed her money to the bored-looking cashier before Dylan could get his out. "You can buy the sodas and popcorn in the second period and ice cream in the third."

"You sound like you have a routine when it comes to the games." Dylan took the box holding their food while Ems took the two bottles of water. He followed her to the condiments stand, and they each doctored their dogs—Dylan adding only ketchup and mustard, and Ems adding almost every condiment available except onions. He tried not to be grossed out at the amount of pickle relish she added to the dog and instead concentrated on pumping ketchup and mayonnaise over his fries.

"Mayo on fries? Gross." Emerson wrinkled her perfect example of a nose. Her face was so symmetrical, he really should get her into his portraiture class for a study in creating a full-face portrait only from one side of the model's face.

"I picked it up in Philly. It's best when I can mix the ketchup and mayo together."

"Add relish to it and you'll have Thousand Island dressing."

Now it was his turn to wrinkle his nose. "I'm not a big fan of pickles—of any kind."

Though he'd been worried about what he might find to talk about with this stellar physical specimen of womanhood, the topic of food preferences—especially those they couldn't stand—took up most of the remaining time before the game began, interspersed as it was with eating.

The seats were fabulous—only a little off center ice—and Dylan's heart raced as the teams were introduced and the national anthem sung. He'd fallen in love with the game in New York, so naturally his loyalties still lay with that team. But he couldn't care less about the other visiting team on the ice tonight, so he had no problem cheering for Nashville.

The game started off slowly, but a couple of good fights broke out. Ems was at least as fanatical as the rest of the fans sitting this close to the ice—definitely more avid than Dylan. She seemed to take it personally when a call went against Nashville or she saw something she deemed unfair done by the other team. Dylan enjoyed the game, but he'd never get that wrapped up in it.

With only thirty seconds left in the first period—and the score still sitting at 0–0—play on the ice stopped for a penalty. All wound up from the infraction perpetuated on one of her beloved players, Ems pressed her forehead against Dylan's shoulder.

"I don't know if I can watch." Belying her words, Ems hooked her arm over Dylan's shoulder and pressed herself even closer to him.

Dylan's arm, shoulder, and torso tingled—but not in a good way. When the player scored a goal, Ems leaped to her feet, ending the contact, and Dylan started breathing again.

The period ended, and he cheerfully jumped up to go get the requested popcorn and sodas. Standing in line, he could hear the voice of Ken that lived in his head coaching him on being assertive. If Emerson's contact made him uncomfortable, he needed to speak up. Be kind but firm.

The second period brought more nail-biting moments for Ems when the other team scored, tying up the game again. During one particularly tense advance, Ems wrapped her arm through Dylan's, once again pressing her side against him. Once the play ended with the other team regaining the puck, Dylan waited for her to remove her arm from his.

She didn't.

"Be kind, but firm." He pulled her hand from around his upper arm and untwined her limb from his.

"I'm so sorry, Dylan. I didn't even realize—I'm a very touchy-feely person, especially when I get worked up over a game. I should have warned you." Ems smiled at him.

He smiled back. "I just didn't want you getting the wrong message from me. I'm glad we're getting to know each other, but there can never be anything but friendship between us." Had he actually just said that? To a girl? To beautiful, perfect Emerson Bernard?

Why yes. Yes he had. A sense of accomplishment, of maturity, flooded through him.

"Oh—you don't need to worry about that. I never thought of you as anything but a friend." Her smile broadened.

The flood of good feelings ebbed a bit. Had she just insulted him?

Though Nashville ended up winning the game by one goal, the rest of the evening wasn't as fun for Dylan as it had started out. And as he lay in bed later, reviewing everything that'd happened, he couldn't help wondering if Caylor was still in New York or if she'd come back and would be at church tomorrow.

Caylor or no—he'd enjoyed the service at Providence Chapel last week, and for the first time since coming back home, he decided he'd return to a church for a second visit.

Dressing with care the next morning—he should have made the time to go get his hair cut this week—he reminded himself that he was supposed to be creating emotional distance with Caylor.

While the disappointment at not seeing her in the choir loft wasn't crushing, it did put a damper on how much he enjoyed the worship service—though the pastor's talk about doors and windows, and how God opened and closed them all the time, did remind Dylan a little too painfully of his own life.

During the benediction, Dylan prayed for guidance—visualizing the doors and windows and gateways opening onto darkness from the paintings he'd set aside for the auction. He was tired of all the doors he tried to go through being dark on the other side. Maybe that's because he'd been letting someone else open them for him and following blindly through rather than opening his eyes and looking to see if what lay on the other side was from God or not. He promised himself, and God, that from now on he'd do his best to make sure he followed only God's will for his life.

After service ended, he decided there was no better time than now to talk to the pastor and set up a meeting to discuss joining this church. But since the pastor stood at the back of the sanctuary shaking hands with everyone as they exited, Dylan waited until the crowd cleared.

Nearby, he recognized a head of blue-gray hair. "Good morning, Mrs. Morton."

"Humph." The elderly lady looked him up and down, raised her nose in the air, and turned away from him. The gaggle of women around him did the same thing.

What was *that* all about? Dylan watched, bemused, as the ladies walked away. He followed at a distance behind them until he was the last person to leave the sanctuary. He shook the pastor's hand and introduced himself.

"I'm interested in talking to you about the church. I'm thinking about joining, but there are some things I want to talk to you about before I do." Dylan stuffed his fists into his pockets, not wanting the pastor to see how nervous this made him.

"Call the office first thing tomorrow morning and set up an appointment with my secretary. I'm usually out of the office on Mondays—that's my day off—and at the hospital and nursing homes visiting members on Wednesdays. But we'll find a time this week to talk." The pastor excused himself, and Dylan bounded down the front steps of the church, dashing to the SUV before the light sprinkle turned into a full-blown spring rain.

When he got to the restaurant, only Gramps, Perty, and Sassy Evans were already there—and Sassy gave him the same kind of look Mrs. Morton had.

The gravity in his grandparents' expressions wiped out his excitement to tell them he was thinking about joining Providence Chapel. "What's wrong?" He took the chair beside Gramps across from Perty and Sassy.

Perty handed him a folded piece of newspaper. "That was in the Style section this morning."

Dylan looked down at the page—and his stomach sank. In color on the front page of the section was a picture of him with Emerson Bernard, her arm wrapped cozily through his.

But the caption was what nearly did him in: WEDDING BELLS IN THE NEAR FUTURE FOR SON OF STATE SENATE CANDIDATE? JUDGE GRACE PAXTON-BRADLEY'S OLDEST SON ATTENDED LAST NIGHT'S HOCKEY GAME WITH MAIN SQUEEZE EMERSON BERNARD, AND BOTH LOOKED QUITE COZY.

Oh, he might be sick. "It's not true. She's not my main squeeze. She's Mother's event planner. I've only been talking to her about the art auction. This is horrible." He looked at the picture again. "Thank goodness Caylor is in New York."

Sassy's pale eyebrows shot up. "Yes? So she wouldn't see that you've been stepping out on her?"

He wasn't certain exactly what that meant in this context, since he and Caylor weren't even dating. "No, that's not what I meant." He set the page down in the middle of the table. "I'm not seeing Emerson Bernard. She had gotten two free tickets to the game, knew how much I like hockey, and invited me."

"Uh-huh." Sassy folded her arms.

Dylan wasn't sure what else to say. But his silence didn't extend too long—because Mother and Dad arrived.

"Did you see it?" Mother beamed, her eyes sparkling. She saw the page on the table and snatched it up. "Do you know how many points a candidate can gain in the polls with even a rumor of a child getting engaged or married?"

Dylan stood so fast, his chair toppled over behind him, drawing the looks of the other diners. "You did this? You set this up? You set *me* up?"

"Please, do lower your voice." She smiled at the other diners and leaned over to set his chair upright again. "*Set up* has such a negative connotation. I might have traded a few favors to get the tickets and mentioned to a reporter that my son would be at the hockey game Saturday night with a beautiful young woman." Mother patted his cheek. "After the election this will all blow over. Ems fully understood the necessity of this, and she doesn't expect anything from you. So there's nothing to worry about."

He backed away from her. "Nothing to worry about? Didn't you even once consider the ramifications this kind of publicity stunt would have on my life? On my future happiness?"

Mother laughed, though her eyes shot fire at him. "Now you're just being dramatic. Maybe you should have majored in theater instead of art."

Dad stepped forward and wrapped his hand around Dylan's upper arm. "Dylan, you're making a scene. Sit down. There's nothing to be so excited over."

Dylan wrenched himself loose from his father's grip. "Nothing to be. . . ? How can you not understand? The woman I'm in love with could have seen this and been devastated by it."

"In love again? So soon?" Mother's voice came out almost as a sneer—and she seemed to have stopped worrying about the audience of other diners, now whispering behind their hands and menus. "Dylan, dear, just play along, and by the time the election is over, maybe you'll have grown up a little bit and realized that love is not the be-all and end-all."

Dad once again made a grab for Dylan's arm—but was intercepted before he could touch his son. Dylan hadn't even heard Gramps stand up, but there he was, holding Dad's wrist.

"Over the years, I've privately questioned some of the decisions and choices you and Grace have made, Davis. However, I believed that you needed to strike out on your own. Make your own decisions. This time, you've gone too far. I should have stepped forward years ago when you refused to pay for Dylan to go to college because of his choice of major." Gramps settled his free hand on Dylan's shoulder. "And I truly regret that I didn't."

Dylan reached up and squeezed his grandfather's hand in acknowledgment and acceptance of the apology.

"But I refuse to allow you to use your son, your own flesh and blood, as a pawn in this game of politics you've decided to play." Gramps released Dad's wrist but kept his hand on Dylan's shoulder. "You should be proud of Dylan, of all he's accomplished. Even if he hadn't accomplished anything, you should still be proud of him. Because he's your son. And you should love him unconditionally, just the way I do."

Gramps looked across the table. Perty and Sassy stood. He turned back to his son. "Now, if you'll excuse us, I believe we've lost our appetites."

Dylan allowed his grandparents to usher him out of the restaurant. But he couldn't resist one glance back over his shoulder to see his parents standing in the middle of the restaurant and the other patrons watching them with bemused pity.

In the small chamber between inner and outer doors, Sassy turned and stopped Dylan, pressing her hand to the middle of his chest. He'd never noticed before how much taller she was than Perty.

"Did you mean what you said in there?"

"About what?" Though he was pretty sure he knew.

"About being in love."

"I'm not supposed to be. It's too soon." He rubbed at the ache forming in the back of his neck. "But. . .yeah, I think I am in love."

"With Caylor?"

He nodded. "With Caylor."

Instead of looking happy or excited, Sassy's expression turned shrewd. "Then we'll have to see what we can do about that."

He cocked his head and narrowed his eyes, unwilling to mask his uncertainty. "Do about it?"

"Yes." She nodded, and then her eyes sparkled. "And I know exactly how to start. You're going to paint my portrait."

"Um, okay."

"Now, come on. I've been wanting to try that Five Guys Burgers place just around the corner, and I'm starving."

Obediently, Dylan followed Caylor's grandmother up the sidewalk. One thing was certain: if he did indeed have a future with Caylor, it wouldn't be boring.

Chapter 25

"How was New York?" Bridget puffed, out of breath from speed walking to catch up with Caylor—even though Caylor had stopped to wait for her.

"Cold. Slushy. Gray." And depressing in more ways than just those. Caylor forced a smile. "We found the perfect dress for Zarah. And her mother-in-law finally convinced her to go with a black-and-white color scheme when we ran across the perfect black dress in a shop in the Fashion District. It's the only color both Flannery and I can wear and look halfway decent. Plus, if the trend of evening wear continues at the faculty holiday party this year, I can wear it again."

"Did you make it to any shows?"

Caylor shook her head. "We weren't there long enough."

Bridget twisted her mouth in comical disappointment—and then an odd gleam came into her eyes. "Hey, did you hear about Dylan Bradley?"

Caylor tripped over a shadow on the sidewalk. How could Bridget have learned about Rhonda Kramer—and more importantly, did she know more than Caylor had learned? "H–heard what?"

"Dr. Holtz offered him the assistant professor position. So it looks like he'll be sticking around for quite a while longer." She nudged Caylor with her elbow.

"Oh. . .really? That's—that's great for him." But what about for her? If Dylan had been living with a woman as recently as Thanksgiving, he could easily be on the rebound from a bad breakup, and all the sparks she'd felt between them could be nothing more than his own subconscious need to feel he was still attractive to the opposite sex.

God, I want this to be real.

"Of course, from that photo in the newspaper, it looks like you may have some stiff competition. See you later," Bridget called, heading off toward Rutherford Hall.

Caylor's feet dragged as she mounted the front steps of Davidson. For the first time, she'd admitted to herself—and to God—that her feelings for Dylan Bradley went deeper than the visceral attraction she'd always felt toward the hand-drawn self-portrait of him she'd had for so many years.

Argh. She shouldn't have kept everything bottled up this weekend—she should have talked to Zarah and Flannery about what his former roommate had told her.

And she needed to talk to Dylan. Maybe tomorrow night after the painting class—

But no. She'd agreed to go out with Riley Douglas tomorrow night.

At the second-floor landing, Caylor almost dropped her keys when her cell phone started buzzing loudly in the outside pocket of her bag. She dug for the phone while trying to unlock her office door.

She looked at the screen before answering.

Dylan Bradley calling.

She paused, thumb hovering over the button to answer the call. What had Bridget meant about the photo in the newspaper and competition?

"Dr. Evans." A student hurried up the stairs. "I hope I'm not late for our appointment."

Caylor hit IGNORE and dropped the phone back into her bag. She smiled at the young woman who would be graduating with top honors in a few months. "No, I haven't even gotten my door unlocked yet."

She finally got the right key into the lock and opened the door, ushering the student in. Dylan Bradley would just have to wait.

After a full afternoon of student meetings—most of them having put off coming up with their thesis topics until as late as they possibly could—Caylor finally had time to get on the computer to take care of her e-mails and. . .oh, yeah, that thing Bridget said.

She pulled up the web browser and went straight to the newspaper's website, where she searched for Dylan's name. Though it took a little doing, she managed to find it—a picture of Dylan with a beautiful blond woman, her arm looped through his. Caylor read the caption twice.

Wedding bells? Main squeeze?

Caylor's mood plummeted lower than it had been all day. Why hadn't he said anything to her about being involved with someone? And then. . .what was that article?

She clicked on the related link at the bottom of the page and read the short blurb posted by one of the newspaper's political bloggers today:

> State senate candidate Grace Paxton-Bradley had an altercation at Pei Wei restaurant in the Hill Center at Green Hills Sunday. It is believed that the fracas happened between Judge Paxton-Bradley and her son Dylan Bradley, whose photo appeared in the newspaper yesterday. According to witnesses, Paxton-Bradley and her son seemed to be arguing about the photograph.

Caylor turned off the computer, more confused than ever. She locked up her office and headed home, head spinning. She passed Sage coming out of the subdivision onto Granny White Pike. Sage waved as she pulled Sassy's classic Ford Falcon onto the road, headed who knew where. Caylor had a hard time believing Sage spent every evening studying as she claimed. And so far, other than the six hours a week she sat for Dylan's portraiture studio, she hadn't gotten another job.

Dylan. The day Caylor had sat for his class, the intensity with which he'd studied her as he created that extraordinary sketch of her—had that been merely an artist's critical gaze? Had she read too much into his reactions to her?

Or was it possible that Wyatt Oakes had been misinformed about Dylan's relationship with Rhonda Kramer? But what about the blond in the newspaper photo? The argument with his mother?

She turned into the driveway—and came to an abrupt stop. A bright blue Ford Escape sat on the parking pad beside the carport. Of course he wasn't the only person in Davidson County who drove one of those, but. . .

Once parked, she sat still for a moment, steeling herself to come face-to-face with him without immediately grilling him about what she'd heard and read. She pushed papers that had slid out back into her bag and, taking a deep breath, got out and headed for the door.

She draped her coat over one of the chairs at the table in the new breakfast room and hooked the strap of her bag over her shoulder, pulling the bag in front of her as if it could shield her from finding out something she didn't want to know.

Soft voices came from the living room at the front of the house. Caylor stepped into the kitchen and, beyond the staircase that now created the only separation in the main portion of the house, saw Dylan adjusting a lamp to shine on Sassy, who sat in front of the fireplace in the dusty-rose wing chair from her bedroom. An easel sat a few feet away from her with a large canvas clamped onto it, and beside that stood a rickety-looking table holding an artist's paint box.

"Caylor!" Sassy waved at her. "I wondered when you might get home. There's a plate for you in the kitchen."

"Sassy—what's going on?" Caylor had to fight against her own body to keep from looking at Dylan.

"Oh, didn't I tell you? Dylan is going to paint my portrait. He's also going to do one of Papa and one of the two of us together—from photos. And I might have him do one of you and Sage."

Caylor leaned against the bottom newel post of the stairs and crossed her arms. Even from here, she could see the glitter in Sassy's eyes. "No, you didn't tell me."

Okay, she couldn't be rude. She allowed her eyes to drift to Dylan—where they'd wanted to be ever since she walked into the room. "Hey, Dylan."

"Hey, Caylor. How was New York?" He made one more adjustment to the lamp and then moved around to the canvas, his gaze locking with hers.

265

"Fine. We got what we went there looking for." And then some. "I'm sorry I didn't call you back earlier today. I understand congratulations are in order. Bridget told me Dr. Holtz offered you the assistant professorship." She picked at a worn spot on the strap of her bag.

"Oh—yes. Thank you. I called to see if you're planning on going to one of the performances of the winter concert at school this weekend. I've heard it has a World War II theme, with music from that era and readings from actual letters from the front lines. I thought we might. . .sit together if we're both going."

He was asking her out—or was he? Sit together if they were both going? What, couldn't Blondie go with him? Her head and heart warred with each other. Until she had confirmation or denial of what she'd heard about him, she couldn't risk losing her heart to him even more by spending time with him on a quasi-date.

"I. . .I'm not sure. I think I might, but I'll have to get back to you." She needed to be proactive here, not put her fact-finding mission on hold too long. "Are you busy Wednesday afternoon? Maybe we could grab some lattes in the student center and talk for a minute."

"I'd like that. My studio lets out at three thirty. Meet you there then?"

She nodded. "I'll see you then."

Turning her back on her grandmother and the man she'd love to spend time with—a whole lot of time, like maybe forever—she pulled the waiting plate of dinner from the warming drawer and carried it and a bottle of water upstairs.

She hadn't been this uncertain about her feelings toward someone—well, about his feelings toward her—since high school. And this whole situation made her feel like that gangly, awkward sixteen-year-old again. It had helped that she'd gone to an all-girls school—so the fact that boys avoided her hadn't been quite so painfully obvious to everyone. There had been a boy at church she'd had a crush on for a few years. When her mother encouraged her to take the initiative and ask him to prom her senior year, she'd done it—and been soundly rejected. No teenage guy wanted to be asked out by a girl who towered over him. In the end, she'd had to ask Flannery's boyfriend to go with her. It helped that he already had a tuxedo for prom at their high school the next weekend.

Caylor left the full plate on her desk, hooked the bag on her chair, and returned to sit on the top step. Sassy and Dylan spoke in tones too low for her to make out what they were saying, but just hearing the deep timbre of his voice made visions of highland warriors, English barons, and Italian painters dance through her head.

≈

Seeing a Monte Christo—a club sandwich that was battered and then deep-fried—on the menu at the Wildhorse Saloon brought the most excitement Caylor had been able to muster since yesterday. Even though she and Riley arrived early enough to get a good table on the second floor overlooking the dance floor and stage below, the noise in the tourist trap wasn't doing her headache any favors.

"Isn't this fantastic?" Riley swept his gaze across the room, beaming. His sweep stopped on the large table beside them—a table full of twentysomething women dressed in too-tight tops and too-short skirts. "Looks like a bachelorette party."

Caylor squeezed her face into a smile. "Looks like it."

Riley turned back to her, though it took his eyes a little longer to turn her direction than his face. "So. . .you teach English, huh? I hated learning grammar and stuff when I was in school. You must really like it."

"I do. But I mostly teach literature and writing. Because I teach upper-level students, most of them come to me having already learned 'grammar and stuff.'" She looked up and leaned slightly to the side when a server brought her iced tea, Riley's beer, and the order of fried dill pickles.

If she'd known he'd planned to drink tonight, she would have insisted on driving herself. Today's heavy rain had made the streets dangerous enough without having an intoxicated driver adding to the peril.

"Did I tell you about the new job I started on this month?" Riley launched into a description of the kitchen he'd spent the better part of the last few weeks tearing apart—and all of the foibles, problems, and near-death disasters it entailed.

Their food arrived. She'd barely had time to grab a sandwich from the snack bar in the student center between classes today, so she'd inhaled the first half of the Monte Christo before Riley had finished doctoring his hamburger and drowning his fries with ketchup.

"I figured you for a gal with a healthy appetite." Riley reached over and squeezed her waist with his right hand, grinning.

She wouldn't smack him. She wouldn't. She wouldn't. Forcing her fists to unclench, she reached for her glass and took a sip of tea to wash down her pique. "I've never believed in going hungry just to try to impress someone." And frankly, the sandwich would probably be the most pleasure she'd get out of this evening—especially with the chipotle-spiced raspberry dipping sauce.

So far, she'd been pleased with herself for taking off another five pounds since Christmas—the lowest her weight had been in more than ten years. She wasn't about to let Mr. Fantastic ruin that sense of accomplishment. She picked up the second half of the sandwich and dunked the corner into the dipping sauce. She savored the bite, truly allowing her tongue to experience the diversity of flavors—sweet, salty, spicy—of the food.

"So, anyway," Riley picked up his hamburger and took a huge, sloppy bite of it. "I got the wrong-size pipe and had to go back to the plumbing center. . . ." He chewed as he talked.

Caylor almost gagged but moved her focus to her own food and finishing it. Which she did. And he was still talking.

Why was it that sometimes, when taken in small chunks—and when "on the job"—some people seemed perfectly nice, perfectly normal? But get them out into a social situation and they completely changed?

As unobtrusively as she could, Caylor reached for her purse, pulled out her journal, and wrote those questions down. Since she couldn't stomach writing romance right now—because she couldn't do it without thinking about Dylan—maybe she'd see if she could work that dichotomy into some kind of idea for a new novel.

"Come on, let's go down for the dance lessons. They'll save our table for us." Riley grabbed her hand and started pulling her off the high, bar-style chair.

Caylor grabbed for her purse and looped the long strap over

her head and across her chest. She already knew the dances they'd announced they were going to teach, but what the heck. This would give them something to do that didn't involve Riley talking about plumbing supplies or nearly exploding gas lines.

Down on the dance floor with a couple dozen other people, Caylor actually started having fun. Most of the young women from the bachelorette party had come down also, and several of them managed to work their way between Caylor and Riley during one of the line dances.

She supposed she should make some nominal effort to "fight" for him, but she just couldn't bring herself to do it. She was having too much fun dancing and helping a few middle-aged couples with the steps.

When it came time for learning the two-step, Caylor begged off and returned upstairs to their table. She ordered another iced tea—going wild and having them add raspberry flavoring to it—and perched on the chair at the high table and watched the dancing going on below.

Riley looked up a few times and waved. Impressive—even surrounded by the bachelorette party girls, he still remembered he was here with Caylor. He pulled out his phone and texted someone.

Caylor's phone chirped. A new message. From Riley. IF YOU COULD ORDER ME ANOTHER BEER, THAT WOULD BE FANTASTIC.

It would only be his second, and they'd be here for hours yet. It would be through his system by the time they left.

Or she could just pretend that she hadn't seen his text. She shoved her phone back into her purse and pulled out her journal. It fell open to the pages she'd filled up back in December and January with descriptions and story ideas for Giovanni and Isabella's story. She made the mistake of starting to read it—and lost herself. The bar, the noise, the music, the woman calling dance steps below—everything around her disappeared as her mind traveled back to Renaissance Italy.

Suddenly she was yanked out of her fictional world when someone grabbed the sides of her waist and squeezed. She stifled a scream and turned, ready to defend herself.

"Hey, you." Riley's forehead dripped sweat, and he leaned

forward and kissed her cheek. "The girls want us to do some shots with them."

"I don't—No Riley, I don't do shots." Honesty time. "And I don't think it's a good idea for you to have anything else to drink tonight if you're going to be driving me anywhere."

"Aw. . .I'll be okay. I can hold my alcohol. Speaking of. . .Where's my beer?" He lifted the first bottle and shook it, then looked around the almost empty table.

"The server hasn't been back yet." Lame excuse, considering she sat only a few dozen feet from a huge bar.

But he bought it. "Oh, okay. I'll order it when I order the shots. I told them I'd treat them since it's a celebration. You sure you don't want one?"

"I'm sure." Caylor capped her pen, stuck it and the journal back into her purse, then crossed her arms and leaned on the table.

By the time the warm-up band was halfway through their set, one shot had turned into four, and Caylor was pretty sure Riley had forgotten he hadn't been hired to be the entertainment for the bachelorettes.

Caylor's head throbbed worse than it had all day. She'd known this was a mistake, that she should have canceled. She should have trusted her gut instincts on this. Hers—and Sassy's.

When Riley ordered another round of tequila for the table, Caylor couldn't deal with it any longer. She pulled out her phone.

But whom could she call?

She tried Sage first. No answer. She waited through the voice mail message, swinging her foot in agitation. "Sage, it's Caylor. It's. . .almost nine o'clock. If you get this message in the next twenty minutes, please give me a call. It's urgent."

But she really didn't want to wait twenty minutes. She scrolled through the list. Zarah was teaching tonight. Flannery had an author in town whom she was treating to dinner. Bridget was at play rehearsal. Who could she. . . ?

She stopped scrolling through the contact list at the end of the Ds. Dylan Bradley. He should be home by now. She hit call before she could talk herself out of it.

"Hey, Caylor." Dylan's voice sounded either amused or curious—she couldn't tell.

"Hey, I hope I didn't interrupt anything."

"No. I was just doodling around with a new project. What's up?"

Caylor glanced over at the bachelorettes' table. Riley seemed to be the life of the party. He staggered a bit as he slammed back another shot of liquor. "Um. . .I hate to ask this, but I'm kind of stuck and need someone to come pick me up."

"Is everything okay? Did your car break down?"

"No—my car's over at school, so that's where I need a ride to. I'm in downtown, at the Wildhorse Saloon, and my. . .the person who was supposed to drive me back to campus isn't in any condition to be driving me anywhere." Caylor pressed her hand to her free ear to try to block out the overpowering noise.

"It'll take me at least twenty minutes to get there. Where should I meet you?"

"If you will call me as soon as you pass Tootsie's on Broadway, I'll meet you down on Second Avenue just in front of the Wildhorse." She cringed as a loud, shrieking *woooooooo* went up from the table beside her. Riley had just chugged a beer into which a shot had been dropped. He'd be dropping soon if his unsteadiness was any indication.

"Are you sure? I don't mind parking and coming in to meet you."

"No point in you paying to park and having to buy a ticket or pay the cover or whatever to come in." Besides, she didn't want him to see the condition of the guy she'd agreed to go out with on a date. "I'll meet you on the street."

"Okay. I'll call you when I pass Tootsie's. I'm in the car and headed your direction now."

"Thanks, Dylan."

"My pleasure."

After hanging up, she kept the phone wrapped securely in her hand, checking the time every couple of minutes. She couldn't wait until he called to say he was just a few minutes up the street before telling Riley she was leaving.

Fifteen minutes after talking to Dylan, Caylor stood and shrugged into her raincoat. She checked the time again. Based on how long it took her to get into downtown from Sassy's house—which was a little farther away than Perty's—Dylan should be approaching the Broadway exit on I-40, which meant he'd be calling her in a couple of minutes.

Tucking her purse under her arm—she didn't like to leave it hanging for anyone to try to grab in a crowd like this—she slid down from the chair and squeezed through the crowd that had gathered between the tables and the bar to get to the bachelorettes' table.

It took a couple of attempts to get Riley's attention. When she finally did, she wished she hadn't.

"Hey babe." He wrapped his arm around her waist, pulled her to him, and gave her a smacking kiss—which missed her mouth only because she turned her head at the last moment. The overwhelming stench of alcohol on his breath turned her stomach.

"Riley, I'm leaving. A friend is coming to pick me up." She had to use both hands to pull his arm away and free herself from his painful grip.

"No—stay. Have a drink." He thrust a half-full beer mug toward her. It sloshed over the side, but she jumped back in time to keep from being splashed.

"No thank you. I've got papers to grade tonight, so I really need to get going. Thank you so much for dinner." Which she'd gone ahead and paid for because the server really wanted to clear the table so someone else could have it.

One of the bachelorettes pulled Riley's attention away, and Caylor's phone started ringing.

Dylan Bradley calling.

What a difference a day could make. Yesterday, seeing that on her phone had brought anxiety and uncertainty. Now—relief, gratitude, and an overwhelming desire to be with him. She answered and wended her way through the burgeoning crowd.

"I'll be there in about a minute." Dylan's voice acted upon her like a soothing nerve tonic.

"I'm on my way down now. Thank you so much for doing this for me."

"As I said, it's my pleasure. I just stopped at the red light on Third, so I'm about a block away."

Caylor pushed through the crowd coming up the stairs. "Is it still raining?"

"Just a light drizzle."

"Good. I just realized I left my umbrella in Ri—in the car of the person who brought me here tonight." Why couldn't she bring herself to tell him she'd been on a date with someone else? It wasn't as if she and Dylan were anything to each other but friends and colleagues. It wasn't as if she hadn't just seen a picture of him with some blond bombshell hanging off his arm. And besides, there was still the little matter of Dylan's former department chair to contend with.

"I'm turning left onto Second Avenue."

"I'm at the front doors now." Caylor stepped out into the cold, damp air and took a cleansing breath. She'd have to shower as soon as she got home and throw everything she was wearing into an incinerator—well, the washing machine would probably do fine—just to get the stench of alcohol out of it.

Dylan's bright blue Escape pulled to a stop on the other side of the cars parked along the curb. Caylor hurried to it and climbed in. "Thank you so much."

"I've always wanted to be the hero who rescues the damsel in distress. Just like you always wrote about me doing."

Caylor whipped her head around. Dylan's eyes sparkled in the lights from the signs on the buildings lining the street.

Riley behind her and Dylan before her, Caylor rediscovered her good humor. "But I always pictured you doing it on horseback. Don't you think an SUV is cheating?"

"An SUV is faster—and more comfortable." He put the car in gear and eased forward to the next traffic light, which turned red as they approached. "And besides, putting it into that context, aren't cell phones cheating? Shouldn't you have sent me something scrawled on parchment with a quill pen and sent by carrier pigeon?"

Caylor didn't want to break the comfortable banter, but she couldn't stand not knowing any longer. "I have to ask you a question, and I really need you to be completely honest with me."

The humor left his expression, replaced by seriousness with a hint of fear.

"Who's the girl with you in the picture in the newspaper?"

Dylan groaned. "I was hoping you wouldn't see that. She's my mother's event planner. Mother gave her tickets for the game and told her to invite me. If I'd known she'd morph into a clinging vine, if I'd known Mother had planned it as a publicity stunt, I never would have gone." His eyes bored into Caylor's. "There's nothing going on between me and Emerson. I promise."

"Was that why you argued with your mother at the restaurant?"

Dylan's groan lasted even longer this time. "You saw that, too? Yes—I publicly embarrassed Judge Grace Paxton-Bradley by arguing with her and accusing her of setting me up. Because I was afraid of what you would think if you saw the photo." He turned and drove another block to another red light. "You aren't mad at me, are you? You do believe me, don't you?"

"I'm not mad at you, and I do believe you." But what about Dr. Kramer? She longed to ask, but her mouth wouldn't form the words.

Dylan braced his elbow on the center console and leaned toward her, his brown eyes as warm as hot fudge.

Caylor no longer cared about the past or what Dylan had done or whom he'd dated. Only the present mattered—the present and the very, very near future.

Did she dare?

His eyes searched hers.

Oh yes, she dared.

Ignoring the car horn blowing behind them, Caylor leaned forward and kissed Dylan. Heart pounding, skin tingling, she pressed her lips to his and reached over and threaded her fingers through the short curls at the back of his head. He stiffened for a brief moment then relaxed, smiling against her mouth, and returned the kiss with equal gusto.

And it was better than she'd ever imagined.

Chapter 26

❧

ust like that? She just up and kissed you?" A grin played around Tyler's mouth. "Way to go, bro."

Dylan jumped up from the wooden chair and paced to the art wall, then returned to the open laptop on the table. His brothers looked at him from three boxes on the screen. "No—this isn't a good thing. I can't do this again. I can't go through this again."

"Go through what?" Pax asked. "She's beautiful, she's funny, she's talented, and for some reason, she seems to like you."

"She's older than me, and she's moving our relationship ahead without asking me what I think of it or what I want." He dropped back down onto the chair, trying to push past the memory of the elation that had washed through him after the brief blip of shock when Caylor kissed him.

"What happened after she kissed you?" Spencer, who'd just gotten home from a date, pulled a ratty old Hume-Fogg High School T-shirt over his head, mussing his usually perfect hair.

"Well, we were sitting in the middle of the street, so I started driving. There's some road construction in downtown, so I got a little turned around, and we talked about how much downtown has changed over the years." Oh, but his mind hadn't been on downtown or the condo buildings or the new convention center. His mind had been on the kiss and hoping that one of the traffic lights would turn red so that he could kiss her again.

And that had scared him more than anything. "It isn't a very long drive to campus from there, so we were still chatting when I pulled up to drop her off."

"And. . . ?" Pax prompted.

"And what? We said good night, and she got out and got into her own car and drove off." Dylan ran his hands over his rough cheeks. Ugh—he should have shaved today. Probably grossed her out when she kissed him, feeling that stubble against her perfectly porcelain skin.

"You didn't open the door for her, walk her to her car, give her a good-night kiss?" Spencer shook his head. "Dude, you're so lame."

"No, actually, she practically jumped out of the car as soon as I pulled it to a stop in the parking lot."

"Probably because she felt weird because you didn't do anything about it but just let it hang there between you." Spencer dragged his fingers through his hair, and it fell back into perfect alignment.

Dylan rubbed his eyes. "Y'all have to understand. The whole thing with Rhonda started because she initiated everything. She took me to art shows and the symphony and out to dinner—she informed me, never asked me. She instigated the physical contact between us. She kissed me. She. . .made me believe that moving in with her was the natural progression of our relationship, even though there was a tiny voice in the back of my head telling me it wasn't what I wanted." Dylan slumped down, resting his head against the top slat of the tall, ladder-back chair.

Pax leaned his elbows on his desk, putting his face closer to the camera on his computer. "And did you hear that voice tonight when Caylor kissed you?"

"No." He didn't even have to think about it.

"Why not?"

He heaved a sigh. "Because I've been wanting to kiss her for a long time. I just wasn't sure how she felt about me. She's so poised and polished and mature and. . .well, she just has her life together, and mine's a mess. I mean, I'm getting back to a point at which I understand myself. I've been able to separate my disappointment with the church from my relationship with God, and I feel like I'm on good terms with Him again. I've accepted the full-time position at Robertson. But it's like I'm fresh out of college and just getting started with life, while she's been living the life she's chosen for a long time now. She's settled and secure and. . .tenured."

"So why would that preclude her from falling in love with you?" Tyler's voice rasped from the cold he'd had for several days. "What does all that stuff have to do with who you fall in love with?"

"Because I don't want to feel like I'm living off of her the way I did with Rhonda. I don't want her to feel like she has to support me or take care of me. I want to be the provider. I want to be the one who takes care of her." Embarrassment washed over him as soon as the words finished tumbling out of his mouth.

His brothers burst out laughing.

"Good grief, could you *be* any more nineteenth century about it?" Spencer leaned back in his swivel desk chair. "Seriously? You're going to put a damper on your feelings for this girl because she makes more money than you? Because she has tenure and you don't?"

"No—you're being obtuse." Or was he? Spencer had a point— Dylan was putting a little too much emphasis on external values instead of focusing on Caylor herself. "I just don't want to find myself in the same situation I was in with Rhonda."

"Oh, so you're saying Caylor is just like Rhonda, then?" Spencer's tone changed from mirthful to challenging. "That she's going to dictate to you what you should paint, where you should live, and who your friends should be?"

Dylan wanted to shout at his brother. He gripped the edge of the table. "No—she's not like that at all. She's kind and considerate and funny and selfless. She gave up her own life to move in with and take care of her grandmother five years ago. She stepped in and picked up the slack for her younger sister when Sage didn't show up to model for my studio class. She loves my paintings." She loved the sketches he'd done of himself—slightly disguised—so much she'd based her characters on him.

"So she's not anything like Rhonda." Tyler's soft voice broke through Dylan's memory of Caylor telling him about her books. "Yet you still believe your relationship with someone who's the total opposite from Rhonda will turn out the same way. That just doesn't add up for me."

"The scientific approach would be to try it out—look on it as an experiment—and see if you get a different result with different components." Pax's mouth quirked to the side, an obvious attempt to try to hide his humor.

"Shall I give you a business analogy to go along with math and science?" Spencer asked.

"No. Please don't." Dylan's bottom lip trembled with his effort to keep frowning rather than let himself smile. "We're supposed to be having coffee after I get finished with class tomorrow. What should I say to her?"

His brothers looked around at each other on their own screens.

"Just be honest with her," Pax finally said. "Tell her everything about Rhonda, and then tell her how you feel about her. Let her decide how she wants to proceed based on the absolute truth. Don't gloss over anything."

Pax's last statement sucker-punched Dylan. He thought about all of those canvases downstairs he'd painted over, covering the original artwork and preparing the canvas for a new image. That's what he'd been doing with Caylor—only letting her see a veneer, the top layer of the image of his life when what he should do was let that layer become transparent so she could see the pentimento of false starts and mistakes he'd made and then painted over.

Even after the pep talk from his brothers, Dylan had trouble sleeping. He should talk to Ken about this. The advice he'd gotten in the counseling sessions, the things he'd learned about himself in just a couple of months had made Dylan feel like a different person—or like Rip van Winkle waking up after a twenty-year sleep, or five in this case.

But Ken wouldn't be able to give him advice that was any better than what his brothers had told him. It wasn't advice he needed. It was guidance. He rolled onto his back and stared at the ceiling.

"Lord, I know I haven't been on the best terms with You over the last several years, but I can't deny that You've managed to take the mess that I made out of my life on my own and turn it into something good. I don't want to assume too much, but I think You put Caylor in my life for a reason. And I want to make sure I do this on Your terms, not mine—because I don't want to mess this up by moving outside of Your will. So if You'd see fit, I'd really appreciate it if You could give me some clarity on this. . .thing with her and show me where You want us to go with it."

His eyelids drooped, and he yawned. "Thanks. Um, amen."

❧

She might as well have canceled classes today, for all that she was able to pay attention during them. Caylor paced the cramped confines of her office, tempted to call Zarah or Flannery and tell them what had happened last night. But she just couldn't bring herself to do it. Not when it would most likely mean humiliation when Dylan didn't show up for coffee this afternoon and never wanted anything to do with her ever again because she'd completely offended and embarrassed him.

What had she been thinking, kissing him like that?

Goose bumps ran up her arms. When he'd kissed her back, she could have died a happy woman. But then they'd both fallen back on inane chatter to keep awkward silence at bay, and by the time they got to campus, Caylor's mortification had been complete. How would she ever be able to face him again—even just to apologize for her rash action?

Oh, but what a kiss it had been. Would she be able to apologize for something she wasn't sorry she'd done?

Three twenty-five. She should probably go—though she'd most likely beat him there, since a teacher rarely managed to get away from the classroom right at dismissal time. She grabbed some cash and locked up her desk and the office. She almost wished for a student to come around the corner at the top of the stairs and stop her with a life-or-death issue.

But no student materialized.

No one stopped her on the way to the student center, diagonally across the quad from Davidson. The food court area in the lowest level of the student center buzzed with activity, but even it wasn't as crowded as usual. She ordered a caramel latte at the coffee kiosk and stood to

279

the side to wait for it, greeting students as they recognized her.

She'd just picked up her coffee when Dylan entered. Taller than most of the people in the room, he was hard to miss. A few drama students gathered around a table nearby stopped him to say hi, but he didn't linger.

Their gazes locked. Caylor's breath caught in her chest. Then he smiled at her. Not a tight, nervous smile, but a genuine, warmth-filled smile.

Unlike every other time they'd ever seen each other, Dylan came close, placed his hands on her upper arms, and kissed her right cheek. "Hey." He stepped back.

Caylor had to clear the gleeful surprise that clogged her throat. "Hey, yourself."

"Want to grab a table? I'll join you as soon as I get my coffee."

Though she'd never thought him immature, something about him was different today—maybe the assertiveness in his manner or the confidence in his voice. Different in a good way, because it made Caylor believe that the seven years' difference in their ages really wasn't an issue at all.

She picked a table in a back corner where they could have a modicum of privacy for their talk. Their talks. Because after last night, two things needed to be discussed.

A few minutes later, Dylan joined her, stirring the whipped cream down into his frozen latte. He set a few extra napkins down and sat across from her at the small, two-person table.

"I know you probably have a reason why you wanted to get together and chat today before deciding whether or not to go to the World War II concert with me this weekend." Dylan took a sip of his drink through the green straw. "But there's something I want to talk to you about first. Something I need to tell you."

Her heart sank. Here it came—the let's-just-be-friends speech.

"At Watts-Maxwell I was an assistant professor in the painting department under the direct supervision of Dr. Rhonda Kramer, the department chair. . . ." Dylan's eyes hardly wavered from Caylor's as he told her what she'd wanted to know without her asking about it.

Latte forgotten, Caylor leaned forward, bracing her elbows on the table, resting her chin in her hands. She ached for the impressionable young man he'd been, falling into the clutches of an overbearing, manipulative woman like Dr. Kramer. Now what Wyatt Oakes had told her made sense. That's why Dr. Kramer answered Dylan's personal phone and told Wyatt to stop calling. She'd been trying to isolate Dylan from anyone who might be able to show him what she was doing to him.

"I knew better than to let the relationship go as far as it did—to become intimate, to move in together—but I was so far in it at that point, I didn't see any way out. She had changed everything about me—my painting, my friends, my whole being." He watched his hand as he moved his straw in and out of the cup, making it squeak against the lid holding it in place.

"How did you get out?" Caylor lifted her cup to drink and soothe her throat, dried out from the anger building there.

Dylan looked up from his cup, a wry expression pulling at one corner of his mouth. "I wanted to come home for Thanksgiving and Christmas this year. Rhonda told me she was my family. She'd made me who I was, and if I left the apartment, she'd ruin me. I packed up my few belongings, threw them in the truck, and drove over to a friend's place where I crashed for a few days until my employment was terminated due to her going to the human resources department and invoking the nepotism regulation to get me fired. And then I came home."

He moved his empty cup aside and traced the condensation ring with his forefinger. "I was so angry and resentful when I first got back. I thought everyone had an agenda and was working against me—even my grandparents, who've always been the most supportive people in my life. It got so bad, my brothers had to hold an intervention with me and suggest I go into counseling."

Caylor smiled at the mention of his brothers. "It's good to know that you have people in your life who care that much about you." *Like me*, she wanted to add.

He reflected her smile. "I don't deserve them. But they're my best friends. I couldn't have gotten through this recovery without them." His smile faded. "And I am still recovering, Caylor. I still have hang-ups and issues and things I need to work through. And a mother who does have an agenda and may still be working against me."

"That can't be true." At least Caylor couldn't believe a mother could do that to her son.

Dylan quirked a brow. "You haven't met my mother."

Caylor knew she couldn't wait any longer to broach the other topic of conversation they needed to explore. "I'm sorry about last night. I'm sorry if I complicated things for you by what I did. . .by kissing you."

The tension in his face eased, his eyes softened, and he leaned closer, taking her hands in his across the table. "Don't be sorry. I'm glad you did it. I've been wanting to kiss you for a while now."

Her heart sped up a little, though she tried to control it. "But it isn't the right time."

"Not the right time for us to be moving forward that quickly, no. Caylor—I need to take this slowly. I need to figure out who I am, what I want out of my life, and what God wants me to do before I can make any commitments to a relationship between us." He squeezed her hands then released them. "But I can tell you that I do want a relationship with you. An old-fashioned, Saturday-night-date, we-can-hold-hands-at-the-movies kind of relationship—because I can't imagine not spending time with you."

Caylor's joy swelled—then deflated. "Dylan, you know I live with my grandmother, right?"

He nodded.

"And she depends on me. I've committed to staying with her until. . .well, until she doesn't need me anymore. And that may be ten, fifteen, or even twenty years from now." She wanted to cry—overwhelmed by the idea she wasn't free to promise Dylan anything more than just the casual dating relationship he'd described, not for many, many years to come.

"I understand." He reached for her hands again. "I'm still getting back in touch with God right now, but I truly believe that if He means for us to be together, He'll make a way for us to be together. Besides," he grinned, "I like Sassy."

"Good. She likes you, too." Caylor turned her hands over and squeezed his. "Since we're baring our pasts, I should probably tell you I was engaged twelve years ago. He played baseball for Vanderbilt when we were in college there. He was the first guy who ever showed any romantic interest in me. We were together three years, and I'd already started planning the wedding."

Sympathy filled Dylan's brown eyes. "What happened?"

"He met Sage."

"He met. . ." Comprehension eased the lines of confusion between his brows. "Oh. She flirted with him, and he fell for her."

"Yep. And then she ran away. Packed up her car and drove off in the middle of the night. Mama and Daddy were in the final stages of getting ready to move to Switzerland, I was getting ready to go back to the UK to finish my PhD, and Papa—my grandfather—had just been diagnosed with cancer. And of course Sage left me to do damage control—to try to find out where she'd gone, to clean up the mess she'd left between Bryan and me."

Caylor looked down at their joined hands, unable to look Dylan in the eye for the next part. "I. . .I tried to win Bryan back. I threw myself at him. He'd wanted to be physically intimate almost from the beginning of our relationship—and sometimes I wonder if he proposed to me to see if I'd sleep with him once we were engaged. But no matter how hard I tried—and I tried everything short of taking off my clothes and climbing into bed with him—he didn't want me anymore."

Dylan's hands tightened around hers. "Then he's an idiot, and you're the better for it. You aren't damaged goods, the way I am."

Caylor lifted Dylan's hands and kissed the backs of them. "My pastor has a verse he likes to quote. It's from 2 Corinthians, and it says that in Christ, we're new creatures; the old passes away, and He makes us new. I believe that. I hope you can come to see the truth of it in your life. Because you aren't damaged goods."

Moisture gathered along Dylan's bottom lashes, and he blinked a couple of times. " 'Love sees perfect that which is imperfect.' "

"I've never heard that before." Caylor ran the saying over and over through her mind, wanting to correct the grammar of it.

"It's something Perty always told us boys. She said that though we're always going to be imperfect, when someone loves us, they don't see the imperfections—they see us as perfect."

Silence fell between them for the first time in almost an hour, their hands still clasped on the table between them.

"Dylan?"

"Yes?"

"How long do we have to do just the hand-holding part?" She let only one corner of her mouth quirk up.

He blinked then grinned back at her. "I'll ask my counselor on Friday."

Chapter 27

Dylan paced a circle in the small, dim room. The shirt collar shouldn't feel so tight, so rough against his neck—not with as much money as he'd paid for it. Of course, this was only the third time he'd worn this suit, and he was unaccustomed to dressing up like this for art showings, so he wasn't surprised at his discomfort.

He could hear the guests arriving—the voices, the clink of glasses at the makeshift bar. He clasped his fingers behind his neck and took several deep breaths. He'd never been this nervous at a show before—because even though it had been his art on display, Rhonda had always taken center stage.

Though, he supposed, Mother would do the same thing tonight. But he'd never had to make an entrance before.

A light tap on the door gave him half a second's notice before Emerson entered the back room. "Are you ready to be introduced?"

He dropped his arms to his sides and backed up a step when she stopped just a bit too close to him. "Ready as I'll ever be."

Emerson reached up and straightened his tie and shirt collar, then smoothed her hands down the lapels of his jacket. He'd made it clear at the game he wasn't interested, yet she still seemed intent on making people think they were together tonight. And Mother was nearly as bad—even after she'd paid lip service to him by way of an apology at church on Sunday the week after the newspaper photo fiasco—encouraging the photographer to take pictures of Dylan and Ems together before the event started.

Oh how he wished Caylor were here.

His mother's voice, magnified by a borrowed PA system, silenced the crowd beyond the door.

"I want to thank all of you for coming out tonight. If you haven't already, please be sure to get a glass of wine and some of the lovely canapés made for us by Chef Christy." A light smattering of applause followed this.

"Now, the moment I've been waiting for. As many of you know, my oldest son left Nashville, studied art in New York, and has been living in Philadelphia for the last several years honing his craft. As you've seen here tonight on your way in, his talent far exceeds his reputation. Some of the reviews that have been written of his previous shows back East call him 'brilliant,' 'an audacious talent,' 'in company with the masters of technique,' and 'an exciting new talent for the new millennium.' "

Dylan jolted at those words being spoken in his mother's voice—until he noticed Emerson was mouthing the words along with her. Obviously, Mother had not written this speech herself.

"So tonight is your opportunity to acquire a painting by this up-and-coming artist before his art hits the mainstream and the prices skyrocket. And your money goes toward a wonderful charity." Mother spent a moment talking about the crisis pregnancy center she'd supposedly been donating to over the years.

Dylan wiped his hands on the handkerchief Gramps had given him earlier for that very purpose—when he had seen Dylan wiping his hands on his pants legs.

"Without further ado, it's my very great pleasure to introduce our guest of honor tonight, our artist, Dylan Bradley."

Emerson threw the door open, and Dylan walked through with as much dignity as he could muster. Rhonda would have been profoundly mortified by the spectacle his mother made of the introduction—having him make an entrance to the applause of the exhibit attendees.

Frankly, he was mortified. And he'd much rather be at JRU at the opening-night production of *Much Ado about Nothing*—sitting with Caylor, his arm around her, as he had last weekend at the World War II program.

He raised his hand in a wave of acknowledgment of the crowd's tribute to him. "Thank you all for coming tonight. I hope you all enjoy viewing the art."

Mother rolled her eyes and turned away from him. "Enjoy yourselves—and try not to fight over the pieces," she quipped. A few people laughed politely as they dispersed to wander among the temporary walls displaying the pieces Dylan could barely remember painting and really hoped he wouldn't have to take home tonight.

"Dylan, darling." Grandma Paxton took him by the hands and made him lean over and kiss her cheeks. "I'm so pleased your mother invited us to come down for your little show, since we've never gotten to see any of your work. I have to say, it is very. . .interesting."

"Thanks, Grandma. Is Grandpa with you?" Dylan glanced around the room, looking for his mother's father—so he could avoid him.

"He's back by the bar, chatting up some tall redhead."

Tall redhead? Dylan spun on his heel. Sure enough, towering over his grandfather, a bottle of water in her hand, stood Caylor, wearing the dark aqua cocktail dress she'd worn to the faculty holiday party at school. She looked up and locked gazes with him over his grandfather's head. As tactfully as she could, she excused herself from Grandpa Paxton and made her way through the crowd over to him.

He shook a few people's hands before she got to him, but he couldn't get rid of them fast enough. Slipping his arm around Caylor's waist, he closed his eyes and took a slow breath in through his nose. She smelled like raspberries and vanilla tonight.

He leaned over and kissed her temple. "What are you doing here? I thought you were going to the opening-night production."

"I went to the preshow rehearsal and wished everyone luck and went over a few pronunciations with people. But once the show started, there really was no reason I needed to stay, since we plan on seeing it tomorrow night. Besides, coming and supporting you in this is much more important than sitting through the shake-out performance." She leaned closer, pressing her lips close to his ear. "I have to tell you, though, I like your other work—your *real* work—much better than these paintings."

He laughed and hugged her. Ken had told him to look for and

make note of the ways in which Caylor was different from Rhonda—the ways in which Caylor was more positive, more beneficial for him. The list just kept growing.

His grandmother cleared her throat.

"Oh, sorry. This is my grandmother, Vera Dillon-Paxton, Mother's mom. Grandma, I'd like you to meet Dr. Caylor Evans. My girlfriend." It was the first time he'd called her that. It felt a little strange calling a thirty-five-year-old woman his girlfriend. But the way she blushed and smiled self-consciously when he said it made him want to call her that at every opportunity from now on.

Grandma's expression turned from curious to forbidding. "*Doctor* Evans?"

Caylor withdrew her hand from Grandma's. "Yes. I'm a professor of English at James Robertson University here in Nashville."

"So. . ." Grandma looked speculatively from Caylor to Dylan, "she's not in your department? Not your supervisor?"

Thank goodness he'd already told Caylor everything—including how his parents and maternal grandparents had taken it. "No Grandma. We're in completely different departments. Colleagues. And I've already checked"—he cut his gaze toward Caylor, who hadn't heard this before—"and there's no rule anywhere in the faculty handbook forbidding professors in different departments from dating."

Caylor's smile returned full force.

Mother chose that moment to walk by. Dylan stopped her to introduce her to Caylor. Mother pasted on her best politician's smile, clasped Caylor's hand in both of hers as if they were long lost friends, and said she was looking forward to getting to know Caylor better. She barely glanced at Dylan, whispered something to her mother, and then moved on to another group of people. Typical. Lavish praise on him and his work in front of all of the guests, but still give him the personal cold shoulder.

The shawl Mother wore over her strapless gown slipped, revealing an expanse of right shoulder and back.

Dylan frowned, reaching for Caylor's bottle of water to quench his dry mouth and throat. "Grandma, how did Mother get that scar on her back? I've never seen it before."

Grandma harrumphed. "That's where she had that hideous tattoo removed."

He inhaled half the mouthful of water, choking and sputtering, eyes watering. "Tattoo? Mother had a tattoo?"

Grandma glared at him. "Yes. When she was young and stupid—eighteen—she eloped with a young hooligan she'd been dating for all of two weeks. They drove all the way from Cleveland to New York in one night and got tattoos to commemorate the event."

"What was it?"

"An angel and a demon sitting on a motorcycle kissing." Grandma narrowed her eyes. "But if you ever tell her that you know anything about it, that I told you, you will be cut out of the will. It goes no further." She turned her scowl on Caylor, who raised her hand as if being sworn in by a judge.

"Wait—she *married* this guy?" Dylan dropped his voice so no one would overhear them.

Grandma closed her eyes as if the memory pained her. "Yes. But as soon as your grandfather found them, he began the proceedings to have it annulled. That's when we made the decision to send your mother to Vanderbilt for college. Grandpa and Gerald Bradley were old school chums, and he knew Gerald would keep an eye on Grace for us. And it all worked out in the end, didn't it?" Grandma looked past Dylan and Caylor toward the bar.

Dylan followed her gaze—Grandpa leaned against the bar flirting with Emerson.

"Now, if you'll excuse me, I must go remind your grandfather to behave himself."

Caylor slipped her hand in Dylan's and turned to face him. "What in the world was that about?"

"The tattoo thing?" Dylan told her the story about the Christmas photo shoot and Mother's reaction to seeing his tattoo. "I didn't tell her I have another one here," he touched his left upper arm, then smiled and leaned forward. "And it was inspired by the art I did for one of your book covers. Next time I wear short sleeves, I'll show it to you." He looked over at where his mother schmoozed with several potential campaign donors. "The hypocrite."

"Dylan—look at it from her perspective. She's probably embarrassed, horrified, by what she did, by the bad choices she made. And in her mind, a tattoo is the physical embodiment of poor judgment and bad decisions. So seeing that her wayward son had a tattoo—no doubt a remnant of what she considers his misspent years away—probably made her relive whatever pain she still carries around with her from her own past."

He wanted to argue, tell her that she didn't know his mother the way he did. But after learning a piece of Mother's past he'd never known before, he had to wonder if he'd ever truly known her. "You're right. I have to give her the benefit of the doubt. But I have to ask—are you always going to be so reasonable about everything?"

She wrinkled her nose and shook her head. "Nah. Only when you're not. And I expect you to do the same for me."

He was about to kiss the tip of her nose when Emerson joined them. She thrust her hand out toward Caylor, who had to extract hers from Dylan's to shake it.

"Hi, I'm Emerson Bernard, the event planner. I hate to do this to you, but we really need our artist to mix and mingle and let the patrons have a few minutes with him. If they feel like they've gotten to know the artist, they're more likely to bid higher on the paintings." She wrapped her hand around Dylan's arm and pulled him away from Caylor without a backward glance.

Dylan shot an apologetic look over his shoulder, and Caylor winked at him. Moments later, she'd joined Perty, Gramps, and Sassy, who were standing near the main showpiece examining it as if trying to figure out exactly what it was supposed to be. Perty gave Caylor a huge hug, and Dylan almost laughed.

When Sassy and Perty came up with the plan to make sure Dylan and Caylor saw each other by having him paint Sassy's portrait, he'd at first been hesitant. He wasn't sure he liked the idea of their grandmothers trying to manipulate their relationship. But he'd come to see they did it out of love—for him and for Caylor—and a desire to see them both happy. That was the kind of love family was supposed to have for one another. And though he didn't experience that with his own parents, from what Caylor had told him about hers, he had a feeling that becoming part of the Evans family would enrich his life in ways he couldn't possibly imagine.

∞

The backstage chaos greeted them when Caylor and Dylan joined the cast and crew in the workshop for the post-presentation rehash of the performance Friday night. Having participated in her share of productions over the years, Caylor understood the need to decompress, analyze each error, and pick on fellow cast mates for flubbed lines and the crew for misplaced props, late scene drops or changes, and microphone malfunctions.

But no matter how occupied the students were with their critiques of themselves and everyone else, no one seemed to miss the fact that Dr. Evans and Mr. Bradley were holding hands when they walked into the room.

Caylor knew the teasing would last only until discussion of tomorrow afternoon's matinee put the relationship status of the English and art professors out of their minds.

Not so with Bridget, though, who hurried across the workshop and gave Caylor a rib-crushing hug. "I knew it. I knew it! I knew right from the very first time I saw the two of you in the same room that you were destined to be together."

"Congratulations on the show, Bridge. They did a great job." Caylor rubbed her sides when Bridget released her to hug Dylan.

He escaped her clutches faster. "Yes, the performance was great"— he raised his voice—"and the set pieces were spectacular."

A cheer went up from the setting design team.

The other drama professors beckoned Bridget to join them. "Excuse me. Time for me to go take my knocks from my colleagues." She shook her head, smiling.

Caylor spoke to several students, particularly the four leads, before pulling Dylan away from the design students so they wouldn't keep Flannery, Zarah, and Bobby waiting too long at the restaurant—since the three had left right after the performance.

Midtown traffic resembled rush hour—even at ten thirty on a Friday night. Caylor directed Dylan to the parking lot behind the row of restaurants and shops on Elliston Place, and fortunately, a space opened up just as he pulled into the lot. Caylor waited for him to come around and open her door. "Are you sure you don't mind eating here? I know it's an expense you probably don't need right now."

He squeezed her hand and shut the door behind her. "It's okay. And don't even think about insisting on paying your own way. I looked at their menu online, and it's actually not that bad. So don't go ordering the cheapest thing they have just because you feel bad for the poor artist."

Caylor did feel bad that he felt like he had to cover her meal because he didn't want her friends to think less of him—but she also knew that if she offered to give him money or, worse yet, pulled her wallet out to pay for *his* dinner in front of them, he would probably never speak to her again.

They walked around the end of the building and down to Gold Rush. The hostess led them back through the bustling restaurant to the round table where Flannery, Zarah, and Bobby sat—a plate of half-devoured chili-cheese fries on the table in front of them.

Bobby stood and shook Dylan's hand. Dylan greeted each of them by name before Caylor could remind him, and she hid her smile when he turned to assist her with her chair. After all, he had spent an entire evening around them at the Christmas dinner and visited their church at least once.

"So, Dylan, I guess you've decided Acklen Ave. isn't the church for you?" Flannery handed Dylan and Caylor the extra appetizer plates and motioned for them to dig into the fries. "At least, I haven't seen you around since before Christmas."

"I've decided I'm going to be joining Providence." Dylan pushed the small plate aside and rested his hands in his lap.

"Of course you are." Flannery winked at him.

"Hey, now, don't you go disparaging my church," Caylor teased, hoping Dylan wouldn't be offended by Flannery's insinuation. "I believe Dylan decided to join the weekend that we were in New York, so it didn't have anything to do with me."

"No—actually, Caylor's nothing but a big distraction. It was much easier for me to find out how much I liked the church when she wasn't there."

Caylor turned, agog, at Dylan's deadpan statement. But as soon as she saw the crinkles around his eyes, she burst out laughing. "It's a good thing I sit in the back row of the choir loft during worship service, then, so that I'm not distracting you from close by."

"I'll just have to resign myself to sitting on the back row—where that pillar blocks my view of you—so I can concentrate on the service." He grinned at her.

Oh, she wanted to kiss him so badly—but it wasn't the right time for that. They'd decided together to wait, to take things slowly. But the fact that he was comfortable enough with her to tease her like this in front of her closest friends made her wish that they hadn't agreed to proceed with caution.

Once Bobby and Dylan found out that they both liked hockey and basketball, Caylor, Zarah, and Flannery were left to their own devices and topics of conversation. Zarah didn't want to talk about the wedding—she'd had lunch with Beth and was wedding-talked out—so they fell back on talking about starting their own book club.

"It's a great idea, but none of us ever has the time to read." Zarah pushed the last chicken tender around on her plate. Bobby reached over and speared it with his fork and chowed down on it.

"Or the energy." Flannery popped her last potato chip in her mouth. "Reading is the last thing I feel like doing when I get home after a long day of editing manuscripts or arguing with—excuse me, *negotiating* with—agents and authors."

"And my agent just told me that I should expect a new contract for the historical romance any day now. With that to write on top of everything going on at school, extracurricular reading isn't high on my agenda right now." Caylor sighed and pushed her plate back. The grilled cheese sandwich had been good—she just wasn't accustomed to eating this late, so the homemade potato chips weren't sitting well in her stomach.

"Trade you." Dylan pushed his plate—with only a lonely pickle spear on it—toward her and nodded toward her chips. She grabbed the pickle and set her plate on top of his. He immediately went back to talking college basketball championship prognostications with Bobby.

Caylor used her teeth to scoop out the soft inside of the spear first, then bit into the firmer exterior.

"What if we do movies instead of books?" Flannery suggested. "We always seem to be able to find the time to go to the movies together."

"But that's not anything new," Zarah said, averting her eyes from Caylor's enjoyment of the pickle. "We've been doing that for years."

"Not with them." Flannery inclined her head toward the guys. "We could start a group blog, and every time we go see a movie, each of the five of us could write a one-paragraph review of it to post sometime during the next week. Caylor could link to it from her blog, and maybe some of her readers would come over and read it."

"I could just make it the Friday feature on my blog," Caylor perked up a little bit. "It would keep me from always having to come up with that fifth topic every week, and my blog readers love discussing movies."

"And we don't have to always go out to the movies," Zarah added, also seeming to warm to the idea. "It could be something we each agree to rent or something that's on TV that we watch."

"What are y'all volunteering us for?" Bobby asked.

Caylor chewed the last piece of pickle, unsure of how Dylan would take such an idea. She was pretty sure she'd heard him say once he liked watching movies with his brothers, but to then be forced to sit down and write about it?

But as Zarah explained the idea, Dylan's smile grew. "That sounds like a great plan. I've toyed with the idea of starting a blog—I always feel like there are things I want to share with. . .whomever. This would give me a good feel of what it would be like to do it. Plus"—he edged closer until his shoulder touched Caylor's—"that means I don't have to put so much thought into what we're going to do on our dates every week."

She leaned forward until her nose almost touched his. "So long as you don't mind Sassy and Sage being there when we watch movies at home."

"You can bring them over to Gramps and Perty's house—there's a fabulous big-screen HDTV in the upstairs bonus room that's great for watching movies." He kissed the tip of her nose then sat up straight again and looked at Bobby on his other side. "And they've got all the video game systems up there, too. When my brothers are in town later next month, you'll have to come over and join in."

As soon as Caylor recovered from Dylan's flirting, she glanced across the table—to see a sappy smile on Zarah's face and. . .Flannery masked her expression too quickly for Caylor to be sure, but it had almost looked like jealousy.

Flannery—jealous? Flannery, who'd once told Caylor she didn't believe true love existed? Or if it did, that she didn't think she was capable of feeling it?

Taking a cue from her grandmother, Caylor made a mental note to start thinking of ways she and Zarah could try to start setting Flannery up. Because now that they'd both found love, there was no way they were going to leave Flannery out in the cold.

Chapter 28

Dylan scanned the crowd funneling past the security gate. Ken had said the time apart—while Caylor was in New York with her friends for dress fittings and stuff for Zarah's wedding—would be good for them. But four days of total separation, including the agreement that they wouldn't talk on the phone or so much as text or e-mail while she was away, had only made Dylan's desire to be with Caylor expand to the point that he could hardly think of anything else.

Except when he was painting. Because of course when he was painting, he wasn't thinking about being with her; he was focused on re-creating her face, her eyes, her nose, her hands. . . .

There—above the crowd, a crown of stylishly messy red hair. Caylor bounced up on tiptoe and waved at him over the heads of the cattle-call crowd between them. He waved back, heart strumming his ribs like an electric guitar.

He yearned to run to her and kiss her when she finally cleared the secured area, but he held himself back to just a peck on the cheek and a long hug.

"I missed you."

"Me, too." She wove her fingers through the hair at the crown of his head, and prickles of pleasure pursued each other up and down his spine.

An anonymous wolf whistle from the crowd teeming past them sent flames of embarrassment licking up the back of Dylan's neck. He reluctantly pulled out of the hug but then wrapped his arm around

Caylor's waist, not wanting any more distance between them than possible.

"Did you have a good trip?" They strolled toward the escalator that would take them down to baggage claim. Several people brushed past him, obviously annoyed with their slow pace. But he didn't care. All was once again right with the world.

"Zarah's dress needs more alterations—she's been so nervous and consternated about this whole wedding that she's lost about fifteen or twenty pounds." Caylor dug her knuckles into his side at his chuckle. "Yes junior high boy, I said *consternated* not *constipated*."

Dylan couldn't help his amusement, still giddy from simply being in Caylor's presence again. "You English professors and your big words. But I do feel sorry that she isn't enjoying this more. I always thought brides liked doing this kind of stuff."

"If Zarah had been able to have the kind of wedding she wanted— small, just family and a few close friends—she'd be much happier right now. But Bobby's an only child of wealthy parents, and Zarah's a people pleaser. So they're both trying to make his parents happy."

Dylan had met Bobby earlier that week at a place where they could eat all the hot wings they could handle and then played darts and pool afterward. Bobby had told Dylan all about his past—about getting in trouble his senior year of high school, which led him to having to enlist in the army, meeting Zarah, their breakup, and the subsequent fourteen years he'd been away from Nashville and his parents. So Dylan could understand why Bobby wanted to give his parents as big a role in the wedding as possible—to make up for lost time.

"Speaking of parents. . ." Though, really, he didn't want to ruin this reunion with Caylor. "I finally heard back from mine about dinner."

"Really? When do they want to go?" Caylor handed her soft-sided briefcase to Dylan and stepped toward the luggage carousel.

"Um. . .tonight." He looked down and picked at a spot of brown paint on the base knuckle of his left thumb. "Mother really wants to do it before the election at the beginning of April because she's worried about how busy she'll be after that. Assuming she wins."

Caylor looked over her shoulder. "You think she won't?"

He shrugged. "This morning's newspaper said the poll numbers spiked two weeks ago after the art auction—that it was the biggest single donation the crisis pregnancy center had ever received—but that since then, the numbers have been sliding back down to where they were around the time they busted her for the scene in the restaurant almost two weeks before that. Where she's polling right now, it doesn't look like she'll win."

Caylor turned and lifted a bright red suitcase off the belt. Dylan stepped forward and took it from her and handed the smaller bag back to her.

"How do you feel about the possibility your mom might lose the election?"

He shrugged again. "Sorry for her, I guess. She really wants this." Of course, she'd never seemed overly concerned with what he wanted, so why—

No. That was a very unproductive line of thinking, something he'd written about several times in the journal Ken made him keep. It didn't matter if his mother had never supported him in what he wanted. She was his mother. He would support her dream to be elected to the state senate.

"I hope she wins."

Caylor wrapped her arm around his waist and squeezed. "What time are we meeting them for supper?"

"Six. So we have just enough time to get you home to drop off your stuff and change before we meet them."

Caylor looked down at her well-worn jeans and long-sleeved, gray, JRU T-shirt. "What, this isn't good enough for your parents?" She reached over with her free hand and smoothed the lapel of his steel-blue corduroy blazer. "I wondered why you'd gotten all dressed up just to come get me. Not that I mind, at all. Where are we meeting them?"

"Sunset Grill. And before you offer"—because he knew she would, and unlike with Rhonda, it really didn't bother him—"you don't need to offer to lend me money to pay for your dinner tonight. I sold a couple of paintings while you were gone—to someone who'd bought a piece at the auction."

Caylor stepped in front of him and stopped, facing him. "Dylan, I hope you know that I don't do it to make you feel bad or to belittle you. That's the last thing I want you to think. I just don't want you eating nothing but ramen noodles and macaroni and cheese because you feel like you have to pay for me whenever we go out. I know that, as soon as you start working full-time in August, it won't be an issue. I just don't want to be a financial burden on you."

He reached up and ran his thumb over the worry lines creasing her forehead. "I like ramen noodles and mac and cheese."

She started to protest again, but he stopped her by pressing his fingertips to her lips.

"It's okay, Caylor. Yeah, I wish I made more money"—*than you*— "but I don't mind making sacrifices so that we can go out and have a good time whenever we want to."

Caylor pulled his hand away from her mouth. "But it's not okay with me, Dylan, knowing that you're struggling to make ends meet as it is. Don't you think it's possible that I'd like to treat you to dinner or movie tickets or something occasionally? What's that Bible verse about where your treasure lies, that's where your heart is? I want to be able to do nice things for you—like treat you to dinner at expensive restaurants or go places you might not otherwise be able to go right now—because I. . ." Her voice faltered. She swallowed, blinked twice. "Because I love you."

His stomach went oozy, and his chest tightened. She'd said it— she'd broken the love barrier.

"And it's not fair for you to keep me from being able to take what I have and put it into this relationship, to keep me from feeling like an equal partner in it instead of someone who needs to be taken care of. It's somewhat insulting." She ran her hand down the lapel of his jacket again.

He caught her hand right over his heart and pressed her palm to his chest. His brothers were right: he was being far too nineteenth century about this money thing. "I never thought about it that way—that I was making you feel like I don't see you as an equal." The way he felt the whole time he was with Rhonda. "I never want to do anything to hurt you or insult you. Because I love you, too." He sealed the declaration with a soft kiss—and forced himself to back away before it got out of hand and took them where they'd both agreed they weren't ready to go yet.

Grinning at the bemused expression in her eyes, he took her by the hand and led her out to the parking garage.

On the way back to her house, she told him about the four days she'd spent in New York. "And I went back to the art museum and did it justice this time. I have to tell you I like your work much better than all those European masters with all their fat, nude women. And considering that was when the Catholic church controlled everything, I'm shocked that they could get away with it."

Dylan had an art-history lecture about that subject ready to tumble forth, but he refrained and let her continue uninterrupted. Someday when they were able to go see the masterworks together, he would explain. But it could wait until then.

At the house, he parked behind her SUV and carried her suitcase in. She took it from him at the bottom of the stairs. Curiosity at what her upstairs "loft," as she called it, looked like consumed him, but he didn't follow her. After all, she needed to change clothes.

The other side of the carport had been empty—and neither Sage nor Sassy was home. Dylan shrugged out of his blazer. For early March, it had turned out quite warm today, making the house stuffy—though it had already started to cool off outside as evening approached.

"There are glasses in the cabinet beside the fridge if you want something to drink," Caylor called down the stairs.

"Nah, I'm good." Dylan draped his jacket across one of the three tall chairs at the island's breakfast bar and sat in another. He hadn't seen this house before the remodeling, but he really liked it now—except that it didn't have enough wall space left for hanging much in the way of artwork.

He didn't have to wait long; and when Caylor appeared at the bottom of the stairs, his breath—and his heart and stomach and shoes—caught in his throat. She wore a dark-green and gold harlequin-patterned dress that, while covering her with long sleeves and a skirt just below her knees, showed off her Rubenesque body to perfection. Worn with tall brown boots with heels that made her almost the same height as him, she looked far too good to be seen with the likes of him.

Balling his hands into fists, he forced himself to stave off that line of thinking. "You look fantastic."

"Thanks. I clean up pretty well." She stepped closer, frowning. "What's that on your arm?"

"What?" He looked down at his left shoulder where she was pointing. "Oh."

Pushing up the sleeve, he revealed his other tattoo—the one Rhonda had never known the meaning behind, the one of a knight holding a medieval maiden to his side with an Irish wolfhound beside them.

"That's. . . ." Caylor ran her finger along the outline of the dog—making his skin tingle—then looked into his eyes. "That's the image from the front cover of *Lady Knight*. When did you get this?"

"About a year ago. I was working on the piece that you saw in my apartment because I hadn't been able to get that cover—or that book—out of my head in the four years since I'd read it and done the cover. Rhonda. . ." He hesitated at the mention of his ex's name, but Caylor didn't flinch. "Rhonda insisted I needed at least one more tattoo to make me look like a real artist. I guess, subconsciously, I already knew that Rhonda wasn't the right person for me, since she never liked this design or the fact I'd painted romance novel covers."

Pink patches appeared on Caylor's pale cheeks. "You permanently marked yourself with the image of one of the covers you did for one of my books."

"Rather fitting now, don't you think?" He pulled her hand away from where she continued to trace the black outlines of the full-color tattoo, knowing he'd have a hard time keeping himself from reacting physically to her touch if she kept it up.

"Has your mom seen this one?"

He released her hand and smoothed the sleeve down. "No. And I don't intend on her seeing it if I can help it—not with the way she reacted to this one." He held out his right arm so she could see the Titian tattoo on the inside of his elbow. She sounded out the Latin, and he explained to her what it meant.

"No wonder you made a bigger deal over finding out your mom had a tattoo and not that she'd run off and gotten married at eighteen." Caylor reached for the dark purple trench coat she'd taken off and draped over an empty bar stool when they'd come in.

301

Dylan assisted her into it and then shrugged back into his blazer. "It surprised me to find out that Mother has a past like that. But it's kind of helped me understand why she's always been so afraid of letting us make our own mistakes. She almost ruined her life. She doesn't want to see her boys do the same thing." He snorted. "Though in my case, her fears were justified."

"Like mother like son? Each flirted with disaster, but each managed to escape before the ruination was complete." Caylor hooked her purse strap over her shoulder.

"Something like that." He settled his hands on her shoulders. "You don't have to do this, you know."

"I want to get to know your parents."

"I'd really rather not expose you to them more often than necessary."

Caylor took his hands and pulled him toward the door. "Don't worry. Between your stories and Perty's warnings, I don't think there's anything they could do or say that would shock me."

At Caylor's prompting, Dylan told her about the paintings he'd sold and the two gallery showings he'd lined up while she was in New York. "I still have a bunch of the old stuff to get rid of, and if people are willing to pay me for them, why throw them away?"

"But you're not planning on doing any more in that style, are you?"

"No—that's my past. I'm back to doing what I love: portraits and historical."

"Good. Those are the ones I like best." Caylor indicated the turn Dylan had almost missed.

Even for this early on a Thursday evening, the parking lot behind Sunset Grill was full, so Dylan pulled up to the valet stand. He grinned at Caylor as one of the valets opened her door. "Mother would be scandalized if I self-parked."

He met her on the sidewalk, offered her his arm, and escorted her into the restaurant.

"Table for two?" the hostess asked.

"Four—there should be a reservation under Bradley."

She looked down at the book. "Oh yes. This way, please."

Dylan took several deep breaths as the hostess led them through a couple of crowded dining rooms and to. . .an empty table.

"We'll bring the rest of your party back when they arrive."

Speechless, Dylan stared at the empty table, then looked at his watch: 6:05. He'd been certain Mother and Dad would be sitting here, glaring daggers at them for daring to arrive late.

"Thank you." Caylor's voice broke through his shock.

He turned to look at her.

"Are you okay?" She touched his cheek and then his forehead.

"I can't believe they're not here yet."

She laughed softly. "I'm sure they'll be here in a minute." She sat before he could collect himself enough to assist her with her chair.

As soon as he gained his seat, he looked up to see the hostess leading his parents through the room. A couple at the table near the door stopped Mother to speak to her, and everyone else turned to look—but apparently since she wasn't a music star, she was of no interest, because they all went back to their dinners and conversations.

Both Dylan and Caylor stood when his parents approached their table.

"Dylan, darling." Mother made a big show of giving him a kiss on the cheek. "Forgive us for being late. Court ran late, and then I had a strategy meeting after that."

Dad shook hands with Caylor and greeted her in a stiff, professional manner.

"Now, Caylor, let me get a good look at you, since I didn't get a chance to at the auction a couple of weeks ago." Mother took Caylor's hands in hers and gave her the once over. Her smile grew. "Why, Dylan, I thought you said she was older than you. I refuse to believe it."

Dylan waited until he bent to help Caylor scoot in her chair before he rolled his eyes.

The first several minutes were spent discussing the menu and ordering.

Dad laid his napkin across his lap. "So, Caylor, tell us a little about yourself. Dylan says you're a Nashville native?"

"Yes sir. I was born and raised right here. Harpeth Hall, Vanderbilt, the whole nine yards." Caylor seemed so at ease, so poised, as if she did this kind of thing—impressing someone else's parents—every day.

Both Mother's and Dad's eyes lit up at the impressive educational pedigree. "And you're a tenured English professor at Robertson now?" Mother asked, emphasizing *tenured* as if that were some kind of social status instead of employment designation.

"Yes ma'am. I've been teaching at Robertson since I earned my PhD ten years ago."

Dylan decided to impress them some more. "Caylor did part of her graduate work at Oxford and the University of Dublin."

"Oxford, really?" Calculation darted through Mother's eyes. It was almost as if he could see her comparing Caylor's and Emerson Bernard's pedigrees and attributes—and finding Emerson lacking.

"Yes ma'am. My areas of study were British and Irish literature, so those seemed like the best schools to study at." Caylor reached under the tablecloth and patted Dylan's knee, which was bouncing rapidly.

He stilled at her touch.

"And who are your parents?" Dad asked, still cold and professional.

"Dean and Susan Evans. My mother was Susan Kirkwood before they married."

Dad's eyes went vacant for a moment as he probably thumbed through his mental Rolodex to see if he knew them.

"And what do your parents do?" Mother's voice had warmed about thirty degrees since she'd walked into the room.

"My father is an independent computer software designer in the international banking industry. And my mother is an oncologist who's been a leading cancer researcher with the World Health Organization for about twelve or thirteen years now. They live in Geneva."

Yes! Way to go, Caylor, getting that info in there. Dylan nodded, expression serene, and enjoyed watching as interest flickered in his father's eyes.

After learning of Caylor's impressive pedigree and social connections through her parents and grandparents—because unbeknownst to Dylan before tonight, her grandfather Frank Evans had been rather a bigwig in the recording industry and had, therefore, known lots of important people—Mother acted as if she was trying to make Caylor her new best friend.

After Dylan and Caylor split a trio of half-portion desserts between the two of them—though Caylor devoured most of the chocolate peanut butter cake and left the Boston cream pie and carrot cake for him—Mother surprised Dylan a second time tonight when she grabbed his bill before the waitress could hand it to him.

"This is our treat, son. To thank you for all the time and effort you put into making the auction such a success."

Caylor had to still his bouncing knee with her hand again.

"Thank you, Mother. But really, you don't have to—"

Dad cleared his throat, and Dylan swallowed the rest of his protest.

As they parted ways at the valet stand a few minutes later, not only did Mother kiss Caylor on the cheek—and not an air kiss, but a real one—she hugged her, too.

And Dad placed his other hand on Dylan's shoulder when they shook hands in farewell. Dylan shook his head, trying to clear the buzzing disbelief of what had just happened: a pleasant evening spent with his parents. One he wouldn't mind repeating—a few years from now perhaps.

Maybe given enough time—and enough exposure to Caylor—his parents could come around to being genuinely likeable people.

Chapter 29

Sassy whistled as she rolled the muffins in cinnamon sugar. Caylor's favorite treat—other than peanut butter cups—and usually indulged in only on her birthday. But today called for celebration. Because Sassy had finally figured everything out.

Watching Caylor and Dylan over the past few weeks had been a delight—especially since they didn't mind spending at least one evening a week here with her, watching a movie or playing games. Dylan fit in with their little family as if he'd always been part of it, which, considering he was the offspring of her best friend, wasn't that big of a surprise.

She set three muffins on a plate.

Sage trundled into the kitchen, carrying an overstuffed duffel bag. "Ooh, can I have one of those?"

Sassy jerked her head toward the counter behind her. "Help yourself. How's the move going?"

Her younger granddaughter dropped the bag on the floor. An old, ratty athletic shoe fell out and rolled several inches away. "Fine. Good thing Angie had a bed I could use so I didn't have any furniture to move—just clothes and stuff." She bit into one of the cinnamon sugar–topped muffins, closed her eyes, and groaned.

"Is this your last load?" Sassy moved toward the stairs.

"Yeah. Are you going upstairs? Tell Caylor that I should have her car back to her in a couple of hours." Sage shoved another large bite of muffin into her mouth.

"And then you'll be getting that monstrosity out of my driveway?" Sassy tried to look stern.

"It's a motorcycle, Sassy. And if memory serves, Papa had one for a long time." She winked, finished off the muffin, grabbed a canned soda out of the fridge, shoved the escaped shoe back into the bag, and hefted it up again. "Besides, in this day and age, a motorcycle is much cheaper to operate than a car."

Sassy held up her free hand to keep Sage from going on about the economic benefits of the old, rusty death trap she'd purchased with the first couple of paychecks from her new job as a receptionist at the music company in which Frank—now Sassy—held a large stake. She'd dropped two classes and cut back to part-time school hours, but the company had a great tuition reimbursement program, and her new bosses had encouraged Sage to aim higher than an office-management degree. She seemed to be fully embracing the idea.

"Just be careful."

"I'm always careful. See you in a little bit." The door slammed behind Sage.

Shaking her head, Sassy started up the stairs, rehearsing what she wanted to say to Caylor as she climbed.

"Caylor, can I speak to you for a moment?" Sassy peeked over the edge of the floor at the stairwell.

Caylor finished typing something then turned in her chair toward her. "Yes Sassy, of course. Come on up."

Sassy topped the stairs and sat atop Caylor's credenza, handing her the plate of muffins. "I feel like I've hardly seen you the last couple of weeks."

Caylor's eyes glazed over. "Cinnamon-sugar muffins!" She reached for one then drew her hand back. "What's going on?"

Sassy tried to keep her expression innocent. "Does there need to be something going on to have a treat?"

"Don't tell me, you're celebrating getting your spare bedroom back?" Caylor cocked a brow and took a muffin from the plate.

Sassy swung her feet back and forth like a little kid, her hands tucked under her thighs. "Sort of. But there's something else, too."

"What?" Caylor set down the half-eaten muffin, instantly wary.

Taking a deep breath, Sassy dived in. "Caylor, there's a big decision I've been thinking about and praying about for some time now. And I finally know what it is God is leading me to do."

Caylor leaned back in her office chair and crossed her arms. "What's that?"

"I'm going to sell the house and move in with Perty and Gerald. Perty has been after me to do it for years—we go everywhere together anyway—and they're looking for a more permanent tenant for that apartment over their garage, anyway."

"The apartment—the carriage house? But that's where Dylan lives."

Sassy's heart beat a little faster, hoping Caylor would catch on quickly to what this meant. "I know. So this isn't going to be an immediate move. But I wanted to inform you of my decision to sell the house before I contact a real estate agent. Because I wanted to give you the opportunity to buy it before it goes on the market."

"But Sassy, I can't let you do that. I can't let you give up your life, your independence for me." Tears welled in Caylor's eyes.

Blinking against the gathering moisture in her own faulty eyes, Sassy reached over and caressed Caylor's soft cheek. "Give up my independence for you? Caylor—I've never been independent. But you were before Papa died, and you gave up everything to move in and take care of me. It isn't fair—I never should have let you do it. I should have moved into Trevecca Towers or some other assisted-living facility rather than let you make the decision to give up any hope of a future so that you could take care of your blind old grandmother." She dashed away the tear burning a path down the side of her nose. "I will *not* let you give up on the very real hope of a future between you and Dylan for me. I'd rather die first."

Tears escaped and ran down Caylor's cheeks. "Don't say that. Don't even think it. You're the only grandparent I have left, you know. I can't lose you."

"Then let me do this." Sassy swallowed against the choking emotion blocking her throat. "At Perty and Gerald's, I'll have as much independence as I want—and much less house to have to keep—as well as Perty's kitchen to cook in. And I'll know that my granddaughter has the ability to life a full, abundant life and experience the kind of happiness I had with my Frank." She leaned forward and pressed her warm, smooth palms to Caylor's damp cheeks. "You've sacrificed for me long enough. Now it's my turn to sacrifice for you."

Sassy kissed her forehead. "I'll set up a time when you and I can sit down with the lawyer and discuss the house sale if you decide you'd like to do that. But for now, I'll let you get back to work." Sassy returned to the kitchen and leaned against the counter over the sink. "Lord, please let this have been Your hand guiding everything. And help Caylor make the right decision. I can't live with myself knowing she's holding back her heart from Dylan because of me."

Peace, like that which had come when Perty had offered her the carriage house, once again descended and soothed her spirit.

Yes, God was in this. She now needed to have the faith that Caylor would realize it, too.

Unable to calm her mind, Sassy pulled out ingredients to make bread. When she set the dough aside to rise, she mixed up batter for a pound cake and set it in the oven in time to punch down the bread dough and start shaping it into loaves.

"Sassy?"

She jumped at Caylor's voice. "Yes dearest?" She wiped the flour and dough off her hands onto a dish towel.

"I. . .um. . .I want to buy the house from you. I know I haven't spent a lot of time thinking about it, but I know it's the right thing to do. I feel like this is God's way of telling me that I need to move forward with my life." Caylor gave her a rueful smile. "I've had a taste of what my future could be, and I'm afraid if I don't listen now to what might be God's leading, I'm going to lose everything."

Sassy crossed the kitchen and hugged her granddaughter. "I can't tell you how happy this makes me." She stepped back, holding Caylor at arm's length. "Why don't you call Dylan and invite him over to tell him."

But Caylor shook her head. "No. Sassy, I have to figure out how to tell him in such a way that it doesn't come across like I'm pushing him to move faster with our relationship than he's ready for. I'll tell him soon—probably tomorrow. I just need to work out how to do it."

"And if he decides to take the relationship to the next level when he hears this?"

Caylor shrugged, but a smile danced around the corners of her mouth. "Then I guess you'd better get ready to start meddling in our wedding the way you've been meddling in our relationship."

Sassy pressed her hand to her heart. "Me? Meddle? Why, I can't believe you would even think that." But then she laughed. "You know I would enjoy nothing more."

Oh Lord. Please let that boy see the light and make my granddaughter as happy as I was with Frank. Sooner, rather than later, would be better. I'd like to hold my first great-grandchild while I can still see it.

"Sassy?"

"Yes?"

Caylor kissed her on the cheek. "Thanks for meddling."

Chapter 30

$\mathscr{D}$ylan read the last page with a sigh and then glanced at the clock in the corner of the computer screen. Oh no—he jumped up from the table. Church service started in less than five minutes.

He threw on a pair of khakis, a navy T-shirt, and his brown leather jacket; dug up a pair of matching socks from the nest of them in his top drawer; and shoved his feet into his favorite pair of loafers.

Church started in one minute.

He pulled into the parking lot eight minutes later. And right beside him. . .a white Escape pulled in and lurched to a stop.

Caylor jumped out and met him at the rear of the vehicles. "Well, I know why I'm late—but why are you so late for church?"

He gave her a one-armed hug and kissed her temple in greeting. "Because you sent me an e-mail at two this morning."

"Oh, I didn't realize you'd still be up. You didn't have to look at it right then." She shifted her purse and Bible to her right arm and hooked her left around his waist. "So you didn't get any more sleep than I did."

"Um. . .a lot less, probably. I made the mistake of opening the attachment. Once I started reading, I couldn't stop—I'm lucky to be here at all." He dropped his arm from her shoulders to open the door to the foyer for her.

When he turned to let her go in ahead of him, he noticed her face had gone white. "You. . .you've already read it?"

"I finished it right before I realized I was running late. It's fantastic. I think it's the best thing you've ever written. But I'm biased—you chose my favorite time period to write about." He ushered her in.

"I almost didn't send it to you because of that," Caylor whispered, moving toward the doors to the sanctuary. "I was afraid of all the faults you'd find with my research."

He shook his head. "I haven't seen anything so far. I could probably help you add to the details when it comes to the scenes when Giovanni is painting—it kind of felt like you were shying away from those."

Caylor smiled, pulling the left side of her bottom lip between her teeth. "I so hoped you'd say that."

The congregation started singing, so Dylan opened the door to the sanctuary and escorted Caylor in. With everyone standing, it was hard to see where they might find an open seat, but Caylor walked forward with confidence and stepped into the open end of a pew halfway down the right side—directly behind Mrs. Morton, who turned and gave them an exaggerated wink.

Caylor's eyes crinkled up with amusement. "You realize," she whispered in his ear, "that by walking in late together, we're going to be fending off rumors and demands for a shotgun wedding."

He groaned, and she launched into singing. Dylan held the hymnal in front of him and mouthed the words, not wanting to offend Caylor or Mrs. Morton or anyone else nearby with his tone deafness.

Whether it was his fatigue or the guest speaker's insistence on breaking down the morning's scripture word by word in its original Greek or Hebrew or whatever, Dylan's attention lapsed and his mind wandered back to Renaissance Venice and Giovanni and Isabella. It had been somewhat disconcerting to read the novel, knowing not only that Caylor imagined him as the physical type for Giovanni, but to see some of his own thought processes and ideas and words written down for anyone to read—since she'd just received a contract for this book to be published next year. The strangest thing was knowing that he'd never said many of those things to her; she'd just picked up on them, he guessed.

Some things about Giovanni he could help her improve on—one of which was the reason why he would have fallen in love with Isabella.

He didn't like the fact that Isabella's beauty was what captured the artist first. Sure, aesthetically he'd have felt something toward her, even physically, if she was as beautiful as Caylor described her—though Caylor described her as having long, raven-black hair. Dylan couldn't help but picture her with red hair. However, he'd rather see Giovanni fall in love with Isabella for who she was rather than what she looked like. As a portrait artist, Giovanni would have seen a lot of beautiful women. He wanted Giovanni to see Isabella's character, her kindness and humility, before he started falling in love with her.

He glanced at Caylor. He appreciated the fact that whenever they were out together, she didn't feel the need to try to sit as close to him as humanly possible. Though she usually sat in the choir loft, putting quite a distance between them, this morning she sat a respectable few inches away from him, her Bible open across her lap, a journal on top of that in which she was taking notes.

Or was she? He looked closer at the page. What had started as an attempt to take notes had turned into what looked like a new story idea—or maybe ideas for editing Giovanni and Isabella's story. He returned his gaze to the pulpit before she could see him looking, but he had a hard time containing his smile.

As soon as service ended, Caylor's prediction came true. Mrs. Morton turned around, a gleam of speculation in her eyes. She immediately grabbed Caylor's left hand then looked up at Dylan with an expression of reprimand.

Caylor pulled her hand free. "No Mrs. Morton. We're not engaged. And it was just a freak coincidence that we both happened to be running late this morning." Though serious, Caylor kept her tone pleasant, her expression soft.

"Well, can't help a body wondering," Mrs. Morton said.

"We've only been dating a couple of months. Don't you think we should take more time than that?" Caylor tucked her journal back into her purse. Dylan would *love* to have access to that book to see how Caylor's brain worked.

The old lady cocked her head. "You're not getting any younger, bless your heart."

Ah, the old "bless your heart" put-down. Something Dylan had not

313

missed about living in the South. The way older women thought they could get away with saying something insulting to or about someone if they followed it with that phrase.

"And I don't know how old you are, young man, but if you two want children, you shouldn't put it off much longer." Mrs. Morton nodded her head as if he'd said, *No, surely not!* "Yes indeed. Don't know what you young people wait so long for. Have the children while you're young, and then you get to enjoy your older years."

Another senior lady called to Mrs. Morton, and she left them to consider that pronouncement.

Dylan cleared his throat, not certain if Caylor was ready for them to broach the topic of children. She still acted uncertain about any short- or long-term possibilities for their relationship to move beyond casual dating.

She slipped her hand into his as they walked out of the church, almost the last ones to leave after Caylor stopped to apologize to the music minister for being late and missing choir this morning. A contemplative frown etched lines across her forehead.

"What's wrong?"

"We've never talked about children." Caylor slowed her pace and looked at him, her expression easing. "But before we do, there's something I need to tell you."

She related her grandmother's decision to move in with Perty and Gramps and sell her house to Caylor. However, she seemed to grow concerned as she spoke. "Now, there's no time line on this. Sassy and I are going to go ahead and meet with her lawyer and begin the paperwork for the house sale, but she doesn't have to move out anytime soon. I don't want you to feel like I'm putting any pressure on you to make any long-term decisions about us because of this."

He wanted to twirl her around and kiss her—truly kiss her, not these little pecks on the cheek or forehead he'd been restricting himself to. "I think that's great. Because I am ready to start talking about the long-term and where we go from here. Which leads back to the original question. Kids."

Caylor's face turned bright red, but her eyes beamed with joy. "I am thirty-five years old." She slipped her arms around his waist.

"And I would like to enjoy some time with just you. But I do want a family, too."

"You've seen my family—my brothers. I love them dearly, but I have to wonder what my mother was thinking, having four. I was thinking. . ."

"Two," they both said at the same time.

He kissed her, though kept it chaste, here in the shadow of the church, with a few other congregants still lingering in the parking lot. Pulling her into a quick embrace, he glanced up at the sky and thanked God for giving the guidance and direction he'd prayed for. Because once he'd read the ending of Caylor's novel this morning, he knew exactly what he needed to do.

∞

At least his mother couldn't blame him for her loss in the special election. Caylor set the newspaper aside. Yesterday's election had been a landslide—for her opponent. Being handpicked by the longtime holder of the seat had actually worked against Grace Paxton-Bradley— given that the former senator hadn't been very well liked when he retired.

Caylor glanced around the sparkling, brand-new kitchen. *Her* kitchen as of yesterday when she'd closed on the house, buying it from Sassy for several thousand under the appraised value—Sassy having added a consideration for all the money Caylor had put into maintenance issues in the house over the past five years.

She'd also talked to the lawyer about what she would need to do in the future if—no, when—she and Dylan married to get the house in both their names. She still needed to read through the documents he'd given her about that.

Sassy had moved fast in the past few weeks, getting everything in order and drawn up—and clearing it with everyone else in the family to make sure no one would object, since it affected inheritances, given that the house could have sold for a lot more money on the open market. But Daddy and Aunt Samantha had both readily agreed to Sassy's decision.

"Aren't you going to be late?" Sassy shuffled into the kitchen, carrying a trash bag full of clothes to take to Goodwill.

Caylor glanced at the clock on the back of the stove. "Oops. Yep, I'd better get out of here." She carried the newspaper out to the recycling bin on the porch and then headed out to campus.

The faculty art show was in the gallery on the main level of Sumner Hall. Each art professor and adjunct was asked to create a new piece representing the subject he or she taught each semester to be exhibited for the students, parents, and public. Dylan had been quite secretive about his piece but had checked at least twice a day for the last several days to make sure Caylor would be there for the exhibit's opening.

She hoped he'd decided to go with one of his Renaissance-like pieces, not the modern art stuff he'd given to his mom to sell at the auction.

She parked in her usual space behind Davidson and made her way across the quad to Sumner, greeting several other faculty as she entered the building. Though the flyers and announcements all stressed that casual dress was acceptable at this opening, many of the older people moving toward the gallery were dressed as if for a semiformal event. Caylor hadn't changed from what she'd worn to teach in this morning—black pumps, gray tweed trousers, and a cap-sleeve purple sweater with ribbing from the empire waist to the curve of her hips, giving the illusion she had even more of an hourglass figure than reality.

Dylan stood just outside the main entrance to the gallery, easy to spot in the milling crowd in the hallway. His hands shook when he took hers and leaned forward to kiss her cheek. "I'm glad you could make it."

"Sorry I cut it so close. I meant to be here early, but I sat down and started reading the newspaper and lost track of time."

Dr. Holtz stepped through the gallery doors and asked for everyone's attention. "Thank you all so much for coming out tonight. I know I say it every semester, but inside this gallery, you'll find the best faculty art exhibit we've ever boasted here at James Robertson University. I know you didn't come to hear me talk, so without further ado"—he waved his arm, and two of the art faculty pushed the etched-glass doors open—"I give you the exhibit."

Instead of taking her straight back to his piece, Dylan stopped to look at all of his fellow adjuncts', instructors', and professors' pieces. Caylor found most of them vaguely interesting, but she wanted to see Dylan's piece. She could enjoy the rest of these later. Finally, he gave in to her badgering and led her to the back of the gallery.

On a temporary wall hung a huge, framed canvas. From what she'd seen at the Metropolitan Museum of Art, Dylan's painting could have hung in the room with the Italian Renaissance masters and no one would have been able to tell the difference—except the paint wasn't crackled, and everyone in the scene was clothed.

"Wait—that's. . . ." She stepped closer to it, studying the woman in the center of the painting.

"That's you, yes." Dylan moved behind her, his hands settling on her shoulders. "I never would have been able to pull it off if Sage hadn't flaked out, forcing you to sit for my class that day."

She looked to the right of the Renaissance version of herself. "And that's. . .Giovanni—you—painting my portrait." She turned to face him. "But you didn't read the manuscript until two weeks ago. How did you do this?"

"Believe it or not, I had a vision for this painting shortly after I met you."

His artwork for her books had always seemed to speak to a telepathy between them. Why should she be surprised that now that they were both making a concerted effort to follow and honor God with their talent, He would lead them to the same story?

With sixteenth-century Venice behind them, except that the central figure had red hair, this painting would be the perfect cover for Giovanni and Isabella's book. She stood for what seemed like ages, letting her eyes rove inch by inch over the large canvas.

But when everything behind her grew silent, she turned to see what was happening.

"Daddy? Mama? What are you—Flannery? Zarah?" And Bobby and Sassy, and Perty and Gerald Bradley. What were all of them doing here, standing in a semicircle around Dylan and Daddy?

Dylan faced her father as if about to debate him. "Mr. Evans, I know you always hoped your daughter would marry well—for wealth and power and prestige."

No, he hadn't—wait. . .Giovanni said those exact words to Isabella's father.

"I know you wouldn't have wanted her to fall in love with a penniless artist who can offer her nothing but himself. But sir, I love your daughter, and she loves me. And I would like your blessing to ask for her hand in marriage."

Caylor didn't realize her knees had given out until they hit the floor and sent shockwaves up into her hips.

Flannery and Zarah rushed to her side and helped her back up to her feet, both grinning like fools.

Daddy eyed Dylan critically, as if taking his measure, weighing his value as a man. Caylor wanted to cry out, wanted to run to her father and make him say yes. But her shock, as well as Flannery and Zarah, held her rooted to the spot.

"There is much to be said about wealth and power and prestige," Daddy said in the words of Isabella's father. "But as much as I want my daughter to have those things, above all else, I want her to have love." Amusement danced around Daddy's lips. He reached over and laid his hands on Dylan's shoulders. "You have my blessing."

Zarah and Flannery moved away from Caylor as Dylan approached. Everyone else in the room seemed to disappear when Dylan's gaze locked with hers.

Her heart raced, and tears streamed freely down her cheeks. He sank to one knee and held something small and flat, enclosed in a velvet drawstring bag, toward her.

"Caylor, you know all my flaws and failings, yet you've stuck with me and shown me the true meaning of love." Dylan now stopped quoting Caylor's characters and spoke from his heart. "Like Giovanni, I have nothing to offer you at the moment. But if you're willing to take me as I am, I will spend my life doing whatever I can to be worthy of your love. Please be my wife."

Caylor couldn't breathe, but she managed to step forward and press her hands to his stubbly cheeks. "Dylan, you say you have nothing to offer, but the richest man in the world could offer me everything he owns, and I wouldn't take it. Because I love you, yes, I will be your wife."

She leaned down as he started up, and their lips met, sealing their love and their vow.

Around them, their friends and family cheered and clapped.

Dylan opened the velvet bag and pulled out a small, framed painting—of an engagement ring. "I can't afford to buy you a ring yet, so take this as a promise that one day I'll buy a ring worthy of your hand."

Caylor took the painting from him and flung her arms around his neck. "I'll be happy with a plain gold band, as long as it means I get you."

They broke apart to accept the congratulations of those surrounding them. After several minutes, they managed to escape the gallery for a few minutes alone.

"I thought of a title for your book." Dylan ran his finger down Caylor's cheek.

Who cared about books and titles? She just wanted to kiss him again. "What's that?"

"*L'Arte del Romanzo.*"

"That's. . . " She chuckled. "Maybe it should be in English, though."

"*The Art of Romance?*" He tilted his head, considering. "That has potential. But if you use the Italian—"

She stopped him with a kiss. For a guy who used to have problems with expressing himself, he sure seemed to be talking a lot tonight.

But that was okay. Because the true art of their romance was in discovering the trust and respect that came with being completely honest with one another and trusting God to take care of everything else.

Kaye Dacus is a graduate of Seton Hill University's Master of Arts in Writing Popular Fiction program. She is an active member and former vice president of American Christian Fiction Writers (ACFW) and current president of Middle Tennessee Christian Writers. Her *Stand-In Groom* novel was a Christy Award finalist in 2010. Find out more at kayedacus.com.